LOUIS RIEL

DANZIG

CIRCA 1810

✣

Sweeter Than
All the World

BY RUDY WIEBE

FICTION

Peace Shall Destroy Many (1962)
First and Vital Candle (1966)
The Blue Mountains of China (1970)
The Temptations of Big Bear (1973)
Where Is the Voice Coming From? (1974)
The Scorched-Wood People (1977)
Alberta / A Celebration (1979)
The Mad Trapper (1980)
The Angel of the Tar Sands (1982)
My Lovely Enemy (1983)
Chinook Christmas (1992)
A Discovery of Strangers (1994)
River of Stone: Fictions and Memories (1995)
Sweeter Than All the World (2001)

NON-FICTION

A Voice in the Land (ed. by W. J. Keith) (1981)
War in the West: Voices of the 1885 Rebellion (with Bob Beal) (1985)
Playing Dead: A Contemplation Concerning the Arctic (1989)
Stolen Life: The Journey of a Cree Woman (with Yvonne Johnson) (1998)

DRAMA

Far as the Eye Can See (with Theatre Passe Muraille) (1977)

RUDY WIEBE

Sweeter Than All the World

ALFRED A. KNOPF CANADA

PUBLISHED BY ALFRED A. KNOPF CANADA

Copyright © 2001 by Jackpine House Ltd.

All right reserved under International and Pan-American Copyright Conventions. Published in 2001 by Alfred A. Knopf Canada, a division of Random House of Canada Limited, Toronto. Distributed by Random House of Canada Limited, Toronto.

Knopf Canada and colophon are trademarks.

NATIONAL LIBRARY OF CANADA CATALOGUING IN PUBLICATION DATA

Wiebe, Rudy, 1934–
Sweeter than all the world

ISBN 0-676-97340-X

I. Title.

PS8545.I38S93 2001   C813'.54   C2001-930597-4

Page 437 constitutes a continuation of the copyright page.

First Edition

www.randomhouse.ca

Drawing of Wybe Adam from *Die ost-und westpreussischen Mennoniten* by Horst Penner, Mennonitischer Geschichtsverein, vol. 1, Weierhof, Germany, 1978
Drawing of cable car from *Der Stadt Dantzig historische Beischreibung* by Reinhold Curicke, J und G. Janssons von Waesberge, Amsterdam, 1686
Map of Danzig from *Geschichte der Befestigungen und Belagerungen Danzigs* by Karl Friedrich Friccius, Veit & Comp., Berlin, 1854

Text design: CS Richardson

Printed and bound in the United States of America

10 9 8 7 6 5 4 3 2 1

TO THE MEMORY OF

Wybe Adams van Harlingen
1584?–1652

CONTENTS   ⊹

✦

SWEETER THAN
ALL THE WORLD

You're coming home again. What does that mean?
　　—Joseph Brodsky, *Selected Poems*

Turning to the open sea
she speaks in low German.
No one can hear us now she says
except God who already knows.
　　—Sarah Klassen, *Journey to Yalta*

Dwell on the past and you'll lose an eye; forget the past
and you'll lose both eyes.
　　—Russian proverb

ONE

SPEAKING WASKAHIKAN

Waskahikan, Northern Alberta
1942

IN SUMMER THE POPLAR LEAVES CLICKED and flickered at him, in winter the stiff spruce rustled with voices. The boy, barefoot in the heat or trussed up like a lumpy package against the fierce silver cold, went alone into the bush, where everything spoke to him: warm rocks, the flit of quick, small animals, a dart of birds, tree trunks, the great fires burning across the sky at night, summer fallow, the creek and squeaky snow. Everything spoke as he breathed and became aware of it, its language clear as the water of his memory when he lay against the logs of the house at night listening to the spring mosquitoes find him under his blanket, though he had his eyes shut and only one ear uncovered.

Everything spoke, and it spoke Lowgerman. Like his mother. She would call him long into the summer evening when it seemed the sun burned all night down into the north, call high and falling slow as if she were already weeping: "Oo-oo-oo-oo-oo...."

And when he appeared beside her, she would bend her

powerful hands about his head and kiss him so warm his eyes rang.

"Why don't you answer, you?" she would say against his hair. "Why don't you ever answer? The bush is so dark and I listen and listen, why don't you ever say a word?"—while he nuzzled his face into the damp apron at the fold of her thigh. And soon her words would be over, and he would feel her skin and warm apron smelling of saskatoon jam and dishes and supper buns love him back.

His sister laughed at his solitary silence. "In Waskahikan School are twenty-seven kids," Margaret said, "you'll have to talk, and English at that. You can't say anything Lowgerman there, and if you don't answer English when she asks, the teacher will make you stand in the corner."

"R-right in f-f-f-f-ront—of—people?" he burst out fearfully.

"Yeah, in front of every one of them, your face against the wall. So you better start talking, and English too."

And she would try to teach him the English names for things. But he did not listen to that. Rather, when he was alone he practised standing in the corners of walls. Their logs shifted and cracked, talking all the time like happiness; logs were very good, especially where they came together so hard and warm in winter.

Outside was even better. He followed the thin tracks of a muskrat that had dented the snow with its tail between bulrushes sticking out of the slough ice, or waited for the coyote in the field along the hill to turn and see him, one paw lifted and about to touch a drift, its jaw opening to its red tongue smiling with him. Then suddenly cock its ears, and pounce! double-pawed into a drift, burrowing deeper. In summer he heard a mother bear talk to her cubs among the willows of the horse pasture near the creek. He did not see them, but he found their tracks in the spring snow behind the spruce and his father said something would have to be done if they came any closer to the pigpen. The boy knew his father refused to own a gun, but their nearest Ukrainian neighbour gladly hunted everywhere, whatever he heard about, and so he folded his hands over the huge pawprints and whispered in Lowgerman.

"Don't come here, not any more. It's dangerous."

The square school sat at the corner, below the hill where the road allowances crossed south over the creek and bent around the spruce muskeg towards their Mennonite church, and the store. Inside the church every Sunday there were hands waiting for him. At the top of the balcony stairs—which led up from the corner behind the men's benches, under the sloped roof with the church Highgerman of people murmuring like rain below them and poplar leaves at the window—were the hands that found things inside him, and let them out. Thick hands with heavy, broad thumbs working against each other on his neck, pressing down, pressing together, bending his small bones until through his gaping mouth they cawed:

"C - c - c - - *cat!*"

"Yes, yes, like that, try to say it again, 'cat.'"

And he would try, desperately, those marvellous hands holding him tight as if everything on earth were in its proper place, and all the brilliant sounds he could never utter when anyone listened coming out of him as easily, deeply, as if he had pulled a door open.

"Cat."

"Yes, very good, now say, 'Be sure your sin will find you out.' Say it: 'Be sure…'"

He knew *find* and *you* already, but *sin?* No one could find him in the bush, he did not need to say that; those English words, whatever they were, would never have to sit on the edge of his lips hissing. He drew his breath down, deep and safe.

"Ca-a-at," he said firmly.

The post office was a wooden wicket folded open on Tuesday and Friday at the back of the store. There they got the Eaton's winter or summer catalogues, and letters with stamps from Southern Alberta where his oldest sister Helen lived with her husband and Raymond, who came every summer to play with him in the bush behind the house. Mail came on the train, which he had never seen, but he heard it wailing faintly in the west, like an evening animal lost when light rises into mist along the creek. A sound so strange and far away that when it was gone he thought he might not have heard anything at all, it was only his longing for the white clouds of steam his oldest brother Abram had told him blasted out of the train when he worked laying steel rails on the ground for it, and blasting even whiter when it brought Abram back from Bible school at Christmas and he read the story of the Wisemen aloud in church and then prayed. The train, his brother said, went through the town of Boyle, three rows of houses on the edge of a wide valley. Almost a hundred people lived there, and the train ran along the big lake beyond it on steel straight as string. His father drove a wagonload of grain, or pigs, to that town in fall when the mudholes on the road were frozen but the snow not too deep yet. And when he came back he said he had looked far across flat miles again at the rich valley farms they'd cleared there, red hip-roofed barns and white houses, all Swedes and Ukrainians because they got to their homesteads first, on the deep soil, not like their stone and clay where it wasn't creek or slough or muskeg.

But the school had been at the crossroads since before the boy could remember, and now he tried not to look at it when they drove down the hill, though he knew the small panes of its five large windows stared at him as long as they passed. It was the Friday before the Monday when he would have to go there every day, like Margaret, that the planes came for the first time.

He was holding the parcel from Eaton's, which he was certain contained the flannel shirt they ordered long ago for his first day in school, red check with black buttons, but his mother— "Don't tear the paper!"—would never let him open anything before they got home. Their horses were so slow, good farm plugs, *Schrugge*, his brother John called them, pulling the wagon up the school hill as steadily as they always did, and it happened very fast, almost before he could look around. There had been a rumble from somewhere like thunder, far away, though the sky was clearest sunlight. His father had just said that in a week they might start bindering the oats, the whole field was ripening so well, and his mother sat beside him broad and erect, her braided hair coiled up in a bun under her hat, when suddenly the planes were there as a light flashed and he twisted to see, one after the other like four yellow-and-black fists punching low over them, louder than anything he had ever heard in his whole life. Roaring away north above the school and the small grain fields between poplars and sloughs and pastures and over all the trees to the edge of the world.

His father did not look up or around. His hands doublewrapped in the reins and his body braced to hold the terrified horses down, his voice was as sadly angry as an echo.

5

"Russia wasn't enough, here they come out of the air."

But the boy was looking at his mother. Perhaps his own face looked like that when next morning the yellow planes thundered over the school at recess, so low he saw horrible glass eyes in a sleek leather head glare down at him before he screamed and ran, fled inside to the desk where Margaret had told him he must sit. When he opened his eyes the face of the teacher was there, her gentle face very close, smiling almost upside down at him between the iron legs of the desk beneath which he curled, his new red-check shirt against the floor. Her gentle voice speaking.

"Come," she said, "come."

Her fingers touched his hair light as wind, and after a moment he twisted out and scrambled to his feet. He thought she was speaking Lowgerman because he did not yet know that what that word meant sounded the same in English. "Come."

She led him past the amazing front wall that was "black-board," where that morning the white chalk between her fingers reaching out of her sky-blue sleeve drew the large letters of their school name:

WAS-KA-HI-KAN = HOME

She guided him through the rows of desks to a narrow cupboard against the wall opposite the windows, raised her thin hands, pulled, and two doors unfolded both at once. Books. He had never imagined so many books. Maybe a million.

She was, of course, speaking to him in English and years later, when he remembered that moment again and again, he would never be able to explain to himself how he understood what she was saying. The book opening between her hands showed him countless words: words, she said, that he could now only see the shape of, but would be able to hear when he learned to read because, she told him, the word *read* in English was the same as the word *speak*, *räd* in Lowgerman, and, when he could read, all the people of the world would speak to him. When he opened a book, he would hear what they had already said and continued to say, and he would understand.

He was staring at what he later knew were a few worn books on a few short shelves, and then looking back at the visible but as yet unintelligible words revealed by the book unfolded in her hands. And perhaps it was when her right hand reached down to touch his, hidden in his new shirt cuffs with their amazing black double buttons, when her fingers tightened and his hands clutched hers, perhaps then he slowly began to comprehend that there were shelves upon shelves of books on many, many floors inside all the walls of the enormous libraries of the world where someday he would go and read; that the knowing which she could help him discover within himself would allow him to hear human voices speaking from everywhere and every age, saying things both sweet and horrible, and everything else that might be imagined between them. And he would listen.

"A-a-da-a-am."

His mother, calling into the long northern evening.

"Where a-a-re you?"

TWO

SAILING TO DANZIG

Coaldale, Southern Alberta

1953

HIS NAME WAS ADAM PETER WIEBE. When he began school he liked being "Adam." No one else had that name, and everyone called him "Addie," like his sister Margaret who at first knew everything. Then one summer a travelling preacher came driving his thin horse and buggy through the bush to the Waskahikan Mennonite Church and, leaning far over the pulpit, declared that ADAM meant "of the ground," which was how God had created the first man on earth. Out of the ground. And that had happened 4,004 years before Jesus Christ, God's Only Son! was born in Bethlehem of Judah.

The way that huge man told the first story in the Bible stayed with Adam all his life like a memory of blue and golden light. He never wanted to read it in *Hurlbut's Story of the Bible*— which his mother ordered for him from the catalogue when she realized he would never stop reading—or spoil the story with heavy Luther Genesis. Adam, made of ground, moist earth changed into flesh by God breathing warm breath into a mouth cupped open between His great, all-powerful hands! Adam's first job was to name every animal God had already created, such easy work, and then, as a reward, God fingered the most perfectly beautiful woman that ever lived—that was the Highgerman word the preacher used: God touched Adam under his left middle rib and He "fingered" it out to make Eve—and the preacher stepped away from the pulpit, lifted his huge hands high and shaped Eve's head in the air between them and then slid them around her shoulders, down over her pointed breasts—all his life Adam would remember his hands' turn there, so slow, ineffably gentle—and over her hips and along her long legs to her toes. And then, ahh then! Adam and Eve lived together in the most beautiful garden on earth, eating fresh fruit and playing with the gold and sweet gum and pearls and onyx stones that were in the four rivers that flowed out of Eden, and bathing in them too. It was always the perfect seventh day of creation, forever rest, forever summer.

Travelling preachers came to Waskahikan between haying and harvest. Sermons were every evening if it didn't rain too hard and three times on Sunday. This evangelist, Groota Donnadach Peetash as he was called in Lowgerman, Big Thursday—thunder-day—Peters, said the title of his next sermon would be "The Heaviest Word in the World." He was preaching in Highgerman of course and so when he said, "Sünde," exactly that word was the heaviest, and the apple tree and Eve and the slimy snake and Adam eating, that was truly *Sünde, der Grosse Fall*, forever and all eternity for all men and women ever born and all nature, even for trees and small animals, the very mosquitoes were all groaning and travailing in pain to be delivered from man's bondage of putrid corruption!

Instantly, small Adam detested that second part of the story; he knew he'd never be like that stupid First Adam and eat a snake's apple. He'd stick with God; if He had the power to make it He had the power to take it away, and if Eve couldn't figure that out, Adam certainly could. And at that moment, as he sat with the other small boys on the narrow front bench with Big Thursday looming over them, it struck Adam that if exactly *Sünde* was the worst word, he would from now on live only in English where exactly that word didn't exist, and he could stay with beautiful Eve and nice God Almighty in the Beautiful Garden forever, no gigantic angels with flaming swords that turned every way east of Eden.

Die Sünde Adams! That was Big Thursday Peters, weeping and blowing his nose like a trumpet-blast into an enormous blue-striped handkerchief, thundering God's eternal damnation and endless grace all at the same time. But it was Lowgerman that quickly betrayed Adam's thinking; after only a year of learning to read English in school he was no longer aware of what language he thought in, nor even how he dreamed, and looking up from the church bench and seeing the setting sun flicker the fine spray of Big Thursday's mighty words into intermittent, visible rainbows around his mouth, he was convicted in his heart that *Sind* was too close to *sin* for a simple English escape. Especially with his name.

Adam Peter: "ground," "rock." Adam realized his names were basically the same, one merely a more stubborn form of the other. And *Sind* or *Sünde* or *sin* were of course all one too, abominably everywhere, in any language; as his mother steadfastly reminded him.

Four summers later Aaron Voth's overloaded truck hauled them away from their bush homestead, two days of gravel roads south to the irrigation prairie town of Coaldale, Alberta. There his names, including Wiebe, were not at all unique. At school recess the descendants of twenty different races and religions, including Mormons and Mennonites, Czechs and Chinese, squabbled and fought and played themselves into uneasy games and sometimes friendship, but the shifting alliances of grade school became even more complicated when Adam entered Coaldale Consolidated High. There a smart-alec Anglican, who remembered his catechism, swore at him, "You're just plain dirt and filthy sin, you big shit A-damn!"

All the other guys with English surnames howled and hooted, and it didn't help when Adam yelled back, "You're just as much dirt as I, shithead!" because no one laughed.

Few as the English were in that flat Alberta of immigrant farmers and itinerant sugarbeet workers, they considered themselves the ruling class of the school and no Mennonite would play first-string basketball if they could help it. The coach, who was Japanese Canadian exiled from Vancouver by the World War, had other ideas; Adam was too tall and strong not to include. But the "A-damn" stuck whenever it suited anyone and until grade twelve, when he went to the small Coaldale Mennonite High School north of town—as his mother had begged him to do for two years—he had more time than he wanted to consider his first name. How he liked and also hated it; how it so easily shifted into a curse.

He realized then it did not fit with their family names anyway. Adam's father was Abraham Jakob Wiebe, which in the Russian Mennonite tradition of naming meant that his father's name before him was Jakob, and so his oldest brother, who was born in the Orenburg Mennonite Colony village of Number Eight Romanovka in Eastern Russia, was named Abram Abraham, his second brother John Abraham, the John coming from their mother's father David John Loewen. So where did his come from, Adam Peter?

His mother looks up at him without a hesitation in her knitting. Though he has never before asked her anything directly about their past, she shows no surprise at Adam's question. As a child he had overheard endless Russia stories when their Waskahikan neighbours came to visit, and in Coaldale there were more than enough Mennonites talking about themselves and their history, all the time, hundreds of them, with three different churches for them to be happy or to disagree in.

She says, without hesitation, "Actually, you weren't Adam Peter. In the government papers in Edmonton, or wherever they have them, your name was Heinrich."

"Heinrich?!"

"In the papers, yes, and Abraham your second, like always. You were Heinrich Abraham Wiebe."

"I'm not Adam?" He's seventeen and his mother is finally telling him his real name?

"Of course you're Adam," she says calmly. "That was just those government papers, then. When you were born we were living so far in the bush it was seven weeks before your father got to Boyle and then he registered your name, 'Heinrich Abraham.'"

Across the kitchen table Adam's father continues to study *Die Mennonitische Rundschau*; his reading glasses, bought at a counter in Eaton's in Lethbridge, tilt at the end of his long, almost patrician nose. He sits this way every Sunday afternoon, the only day of the week he does not have to feed cattle on the farm where he will work as a hired man until he is seventy, another eight years, never able to find the one Canadian dream he has ever had: a job where he can work inside and be warm all winter. He refuses to speak now, though they all know Adam's mother's teasing irony will eventually prick him into a response.

"He had the day wrong, too." She smiles suddenly. "He remembered it was a Friday, but he got your date wrong a whole week, and when we got the registration when he was going to become a citizen, then Lena Voth said to me, 'My Willm was born the same day as your Adam, the midwife came from you to me, how come your day is wrong?' and then I noticed that, too."

"It was eight weeks after, not seven," his father mutters finally, as if correcting her small mistake would balance his gross one.

"Eight weeks, and you didn't know my name yet?"

He seems particularly intent on the *Nachrichten* column. He will never understand more than a few words of English, and it is in the weekly *Rundschau* that he learns the minimal news he knows of the turmoil in the world.

"Aaron Voth wrote the names in right then," his mother says. "'Adam Peter.' And so we corrected both the date and your names too."

"When was this?" Adam asks.

"*Na* Pa, when was it you became a Canadian citizen?"

"Nineteen forty-three. You want my registration number too?"

Adam's mother is knitting and ignores his growling, easily. A sagging red line connects her unstoppable hands with the thick skein of wool looped over two chairbacks. Adam knows that when his father at last saw his name on the Certificate of Canadian Citizenship, he memorized the number 44988 immediately, in case he was ever forced across a border again; thirteen years before, when they reached the harbour of Saint John, New Brunswick, from Hamburg on February 24, 1930, and finally Waskahikan, Alberta, by train on March 14, he vowed he would never leave Canada of his own free will; and he never has.

"But you always called me—"

"Yes, we always have."

"Why did you call me that, Adam?"

"Oh," his mother looks up from the ritual movement of her knitting. She seems dreamy; Adam will contemplate that same look on his daughter Trish's adult face many years later, something of both distant past and future, like a former anticipation that is already there, an aching present of much more to come.

"You were our first and last in Canada," his mother says. "I thought, something new after all that old...oh, so much, of everything...and there was a little Wiens, our neighbour's, he was born here too but Katya Wiens told me he was started on the ocean, he was a little Adam he was so beautiful, always singing and only four and so good, laughing in the children's room in church and playing with all the babies to make them laugh. It was so sad when he fell into the slough behind their barn. He sank away in the moss and swamp water, he was gone there, they couldn't see him, only the dog jumping and barking. Just before you were born—such a nice name, he was a little Adam, and so good."

"'So nice and good,'" Adam says bitterly. "Well, you tried your best, at least with the name."

"Adam," his mother says softly, reaching to touch him. And for an instant it seems her voice and fingers will find tears behind his eyes.

His father says in his gravel voice, "Where did you find him, this old Adam Wiebe you say was in Danzig, Poland?"

"Where do you think? In a book."

"Books, books, all your books they'll ruin you."

Adam thinks: Old man, just give me the chance—and what's ruined you? All his life he has heard his father's laments and excuses: born in 1889 in Russia, a Mennonite hauled into the Czar's forest *Forstei* instead of compulsory military service, he had barely done his four years and come back to his village to marry Katerina Loewen in 1914 when World War I erupted and he was dragged back again, a second four years, or three rather because the glorious October Revolution finished everything, they got so busy killing themselves, all those Bolsheviks, and chasing him forever, what could anyone do but do what he was told? But finally, when he was forty, he did do one thing: he left what little he had, they were poorer than Russian meadow mice living at the worker end of Number Eight Romanovka, and with his wife and four kids went on the train to Moscow to try and get out of there. Forever. Astonishing indeed that he did one thing, after a Mennonite patriarch and four older brothers and seven years of the Czar's *Forstei* and then ten years of Communists tearing the world apart, oh, those Communists, he had learned to do what he was told.

His father's brown hands hold the newspaper as if they don't know how, knuckles scarred, broken by worn tools slipping: abruptly Adam feels his thoughts are petty.

"The teacher, Frank Bargen," he tells him, "he gave me this

book. When he saw a man in it had exactly my name, in 1616. Here, you can read it, it's German."

"Now you read German?" As if he has forgotten all the Coaldale Saturdays he made Adam walk to German school in the church.

His mother says soothingly, "What was this Danzig Adam?"

Adam/Peter—names surely heavy enough to sink anyone in the deepest swamp—Adam/Peter/Abraham meaning ground/rock/exalted father of a multitude, dear God, more than enough even in Lowgerman, all earth and exaltation too, with Wiebe, as he has now read in the book *Mennonite Yearbook, 1951*, a variant of the Frisian Wybe. Whatever that meant, probably mud. The article did not say, but it did explain his ancestors were not originally German as he—and most Mennonites—always assumed; they were Frisians, who for two hundred years in the Polish and German worlds of Danzig had spoken Dutch in their church services and their own Frisian language everywhere else, a people stubborn and implacable as the water they had learned to live with on the lowlands along the North Sea. The tightly detailed article, "Die Wiebes," by Horst Penner, which Adam could only plod through by translating word after word, informed him that the first Wiebe Adams, as he signed himself, Wiebe son of Adam, sailed from Harlingen to Danzig in 1616 because that powerful Hanseatic League city needed a water engineer to drain its delta, and at that time the Frisians understood more about water than anyone in the world. An engraving of Danzig in 1644 illustrated the *Yearbook* article: a long, low skyline, with the City of Danzig's coat of arms in the top left corner, and on the top right a head-and-shoulders portrait of Adam Wiebe himself.

"Look," Adam points it out to his mother, and reads around the portrait's scrolled edge for his father's benefit, since he will not look up. "'Wybe Adam von Harlingen,' he's right over the picture of Danzig, a real big shot, see. And he signed his name, big Gothic script, 'Wiebe Adams.'"

"*Na oba*," his mother exclaims, and points with a free needle, "look, that's Pa's nose too, heh?"

Strangely enough, she is right. But a higher forehead, heavier eyebrows in a narrow face surrounded by a trim crown of hair to the nape and a full, patterned beard; an unstoppable genius who served Danzig for thirty-four years and before he died had streets and squares and a huge bastion anchoring the city wall named after him.

"Where's my long nose?" Adam asks her.

His father snorts. "It got lost for a turned-up Loewen, her family."

"Does this book have pictures of a Loewen?"

Thirty years later Adam will remember his mother asking him that while she knit red mittens for children's winter relief on a hot August Sunday in Coaldale, Alberta. He will remember with longing and grief, and think of all he could tell her in 1983 if only she were still alive: that the Loewens were Flemish Mennonites from the great seaport Antwerp, most likely jewellers. Perhaps their shop stood in the wedge of narrow stepped buildings pressed between the Grand Square and Our Lady of Antwerp Cathedral, whose Brabantine Gothic, with the tallest tower ever built in the Low Countries, dominated the great roadstead on the Scheldt River from which wooden ships then sailed to all known and explorable worlds. With so many ships coming and going, it was probably not difficult for her ancestor

Loewens to escape the massive persecution of the Spanish Roman Catholics or the coming Calvinists by emigrating to Danzig; in fact, they probably arrived there decades before Adam Wiebe. In 1983 he could also tell his mother of the beautiful modern town of Harlingen, still so compact inside its labyrinth of dikes and canals thrust out in alternating loops of earth and water into the grey sea; or tell her of the long blond girl named Wiebke den Hoet he and his daughter Trish had met, whose father was the dikemaster on Ameland in the North Sea and who invited them to come, see how the Frisians still make land with the sea; or tell her of Het Steen Castle—now an innocent maritime museum—where in the 1560s the Inquisition chained the "defenceless Christians" in dungeons until they convicted them of heresy and led them out to burn.

All the facts Adam knows later, all the places of the ancestral past he will visit, all the family members scattered in the world he will talk to—but rather than parade the intermittent, infinite details of history he has excavated over years, he will then think only: I should have asked her to sing.

Her beautiful soprano, vivid forever in the folds of his memory. Any of the songs she sang when the leaves came out, green as frogs in the Waskahikan slough and poplar May, and she began to cook in the outside "summer kitchen" to keep their low log house dark and cool for sleeping. It would have been a song from the *Dreiband*, their pocket-size hymnal without notes, but of course a person who sang in a Mennonite church then knew at least three or four hundred songs from memory, truly "knew them by heart" as English expressed it so profoundly. And his father across the farmyard somewhere within earshot would have answered her in tenor harmony, their voices floating like lovers hand in hand high in the bright air. By some genetic shift more drastic than his nose, the musical rock of Flemish Loewen and Frisian Wiebe has faulted into Adam's tunelessness: though he can recognize any melody, he cannot reproduce or mirror one either close or at a distance. Not even the overwhelming choir of twenty-six Peter Wiebe descendants he will discover in West Germany in 1983 will help him to one consecutive tuneful sound, those two dozen Peter Wiebe children and great-grand-children finding hours of harmonies in a tiny apartment, their heads filling endlessly with identical words and running notes, their bodies leaning together like one body.

"Peter Wiebe?" If Adam's father hears that name spoken, he will certainly raise his head from *Die Rundschau*, and glare. "That was my brother, the rich one, with us in Moscow in '29."

"Leave that old story," his mother says quickly, as she always does.

But once the story of the Great Mennonite Flight over Moscow is hinted at, Adam's father is not stoppable, he can only rush on:

"In October '29 my oldest brother, Jakob, the one who inherited the stone house and one full farm, he and his big sons and all his workers were threshing in the front yard when we drove down the street with our little wagon, and you remember, Tien, what I said, I told him, 'Come, it's Moscow now or never!' And he, with his threshing fork high: 'Yes! yes! I just have to fin-ish my barley.' Huh! He was still thinking money would get him out of Russia."

Adam's mother nods sadly. "His wife never got any buns roasted to go."

"Of course not!" His father is triumphant. "And the

Collective with Kolya Wiebe who was still too young to get married but the Communists of course made him kolkhoz boss, Kolya had to take all his grain away from him too, but my brother Peter—"

"Stop it," she pleads. "Don't start with that."

"But that Peter," the weight of his remembering rolls over her, "my second brother, he had inherited our second full farm and he had his money sacks tied up and the travel ham smoked, he had three teams of horses harnessed and train tickets bought ahead from Platovka, and his whole family—"

"We have to forget such things!" Adam's mother interrupts, very loud, her head bent; her needles in the sagging wool no longer move.

"Forget!" His father's worker hands crush *Die Rundschau*. "You can forget? When your own brother who's as rich as the dead Czar says to you all the way to Moscow, 'How do you think you'll get out to Germany, you with your sick Tien and four kids, you don't have three kopecks to rub together?' How do you forget that?"

"Abraham, we know God needs money for nothing."

"And the Communists don't either, thank God." Adam's father laughs, sardonic with his own wit. "Having money in '29 was the end of any going, no beginning."

His mother's steel needles are flying again, as if red wool in her hands could knit the splintered world into goodness. She murmurs, "So forget that old story, it—"

But if Adam could have told them this story, he would have had to interrupt her. "This wasn't your brother Peter, Pa, it's his son. He was in Moscow with you too, a boy then, he survived over fifty years in Russia and just got out now."

"Peter Wiebe is in Germany? He bought his way out, now?"

"Not your brother, Pa, his oldest *son*."

"I remember his oldest son in '29, we always called him 'Young Peter,'" Adam's mother would have said if she had heard. "He was fifteen then, short, thin, and bright eyes. Such an open Wiebe face."

"Young Peter" Wiebe will still have that the first time Adam meets him. In 1983 Adam will see a small man come towards him through a crowd of several thousand Mennonites at their first mass gathering in West Germany to celebrate their escape at last from the Soviet Union, his hands high in greeting, exclaiming, "That's a Wiebe face, a Wiebe face!"

And at that moment he will appear to be Adam's father reincarnated in a slight, short body, with his thin hair that will never turn completely grey and that patrician nose and square jaw, limping through the crowd that parts and turns to stare and then laughs aloud at their happiness, at their embrace and enfolding double kiss. Adam will have to bend down to his cousin Young Peter, over him, his arms surrounding those narrow bones, and suddenly between his fingers there spreads an overwhelming silence. He might be holding his father Abraham, alive again after seven years; though his father never in a lifetime held Adam like that.

"I never wanted another Peter in my family," his father says like a groan over their Coaldale kitchen table. "An Adam I didn't care, but a Peter, another Peter..."

Adam's mother is singing while she knits. She sings not to avoid his father: they will not live sixty-one years together that way. Rather, that sweet sound suspended by her voice, a broadening colour that does not hesitate at sadness or pain, never breaks because of anger, unforgiveness, or even hatred. It is a sound that slowly, slowly threads brightness into the stifling Sunday afternoon.

> "My home is always on my mind,
> Ahh, when will I reach home?
> I long to be in heaven fair,
> With all God's children gathered there
> In blessed harmony, in blessed harmony."

As she knits and sings, Adam unhooks the skeins of wool sagging over the chairbacks, strand by strand, and rolls them into a ball. In the slow, steady tug and rhythm of her needles his mother will sing every verse of her favourite *Heimatleed*. She knows so many Mennonite "songs of home"—which have nothing to do with their home on earth. On earth you are forever a stranger, here you can only endure and sing long, slow songs that in your longing inevitably circle around to your true and only home, which is always "over there," blessed and perfect with God "far beyond yonder sea of stars" where loved ones are already waiting to greet you.

Across their kitchen table, Adam's father refuses to join her, though Adam can see the song's sweet, sad melody tugs at him, that his mother's high soprano holding on "har-mo-ny-y-y-y" is wrapping itself around him, an irresistible, sorrowful happiness. His father does not so much as glance at the *Yearbook* Adam has laid open before him, to see the austere and brooding face of his ancestor Adam Wiebe, who in 1616 sailed east from Harlingen to Danzig. Over years he laid out the city's first wooden water mains, set new flowing fountains in its squares and drained the great marshlands along the Vistula and Motlawa and Radunia rivers by building dikes anchored by roads and great bridges to control the spring and heavy rain runoffs, and dug drainage collector canals and designed wind and horse-driven mills that lifted the turgid water up over the dikes and into the Baltic Sea. Adam Wiebe making dry land, so that the whole Vistula delta of deep river soil could flower into ever more Frisian and Flemish Mennonite farm villages.

"What is this," his mother says, pointing with a needle, "these lines here, these things hanging?"

She is studying the grey picture of the copper engraving of Danzig, the coat of arms in its top left corner, the long, bearded face of Adam in its top right. Across the centre of the picture is printed, "Die Stadt Dantzig," but above that hangs a wide scroll of Latin, some of which in this printed miniaturization is almost legible through her reading glass. Adam can decipher "Nova inventi," and more clearly, "MACHINAE ARTIFICIOSAE," but then lines of scattered dots, something "Exacta delin—" and a sudden "Sacra" and "Adam Wiebe Ha—," the words lost inside their engraved, dotted and multi-copied minutiae. Whatever they were once intended to say, below the coat of arms on the left there remains a line drawing of a high hill labelled Bischoffsberg, Bishop's Hill. The centre is low sagging land along river and marshes with the church spires of the city beyond, but below Adam's picture on the right there is an elevation almost as high as the hill: it is clearly labelled "Wieben Bastion." At the urgent request of the Danzig City Council, in the 1640s Adam rebuilt the walls and that particular fortification to protect the city during the Thirty Years War between the Roman Catholic and

Protestant kings and dukes and emperors and opportunistic generals for hire anywhere in Europe, and since there were no stones in the watery delta, he reconstructed the entire circuit of the Danzig city wall and redesigned and built its twenty military bastions above the flood plains between the rivers by using rocks and earth from the Bishop's Hill. The "lines, with things hanging," across the centre of the picture, are the double cable "Nova inventi" that Adam strung on poles, so that by means of an endless circuit of moving buckets attached to this cable, earth and rocks could be carried from the hill and over the river and the marsh to the bastion walls of the city. So exactly were these buckets designed, so precisely were distance and weight calculated, that no power beyond themselves was needed to make them move: the weight of the filled buckets at the top of the hill carried them down across the valley to the top of the bastion while returning the empty buckets back up the hill. And though the mighty Swedish army under King Gustavus II Adolphus, with its enormous wheeled cannon pulled by six- or eight-horse teams, its cavalry and pikemen and lockstep infantry armed with the lightest, quickest-firing muskets, destroyed much of Europe for pay and ultimately, as they professed to truly believe, for the glory of the Protestant Christian Church, though unnumbered armies trailing even larger rabbles of camp followers ravaged and raped their way, year after horrible year, through the farm villages of the Vistula delta, in thirty years not a single enemy got inside the walls of Danzig: because Adam Wiebe invented the cable car to rebuild the defences of an indefensible city.

"*Na oba doch*," Adam's mother says in utter amazement. "I've never heard of anything like that."

And she reads aloud the Highgerman caption historian

Horst Penner has placed beside the picture: "'Adam Wybe (Wiebe) from Harlingen in Holland was apparently the ancestor of most of the present bearers of this name. He was a highly successful engineer and master builder in Danzig during the seventeenth century.'"

Adam's father can refuse to see or read, but his large ears force him to listen. Adam says, unnecessarily loud, "Adam Wiebe built all that, but he had to live outside the Danzig wall, in a Mennonite village outside. Only after twenty years they finally gave him permission to build a house inside the city, against the wall he rebuilt."

His father asks abruptly, "Why would he want to live in there, with strangers?"

"Walls protected people in war. There were always armies tramping through, they shot and took whatever they wanted, they always wanted food, and animals, women—when people heard armies were coming they left everything in their villages and fled behind the city walls—if the Danzigers opened the gates and let them."

Adam's mother asked, "And the walls, they did keep soldiers out?"

"Adam Wiebe's walls did."

His father pulls the book around; his crooked right thumb rubs the margin beside the portrait. He says at last, "So, when did this Adam Wiebe die?"

"Sixteen fifty-two...three hundred...Pa, he built their city for thirty-four years, and his sons after him too, but Danzig never even made him a citizen."

"*Yo, yo*"—his father draws out the Lowgerman "yes" long and heavily—"that's the way it is, it always was. Those

Communists hammered on our door after we sat in those Moscow summer houses for two months and told us to get on the train to Germany, go! They gave me a yellow card, 'Stateless refugee.' That's all it said. A hundred and fifty years in Russia and they shove you out with nothing, the clothes on your back and a piece of yellow paper, fill in your own names. 'Stateless refugee.'"

Adam realizes he has not known that either. Perhaps, in the face of certain facts, ignorance does not much matter. After all, over how many lakes and rivers and parts of oceans, across how many fairgrounds, up how many mountains on how many continents do millions of people sail through air, suspended somehow from a cable, without ever having heard of his ancestor Adam Wiebe? Their ignorance—or his own when he is carried through air—has of course never made any of those cables less real, the sailing less beautiful or potentially lethal.

Years later he will remember their small house in Coaldale, the kitchen table covered in oilcloth where he ate so often; remember his parents sitting there, suspending the thin thread of their songs across the marshes and bitter rivers of their past. Building what bastions? Against what fearfully anticipated or remembered war, against what memory, what knock at the door by secret police, "We just want to ask you a few questions, come on now, you'll be home for night"? Slight, bent "Young Peter," the once rich Peter Wiebe's son having to live a sort of a life in the Soviet Union, and he—whatever his name was, Adam or Heinrich—the once poor Abraham Wiebe's son living a very different sort of life in Canada and running all over the world: which would one actually prefer? His oldest uncle Jakob Jakob, his beard white as snow, escaping the Communists by a miracle and dying surrounded by his family in 1962, his second uncle

Peter Jakob dragged off by the NKVD in the bloody purges of 1937, and his son, "Young Peter," surviving Stalin's Orenburg prison once and the Gulag not once but twice—these are the facts, were already becoming facts somewhere in the world that August Sunday afternoon when Adam was seventeen and the Coaldale Mennonite High School history teacher gave him a German article to read—one he could never have discovered for himself, not then knowing enough to know he would want to see it if it did exist—seven amazing pages of archival research on the Wiebes in *The Mennonite Yearbook, 1951*. When he glanced at the fiercely bearded man whose picture stood at the head of it, and saw his own name.

The summer Sunday when Adam discovers that, for all their stories, his mother and father can, or will, tell him little about the names he has. What they do is tell him small, personal, contradictory, denied, avoided details of their lives that explain very little; that are, as it seems, less facts than momentary needles tugging at a string of wool, knitting mittens to protect some hand they will never know; less facts than thin images of poles sticking up out of sinking ground, and holding up cables made possible by what genius, what vision, no one can explain, so that all that solid earth could be moved with such marvellous ease over marsh and river from the high cliffs of the Bishop's Hill to build an impregnable Wiebe Bastion.

"So." Adam looks at his mother. "That's my first name, so. why the second?"

"So." After a moment she stops knitting; she glances up at his father, but he continues to stare at the book tilted in his hands, motionless and silent. They hear, outside, a car rush by on the gravel street.

"In 1935, just before you were born," his mother says, "we got a letter from Russia. My brother Peter David Loewen was dead. You were named for him."

Adam studies her gaunt, motionless hands, fingers ringed by the tension of soft wool.

"They said he was killed, in a Communist prison camp on Sakhalin Island."

"Sakhalin...the island in the Pacific, by Japan?"

"Peter and I were the only children of my mother, Justina. She died when I was born and every day, my father told me, he carried me across the village street to your father's mother, Maria Wiebe. She had just had Netta then, and she nursed me too."

Slowly Adam's mother begins to knit again. "I'm sure you can find a map in school," she says, "where that is, Sakhalin. He's been dead so long now, all your life."

THREE

Flour and Yeast

Makkum, Friesland
1527

I WAS BORN ALMOST FIVE HUNDRED YEARS AGO on our farmstead near Makkum, Friesland, now a province of the Netherlands. I am Trijntjen, daughter of Weynken Claes and Wybe Pieters, their first and only child. Two others born after me died before they were one. My mother told me I came on a Wednesday, very early in winter. Ice was forming on the canal but it was still too thin to cross—the midwife had to walk along the dike to the lock by the second windmill.

Not knowing the date of one's birth was common for my time. Not even Menne Simons' birthday is known, and he had all the "defenceless Christians" nicknamed after him because he wrote so many books for them. Countess Anna van Oldenburg called them "Mennists," trying to protect them. Menne was born nine kilometres from Makkum some twenty-five years before me, and at the end of this millennium many Mennonites still say,

"*Ejk sie een* (I am a) Mennist." They number over a million and live everywhere in the world.

But I'm no Menne Simons. I never wrote a word.

My mother couldn't write either, but she has been well known since the day of her death. The exact day was recorded in a book of martyr story-songs, *The Lord's Sacrifices*, 1562, and again in *The Bloody Theatre or Martyrs Mirror of the Defenseless Christians*, 1660:

Weynken, a widow, daughter of Claes, of Monickendam,
burnt to death in The Hague,
the 20th November A. D. 1527

Burnt to death. Charles V of Spain "by divine right," as he said, was then the Holy Roman Emperor of Europe. He also considered himself ordained by God to be the owner of the provinces of Holland. So he in turn ordained Duke Anthony Lalaing van Hooghstraten to be our Governor, that is, our Chief Exploiter. The official records say my mother was brought by cart as a prisoner in chains to The Hague on Friday, November 15, 1527. The Governor arrived in the capital on Sunday, November 17, and on Monday, November 18, my mother Weynken was arraigned before him and the full Governing Council of Holland. Accused of heresy.

It was deep sunset when the Spanish soldiers in their steel helmets hammered on the gate of our farmstead. We had watched for them through the outside window. They came marching along the road on the dike, and the evening light burned red around them. They looked like one huge, thick monster that bristled spears and heads, different heads lifting out of it and pulling back in, heads human, then horse, then steel human again. Growing larger so fast. I had looked out on the dike road all my life, but they seemed to be coming low, flat, on a burnished sea of shining blood.

My mother had sent our farm people quickly to their relatives, so they would not try to defend her. But I hid myself deep in the hay of the loft. By the time she found me, it was too late to run to Auntie Lijsbeth's. My mother kissed me hard and pushed me towards the ladder again. "Deep, deep!" she hissed as I climbed. I was so terrified for her, at their hammering and their smashing the rooms below me, that I was too stupid to look out the roof window. So they dragged her away, and I remember only her face against mine in our terror. And her kiss.

My mother was the widow of Wybe Pieters of Makkum. But she could be arrested in Friesland and taken for trial in The Hague because she was born in Monickendam, Holland. Makkum is eighty kilometres from Monickendam by sail across the Zuiderzee, and during an autumn storm my father's fishing boat was driven ashore there, and they saw each other. She was locking down the shutters of her family's shop against the spume flung by the crashing sea, and she glanced at him with the usual Dutch expression when recognizing a "stumma Fries," no matter how young, long and handsome he might be. The problem was he looked up at exactly that moment.

That's the way she always told the story. He and his two mates walked past, staggering from their twelve-hour struggle to save themselves and their boat. They had thrown all their gear and fish overboard to lighten it in the storm, and his hard body passed nearest her, bent like a tree against the shuddering wind. Then he saw her bare feet, the edge of her skirt, and from under his heavy eyebrows he looked up the length of her dress to her face. Expecting, and seeing, her lip curl. They were so close she would have touched him had she raised her finger. Their looks locked, and she saw light shape itself into an immovable decision in his blue Fris eyes.

That's how our mother Weynken told me the story. What my father Wybe saw he never said. Not that story in her eyes, nor any other. I remember him a little. He would sit with his legs stretched out, long feet naked and toes moving a little as if he remembered a song, staring into our hearth fire where bread baked. He was always mending a fish net, or sewing one. God took him, my mother told me, to Himself in the violent winter water, west beyond the Wadden Islands of the North Sea. I asked her, Does God live in the stormy sea? She said, I've told you and told you, God's home is everywhere.

On November 18 in The Hague, my mother stood alone and chained—there was no place to run, did they think she would attack them?—before the Duke van Hooghstraten and all his Councillors seated high in the Council Chambers. They would not, of course, talk directly to her themselves. As the records show, they had a woman ask her the questions that their learned and compliant theologians had prepared:

> *Question*: Have you well considered the things my lords have told
> you?
> *My mother*: I stand by my word.
> *Question*: You have been warned. If you do not speak differently,
> and turn from your error, you are subject to execution.
> *Answer*: Only if power is given you from above. I am ready to
> suffer.

Question: Do you then not fear death?

Answer: Often I fear it. But I shall never taste it, for Christ teaches
   in his Gospel, "I tell you the truth, if anyone keeps my word,
   they will never see death."

Question: What do you hold concerning our holy church?

Answer: Nothing. I never in my life met a "holy church."

Question: You speak with spite. What do you hold concerning the
   sacrament?

Answer: The sacrament your priest gives is in one kind only, not
   two. And the one he gives, I know it is flour and yeast.

Question: Take care what you say, such answers cost necks. You do
   declare that you do not believe the body and blood of Christ are
   present in the sacrament?

Answer: I verily believe, and hold, that God is not baked.

How could my mother speak before high lords and priests
in this way? A shopkeeper's daughter, the widow of a peasant
fisherman who could write her name well enough but could otherwise write or read not a word?

She'd say to me, "Listen, my sweet Trijntjen, listen," and
then she'd laugh and pull me tight against her. "Our dear God
gave us one good mouth in the middle of our face, see, to talk,
but two good ears, one on either side, to listen. So, two and one,
you listen twice in all directions, and then you speak straight
ahead, but only once." And she'd lean forward, nudge a forefinger into each of my ears—by now we were both laughing—and
she'd wriggle them into rhythm until my head rumbled gently.
And she would speak straight into my mouth, her breath like a
kiss, "Do you hear?"

Since before memory I lay on my blankets and watched her

sell. She sold the cheese and bread she made in the Makkum market, and also our father's fish. After he was gone his partners still brought her their catch to sell, and when I was old enough to walk, she carried the fish with her wooden yoke to Witmarsum and Bolsward as well. She talked to everyone easily, friends, acquaintances, the many strangers who paused, but like all market women she listened more. Especially to travellers shouting aloud in the market news from other towns, or reading out pamphlets on theology, or broadsheets about politics. So she heard, and remembered, when a priest named Ulrich Zwingli began teaching in Zurich far away. He taught that, according to the Scriptures, the Pope himself had no more power to forgive sins than any true Christian believer. She heard that Melchior Hoffman was travelling across Europe saying the Holy Spirit was poured out on every living person, you must listen to God's Word in the Bible and you would feel the Spirit move in your heart, all men and women too, it made no difference! She heard the New Testament read aloud, first in Martin Luther's German translation, and then the reader translated it on the spot into Dutch.

Masses of people were crowding the market square, many with their mouths open, listening. The women especially, as they bought and sold and waited, talked among themselves. Was this what the priests had mumbled in Latin all their lives? What no ordinary person was supposed to hear or understand? The women discussed, they argued, they memorized; they could not speak Latin or read, but they certainly could hear this, and remember.

And, shouted in the market, my mother heard what happened to Felix Manz in Zurich. He was the illegitimate son of a priest who studied theology with the preacher Zwingli. But he went farther than Zwingli, too far. He dared to have himself baptized as an adult by a fellow believer because, Manz testified at his trial, his baptism at birth could mean nothing. No infant could commit itself to a life of discipleship following the teachings of Jesus, as he, a grown person, now publicly did.

On January 5, 1527, Manz was bound with chains and rowed into the middle of the Limmat River. To below the Grossmünster Cathedral where Zwingli preached every Sunday. There the executioners held Manz under the water of the river until he was dead. An unforgettable lesson for the hundreds who watched, and those who heard it shouted in the towns and cities of Europe: if any adult dares the heretical water of rebaptism, the church and the state will give you enough water for a *third* baptism.

My mother heard of Felix Manz's testimony unto death. She heard of Michael Sattler burned alive in Rottenburg, Germany, on May 20 for the same reason. And of his wife forced to watch his torture. She was given the "third baptism" in the Neckar River, though it was reported she had asked for fire like her husband.

I never met anyone with a memory like my mother. She knew exactly how much fish she had sold, and for whom, every market day. If she heard something once and thought it important, she remembered it word for word. She told me these stories, she memorized and taught me the Word of God. By heart, she said, listen:

"Mark 12:30, 31. You must love the Lord your God with all your heart and with all your soul and with all your mind and with all your strength, and your neighbour as yourself.

"Acts 2:38. Repent and be baptized, every one of you, in the name of Jesus Christ for the forgiveness of your sins. And you will receive the gift of the Holy Spirit."

So, when the woman read her the questions before the

Governor and the Council of Holland, and asked, "Who taught you this, Weynken, how did you come by these opinions?" she disdained to implicate anyone. She simply quoted Jesus:

"John 10:27. My sheep hear my voice, I know them, and they follow me."

When he heard this, the Duke Anthony Lalaing van Hooghstraten could no longer contain himself. He leaned forward in his throne and roared at my mother:

"Woman, you would teach us!"

And she dared answer him directly: "Listen to the words of our Lord, Matthew 5:9. How blessed are the peacemakers, for God shall call them his children."

Though she did cry when the guards led her back to the dungeon exhausted after hours of such cross-examination. Those heavy men facing her in their fur and silk gowns, glaring. And especially when Auntie Lijsbeth made the long journey over sea and land to plead with her.

"How is my darling, my Trijntjen?" My mother was chained to the floor, Auntie Lijsbeth told me.

"She's safe. She doesn't go outside the farmstead wall. But she cries for you, so much—dearest sister, why, why? Can't you think what you please and keep it to yourself?"

"How can I be silent, when they ask me what I believe?"

"They have no moral right to ask. . . . Lie!"

"Yes. And then, how could I believe it?"

"I'm so afraid. They will kill you."

My mother wiped her tears, and suddenly she chuckled a little.

"I am learning Latin," she said. "Two Dominican priests come to me every day, and twice at night. One is to confess me—

he's very harsh, with heavy Latin—and the other is very cheer-ful, though full of Latin too. That's the way they confuse you, one rough and the other pretending to be gentle. But the guards are better teachers. They say in Latin 'domini' means 'lord,' and 'cane' means 'dog,' so, they tell me behind the backs of their hands, don't let these two fat *dogs of the Lord* scare you!"

But my aunt said she could not laugh with her. The filthy stone dungeon, my mother clamped by both legs to a huge ring with short irons she could barely lift....

We were with our cows, milking, when she told me. I sat rubbing Oldcow's heavy udder, my face pressed into her flank. The thick warmth of the good animal who gives us God's best food while we feed her hay and hard grain. I could feel life bur-ble inside her, it seeped through the short hair of her hide, warming me, and the barn, and all our living quarters up into the open rafters. Oldcow turned her long head to me, her single eye and blunt nose with its large, moist nostrils breathing, to watch me stroke her. Together we felt the milk gather down into her teats, ready and warm.

> Stripp, strapp, strull,
> Soon the pail is full.

My mother and I always sang that little song when we milked together. I could not clench my hands for weeping.

"What do you hold concerning the holy oil?" the "kind" Dominican asked my mother. He was trying to frighten her about death with his instruction on extreme unction.

My mother answered, "Oil is good for salad, or to oil your shoes. First Timothy 4:4—"

"God be damned!" the Dominican burst out. "Does it say that in the Bible?"

"You should read it, and not curse," she told him. "It says, 'Everything created by God is good, and nothing is to be rejected if it is received with thanksgiving.'"

She would not recant. After three days of trial, on Wednesday, November 20, the other Dominican led her before the court and held a crucifix in her face. "Fall on your knees," he whispered in her ear, "and ask the Lord for pardon."

But she turned her face from the crucifix and answered him loudly, "The just shall live by faith. Hebrews 11:2. For by faith our ancestors were commended."

He told her, "You will be condemned to death!"

She declared even louder, so that all would hear, "If any die by faith, they shall indeed never die but live in the Lord. Hebrews 12:1. With so many witnesses of faith around me like a great cloud, I will run with patience the race set before me."

My auntie Lijsbeth told me that, at these words, there was silence; as if, at that moment, they all knew that the great cloud of witnesses filled the trial chamber, watching. Then one of the Council asked her, softly, "You would condemn us all?"

"My Lord Jesus came to condemn no one," my mother said. "He came to give us peace."

The Governor pounded his gavel. "She has spoken enough! We will hear her sentence!"

The Dean of Naeldwijck stepped forward and read out her sentence to the Council in Latin, and repeated it for her in Dutch. Then he delivered her to the power of the state, adding that he did not consent to her death. When he and the two Dominicans—hypocrites—had left the Chamber, the Governor looked to his Council. They nodded one by one, and he declared:

"The heresy of Weynken, daughter of Claes of Monickendam, her immovable obstinacy of error regarding the sacrament, cannot pass without punishment."

He ordered, first, that her property be confiscated to the state for expenses. These, even before execution costs and including the daily fees of the Lords for Council sessions, already amounted to over fifty guilders. Second, that she be taken to the city square, that she be chained to the stake, and that she be burned to ashes.

I see a grotesque logic here. My mother baked bread all her life. If a man's baptism heresy demanded death by water, then a woman's heresy concerning the bread of the Sacrament could receive nothing less than the most extreme application of fire.

That afternoon on the scaffold she turned to the hundreds of people watching in the square and asked forgiveness of any she had offended. Then with one hand she moved her neckerchief so that the executioner could lay the gunpowder on her bosom. A priest held his crucifix in front of her, but she pushed his hand away. Instead she turned to the bench set against the stake and heaped around with very good wood, and asked the executioner, "Is the bench strong enough? Will I not fall?"

The executioner said, "Hold fast to God, Mother, don't be deceived."

So she stepped up onto the bench. He was preparing the irons to chain her to the stake, and the priest cried out, so that all the people crowded into the square must hear him, women and men and small children held up high in the arms of their parents to see:

"Mother Weynken, do you gladly die as a Christian?"

She answered clearly, "Yes, I do!"

"Are you sorry you have erred?"

"I once did err and for that I am sorry. But this is no error. I hold fast to God."

When she said this, the executioner laid a rope around her neck and in his kindness began to strangle her. When he had finished that at last, and she moved no more, he set the wood on fire.

After Auntie Lijsbeth and I finished milking, we fed our animals in their stalls and pens. The steel soldiers with the confiscation papers had not come yet. My aunt was in the pantry pouring the milk out carefully to cool and set for the night. I sat on my stool in our hearth. I watched our peat fire burn under the cooking grate, so quick and changing, so beautiful. Frisian peasants cannot afford wood. Of course, we are not state executioners.

Many times my mother had told me the Bible story of Moses. He heard the voice of God Himself speak to him from out of the fire.

I began to listen to this fire. From the wide, high darkness of the barn opening behind me I could hear the animals, the sounds of their large, uncomprehending bodies sinking gently into sleep. Otherwise there was nothing; I could hear nothing.

Listen, my mother whispers, her finger in my ear.

So I lean down. At the edge of the grate I point my finger into the low blue flame. Still nothing. I push more of my hand forward into the larger, leaping flames, my finger pointing; I am listening as hard as I can. At last I see that my whole hand is buried in the blazing coals. And then, finally, I hear something, yes, I can hear it more and more clearly. And I recognize it too. It sounds like a scream.

FOUR

ON LASTFIRE LAKE

Northwest Territories, Canada
1961

ADAM'S HEAD RINGS IN ENORMOUS SILENCE. His two rifle shots exploding at his ear have vanished over the land like air; the caribou jerked and twisted a little, staggered, but did not fall. Back sagging lower, but it would not. The immense bow of its six-tined upper rack, the double blades of its lower shovels start to draw its superb head down to the rocky tundra, its breath snores, but its legs are splayed, erect and solid. Adam takes a step, and sees a distant lake between them.

Why won't it—quick, another bullet, exactly behind the front shoulder. He pulls the trigger.

A crack, a thud, and nothing. The caribou bull stands immovable, white neck braced down between its thin framework of dark legs. Nose snoring blood.

Adam mutters, "Good god, why—" staring, and for an instant the caribou's snow-white ruff lurches at him like a childhood memory of a woman's high winter collar and her round face turning—his head spins in vertigo; he crunches sideways in the lichen.

Eric hisses beside him. "Goddamn it, hit the legs!"

But Adam's left arm muscles bunch, cramp, the .306 sinks to point at his own foot.

"Shit!" and Eric's rifle fires. The bull's front leg disintegrates, and it starts to crumple, *again!* and its rear hoists sideways; topples over. On the lip of the ridge where it rose up over them there remains against the far lake only the long curved stem of one antler, the flare of its tined bone flower.

"I told you they're tough." Eric is walking up the ridge, fast. "Rack growing, summer fat, they're full of juice."

Adam clicks his rifle on safety. A wave like nausea soaks through him. He sinks onto his heels, balancing with the rifle clutched erect in front of him, the way Napoleon Delorme showed him the Dene rest when there's no rock handy, rest, but always alert on the open barrenlands. You think you can see everything, Napoleon said, it looks flat and the slopes to the ridges like there seem close and easy, but it fools you, there's wrinkles all over land like any old face—laughing—and gullies and water and niggerheads, a caribou will surprise you, just come up outta nowhere, huh! she sees you and you move and she's gone again.

But this one came up and saw him and stopped. Who can know the way of the wind or the caribou? So the Dene said.

Or a woman. Susannah Lyons. Who had stopped and studied him and said she wanted to marry him. She had.

Their mutual friend Eric Gunnarson is up on the ridge hauling at the antlers of this caribou bull dead at last, twisting him over on his back to butcher. Adam is more than a thousand miles away from her; north, ever north, another thousand and more to the limit of Ellesmere Island and everlasting ice until north bends south into Siberia, the Mennonite name for suffering and the Bolshevik beast Stalin—sweetest shit! as Eric would say. Adam feels himself vertical in flat landscape, an engaged man standing in a museum diorama of Canada with tundra, September shining on the circle of horizon, two clusters of Dene far away skinning caribou; all painted.

But John L in his bright red jacket is moving, coming towards him and Eric and hoisting his rifle over his head in recognition of their kill.

Carefully Adam straightens up. He feels good, the air in his nostrils blue as Edmonton spring, with a lace of Arctic cold. He walks a hoof trail between stones up the ridge. Eric has cut off the dark head with its open eyes and is laying it aside, propped over on the incredible curve of its antlers. Such immense bows of bone sprouting on a slender head, they seem longer than the mound of body; there is still the ragged velvet of growing on the tips of their tines.

"Nice one, you hit him dead right," Eric says. "So dead he couldn't fall over."

Adam can, thankfully, focus on the detached body, the splintered bones. He says, "You really smashed him."

Eric is concentrating on anatomy, not catching his tone. "Lucky shots." He searches in the white hair between the splayed hind legs, finds a hold. "Here's where you start."

And his knife unzips the tight hide, one quick line running open from the back vent and curving close, not touching scrotum or ridge of penis, and through the bullet-smashed blood of the ribs; lays it open to white fat streaked with red, deep blood-cratered muscle. Not slowly, centimetre by centimetre, the way they worked together for months on the endlessly enduring, formaldehyded cadaver in their human anatomy lab in medical school: here Eric is strictly a butcher unparcelling meat, Adam reminds himself, good fresh meat to eat with gratitude.

"Oh, eat your roll!" Susannah exclaimed, exasperated.

"Your dad," Adam muttered into his thick china coffee cup. "He doesn't like me."

"It's not you, silly, it'd be anybody, I'm all he—"

"Thanks a lot, I'm just 'anybody.'"

"I told you, it's my mother." Her long fingers unravelled a University Tuck Shop roll, its cinnamon tang drifting between them. "He's still mourning her."

"He still has you, he'd just gain me."

"He knows that, he does."

"Then why doesn't he like me?"

"He does! You just don't recognize how he is, listen," and she slid out from under her side of the booth and onto the seat against him, "you don't need cinnamon or coffee, you need a bit of osculation."

The mirrors above the Tuck Shop booths multiplied their heads into facing each other endlessly, but at that moment he felt there would never be enough of her. "'Os-cu-la-tion,'" he recited to her lips, "'the mutual contact of blood vessels.'"

"Yes, Anatomy 201, but also geometry: 'One curve osculates the other when it has the highest possible order of contact with the other.'"

"I love you when you recite the *Oxford English*

Dictionary on Historical Principles."

"Just for you," she said, half a breath from contact. "Pure love."

"The *OED* definition of 'love,' please."

"'That disposition with regard to a person which, open bracket, arising from recognition of attractive qualities, from instincts of natural relationship, or from sympathy, close bracket, manifests itself in solicitude for the welfare of the object, delight in his presence and desire for his approval.'"

"Ex-cel-lent." He was eighth-of-an-inching closer. "Love is disposition, desire, delight."

Susannah said into his mouth, "Love is also a decision."

John L in his blazing red jacket stands in front of Adam, his face dark with happiness. Annual fall hunt on the tundra: you get off the plane onto shore and within an hour you have first kills. "Good. Lots of rump fat, that's where they store it." And he laughs aloud. "Power right there for jumping them sweet little cows!"

Eric says, "Adam shot it."

"I hit him, twice, spine and heart I thought, but he wouldn't fall, he just stood...."

John L says, suddenly quiet, "Sometimes they're dead on their feet but won't go down, like, Hey, this is my land, I live here, who are you?"

Adam's mind goes blank; the sky settles over him like a pale, thin bowl. After a time he sees that John L is offering him his hunting knife.

"If you want." His voice in the gentle Dene tone of suggestion. At first Adam thought it was merely their inflectionless way of speaking English, until he realized they did not speak in orders. "You can offer thank you, to the caribou spirit, this gift. You can lay a bit of liver on the ground for him, and eat some."

Eric's knife has stopped unlayering skin from fatty ribs in a hollow of bullet blood. Adam accepts John L's knife, already slippery with other fat, and kneels down on the lichen; he opens the given body and does that.

He carries the caribou he killed but could not make fall. Every bit of its red meat and fat and heart and brain and the rest of the liver he had not offered or eaten, bundled in its own brownish-grey-and-white hide. One hundred and twenty, perhaps thirty pounds, John L said as he and Eric hoisted it carefully onto his lower back and he smoothed the carrying band of the tumpline across his forehead. He could stand easily enough, the bundle such a warm, settled weight squarely on his hips with his back and neck tilted taut in a straight line holding it. You know the direction to camp? John L asked. That ridge with the boulder, from there you'll see, you can rest backed against it so you won't break your back lifting. Eric laughed and said, Next time shoot a smaller one. John L said, balancing him, It's not you, as Adam took his first steps, staggering a little. It's the caribou, caribou test you.

Kathy leans at right angles over a fire between three stones on the open tundra, frying bannock. She slides in another piece of the split spruce they brought on the plane, exactly so the flames touch only the pan, wasting nothing. Sleeves pushed up, black hair tied back, glasses.

"Nice big meat you carried," she says, "and tomorrow your back will feel it!"

"It already does," Adam says. "Not bad, it just knows."

She laughs. He thinks, She could certainly carry a hundred and fifty pounds on a tumpline across the tundra, as many miles as necessary to bring it to home camp, stocky, legs solid and planted like that on the hard ground. Then she straightens up, and her woman's shape moves under her bulky clothing, the neckerchief and thick jacket with white polar bears down the black sleeves and blue pants inside rubber boots doubled over: her brown skin would contain her so perfectly, her arms, shoulders, her breasts, they would be heavy, the push of her knee, the loose pants cannot hide the long, narrow space between her thighs.

"Here," Kathy says. She has cut the golden bannock in the frying pan and is offering him half on her knifepoint. "You work, you get food."

Deep-fried and hot, unfathomably good in the colder air. Napoleon Delorme materializes at the tent opening: Adam has not known he was in there, but where else would he be? As he said, he is long past being a hunter, even now when a plane flew in an hour what was once three weeks of heavy paddling and portaging. Napoleon, resting his ancient bones for the evening.

"I can still smell that bannock," he says. Kathy snorts with a grin, offers him the other half. He takes it in his bare hand and folds himself down cross-legged beside Adam on his stone. "I gotta eat lots now, for all the starving I did when I was a kid."

"No caribou then?"

"Oh, lots, more than now, but you never know where they come, you can't sit and look out of a window and fly around and find them caribou travelling along below there."

Kathy says, "But the Old Ones have power, didn't they, to find them?"

"Yeah, sometimes, sometimes they had power, they could know where they were coming south with their little calves. My grandfather Pierre had power. One fall he told us it would be Winter Lake and we paddled there straight up the Yellowknife River, that's an easy way north, only two weeks and there they came, thousands, we snared them among the last trees around the lake all winter, we didn't even need expensive bullets. But sometimes ..." He shakes his head sadly inside the hood of his huge parka. His face tight and dark like polished stone.

Abruptly he laughs. "That's why I got my name!"

"Oh, Grandpa!" Kathy exclaims, bent at the fire.

But Napoleon has a new listener. "My grandfather Pierre was never happy with his power, the people always needed help and power is always responsibility, it's so much work, and there were the whites, traders and priests and government eating better than he and it looked like they never worked at all, so he sent my uncle Joseph and my mother to school to learn what white people know so they wouldn't have to work either."

Napoleon chuckles. Surprised, Adam asks, "He sent his children to residential school?"

"It was day school then. In winter they'd move to Providence before Christmas and my grandfather Pierre hunted and trapped and the Oblate Fathers taught the kids to read. My mom was very little but she knew her grandfather's name had been Napoleon, and the priests taught her about the first one, a very Big Man they said, emperor of France. She loved that big map they had, they told her it was the real picture of the world, and she drew it exactly on one sheet of paper. I was born a lot later, but she still had her school picture of the world and sometimes when it was so cold in winter I'd sit in her lap and she'd say, 'That's your name, Napoleon, that's a big name, big enough for an emperor.' And she'd laugh and fold open her map. It was grey and pretty worn out, but she'd coloured France and Russia red. 'When you're big you'll march into Russia too, just like the emperor, but you'll come from here, see, from the back, up the long tail of Russia from Alaska, not from the front where they're watching, and so you'll surprise them and take over that big city Moscow easy. Its roofs are all gold,' she said, 'and you'll live there rich all your life and never be hungry!'"

They are laughing around the three-stone fire, their sounds thin as stray hairs adrift in space, taking golden Moscow from the barrens of the Northwest Territories with Dene carriers trudging towards camp packing meat on tumplines as they have for ten thousand years. Flee Canada for Russia—not the story Adam had heard in his Alberta bush, often in icy winter on his mother's warm lap, though he had never gone hungry either. For his parents Moscow was hungry misery and abrupt, inexplicable release into a strange land for a few, but banishment for most. Banished home. How is that possible? Adam is laughing at the Dene conquest of Moscow, but he is also on the edge of crying. Clearly this tundra space, where a person walking is always less than a mere speck, is nevertheless home to Napoleon; and Kathy too.

Legs straight and body bent down to a fire burning under nothing but sky: a beautiful woman. Adam feels Susannah sing in his head, she has taught him how a woman's contained and perfect shape can drench his mind and seep through his body; he has to straighten up, stretch out his legs, the stone under him so hard and raw suddenly he has to stand, move, walk away, down to the narrow sand of the lake where the Otter backed them in on its pontoons, where they grabbed their packs and scrambled through brush up to the level of the tundra and instantly saw the caribou. A line of pencil dots between grey knobs of hills, dots bunching and shifting shapes below the horizon, vanishing as they all stared without even a moment to unstrap binoculars. "Look there," John L said beside him. To the right, there they were too, so close they became huge individual animals walking a steady single line, their brownish-white bodies seemingly so close, their necks and shoulders hung thick as snow, their high shovelled antlers bowed forward over their precise heads, walking south on the skyline as if above and far beyond them, travelling on air.

Susannah, his long-legged Susannah. "I'm all he's got." Bud Lyons, he thinks, you can have every bit of her that's daughter, she has more than enough life and love as wife with me.

Susannah, the intense joy of his life, which for so long had been hardened into nothing but concentrated, laborious study. Medicine. It was impossible, but nevertheless necessary, to know everything concerning the human body; body models did not change every year like cars, they were always all the same, like a smashed caribou chest—and also always infinitely different like every other smashed caribou chest. Every body was capable of growing things until then undreamed of, to say nothing of the brain that controlled the mind or the infinite corpuscularization of feelings. But when they two discovered each other, gradually over months like an inevitability edging closer, in every concentration of endless medicine he began to realize she permeated him with her undemanding or arguing presence like blood beating, she was there in any split-second slit of his concentration. And when they were together every other body vanished, the University of Alberta Hospital with its six or seven hundred beds filled with sick, screaming, healing, dying, weeping or overjoyed people dropped away, gone. Talking, enfolded in arms, twisting wits, the lengths of their bodies, a room, a couch, a bedsheet a world enough.

Then why is he apprehensive? Face it: here on a staggering landscape he has never before seen, he's afraid.

Four weeks from today, on October 7 in Edmonton; Saturday.

"*Na oba doch,*" his mother said softly in Lowgerman, which of course Susannah could not understand. "At least, it has to be in a church. Our last boy and we see his bride once and the second time they're just written together?"

He wanted to yell at her, Because getting written together can be just one more suffering for you, how can this be *God's will* if you don't *suffer?* But he saw Susannah had understood his mother's tone, if not her words, and he controlled himself.

"No, no, Mam, in a chapel, United Church, and you and Dad will come, yes? I'll drive down and get you."

"Where will we stay?"

No relative within three hundred miles of Edmonton.

"It's all arranged," he assured her. "The guest room at St. Stephen's residence, the same hall as my room, I'll be right there and Susannah's father will bring you back, he says he'd like to look around Lethbridge, he'll bring you home."

"What kind of name is that, 'Lyons'?"

"Bud Lyons...I guess it's English, they came from the States after the war. And he'll drive you back in his big car all in one day, he said, he'd be very happy to do it."

Susannah's green eyes watching told him again: I want her there, I want them both there, my mother's gone and she has to be there, so be a good and considerate son to her, try, for once.

"And everything English," his mother said sadly.

"You want to bring Preacher Puddel Reima up there to—" He caught himself, explained again, steadily, "Susannah and I are getting married," and standing there with his right arm around her shoulders, looking into his mother's grey eyes, Adam knew that it would happen. "And Susannah does not understand German."

She said into his ear, "Tell her, in the ceremony we can have a Mennonite German hymn."

"What? Who'll sing it? Nobody'll know a word of German."

"She and your father, they sing beautifully."

"Sing...a duet?"

Adam recognizes his feet walking the curved margin of the tundra lake, along the many shovel-footed tracks left in the sand by caribou. Here and there their trails lead aside, cut up the bank and radiate in worn lines over the tundra; so much like the paths trodden deep into poplar bush where he once brought the cows home for milking that he looks around, almost expecting leaves to flicker above him. But only immense bluish sky streaked with thin, fast clouds; running, like the caribou.

His apprehension wasn't about his mother—and certainly not his father, who looked at Susannah and laughed aloud; to him she was simply beautiful, a golden girl tall and strong and English, you've found yourself such a bride! Their song, Susannah said, would be the most beautiful part of the ceremony.

"They have the steady, delicate sound," she told him, "of medieval angels."

"So where have you heard medieval angels?"

"Goof, you know what I mean."

"It could be...as long as they don't sing Dad's all-time favourite:

> "Here on earth now I am a pilgrim,
> And my pilgrimage, my pilgrimage, is not long."

Susannah said, "You told me Mennonites sing that at funerals. This is our wedding."

"You don't know my mother. Her life motto is, 'We have here no abiding city, for we seek the one to come.'"

Eric, plough-straight-ahead roommate, would have none of that. "Mothers are fine, in their place—the past. So," and he threw his big body on his residence bed set at right angles to Adam's so they could talk more easily, "you graduate in the top third of the class, you can choose anywhere in Canada to intern, and practise, and get rich, a beautiful girl is in love with you, she's so smart she'll have a Ph.D. before you've finished interning, but despite everything she loves you and you love her, so what's the matter?"

"Getting married isn't all-night cramming and you ace a test."

"Hey, I never said it, but hell, this one's made in

heaven, everything right here in St. Steve's Chapel, walk down the hall, just you two and three parents and twenty friends and a minister, a mountain hotel Thanksgiving weekend lovering and you're back in classes, both, the world goes on as it should, but together...so?"

Purest Eric logic: one of the reasons they had roomed together comfortably for three years. Unworried and unhurried, he would certainly make a very good, practical doctor. He was born in Yellowknife where his father managed a gold mine, but there was no way he'd go into a goddamn hole a mile in the ground. His big body had the steady, delicate craftsman's hands of a surgeon; unlike Adam, who certainly didn't want to spend his life searching for and cutting things out of people's bodies and sewing them shut again; who sometimes couldn't remember why he was in medicine at all.

"In grade twelve this teacher, Frank Bargen, got me really interested in history, about the city-state Danzig—" Adam stopped; that was too ridiculously personal even for midnight confidences. "He also got me reading a book, too, called *The Bloody Theatre or Martyrs Mirror of the Defenseless Christians*, a huge collection of stories of people who were killed during the Reformation, hundreds of them."

"Good god," Eric said, "a history of fanatics? And really horrible?"

"Oh yeah, blood and burning and beheading, drowning, lots of it."

"Sounds great for a growing boy," Eric laughed. "Pretty kinky teacher."

"He wasn't kinky at all, he told me history wasn't just

kings conquering worlds, it was people living lives, as they had to, as they believed. Sometimes I think if that first-year university course had been any better, I'd be in history."

"Old fart MacDonald, so mentally constipated he'd just come in and read for an hour from his own lousy book."

"Anyway," Adam said glumly, "what can you do with history?"

"Nothing. Maybe teach. Hey, it's okay," Eric calmed him, "for you medicine's easy. It's a legal profession, very good money, and you can always change and do anything else if you want. In the meantime you get shitloads of respect. 'Oh, you're a doctor!'"

"Yeah, like the Jewish mama, she could just as well be Mennonite, yelling on the beach, 'Help! help! *my son the doctor* is drowning!'"

The crystal water laps at his boots, at the edge of two pawprints. Perfect in impressionable sand and large as his mittened hand, the oval indentation of the heel, each drop-shaped toe pointed deep in a scimitar claw. Adam's feet sink slowly in the soft surface, the lake clicking tiny waves beside him: Susannah, marriage—how can that be, how is that about to happen? Life, past and foreseeable, is organized university routine, classes and study, get drunk and talk about sex and go to dances and drink and sleep and classes—but he detests the stupidity drink blunders him into. He has decided his life into what he thinks a transparent cycle: study, study, in summer dirt and good wages on oil rigs and save and study. A deliberate concentration of books and labs and professors and finally cadavers and precise, clear requirements that can be fulfilled exactly if you concentrate and work hard enough, focus. He can drive three hundred highway miles to Coaldale on a long weekend reviewing definitions and body parts, and leave about the time it is necessary to go to church because his mother understands, yes, of course he has to study. And even Susannah, met when they both were leaving a silly dance and then met deliberately, again and again, until he began to intuit a possible happiness with her far beyond Tuck Shop coffee. Nevertheless, when he is studying she seems a sort of dislocated fantasy. A shadow passing over him, beyond touch and unawares. But then she is actually beside him, with him, and she pushes aside, as it seems then, his ridiculously narrow world so completely that he can for those moments understand, beyond any doubt, his mother's eternal and unshakable faith in the substance of things hoped for as the evidence of things suddenly seen.

"*The Bloody Theatre*," Susannah said in wonder, "what an amazing title for a book. And *Mirror* too."

"It was odd, yeah, but no odder than all the bloody stories."

"All books had those long, complex titles then, in the 1600s...."

"One of those martyrs," Adam told her, "was barely a teenager, they tortured her by 'tearing her tender limbs with cutting hooks,' I remember that, they cut her open to the ribs and she cried out, 'Behold, Lord Jesus Christ! Thy name is being written on my body!'"

Susannah's large, brilliant eyes held him unblinkingly. Adam murmured, "I remember that...story...."

And she responded, strangely, "In a mirror you see the world in reverse."

"Yes," Adam said, "there's that. And also it's always behind you."

They were two people profoundly together, and together thinking beyond themselves; his deliberately cobbled world of medicine gone somewhere then, somehow pale and shallow and gone. But. But. Never as completely, he sensed, never quite gone in the flat, factual way she vanished when he lived hands-on in medicine.

Eric said no worry, they were just up to their goddamn necks in endless minutiae. More likely, Adam thought, he was in over his head. And if he could surface, would a life split with Susannah submerge him as well? How many ways does a person need to drown?

"C'mon, clear your head," Eric pushed him. "A break before term, before the wedding, just relax, hunt caribou on the tundra where there's nothing but horizon. C'mon, Napoleon says sure, if he wants to, you bring your friend along."

Adam hunches down on the soft edge of a lake at the Arctic circle. Huge prints with four toes; grizzlies have five. Napoleon would say: This is our brother, our sister wolf who long ago when the world was new showed us how to hunt the running caribou, taught us how to live as good a life as the Creator has already given us, live it until we die. The relentless hospital wards slide over Adam's thoughts, row on row on corridor of Hippocratic devastation so simple if they could all simply die when their bodies said so, and he simply carry a tumpline of

meat, drag his convoluted life over the moss-and-stony tundra—
sweet shit.

He should go back. Gnaw a roasted rib, listen to hunter talk
and grunt, stare into a three-stone fire. Shut the shit down.

As the autumn night deepens they lie side by side on or in their
sleeping bags inside the perimeter of the tent; it is so compact
that unless they curl a little their feet touch down the centre line.
Napoleon sits beside the barrel heater and tells stories. Some in
English, a few in Dogrib that he has been given to tell only in
that language, but which John L has permission to translate.
Stories about the People, who have always lived here, who know
certain things a little, who have no word for wilderness because
everywhere this land is home. No plane or skin canoe or radio or
bone needle changes land and People. A journey here to Lastfire
Lake for fall caribou once required three or four weeks, paddling
and carrying around rapids and between rivers from Rae-Edzo,
their dogs running along the banks with them in summer clouds
of mosquitoes, fifty-seven portages on tumplines, even the little
children carrying. And on the way they would pass the immense
dam built by the Giant Beavers where the Lawgiver Yamoria
fought them, and also the place where the Dogrib and
Yellowknife Dene a hundred and fifty years ago pledged peace to
each other forever and danced, the circle they pounded into the
earth dancing still rounded deep between the stones. Napoleon's
lips barely move, a mystery of incomprehensible language and
John L's quiet voice speaking his words into the further mystery of English as the spruce snaps in the heater. They are drifting into sleep while the mantle lamp hisses down.

And then Adam is jerked awake, the warm stovepipes

crashing down over them. Storm outside, slamming the tent with boxer combinations *boom! boom! boomboom!* Someone opens the tent flap, in the grey dawn snow is streaking past and John L shouts above the din for everyone to sit up, back onto the floor edges of the tent, the anchor ropes may not hold. Then he tries to burrow out, low, and the wind catches the flap and gets a muscle inside and bulges the tent out of itself with a roar, it will heave them all into the lake; they can hear whitecaps smashing against the shore below. They sit bunched up and as heavy as they can imagine themselves, the canvas pounding continuous ice and thunder back and forth over them, and there is nothing to do but sit, and nothing particular to think about; they are inside and dry and together, nothing to do but smile at each other sometimes a little. Wait.

Napoleon tells Adam, "My grandfather Pierre had power with animals. Mostly with caribou, but he always said to me, power is seeing. There's a way to find anything you need, what you have to do is first see it."

They have re-erected their tent in a hollow studded with brush at the end of the lake. Kathy is showing Adam how to cut meat properly into strips for drying. She laughed aloud when he asked her if he could try; the cutting board is short and for every uneven strip he manages she cuts three. Swiftness matters here, not studied laboratory investigation, though the running muscles of a caribou haunch are stunning in their complexity. They sit shoulder to shoulder on the ground over the cutting board worn thin by long hunts, while the old man lies on his elbow feeding tiny sticks into the fire.

"Everything you need to have," Napoleon continues, "my

grandfather always said when I was a little kid, you need to understand it's already there, you just have to see it and then you'll know how to make it. So, when you need caribou meat, you first have to see the snare, and you braid that, and then you see the right trail going past Winter Lake and down through the trees to Snare or Roundrock Lake, and the caribou will get tangled in that snare because you set it where you saw the caribou was already caught."

For an instant something flickers in Adam, almost a whiff of comprehension, but it is gone.

"You mean . . . dream it?"

"No no, like a dream, but you're not dreaming, no, you see it. And you can't be scared because then you won't see. If you're scared, that always keeps you too small to see anything."

Adam thinks, placing his knife for the next cut, Maybe it was this caribou leg I carried here this morning through the snow on the tundra, where John L shot it and removed the hide as if he were pulling a parka over his head and had it disassembled and bundled in twenty minutes, and then I was staggering off again, over two ridges and along an esker, under the gathering pain of a tumpline and not seeing even one trail found long ago by the caribou for easy travel on this relentless, endless land. I'm blinder than a whole Dogrib tundra of bats.

Napoleon seems to be staring into the flames. Five curved halves of caribou rib-racks surround the leaping fire, lean towards it speared on sticks; looking like oval lyres some bloody-minded giant might play with greasy fingers.

If everything can be seen as having already happened, then there is nothing, further, to be scared of. Napoleon said that, twice.

The old man lifts himself off the ground. "Let's look at the animals," he says, and walks towards the slight tundra rise between them and the lake. Adam follows him. And he's right, there the caribou are against the knobby hills again, where they already were when the plane first landed; but much closer now because the storm forced them to move their campsite.

Napoleon lifts his hand, and stops. The hunters from their camp are black dots far away to the right. Arctic landscape with motionless animals and running sky. Adam walks forward. He keeps on walking towards the caribou.

Walks until one by one and then all together they begin to run. They spread flat like a stream flowing over the tundra before him, the mass of them breaking out into tremendous speed and they are so close he sees how they lay their heads back to run, nostrils high in the wind, and he can hear their hooves thunder and click, running right and vanishing behind a long hill away from the hunters and emerging at last far in the flat distance, still running but turned back again to the left, until they slant up among the erratics of a ridge and their small, huge-antlered bodies walk away south there, high against the wild, cloud-driven sky.

When Adam finally turns, Napoleon has not moved. The old man looks at him silently, without expression, not even his eyes asking Adam what he is asking himself: Why did I do that, walk towards them till they ran? Why am I such a fool?

Beside the fire the dark ribs still roast on their stakes. Kathy bends, gathers up a handful of meat strips they have cut. She begins to hang them over the line they have tied between the tent and a dwarf spruce farther in the hollow. Adam listens to the snow melt, the air peaceful as a blanket.

Kathy asks, "You got a picture of your sweetie?"

"Oh yeah," Adam says. The muscle he sliced looks amazingly like human muscle; he would look like this if he were dead and someone were cutting him into strips to dry, exactly like this, nothing whatsoever special about his muscle; there'd just be a lot less of it to keep someone alive.

"Can I see it?" Kathy grins at him over her shoulder; skin and long profile like any classical Egyptian. "Her picture?"

"Sure." Adam fumbles against the bump of his wallet, and suddenly he is wiping his hands on his parka, down his pant leg as he lifts the edge of it, wiping his greasy hands the way his mother taught him never to do, unthinkable in the lab too, and talking, words running from his mouth. "It's just little, one of those silly things you go into a bus depot, mostly greyish, it's not her alone, in Edmonton and you stick your head behind a curtain, she sat down and I just wanted to too so I stuck my head in beside her and just then the silly flash goes off, Susannah was trying to ask me if I..."

He is nattering as if he has lost his head.

Adam wants to tell this tundra woman he will never see again absolutely everything. The story of the life he has lived until this very moment, the longer story of the life he will live, his singular life, which as he has seen in the running of the caribou, is already, and simply, complete.

FIVE

TONGUE SCREW

Antwerp, Flanders
1573
Danzig
1638

I WAS BORN IN ANTWERP, FLANDERS, in our small stone house on the Oudenaerde Ganck in 1570. They named me Jan Adam Wens. It was the horrid time when the Spanish Fury burned in the Low Countries, driven by the merciless inquisition of Antoine, Cardinal Granvelle of Utrecht, and the Spanish armies led by Fernando Alvaraz, Duke of Alva. King Philip II of Spain and Portugal considered himself the champion of the Counter-Reformation; his armies slaughtered infidel and heretic alike, and he paid his mercenaries with shiploads of gold and silver brought from the Americas. Death by labour in the mines of the New World, death by religious rage in the Old; my brother Adriaen Wens was fifteen years old and I was three when, early in the morning, our mother was led out to be killed.

In the Grand Square of Antwerp, where the unfinished

spire of Our Lady Cathedral towered over the tall seven-stepped houses facing the new city hall, Adriaen climbed up on a bench, holding me as our mother had written him in her last letter: "Take Hansken on your arm now and then for me." He was trying to lift me high so that together we could see her burn. But when the executioner chained our mother to the stake piled around with firewood, Adriaen fainted and fell to the cobblestones, and of course no one in the crowd noticed. So neither of us actually saw it happen.

October 6, 1573. I remember nothing, not even how my head cracked. I was only three.

On the other hand, my wife, Janneken, says she remembers everything. Both how on September 6 of that year her father Hans van Munstdorp was burned alone in such a huge fire that it drove the watchers into the side streets and they feared for the surrounding buildings, and also the four well-controlled fires— the executioner had a month of burning experience—which much more slowly, and with great torture, destroyed her mother Janneken Munstdorp and my mother Maeyken Wens, together with her sisters, my aunts Mariken and Lijsken Lievens.

"It's impossible," I say to Janneken. "You weren't born when they killed your father, and only a month old for your mother."

"I know, I know," she answers in her low, soft voice, her small face looking at me as fierce as any bishop. "But I saw."

"How?"

"I saw him because my mother saw, I was in her womb. That's why they didn't burn her and my father together. For her they waited till I was born and they found a wet-nurse."

"I know that—but how can you say you saw even them? You were barely a month."

"The nurse took me to the square."

"But I was three years, and I remember nothing!"

"If you don't remember, how do you know what happened?"

"Adriaen told me."

"But he told you, many times, he fainted and fell. You have the scars to prove it."

"He saw enough, before and after."

And usually, I don't have to say any more. I can't. We sit opposite each other in our hearth, warm, silent together. She knits, I stir the fire and raise or lower the kettle on the kettle-hook, so it sings. Adriaen told me all he ever will; he's no longer alive. And when Janneken and I speak of that time, sometimes years apart, we talk the way a wife and husband do who have lived through forty-seven years together and who know they will continue to circle back, again and again, to those horrible memories, sometimes by accident, sometimes when it seems they can, momentarily, bear them: this is how we were born, it is our one life. If we cannot by the mercy of God forget, then we have only this past by His grace to remember.

Sometimes, when I'm at work splitting or polishing stone, trying to shape it exactly into what it needs to be, I see my scarred hands and tools chipping away forever at what already exists: our immovable past. Which surrounds Janneken and me like an immense plain of irreducible stone. Hand, hammer, chisel, stone and the years of our life, we keep on trying to split and shape them right; so they will fit.

Fit into what? How? If you could remember perfectly, could you shape a horror the way you work a stone? Shape it for what? To build what?

"They would have killed your father too," Janneken says suddenly, directly to my thoughts. "If he hadn't fled to Friesland."

"Then why—my mother knew that—why did she write to him, asking him to visit her in prison? He never came."

"He sent Adriaen and you, he knew they wouldn't hurt children, especially unbaptized ones."

Why do I have no memory? Not so much as a slant of darkness in her cell, a smell of stone. When I was fourteen and our father died, Adriaen decided we must leave even Friesland, forever, and he took me back to Antwerp so I would have some memory of the place where our mother died. The roadstead of the Scheldt River was full of more ships than I could count, their ordered sails tied up or opened white as the clouds of heaven. But we had no time to watch them glide by, we were staring at the stone walls of Het Steen Castle rising out of the harbour water. Stones well cut, expertly laid, its great arched halls could have been filled with choirs singing praise to God over the water, to encourage travellers leaving for the measureless oceans of the globe. A king's castle for seven hundred years, and now a dungeon. Defenceless Christians chained there to groan, their bodies beaten open and rotting.

Like our mother. Arrested in April, tortured for six months and burned in October. Adriaen told me I was with her inside that stone twice, for several weeks.

Janneken says, "It was all they could do. Your father escaped Antwerp alive, he worked to send money so the four women had better food and a cleaner cell." She smiles at me, certainly the living memory of her mother's face, with no chisel needed. "So I didn't have to be born among the rats in the holes below the river."

"Six months. She smuggled out two letters, and he never came to her once."

"How do you know he never?"

I don't. That's the trouble. No matter how often you turn over what memories you have, you still never know any more; you never know enough to recognize what more you will want, what more you will desperately need to know, later. And when the later arrives and stretches into endless future, what can you do?

Remember what you cannot forget. Every bit you have. When the evening light fell low across Antwerp harbour, the water blazed like polished steel against the castle, and finally Adriaen and I walked away. Through the narrow, high streets to the Grand Market. It was safe enough then, just a young man and a boy walking. The winged, slate slope of the city hall roof, its carved arches and windows, and the tight, beautifully peaked buildings all around us, as if in the level light we were standing inside the darkness of an immense, blazing crown. The Cathedral spire was still not complete; the Calvinists momentarily controlled the city and they had been throwing the Papist furniture out of the church while Antoine Cardinal Granvelle and Philip II were busy ashing Catholic heretics in other parts of the Low Countries. In southern Europe the Calvinists burned Anabaptist believers—rebaptizers, as they called them—as quick as did the Catholics, but not in Antwerp. They used other means, like allowing them no work and hoping they would either starve or leave.

Adriaen showed me where the bench had stood that he climbed on. Where we both, he told me, strained to look over heads to the four tall stakes. They made the four women climb up; they had brought them in carts along the same street from the castle that we had just walked. The fountain was not built yet, nor the statue over it representing the Roman soldier holding the chopped-off giant's hand high over the Scheldt and, in his defiance of tyranny, about to act out the city's name, *hand werpan*, that is, "throw the hand away."

Adriaen and I stood there. Perhaps he prayed. I told my mind, "Here is the place, here," but it would think nothing. After a time he walked away, into another street. Ten slow steps and we were on an open triangle of cobblestones. I looked up, and up, bending back, looking: it was the magnificent Cathedral of Our Lady.

Named otherwise by the Calvinists, at that moment. But as soon as the last Anabaptist-Mennonites were gone and Alexander Farnese and his army in their turn destroyed the Calvinists and most of the beautiful city for the continuing glory of the Roman Catholic faith, Our Lady would arise once more inside her enormous stone diadem. Wearing her blue and golden robes, her crown three times taller than her head, her tiny crowned Child held high on her left arm. If, as they affirm, the Virgin and the Child neither sleep nor faint, how many thousands of people have they been forced to watch burn? They say eighteen thousand by the Duke of Alva alone.

I have learned the tender prayer that can be prayed to Our Lady: "Heavenly Mother Mary, in his last hour on the Cross, your divine Son Jesus committed us to your motherly care. We pray to you, reveal your holiness in this your city, Antwerp." But the prayer helps me little. I have no motherly care to forget.

Janneken says, "But Jan Adam, you do. Adriaen and I have told you the stories."

Sometimes my mind sinks, it refuses even those. The four

chained and violated women whom Janneken says she "knew" for the five months they endured in their dungeon before she was born, and the short month after.

"Your mother wrote to you," Janneken insists. "'My dear children, kiss one another once for me, for remembrance. Be kind, I pray you, to your afflicted father all the days of your life, and do not grieve him.'"

"Adriaen's son has that letter, both the second and first."

She answers, "But you saw the words she wrote, you memorized them. She wrote, 'What I say to the oldest, I say to the youngest. By me, your mother who gave you birth in much pain.'"

And I answer her back, "And your mother wrote your sister, at one o'clock in the morning on the day of her death, 'Here are knitting needles for my daughter. Keep them, and do the best with her, my little lamb which I bore under my heart.'"

"Yes," Janneken says, the needles clicking steadily. "I lay in her lap when she wrote that."

I know the letters by heart, but in a way they will never be more than a memory of paper, of shrivelling ink. Not touch or feeling. But I do know the feel of the ship that brought Adriaen's family and me to Danzig in 1584, its sway and riding of long swells, the sails cracking full, and the ship's lean down before the wind to drive the chisel of its prow *smash!* through the froth into the blue, away. The journey of my life.

Danzig was the wealthy Hansa city-state on the Vistula River, a mile inland from the Baltic Sea, protected by low walls and the salty river delta called the Werder. The Danzigers wanted more productive land for their grain trade, and so they welcomed the Mennonites to dike, drain and farm the Werder more intensively, but inside the confined city they also needed more of the tall houses the Dutch knew how to build side by side on narrow land. So, when I turned fifteen, Adriaen hired me to a builder's stoneyard, on the channel where the Motlawa River flows through the southern wall of the city to form the harbour inside.

I was a labourer. Climbing down onto the barges heaped high with shifting stone, I grappled chains around each rock so it could be hoisted onto the docks of the stoneyard. I had never seen a mountain, nor will I, but as I clambered and balanced among those immense rocks I began to comprehend the jagged spread of the massifs from which they had been cut. My wooden shoes hooked on their sharp edges, my arms were dusted raw from reaching around them. It came to me then that, as far as it was possible for me to think, here the textures of infinity rubbed my fingers.

The Dutch Mennonites who fled to Danzig to escape persecution could work in the city, but were not allowed to live or own property inside it because they were not citizens. So they built their villages outside the walls, as close to them as they could, the Frisians in Neugarten west of the Hagel's Hill, and we Flemish in Schottland just outside the southern Petershagen Gate in the shadow of the Bishop's Hill. It was here, in church one summer Sunday, that I met Janneken.

Met her *again*, she told me. The first time, she said, was in the death cell of our mothers. I cannot even remember her saying that, though she has reminded me often. I remember only her standing there, the wide folds of her long brown dress skirted with a white apron, her reddish hair gathered up under a white cap covering her ears, her small, pointed mouth moving. I did nothing but lift rocks all day, and suddenly before me was a manifestation: I felt as if God Himself had taken my head between His two hands, twisted it right and spoken into my face:

"Jan Adam Wens, look at this delicate woman. She is your wife."

Janneken helped me understand and accept what my father had undeniably bequeathed my body: his mason's hands. I became an apprentice in the Danzig guild of stonecutters. Hand and chisel and rule and line and hammer, I learned not only to see mountains in the stone I handled, but I became content, sometimes almost happy, to shape them. Feel them, in turn, determine the very muscle of my hands and arms and back.

That was the best thing I learned, and perhaps also the most limiting. Because seeing mountains in a stone could not teach me to recognize the smaller, delicately beautiful shapes that the greatest of Mennonite stone masters discovered there. The first master was Willem van den Blocke; he had fled Antwerp to escape the Duke of Alva, and Danzig gave him many building commissions, including the magnificent High Gate through which the annual procession of the King of Poland entered the city. I never worked for old Master Willem, but I cut stone for his son, Abraham van den Blocke. He was, if not as gifted a sculptor as his father, certainly a greater architect; better even than Adam Wiebe of Harlingen would be.

Once, towards the end of Abraham's life, when under Adam Wiebe's rebuilding of the city core we were fashioning the Neptune Fountain on the Royal Processional Route, Abraham said to me, "I thank God for you, Jan Adam. Every day. I can draw the design for a fountain, and Wiebe can bring up the water, but only you can cut the stone perfectly."

He created the figure of Neptune, his trident and small

basin, and had it cast in bronze in Augsburg. I built the wide stone base for the fountain where it still stands after 370 years of war and rebuilding, on the Long Street where it broadens into the central Long Market. I also cut the intricate façade of the Arthuis building opposite the fountain, which has been called the most exquisite Renaissance building that still exists north of Italy. Perhaps it is. When the sunlight reflects across its stones, I always thought any soul must feel its flawless serenity.

Janneken is so tiny, I am so large; across from me at our hearth, she is singing. She threads that old Flemish skipping song into the click of her knitting:

> "Oh, the lice, the lice,
> They were worse than mice,
> For they visited once,
> And they were not nice,
> The high and mighty Bishop of Ronse."

And I sing the proverb of the Bishop Pieter Titelman after her:

> "Pieter, Pieter Longnose,
> Your nose, so high it rears,
> The wind blows through your empty head
> And out through both your ears."

"One evening," continues Janneken, "the high and mighty Bishop of Ronse drove his carriage into an inn." Her voice is lilting as if she were telling this to our six children again, the stories they and their children after them will carry in their blood into coming generations. "And there the Bishop met the Bailiff of Kortrijck, who was already sitting inside, eating an enormous supper of lamb and boiled and rare roasted beef, and chicken and seven kinds of cheeses, both sharp and salty, with mussels as a side dish and white, white bread so soft to sop up all the lip-smacking juices."

I join in her telling, the way we often played the roles together. "'My most merciful Bishop,' said the Bailiff, bowing low to hide his smile, 'you are travelling again.'"

Janneken answers: "'Of course,' said the Bishop as the fawning innkeeper lifted his fur cloak, so fine and churchly heavy, from his broad shoulders. And then he sat down at the table, for the Bailiff was after all close enough to his rank that he could quite properly sit and even eat with him. 'Know you not,' the Bishop told the Bailiff, misusing the words of Jesus, 'that I must be about my Father's business?'"

I speak as the Bailiff: "'Of course, my Lord Bishop! So you are again travelling throughout the land in your sacred concern for souls. And perhaps hunting out and capturing heretics again, is that right?'"

She says: "The Bishop answered, 'You know me well, my son,' and sighed wearily, folding his large, soft hands as if in prayer over his great, round belly. 'The Church must be ever vigilant, it can never rest at ease when sin would abound.'"

I say: "The Bailiff hid his mouth behind his hand and said in a puzzled tone, 'My Lord, I, like you, travel much in my line of duty. I arrest evil men, thieves, murderers, corrupt merchants, violent lawbreakers. Now, I must have at least nine, sometimes twelve men with me in order to effect an arrest, but you never travel with more than two servants and your skilful smith to forge and fit the necessary manacles. If I travelled with so few men, I would not live for a day. How is it possible for you?'"

She says: "The Bishop fondled his great diamond rings one by one, and smiled at such ignorance. 'I need have no fear,' he said. 'Wherever I go, I bear the authority of God Himself, and I arrest only good people who have never yet offered me danger.'"

I say: "'But my Lord,' answered the Bailiff, ever more puzzled, 'if I arrest all the bad people, and you all the good, who then in our land shall escape captivity?'"

Janneken's needles are at rest; I follow her gaze into the low blue flames of our evening fire. She continues:

"And not long thereafter, God Himself visited the high and mighty Bishop of Ronse in his princely palace at Kortrijck, visited him with a miracle. He became infested with lice. They grew on his body like grass, in such terrifying numbers that not even his numberless servants could bring him enough linen to keep him clean, nor wash his body free of them. The more lice they scraped from him, the more the lice multiplied. Days, weeks, months…and at last he died, in his splendid bishop's bed, a most horrible death."

My wife glances at me; is there a slight smile at the tips of her lips? The fire burns too darkly, I cannot tell. I take my turn to complete the story:

"Four women came, albeit in great fear, to lay out the Bishop for burial. And it was to them that the second miracle was revealed. When they drew back the blankets, they discovered his poor shrunken body, but not a single louse."

Janneken and I tell each other this amazing little story quite often; the way we told it to our children, now grown and living around us. For we consider ourselves the third miracle: we found each other in Danzig, far from Antwerp and twenty years after our mothers gave their final encouragement to each other as they were chained, each to her stake. Encouragement with their looks only, and groans; they could not sing or call out their faith to each other through the rising fire because their mouths were transfixed by iron tongue screws.

After I was old enough to know the story, Adriaen told me how he recovered from his faint, got on his feet and found there was no one in the Grand Market. Just the charred stubs of the execution posts and ashes, smoking. I must have stayed beside him all that time, he said, because I came with my bleeding head and watched him search in the ash heap.

I asked him, "What were you looking for?"

He raised me, and even after I grew to be taller than he, and later much broader, he remained my Big Brother, full of exact facts and wise decisions. He said, "There was no…reason, I was blind with tears, I couldn't see, not at that moment. I saw nothing happen, and now there was nothing…the square was empty, no one there, smoke going up from the stump and ashes where I saw her being chained, and suddenly I knew that the dear Lord Jesus had come, He had lifted our mother up in His arms straight to heaven, that was what had happened, she had vanished and so everyone had just left, gone home, and I kicked those stupid ashes, they were nothing! and my foot hit something sharp and hot and I cried out, I was kicking embers away from the black stump over the cobblestones, but then you came closer, and bent over. You picked it up."

I know I did. I have deep scars. I see them every day because I work closely with my hands. I must have picked up the iron tongue screw with my right hand because my right thumb and two fingers are scarred, and then I dropped it into the palm of my left hand because it is burned even deeper. Adriaen told me he could smell my left hand burning, but I did not make a sound.

My Master Abraham van den Blocke died on January 28, 1628, only a week after his father Master Willem. Though neither had been permitted to live in Danzig, because they were not citizens and were neither Catholic nor Lutheran, they were given the high honour of full city funerals, and burial inside the massive Cathedral of St. Mary.

My mother, Maeyken Wens, has no gravestone; nor do her sisters Mariken and Lijsken Lievens; nor does my wife's mother, Janneken van Munstdorp. They were translated by fire from earth to heaven, they parted from us and a pillar of cloud received them out of our sight. But the place of their translation remains: the "hand werpan" fountain in the Grand Market in Antwerp, Belgium, stands on the spot.

Janneken and I have the knitting needles, and also the iron tongue screw. Sometimes I hold it in my hand. My gnarled fore- and middle fingers fit into it as precisely as my mother's tongue, for which it was especially forged. Janneken tells me this: there is no need for memory.

Cardinal Granvelle had ordered that there was to be no more testifying to the crowds by condemned heretics during their procession to the place of execution; there was in particular to be no more singing, especially of martyr songs. They were too disturbing for the church faithful. Therefore, on the ordered day of execution the skilful smith of the Bishop of Ronse came to the cell in Het Steen Castle with his portable charcoal smithy.

The executioner commanded my mother to put out her tongue. She said:

"Love God above all. He Who is, and shall ever be."

And then she did that.

The smith pushed the curled iron onto her tongue until the flanges spread her lips as wide and hard as possible. He pulled it off, hammered it a little tighter, then forced it on again. He was silent, efficient, well accustomed to intimate work on a shuddering woman's face. He screwed the vise down to the point of steady blood, and finally, to make certain it would never slip, with tongs he took from out of his fire a white-hot iron. He laid that iron on the tip of my mother's tongue.

MANHATTAN

Harlingen, Friesland
Danzig
1616

HISTORIANS CENTURIES LATER WILL WRITE that I, Wybe Adams, was born in Harlingen, Friesland, in 1585, but my mother told me it happened on July 12, 1584. A day easy to remember, she said, because she gave birth to me when she heard the runner cry out in the Harlingen fish market that our Protestant Prince Willem of Orange and Nassau had been assassinated two days before. Killed by the bullets of a Catholic fanatic; his death was most certainly paid for by our relentless enemy Philip II of Spain.

It happened in Delft, which is barely an hour's walk through fields and along dikes from The Hague, where the Spanish Inquisition tried and burned my great-grandmother Weynken in 1527, for confessing only to her living faith in Jesus and the reality of flour and yeast in the bread of the mass.

For thirteen years Prince Willem had led the Dutch in negotiation and in relentless war until Spain and the Roman

Church gave in and agreed that he would become the independent Governor of our United Provinces of Holland. How often, both by sword and by negotiation, had he not protected Mennonites from persecution. Now, at the crying of the news of his death—and especially at his last words: "Oh, love of God, have pity on my soul and on this poor country"—what a wail ascended to heaven. My mother screamed and fainted in her market stall, and when she regained consciousness she was in labour.

"So why didn't you name me Willem?" I asked her.

"Oh no, you had to be Wybe," she said. "Wybe was your great-grandfather, as Trijntjen Wybes became your grandmother's name after he died. You were the first boy in two generations. Wybe Pieters was lost at sea in 1526 or the Inquisitor in The Hague would have burned him together with Weynken."

"Either way, he was dead."

"No no," she said at my tone, "it's all different. The sea is forever what God made it, but people...we people can decide for good, or too often for evil. War, hatred, revenge, fear...our good Prince Willem wrote to King Philip when he was fighting both the Spanish armies and the Jesuits: 'God did not create people to be slaves to their prince or bishop, to obey their commands whether right or wrong, but rather the prince for the sake of his subjects, to love and support them like a father his children, a shepherd his flock as Jesus taught.'"

"Nice Christian words," I told her, "and so now the Calvinists, not the Papists, can laugh at us."

"A little laughing is no sword in the belly. If it makes them happy..."

"Happy! They yell 'Mennonite wedding' at me when they pour their morning shit bucket into the canal!"

"Wybe, Wybe," she sighed. "Names don't burn us alive."

"I can turn my teacher into knots with his own numbers and I can't go to Leyden because I'm a Mennist!"

Without raising her head from her endless knitting, she stared up at me through heavy eyebrows. She read the Bible in German and Dutch and Frisian, and could multiply five numbers in her head faster than I could write them down. Her hands continued the rhythms of tugging, knitting the line of wool into a sweater for me thick enough for any of God's storms on His endless ocean. She told me, again:

"We have been given the good fish in the sea. You don't need a conceited professor lying to you in a university."

Are professors liars? I was never able to prove it for myself, because I never went there, and after I was sixteen I had no time for good fish either. When violence threatens you, there are two things a defenceless Mennonite can do: run away if you can find a place to run to, or try to build a shelter to protect yourself. For fifteen years I helped dig moats, built walls in Franeker, Leewarden, Bolsward, Sneek. The war engineers of the world were making more and more powerful cannon, so I redesigned the walls and corner bastions of our small fort at the head of Harlingen harbour, the last refuge for citizens who could not escape by sea. When I was thirty I was invited by the Danzig Council to come work in that city, and the Mennonites who had fled to the Vistula delta to escape the Spaniards wrote to me as well. They said that perhaps they had not fled far enough: around Danzig they were not persecuted for their faith, but nevertheless their villages were overrun by more political wars than ever.

You know how to build dikes and walls, they wrote, to

channel and control water. Please, come. Protect us, and the good people who have given us refuge, from violent princes.

Strange, strange. My grandmother and mother and later also my wife knitted sweaters, mittens, scarves, hats; they sewed cloth and leather clothing to protect me from cold and water while I worked. Without that protection I would have suffered and died, at sea or on land, as surely as the thousands of people I protected by building walls against the annihilation of armies. I have been praised across Europe for what I built of earth and stone, princes have called it extraordinary, but my mother and my wife built the "walls" that fitted my single body so perfectly that I forgot to notice how well I was protected, and they were never praised. They were merely doing the woman's work expected of them. Protecting.

My head swarms with the perpetual wars of my life, war perpetrated with every imaginable brutality by self-centred princes and bishops and popes and sultans and kings and emperors and counts and the "great liberating Christian" preachers Luther and Calvin, even though they are both already long dead, and by shiploads of gold and silver hauled from the new Americas, to pay for more and more soldiers to destroy villages and slaughter animals and ravage women and children, pays for designing more horrible guns, so that now a soldier can actually carry one on his shoulder, aim it, kill with it all by himself. In 1615, while I was pondering the Danzig invitation, Europe was about to plunge into the deep and bloody canyon of the Thirty Years War.

I did not know that, of course. But I think my brilliant engineering master, Jan Adriaenz Leeghwater of De Rijp, anticipated it.

Jan Adriaenz taught me what I comprehend about building; how to desire the logical, reasonable beauties of the things that are given us, especially the reliability of water, its absolute and inviolable constancy; how to sense the spirit in discrete things, the shards of the seemingly impossible that glitter beyond the edge of imagining. When he heard of Galileo and his discovery of the telescope, he could not contain his joy.

"Think of it!" he exclaimed. "Some day soon we will see past the stars, perhaps see far enough to understand how we are alive, and why."

I could not understand him then; he seemed to be thinking in circles, and the genius of the telescope, as far as I could comprehend, lay in looking as far as possible in a straight line. When I was apprenticed to him in De Rijp, I saw the same puzzlement in his Mennonite congregation when he occasionally preached. Not often, for it seemed his practical brilliance—which could design a city hall or a mill or an overflow canal, or sketch the sluices and dikes that would drain the enormous Haarlemer Lake so that the island town of De Rijp could become the centre of the richest grain field in Holland—lifted his spirit beyond language into mystifying mystery. His pulpit contemplations did not open the minds of the hard-working men and women of De Rijp; rather, they became uneasy, and settled themselves all the more firmly into a spiritual position of stubbornness.

That has never been a particularly difficult position for any Holland people to achieve, and it is almost habitual for us "stumme Fries." Jan Adriaenz was never invited to preach at any Harlingen Mennonite meeting—by 1600 there were several Mennonite congregations in our town; they had fractured not about baptism or refusal to bear arms in war, but upon some extremely fine biblical interpretations that for me were theologically indiscernible—and the last time he came to Harlingen he and I did not go to Sunday worship at all. Rather, we walked in the spring air all afternoon, until towards evening we stood on Harlingen's outer harbour wall.

The burning ball of the sun nestled between the black smudged islands of Vieland and Terschelling on the farthest edge of the Wadden Sea. Its level light glazed the sea into a crimson mirror.

We were surrounded by the landscape of my life. We could hear the water of the canals that drained the land being lifted everywhere around us by creaking windmills, their last small step up into the sea. A cloudless evening, but we would have stood there in rain or storm, for Jan Adriaenz loved to watch water fall from the sky to the patient earth, or contemplate the enormous power of wind and tide driving wave after wave of it, over the sand, against the land, endlessly. If you could only, he said, build a machine to catch a few strands of the power of that water the way our enormous, balanced windmills caught a bit of every passing wind, you could grind all the grain in Friesland into flour with the roaring sea that smashed itself against our short harbour dikes. But there was sometimes nothing and sometimes too much overwhelming power in the sea, and after twenty years of thinking he still could not see how it might be held, even for a moment.

But that evening he did not muse about machines to channel the unfathomable power in all creation. Rather, he told me of the diving bell he had at last perfected, which held air in its dome like an overturned cup so that he had been able to walk on the harbour floor at Hoorn for almost an hour. And beyond its breakwater, he had stood deep in absolute water silence, on the sunken ship that had foundered a year before in the shifting shallows of the harbour mouth.

"With the diving bell we can inspect any harbour floor," he said. "And need never again lose men or a ship to sand."

"You went in it yourself? To the sea bottom?"

"I had made it, I could not send an apprentice down first."

"You are now," I said, amazed, "a man who walks under water."

In the level light his moustache and pointed beard seemed to be, like the far islands, on golden fire. And I saw he was thinking of something altogether different.

His burning mouth opened. "Adriaen Block has returned. With all his men alive and his ship full of fur and strange plants."

Hoorn's most daring sailor, two years gone and almost given up for lost.

"Where was he, how far did he go?"

"He explored very slowly where the Englishman Heinrick Hudson sailed past and up a river so fast. He says the New World and the oceans are far, far larger than we can imagine. That if it takes three months to sail to America, as it does, then China, he thinks, is still half a year farther, if you could find the direct water to it."

"Did he bring back people?" At thirty-one I had never yet travelled farther from Friesland than Amsterdam or met any strangers beyond sailors, whose stories simply grew more fantastical with every league they had sailed and every dram drunk. A Mennonite like Adriaen Block would drink only beer.

"No. He said he would not bring any away, they always die in Europe. They were very good to him, they traded furs and helped them live easily through a winter in their country. It's a beautiful island. They call it Man-a-hat-a; in their language it means 'the heavenly land.'"

"Those people know of heaven?"

"On earth, Adriaen Block says. Endless giant trees like we have never seen in Friesland and deep, rich soil, a harbour sheltered from the ocean and faced by great rivers thick with fish. Heavenly."

My eyes were almost blinded by light; the western islands beyond which my great-grandfather vanished were now like black, narrow clouds running out to sharp points in the sky of the sea: heaven indeed, with every upper edge blazing fire. I could not imagine what else Jan Adriaenz was thinking until he said it.

"The Inquisition," he said, "and then the Lutherans and Calvinists burned us, but now, between ourselves, we argue much thinner theology than baptism or bread or state citizenship or pacifism. We ourselves have learned to make the immense teachings of Jesus into small, sharp knives to slice ourselves apart. If someone does not agree with us, we hit them with the Scriptures. You, we say, you are now banned from the believers, you must now be shunned! Then we cannot eat with you or even speak—for what reason? With every theological debate the list of little reasons grows longer, and smaller."

"You think…" I was trying to catch his tone. "You think there is a new world? Possible?"

"Perhaps. As Adriaen Block says, perhaps if we had to sail for three or six months more and the terrible ocean made us vomit out enough of ourselves."

We chuckled a little. We both doubted that even the

world's greatest oceans were large enough to purge most Christians of their smallness.

"And he said the people who live there invited him."

So I reminded Jan Adriaenz, "I've been invited too—because you won't go—in the opposite direction."

"Danzig," he said like a deep sigh. "The great city on the Baltic."

"They do need help, and so many Mennonites have found refuge there."

"Yes," he said, "they fled there because they were offered protection by a city and a Polish king who did not believe in the Inquisition if they could get industrious people. So now they're surrounded not by Spaniards and French and Germans, as we are, and the English across a narrow sea, but by the lands of the Swedes, Danes, Finns, Russians, Poles, by the Prussians, Saxons, Estonians, Latvians and Lithuanians, to say nothing of hounded gypsies and Jews, and the brutal Hapsburgs and the Hohenzollerns who have been killing each other for centuries to prove they alone are God's elect to rule the whole earth no matter how enormous it may be—a small corner of Europe and such a past. As full of slaughter as the Mediterranean, or Jerusalem itself."

"Why?" I asked him then. "We keep killing each other—why?"

"Why." The sun was gone and we were fading into darkness. "In all of Europe, now, God is every reason."

"You think we wouldn't drag that to this 'New World'?"

"Of course, of course, it's happened already, for over a hundred years. But…it sounds like a story in the Bible, so beautiful if it were far enough away, a hidden corner of earth. Man-a-hat-a."

"Anyway, how long could you hide heaven?" I said, and I

knew the tinge of bitterness was in my voice, but I could not help it. I had been dreaming of all that might be built in a great city since the Danzig delegation came to Harlingen, after he refused them but suggested they consider me. "John in the Bible saw heaven. An immense city with very high walls."

"The new Jerusalem," Jan Adriaenz murmured. "I have read the Book of the Revelation often, and pondered it. Heaven is not shown as a garden, or a deep, hidden forest. The angel says to John, 'Come, I will show you the bride, the Lamb's wife.'"

I looked at him; I did not remember that.

"Heaven is first of all a woman, the Bride of the Lamb. And after that it is also a city."

All I could say was, "What can that mean?"

He smiled wanly. "You see why we studious readers of the Scriptures, we Menniste literalists will have problems between us forever. What I think is, these are all pictures, and on earth no one picture of heaven can be enough; we need many. For me, the simplest is heaven as a city—and that is complex enough—a huge city brilliant as jasper, square and hard…but also," he added abruptly, "trees of life grow on the banks of the river that runs through it. If we built a beautiful city with a river…"

I said, into his silence, "A river runs through Danzig."

On the Bay of Danzig our ship caught the morning wind off the Baltic Sea and under full sail moved slow as a procession between the sand dunes of the Wester Platte and up the bent throat of the Vistula River. The church spires and towers of Danzig—I counted more than thirty-seven—blazed in the sun standing low over the delta and outlining the three peaks of western hills, against which the city lay, and the tips of the masts of ships anchored there from every ocean on earth—I saw twenty-two of them along the river quays, their wrapped sails glowing into a deeper brilliance as we moved between them. I thought of small, flat Harlingen, its houses squeezed between the four fingers of the van Harinxma Canal, its tiny fortress above the Wadden Sea. Danzig was huge, it was walled and bastioned below the hills a mile inland from the sea, and it stretched out farther than that. When we turned right from the Vistula and sailed into the Motlawa River and between the towers of the city walls, the harbour narrowed before us into a molten street of welcoming light. Our long bowsprit pointed between stepped Dutch houses on the right and the huge granaries along the left quays, between the silent men and women and children at windows and standing motionless watching us arrive in our tall blue ship. Verily, in 1616 Danzig seemed to me a city of beaten gold floating on the long, northern-summer light.

But my engineer's eye recognized it had by no means "come down to earth adorned as a bride." Its walls were not two hundred cubits high nor its gates made of pearl. The river was thick and sluggish, the gate irons rusted thin, the stone lintels and pillars cracked by age and cannonballs. Inside the low walls, as we bent away from the old, glowering castle, there were so many houses and markets and tight cobbled streets and granaries and immense wood and iron cranes so crushed together upon each other that not a single green tree could possibly have found a place to root, anywhere.

A most earthen, stone, and muddy water city. I had come to the heart of my life's work.

SEVEN

BELIEVING IS SEEING

Edmonton
1986

"HAVE YOU EVER," SUSANNAH ASKS, "seen a row of dead people?"

Adam looks past his nightly day-old newspaper; her profile as if dreaming against the low bedside light.

"I see enough bodies," he says. "More than I want, alive and dead."

"No, not one dead at a time, I mean a row of them, a long row."

"A long...everybody dies, everybody runs to the doctor, you can never stop it for good...what is it?"

Susannah is staring immovably into space. "No. I mean"—her hand makes sharp chopping motions across the width of their bed—"people, laid out in rows one beside the other, full length on the ground, say hundreds of them, dead."

"No, where would I?" Adam murmurs. "Yes, of course I have."

"Where?"

"TV news, everybody sees it, practically every evening."

"No, TV doesn't count."

"Not count? The first TV we bought, the first thing we saw was Lee Harvey Oswald shot between those Texas cops, live on TV, and now it's twelve-channel reruns of news bodies, all the time."

"I know, but television's just an electric shimmer, like a voice on an answering machine, I mean human bodies, that's what Dad said once, like this."

She makes the chopping motion again, across into his paper; despite the elegance of her hand, the gesture strikes him as grotesque.

"What, your dad?"

But she continues, obliviously, "And your doctor training wouldn't help, there'd be so many you couldn't believe your trained eyes and you'd have to touch them, one after the other." Her fingertips rest momentarily on his skin. "Every one dead human flesh."

"The fact of touch, that's proof, yes."

"And the fact of smell," she says.

"Oh, there'd sure be that, in no time."

"Yes, that."

Her quiet voice seems to have turned the bedroom light so dim they might be between candles in a chandeliered dining room again, her face a Pre-Raphaelite vision over the table, a face he can, for the moment, barely recognize in its incomprehensible beauty.

Adam has to look away; years ago they were like that, and not in bed reading either.

"Unless it's very cold," she says, "like February, bodies swell up, there'd be an extremely strong stench very fast."

"And flies and maggots." He hesitates, but her lengthening stillness is some consideration he must break. "A Dene from Fort Good Hope, I was sewing his knife cut, he told me a body even in cold water like the Mackenzie will come to the surface from stomach gases, you often can't recognize the face after the fish find it but the body will certainly rise again...." He laughs, realizing what he has said. "At least in water!"

"In Canada," she says deliberately, "we see rows of bodies only in industrial disasters, like Springhill, or the Hillcrest coal mine in 1914...."

His long wards at the Royal Alex Hospital, suffering flesh laid out row on row and never permitted to simply die; it was worth your life in lawsuits not to multiply attaching, supposedly succouring, machines—Adam crushes the newspaper and drops it to the floor, but Susannah continues:

"... one hundred and eighty-nine men in Hillcrest. When they brought them up from the exploded shafts inside the mountain they laid the body parts out in the mine washhouse and tried to reassemble them, arms, legs, heads, so relatives could identify—"

"Susannah," he has to interrupt, "why are you talking about this?"

"We could drive to Hillcrest, five hours, it's more or less a ghost town, and see all the graves," she says. "A long double row with little pickets, hardly any tombstones or names, just Crowsnest Mountain and the lovely valley and grass sunk in like giant footprints, side by side."

Her shoulders beside him are bare, and fuller, arms a bit shorter and hands much more worn, not quite the same as Jean—who would also never talk her way into an abstract reverie on bodies! He speaks quickly to avoid his betrayal:

"We drove through the Crowsnest, years ago. Why are you saying this?"

She touches him. "I remembered that beautiful graveyard, thinking about bodies."

"Is it Cambodia, those horrible pyramids of skulls?"

"No, bodies. Laid out side by side, row after row."

And his mind flips. "You said your dad"—he chops his hand across the bed, across her legs—"he saw this?" She nods. "About the war, he saw rows of bodies?"

"Uh-huh. Dresden. A Tuesday in February, 1945."

"He was ground crew for Flying Fortresses, in France, how would he see Dresden bodies?"

She knits her fingers into knots. "And he said many were twisted together. One hundred and thirty-five thousand people burned alive."

"He told you he saw them?"

Her endless father, his endless silence about "his" war. A new evasion?

It was so dark they could no longer distinguish each other's face when they finally heard the beaver coming.

The sound of the creek running over stones played back to them from the cliffs in an endless lullaby and they stood motionless as trees against the birches, their shapes gone from dark into darkness. Adam was certain they would never meet anyone here. In this night silence they had no names, they had disappeared. They could simply stand with the length of their bodies touching, and wait.

And it seemed they had waited so long for that quiet splash, that imperceptible breaking of surface in the pond before them that at first they did not recognize the sound: It seemed barely a skiff…white noise coming over the narrow water from the sand-bar overgrown with willows, a small racket as if something were being dragged, perhaps a body being lugged through willows and alder brush, slightly louder bumping between birches. And then nattering as if, walking along a hospital corridor at night, a young technician and an older doctor were coming closer, anticipating what would now happen after a long shift. And then there fell into the indecipherable black sheet of water before them a plop! so clumsy, one seeming bellyflop and then another, that they nudged each other in astonishment: could this be the secret beavers no one ever saw, whose dams measured and tiered the creek in water steps around every bend, every rapid, where twenty-metre poplars lay as devastated as wheatstraw, mown down and hurled against others still, temporarily, standing? They strained forward, touching more lightly now, both anticipating and warning each other not to make a sound, and they saw on the still invisible, suddenly silent water a string of starlight slowly being drawn.

"There," Jean breathed.

Adam felt her arm rise, a click, the black-green water surfaced in one spot of brilliant light. A beaver head, a small, pointed blotch quickly turning and gone, the black hump of back and tail flipping, *smack!* into a roil of water and gone, nothing but spreading ripples, Adam was cursing almost aloud but unable to finish an oath before the head again surfaced, the light centred on it, *crash!* the cliff pounded the tremendous sound back like a club and the water exploded, seemed to smash in pieces out of the yellow light. And then again, a beat too late, another *crash!* smashing the pieces further into pieces.

"Did I hit him?"

"I don't—shhhh!" Jean hissed.

A head again, nose circling high in the broken water. Was it the first? Was it the partner? Stupidly nosing the naked light to smell its way into invisibility there?

Adam pulled the trigger and held steady: the tremendous crashes this time were almost simultaneous and so overwhelming that the clang hammered in their heads, on and on, while the light wavered, searching over the pond. Gradually the sound of the rapids returned to its gentle insistence. There was nothing on the stirred surface of the water.

Jean had her arms wrapped around her head. "Sweet Jesus and Mary, is that automatic?"

"Semi," Adam said. "When I shoot, I want it dead, quick. You think I hit him?"

"Too loud to see. Could be a her."

"Good, then her babies are finished too."

"You're a heartless man."

"Not utterly." His tongue in her ear tasted wild raspberries. "Only with dam-building animals."

Jean eased her sturdy body tighter into his, while her light searched the restless water again. A dark green sheen, with seeming bits of white bobbing. They could be bleached late-summer leaves, or perhaps bone.

"A mine disaster isn't massacre or war," Adam insists. "A mine has a working civil order in place, rescue parties, doctors—"

"It's no Final Solution," Susannah concedes, "but—"

"There's a living community, police, firemen, elected officials, whoever, families and relatives are there, the only dead are the miners who know perfectly well every time they go down is very dangerous."

"Knowing it doesn't make them any less dead."

"Okay, but *dead* is the given hazard of their job—like you, much milder, flunking students. Underground miners, in a mountain or under the sea, always work in danger."

"Danger like being a citizen in Vietnam? Or an African country we haven't heard about yet, or Chile? They're just living too, trying to work to feed their children, and all of a sudden the world explodes, there's fire falling out of the sky like water and they're laying bodies out in rows. Since the forties it's women and children and old people dead too, more than working soldiers."

"That's all different, that's war."

"I don't think it's so 'all,'" Susannah says quietly. "It has to do with men walking a dangerous line, knowing people will get killed, and still they do it."

"Oh, men," he says. Discouraged already. He never has to argue women and men with Jean, especially in a sleeping bag.

"Yes," Susannah says. "Men run the businesses where people have to work, they control countries and they kill to keep power."

He deliberately pushes his right arm around her waist and nuzzles his head tight into her back; the warm smell is his sweetest and safest memory of her.

"Yeah yeah," he says into cotton, "and men know best how horrible wars are."

"Oh, they're horrible all right."

He hoists himself on his left elbow, still behind her. "All those men in all the wars, even good ones fighting fascists, your dad holding those Flying Fortresses together so his buddies could drop bombs all over Germany, it was horrible, but they had to do it."

"If he could only have stayed in Edmonton," she says, abruptly inside the good memory her father can sometimes be now, after fourteen years dead. "Just kept his head inside a DC-3 engine. He said one day in 1942 over eight hundred planes landed and took off here, minute after minute, for Alaska."

"So what was in them? Milk for burbling Russian babies?"

He feels a lurch of regret—too smart-ass sardonic again by half—but Susannah only shrugs; the length of her legs under the thin blanket remains warmly against his. She says, "Two years in Edmonton he could pretend he was just fixing engines. But then the U.S. Air Force sent him overseas."

"His luck it wasn't the Pacific," Adam says quickly, trying somehow to extricate them both from her father and his thoughts against her back into a bland generality. "That's what I mean, when he was really in it, war, nothing but shot-up Flying Fortresses his buddies flew, all he said was they hated it."

"Oh, they hated it, of course. But...maybe they loved it too."

"Well, love..."

"It was fun for them, finally. Years of boredom waiting in England, then the ultimate game, hunting humans. And they were so quiet when they came home, everyone at home knew the worst about war, today we're supposed to hate it, and there was so much violent death, so they don't dare tell anyone how much they liked about it."

Adam hunches up a little; in bed, silent Bud Lyons is one of several subjects they usually avoid. "Well...you know how Tom's dad is."

"Yeah, Tom's dad. He never says anything either, just goes to Remembrance Day parades with the other vets and cries and has a drink with his old buddies—flying over Germany at eighteen, you think he ever had that much living intensity again? Selling furniture in Eaton's for forty years?"

Try sixty patients a day repeating a cough or a bee sting or a sliver, or depressed by one smaller breast, an indefatigable wart, a penis limp once too often.

Susannah pulls his arm tight across her stomach, never again so taut after Trish and Joel, but soft, surrounding as love. What kind of a stupid ass is he?

She talks into the dim room, away from him. "Tom's dad never tells what fun flying a Spitfire was for a prairie boy, in the air over the burning cities of Europe, and life-and-death dogfights and watching the bright streaks of bullets, his bullets, and seeing those Nazis falling, trailing fire and exploding when they smashed into the ground, monsters who shoved people into ovens."

"They didn't know about ovens when they were flying."

"Don't quibble, they knew it all later and it just made their memories better, their intensity more moral."

"Well, aren't they right? They were doing a good thing, stopping unspeakable genocide. Many with their own death."

"But what 'unspeakable' did they do too? One Hitler, and millions of children."

"They had to. There was no other way to stop him."

"Oh? Listen, *Bengjeltje*," Susannah says. Lowgerman she learned from his mother and always a caress, but under the blanket she is drawing away from him. "Don't argue. You know it, women never get into situations where they have to do that to each other. War is the ultimate male business."

"Okay, okay…but fun? Tom's dad is so gentle he'd never hurt a fly."

"Yes! And a man never wants his son to be in a war, I know, and yet in a way I think maybe he does. Comradeship, life-and-death terror, intensity together, the most paralysing fear and still knowing, if you live, that you found the courage to go through it. Together with someone. How can shopping till you drop at the mall, playing golf—for God's sake!"

He reaches, wraps his arms around her distant body too hard, too hard. She has boxed him in: he can only grope for a speakable moment. "Sometimes…when I'm pounding a chest, and suddenly I feel that, the heart beat, and beat…."

She says gently, "You're a good doctor."

"Hospital teamwork, when someone really is sick or injured, that's intense enough."

"I meant," she says, "who in our generation besides you medics ever sees a corpse? We lock the coffins, we sing 'There is no death, though eyes grow dim,' from the ridiculous *Student Prince*. There is no death!"

"That's the mourners, they're in shock, they reach for anything from their happy past to help—"

"Listen," half turned to him, "Robert Graves wrote his major inheritance from World War I was 'a difficulty in telling the truth.' Tom's father won't lie outright, he just doesn't tell anything."

Adam says, "Nobody needs a war to have 'a difficulty in telling the truth.'"

Susannah looks at him sharply, the upper slant of her eye. "Surely not," she says slowly. "Not in your office."

"Oh my office, hell, that's just S.O.A.P. ritual, scribble scribble sixty times a day SOAP!"

Susannah laughs out loud. "It's so cute! Your perpetual of cleanliness, S for subjective, 'And how are we feeling today?' O for objective, 'Does this hurt when I press, here?' A for assessment, 'Now, there may be a heart murmur, or an ulcer...' P for prescription, 'An antibiotic—'"

"It's ridiculous. Your leg is broken, but there is order, I have to inspect your inner ear."

"How's our whining friend Andy T with his ulcer?"

"He's okay. You know what they say, 'Assholes live longer.'"

"I know, but I think he wants more of him than that to survive."

They are laughing together, and for a moment lightness settles over them like intertwining sleep. But Susannah stirs out of it, as she always does. Once she's started something, she can never leave it alone.

"You remember," she says, "Tom's father hinted at a story, he escorted a bomber squadron and his best buddy from Thorhild was the pilot in one of the Lancasters? He got back okay, no dog-fights, and then his buddy's bomber returned all shot up and more or less crash-landed, with only the navigator alive, and then he died too before he could tell what happened. That's the classic war story: never talk, and when you do, only about death. That way you tell nothing. It's told to keep us, who weren't there, ignorant. He's saying, 'That's the way war is, it means nothing.'"

"You think that's why your dad never spoke?"

"Nothing can mean anything."

She is talking about her father and war, but Adam senses she is talking men and women more; he feels her leading him along the high sharp ridge of what their life together is no longer; if either of them slips, they may fall, and split.

"Did you ever ask him," she persists, "sort of 'between men'?"

"He was always easy, he sounded so open, but he deflected things. I'd ask something and he'd explain the difference between a B-17 and a B-24, again. Never about loading bombs he knew would kill civilians. He couldn't be pushed, I never heard him say 'Dresden.'"

"He told me 450 Flying Fortresses and 764 Lancasters flew that night, packed with 650,000 firebombs."

Adam feels a surge of emotion rise, twist in his throat.

Susannah feels it too. "You loved him, I loved him." Her hand brushes his face. "He talked even less after Mom died."

"I wish I'd known your mother."

"I knew yours, so good."

"I know, I know. Yours would have said I wasn't good enough for her 'golden princess.'"

She hiccups, stirs in his loose arms. "That was just Dad, a joke."

"Well, whoever it was."

For once she does not pick up, thank god, on the opening for disagreement, perhaps argument, he has blundered into again. His arms are still around her, if he leaned lower he would hear her stomach gurgle as stomachs do, but as usual now she feels very far away and in one lurch he decides—he overwhelmingly wants to push her, out of or into what or where he is not thinking—and he reacts quick and deep as a kitchen knife turning.

"You're right, that's the classic war story. Tell nothing and your life is a secret and—" Adam catches himself, his voice rougher. "Is that why he never said anything about Idaho, about

Pocatello? He had some kind of personal 'war' there, is that why he said nothing? Just nothing? That's an American past?"

Susannah seems to be returning from some other place even as she shifts almost imperceptibly under the sheet. "I've told you," she says calmly, "we never lived in Pocatello, that was just the hospital where I was born."

"A mother tells her child no more than a birth certificate? What about the green town you remember? The big lake?"

"I was barely four when we left. I don't know."

"How about," and he says it fast, so he won't think what this means, "you delay Europe a week, I exchange time with somebody and we drive to Hillcrest? Then through the mountains, all the golden fall leaves into Idaho?"

"I told you, he liked Edmonton so much, when he got out of the Air Force he went back to Idaho, married my mother and brought us here."

"Where in Idaho, what lake?"

"You know I don't know."

"And you'd never met him, or seen him before he showed up in 1946 and married your mother?"

"That's what Mom told me."

"But he was your biological father?"

"That's what Mom told me. I don't remember meeting him, I was four and we lived here, in Edmonton."

"And you never looked at a map together? The only place is on your birth certificate?"

She is staring at him so fixedly he cannot face her eyes. "Adam," she murmurs at last, "he was my father, and they're both gone. And next week we've been married twenty-five years."

"I know. God, I knew him eleven years and he never told me anything except motors."

"In Canada twenty-five years is a life sentence."

"Only in the Criminal Code. Your parents were immigrants from the States, and they just never talked about a past, not a word about family?"

"Adam, why are you cross-examining me?"

Her abrupt hardness, like a body tremor, jolts him. What if she were to cross-examine him? But even as her body straightens slowly under the sheet, her voice finds its habitual understanding. "You're just so sick of that office, your hypochondriac patients, the only time you can even read the newspaper is falling asleep in bed—your obsessed keep-every-waiting-room-full, pile-up-the-money partners."

His stupid partners—his guilt can explode in defensiveness: "I don't give a shit about them! How can you know nothing about your grandparents? Everyone has to have them. So okay, you're not Russian Mennonite, they hear a name and they're sniffing for relations way past the third and fourth generation, but Bud Lyons—what kind of name is that? Is it English?"

"We're not criminals."

"Was I implying that? War trauma can beat a person into silence—god knows in this century there's enough—but he helped win the war for the good guys. So why? In Idaho are there any Jews?"

"The trouble is," she says slowly, "no fire ever burns clean. Not even the best firebombing." Abruptly her body lengthens out straight and hard. "It's been twenty-five years."

"And I've practised, as they say, medicine for twenty-four years and four months."

"It's still a life sentence."

Adam's memory is reeling back; he peers at her staring up, as it seems, into a beyond. So close he smells her, but indecipherably far away. It will be some time yet before he understands what he has been hearing; what has happened before his very eyes while he was so carefully protecting his "this-has-nothing-to-do-with-her" life. His secret life, lived not previously like her father's, but parallel.

"Am I," he says with particular care, "am I supposed to be getting this? You don't want to serve a longer 'life sentence'? With me?"

Susannah does not move. She seems to be looking down the length of her body under the thin cover, at the twin peaks created by her feet.

"You know that's a mirror question," she says. "Do you, with me?"

Under Adam's quick knife the inner body of the beaver slowly revealed itself. It was a knifepoint unzippering, the gradual removal of a rich fur coat to expose a glistening, pale yellow nakedness.

"You ever see a seal lying on a rock?" he asked. "In a zoo maybe?"

Jean was looking intensely at the body and his curved knife with a certain abhorrence. She said nothing, as usual, but Adam sensed the slight shake of her head, which might be little more than a suppressed shudder.

"They're a lot bigger, but they have the same fat-layered, seemingly boneless body," he explained. "Water mammals. When I was a kid, north of here, there were no beaver at all, now they're ubiquitous pests, dams and houses everywhere, and look. An inch of fat, turning beautiful trees into lard, the bugger."

Jean said nothing. His left hand, clenched in the roll of greasy fur, was trying to tear it aside over short slashes of the skinning knife. Both his hands were thick with fat and blood.

"'I'd rather be in Idaho,'" he sang in his monotone, "'than any other place I know, in Ida-Idaho...'"

He had worked his way around to the head, more carefully now, slicing to leave the tiny ears in the fur, and towards the eye. "See," he pointed with the knife-tip, "transparent eyelid, they can see perfectly under water. And here," he lifted the mouth wide behind the two enormous cutting teeth, "a second set of lips too, behind these daggers," he tapped them, like steel on steel, "so they can carry wood or stones between them under water and never get water in their mouth. That's real evolution, millions of years of purposeful—"

She interrupted him, "You cut a hole in it, there."

"Ugh! Good thing I never tried to be a surgeon." Adam's hands stopped and he looked up. Stocky body, but that face could sell any man TV toothpaste—and he ducked his head, ashamed of his thought. "You're too close," he said, "watching me."

"You don't like it?"

"Maybe you don't like it. Anyways, trappers always cut the head right off, this fur's no good for anything."

"So why leave it on?"

"I'm not a trapper." And added, suddenly annoyed with her, "Don't you think even a skinned animal deserves a face?"

For a moment only the sound of the creek, and a movement of air as if it had turned to ice below them, rising. Adam covered up quickly. "I always hated skinning. I was on a caribou hunt once, a century ago, up north with the Dene, and all I could do was pack out the butchered meat."

"Being a doctor hardened you?"

He guffawed without humour. "Oh yeah, killer medicine." And he returned his knife to the opened stretch of the hide. Why was he here with her?

"It's just a tiny cut," he said, "not like the bullet hole here. That won't close, but I'll stretch the hide out tight and you can sew this nose nick shut with two stitches. When it's cured no one will notice."

"What makes you think I'd touch it?"

"It's woman's work, the Dene teach that, sewing...and when it's stretched dry you have to scrape it and then chew it, for days, human spit is part of the curing, till it's chewed all soft and cured and we can wrap it around our feet, keep warm at night."

"Seven years of braces to chew a beaverskin?"

He laughed out loud. "What are beautiful teeth for?" and saw her baring hers at him.

Sure, Eric said, use the cabin. And the rifle's locked in the chest, do something useful with it—if you have time on your hands. So to speak.

Jean pulled her sturdy legs up against her breast, wrapped her arms around them. Her chin found the notch between her knees.

"Would your wife chew it?"

She surprised Adam, but only for a hesitation.

"My wife is going to Europe, to the archives in Madrid, Toulouse and Milan. Working on an obscure literary subject."

"One a lab technician wouldn't understand."

Adam snorted. "I'm not sure I do."

"She speaks all those languages?"

"And a few more. It's useful for a professor of comparative literature."

"Which language does she still speak to you?"

"What?" he said, intense. "What is this in aid of?"

"Me."

"What language do you speak, to other men?"

"Any they understand."

"Okay. My wife's going to Europe for four months."

"Did you or did she decide that?"

"It's professional research, there's nothing to 'decide.'"

Jean was doubled and wrapped about herself, staring across the brown water at the high, eroded cliffs, the coal seam a thick black stripe holding the grey clay and bushes and poplar trees in the sky. Seated woman in landscape, brooding on the approach of winter. Adam reached out, almost touched her rusty hair with his fat-smeared, bloody hand, but resisted.

"Listen," he said as gently as he could, "this skin will cure softer than layered silk, you'll see, this inner fur's so soft...have you ever made love on beaver fur?"

"I'm not sure," she replied carefully. "I don't know if I could make love to a beaver."

"That's not what I meant. That is not what I meant at all."

They both chuckled a little, but not together. He lifted what was left of the skinned beaver from its hide and laid it on its back, beside the others in a row under the pale birches that leaned over the slipping edge of the creek. They looked like no animal that could have lived, not even a lab specimen; they were four elongated sacks of bruised fat sheared with uncountable cuts. But through half-shut eyes Adam saw them change, strangely, into yellowish, bloated children...each with two enormous buck teeth and black gaps for nostrils, their small, naked arms folded high over their distended bellies in a prayer of desperation, please… please…and his mind flipped. *What am I doing, I'm stupid, what have I done, just turned fifty and hiding in the bush with a woman I pass in a hall ten times a day, what an idiot, what am I doing—*

The row of beaver bodies laid out on the mud changed yet more strangely; in the level evening light glancing off the creek and the blazing birch leaves they were gradually, one by one, catching fire.

Adam struggled to twist himself into his standard every-waking-hour oblivion. He grumbled in his monotone: "'I'd rather be in Idaho a'eatin' baked potatoes! Oh, I'd rather be in Idaho than any other place—'"

"Marilyn Monroe!" Jean exclaimed. "In her first famous picture as a model, she wore a Idaho potato sack."

He shook his head. Famous dead Marilyn. "Would you believe it, I've never been there? It's just a silly song running in my head. What do we do," he gestured, "with these?"

"They'll be gone overnight," she said. "The coyotes will take them."

"Good. Coyotes. Four-legged vultures of Alberta."

The bodies were again what they had been, four greasy, skinned beavers.

"Look," he said, getting back into it and pointing with the knife, "the tiny anus, a very special evolutionary adaptation there. Because the beaver can't digest bark, though that's what it eats. Bark and wood fibre have to be broken down by bacteria, and the bacteria that do this can live only in the beaver's lower bowel, so every day it has to nuzzle its anus until certain faeces containing the bacteria come out. Then it eats the faeces to get the bacteria into its stomach, to break down the bark, so it can absorb the nutrients in the wood, and not die of starvation. Great, huh?"

Jean's carefully made-up eyes were incredulous. Adam continued, "Canada's national beast, it's survived forty million years because it learned to build wood and mud and stone dams to protect its houses. And to eat its own shit, every day."

She tilted to him, tried to wrap herself around his head, but he got one arm up between them. They stared at each other.

"I mean, you do what you have to, to survive."

She does not blink. "Will you please shut the hell up."

The bed feels so huge, they might as well be lying in separate rooms. Adam knows Susannah is no more asleep than he, though he has hopes his exhaustion will submerge him soon. Then she speaks, without moving.

"Have you read anything in your *Martyrs Mirror* lately?"

"When would I have—" he begins, but stops. "Not for years."

"You remember the Cathari believers, of the thirteenth century?"

"Not much. They were in southern France, sort of Waldensians?"

"Yes, but stricter. They ate no meat, never married, tried to live absolutely moral lives. Real goodness was a bad example for the clergy, and Innocent III organized a crusade against them."

"I don't remember a Cathari martyr story."

"They're in the survey chapters. One of the worst was 1243, when Pope Innocent's army drove over two hundred of them out of their castle near Toulouse into a village. But then the soldiers didn't want to kill them because, they said, how could they distinguish between Christian and heretic? So the Bishop decided. He ordered, 'Kill them all, God will know his own.'"

Adam's eyes are wide open, it seems he is in a strange night room, perhaps a hotel, he has been awakened by the sound of footsteps in the hall, approaching, and instantly he thinks, The telephone is going to ring.

How did you know I was here?

Why did you answer?

Whom were you calling?

"Sometimes," Susannah says from the far side of their bed, "I think Churchill and Bomber Harris with all his planes made a decision like that bishop."

"What about Hitler and Hermann G?"

"There's Truman too, and Colonel Tibbets flying the *Enola Gay* to Hiroshima."

Aren't you there?

Where are you?

"And Stalin," Adam says, much too loudly. "But he sure as hell didn't bother with God deciding."

"How do you know? He studied four years in a theological seminary. They prayed twelve times a day."

"Then that did it to him for sure, for life!"

But Susannah does not respond to his throwaway cynicism. Rather, in a voice irrefutable as a needle she opens the mantra they first discovered together between the mirrors of the University of Alberta Tuck Shop.

She says, "Love is disposition, desire, delight."

And Adam must respond, "Love is also a decision."

How did you know?

Because you answered.

In the high glass and concrete international departure area of an airport echoing with arrivals and leavings, with persons repeatedly paged but apparently never willing to lift receivers waiting for a voice, there is a small circle of people. If they were facing outward they would resemble muskoxen of the High Arctic backed around young to confront relentless enemies, but these face in only upon themselves: they are bending gradually closer and closer together, intent upon the slowly tightening sphere they make, close feet, rounded bodies, bowed heads. It could be a family: a mother, a son, a daughter, a father. Between the slabs of echoing airport glass a film of quiet gathers about them; it may be that the son or the father is leaving. Certainly none of them has the worn, devastated skin of someone recently hurled for hours along the edges of space. Perhaps the daughter is leaving, and they are trying one last time to look into one another's eyes, to search out, as they may never have before, all of themselves at the same lingering instant, while their hands and arms reach around the person pressed closest to them for the next, trying to feel every bone in every individual body they know they love with the overwhelming conviction of their own fingers stretching to touch themselves.

"Trish," the woman says. "Joel."

They tighten slightly, as if they long to become hollow globes, every surface inside and outside every one of each other touching.

"Have some fun," the girl says. "Archives in Europe never run away."

The boy shuffles tighter. "Right about now," he murmurs, "if Grandma was here, she'd be saying a long prayer."

The man says nothing. The woman is leaving.

EIGHT

LEFT-HANDED WOMAN

London

1744

WHEN WAS I BORN? In *The Dictionary of Art*, New York, 1996, volume 28, page 352, I am listed as: "b. Danzig [now Gdansk, Poland] c. 1694; d. London March 1744. English painter." The "Danzig" is close, but the "c. 1694" isn't.

My Grossma Triena knew the exact date; she was the midwife at my birth. But she always told me not to be bothered by careless or deliberate ignorance.

"Enoch," she would say, "you paint. Everyone was born sometime, but you, you are a painter."

"English painter" would for her have been laughable. "A cat moves into a cow stall in the barn and turns into a cow?" Nor would the *Dictionary*'s statement that "Enoch Seeman maintained his position in the second rank of portrait painters" have disturbed her. She often said to me:

"You are who you are. You just work hard, like your father and grandfather and brother, and when you paint a good portrait, that remains. It's like you're never tired, you never need to sleep—you paint someone's family and you'll have four or five, maybe six more friends forever."

At first I did not understand what she was really telling me: that worlds end. They don't change, they keep ending all the time, and children especially are aware of it. When we sailed the length of the Baltic and North Seas to England, after our painter family troubles in Danzig and Warsaw and Dresden, I felt what it was she said: this is truly an end. Though when I saw the Thames River opening into greater London I realized it might be a beginning also. As it was.

My first major commission came in England in 1708. I painted *Colonel Andrew Bisset and His Family*, which remains in the family Castle Forbes, Grampian, in the easternmost corner of rocky Scotland. The *Dictionary* calls it "an ambitious group portrait of somewhat uneven quality in the manner of Godfrey Kneller." "Somewhat uneven" indeed—what else would you expect, since according to their date I was barely fourteen when I painted it? And certainly Godfrey Kneller, that silly sop, had nothing to do with my style: it was my father, Enoch Seemann the Elder, who taught both Godfrey and me as much as we, with whatever talent we had, could put into practice.

My father told me, "When you paint something you're not ashamed to show the world, declare it. In your own hand."

When I showed Grossma Triena the painting, I asked her again, "What day was I born?"

"Yes," she said, "now you should know. This portrait will last longer than a baptism record in the Amsterdam Mennonite Church."

"I don't want to be baptized, not in Amsterdam or anywhere else."

She peered up at me from under her eyebrows. She was a left-handed woman and her eyes could be sharper than her knitting needles.

"Your brother Peter," she said, "has already talked about catechism, and he's younger than you."

"He likes numbers, he likes business, he even wants to go back to Danzig if he ever can."

"You're sure you don't?"

"Why? In Danzig I'd be nothing but a Mennist."

"Well, you are one."

"I'm a painter too."

Grosspa Isaak Seemann had pulled his long hair forward over his shoulder and was braiding it. He lived in London for twenty-five years, but he would never wear a wig. He listened closely, as always, but I knew he would not say a word. Grossma continued knitting, good Danzig gloves for endless London rain. She said quietly, "September 9, 1689. The clock struck four in the morning when I first felt your bloody head coming."

So I inscribed my first commission: *Enoch Seeman, pinx. AE 18 1/2. 1708.* Which translated means: *Enoch Seeman* (my father dropped the second *n* when we moved: "Double anything is too confusing for the English") *painted this* (Latin: pinxit) *at the age of* (AE, Latin: aetatis) *eighteen and a half years, 1708.* Both the *Dictionary* and the even more massive *Künstlerlexikon,* Leipzig, 1936, record my inscription, but both insist on "c. 1694" as my birthday. Perhaps it's not Latin that is beyond historians, it's mathematics.

A portrait painter lives by his commissions; mine grew

gradually from minimal nobility to the climbing rich to royalty. I painted Elihu Yale full-length, the old tyrant of the East India Company who gave so much of the money he "made" (some say stole, but legally of course) in Madras to a school in the United States that they named it after him. My portrait of him still hangs in the Yale University Art Gallery. Some years later George of Hanover, the great-grandson of James I, became my patron; during one of his rare visits to England, shortly before he died in 1727, I painted him as he wanted it: much younger, wearing his coronation robes as King of England. He talked to me congenially in German while I worked—talked about nothing, the way royals speak to commoners. Squalid, cramped London depressed him, so he would not live here, and he never learned English. His son, George II after him, liked the portrait so much he commissioned me to paint him too, together with his beautiful Queen Caroline of Anspach. Both full-length and bust.

Grosspa Isaak would likely chide me for being *prautzijch*— vain—for listing myself in this way. Too unhumbly un-Mennonite. But in lands devastated by war, memory is never more than one last thought away from disappearing. The corner of the Baltic where I was born has often been destroyed: a form of Christianity arrived there in the thirteenth century when the Teutonic Knights received the blessing of the Pope to become "missionaries" among the Lithuanians and Old Pruzzens who lived their pagan lives at the curve of the Baltic Sea. Within two centuries the Order had either forcibly baptized them or killed them. The atrocities of war often memorialize a man in history, but I, Enoch Seeman the Younger, was a defenceless Mennonite and a painter. So I hereby affirm my existence.

For centuries Mennonites in both Europe and the Americas

have been known as peasant farmers. They grow grain and milk cows, and some of them have pithy Lowgerman sayings like *"Wann wann nich wia, dann wia Kusheet Butta"*—"If 'if' wasn't 'if,' then cowshit would be butter"—but my grandfather, Isaak Seemann, though he inherited a village estate and farm, was no farmer. He was a lay preacher in the Elbing Mennonite Church and, even more importantly, an excellent painter. His wife, my grandmother Triena, was the granddaughter of the Danzig engineer Adam Wiebe, and the Wiebes only became farmers because the Danzig City Council—all Catholics—was too apprehensive of his genius, and the craft guilds too afraid of Mennonite competition, to grant citizenship to him or to any Mennonite. Grossma Triena had years in London to tell me our story:

"Adam and his two sons, Abraham and your grandfather Jakob, bought six miles of floodplain along the Nogat River, across from Elbing. Fifty years before you were born, the Wiebes and the other Mennonites who settled there diked that floodplain and made it so marvellously arable that the old landowners nearby protested: our dikes were too strong! So when the spring run-off poured from the mountains down the Vistula and into the Nogat, the old dikes burst and flooded the Polish farmsteads, sometimes with great devastation."

"Why didn't they hire the Wiebes to build better dikes then, to protect them too?"

Grosspa Isaak explained that it could not work, because at some time every river carries too much water and needs a floodplain. But Grossma insisted no no, it was envy.

"The King of Poland never had a quarrel with us," she laughed. "Unused marshlands pay no taxes."

The fact is, by the time my father Enoch Seemann ("the

Elder" as they called him later) was born in 1661, many families had left the Mennonite villages in the shadow of Danzig's walls. Not only the Wiebes, but also the Blocks, who were architects and sculptors; the Esaus, garment-makers; the Penners, ship designers who sailed as far as the icebergs of Greenland, hunting whales for oil; the Dirksens, who were among the wealthiest bankers of Danzig—all these and more had chosen the relatively unregulated freedom of farm-village agriculture in the vast delta of the Vistula and Nogat Rivers.

My great-grandfather Jakob Wiebe and his brother Abraham were both widely known as outstanding engineers and farmers, but it was Jakob's youngest daughter who truly inherited the imagination of our great-great-grandfather Adam. Triena Wiebe was Grosspa's second wife (the first died in giving birth to my half-uncle Isaak), and she dared to imagine that her husband need not be a farmer: that he could be a preacher in the Elbing Mennonite Church and also an artist; that their children must not only learn to read but have an art education as well; that her firstborn, Enoch, could be dedicated to God and to art, that he must go abroad to study not only with the Mennonites in Amsterdam but as far away as classic Italy itself. And when my father returned home to Elbing at twenty, was baptized, and for two years tried to establish himself as the painter he already knew he was, which his father and half-brother were still struggling to become, she recognized an end before a beginning.

"Elbing is impossible," she declared. "It is too small. We must return to Danzig."

Spring 1683. The village of Stolzenberg. I always thought that a strange name for conservative Flemish Mennonites— "Haughty Hill"—in the morning shadow of the Bishop's Hill.

Just beyond that hill the moated fortress of the city spread itself out between the rivers, and at its base the earth and stone Wiebe Bastion. Our bastion, as we called it, was around the corner from the Maidlock and Wolf Bastions where the inland barges on the Motlawa River passed through the walls and tied up along the wharves of the harbour to unload their grain and building stones.

So Stolzenberg—not quite Danzig—is where I was born. My quiet mother was Susanna Ordonn, who had married Father soon after they came from Elbing. I was second, my brother Isaak was already three on my birthday; left-handed Grossma was the midwife to us both.

My first memory is the smell of light. Like the colours of a palette, the smell of oil paints and the glass windows, floor to ceiling, of Father's studio built against the side of our house, a wall of light that opened on our driveway and the garden of apple trees and roses. Sometimes our matched team of greys would appear there, necks arched high, nostrils flaring, followed by the carriage with our coachman up on the seat, his enormous hair and beard like the fur helmet of a uniformed hussar. Then my father would come out of the house, the footman handed him up, and the carriage drew away until there were only trees and roses again, with the slender footman standing at attention. And light.

Holding my grandmother's hand, from the crest of the Bishop's Hill I saw tall three- and four-masted ships sail through fortress walls below us, sail between distant gardens and grazing sheep and huge granaries and cranes, past churches and tall Dutch-gabled houses like immense birds with their white wings spread, moving quiet as wind, but creaking; sail east into the shining Vistula and be carried along the bend of that river north, to pass between the cannon of Fortress Weichselmünde, and away, Grossma said, to the spice seas and golden oceans of the world.

Like any beloved child, I simply accepted that ours was a large, happy family. I don't believe that even my grandmother surmised then that every Seemann who dared to paint, with the exception of my youngest brother, would die far from this place of our heritage: my father Enoch, my brother Isaak and his son Fiorillo, I and my son Paul, and saddest of all, my grandfather Isaak Seemann. He spoke Dutch and High and Lowgerman and Polish fluently, he preached and taught in the Mennonite church for two decades, but he died in 1730 at the age of ninety among English people he could barely understand, and to whom he could not speak.

Our enduring problem was not the people of Danzig, though at first it seemed that they would be. The Danzig Painters' Guild refused to accept Grosspa Isaak as a member; as a result, no Danzig citizen could commission a portrait from him, and he could not make a living. In consequence, my father disdained to seek admission to the Guild, and instead painted a picture no Danziger could ignore. It was an immense vista of the city as seen from the south, from the Bishop's Hill on the left to the curtain wall of the Wiebe Bastion on the right, with the massive tower of St. Mary's centred over the suspended cables and buckets of Adam Wiebe's *machina artificiosa* that had built the city walls, walls which in half a century of religious and political wars not even the Swedes had been able to destroy. Every Danziger knew that. Then, going over the head of the Guild, Father presented this beautiful painting—I never saw it, only copies of the many copper engravings Danzig had made of it—

directly to Danzig City Council. His Honour Mayor Christian Schroeder was himself, as they say, *"een aufjefollna Mennist,"* a fallen-off Mennonite, but his and the Painters' Guild's opposition could not prevent the Council from granting Father a special "Independent Master Painter" permit. Its only restriction, to avoid competition with Guild members, was that he should neither train apprentices nor paint landscapes. And then, immediately, the Council commissioned him to paint individual portraits of every councillor and hang them all around City Hall!

By the time I was born, Father and Grosspa Isaak were so well known, and painting portraits so widely, that the Danzig Painters' Guild could do nothing. It was our own people, who in the century before had fled arrest and fire in Flanders, who became their persecutors.

Not that Mennonites ever arrested or burned anyone. Oh no, my father said bitterly, the now prosperous Mennonites of Danzig were certainly not the cruel hounds of the Inquisition, and they would call on no civil authority to execute anyone. But they could put you on trial: a trial not conducted in the theatre of public exposure and official report, but in the narrow confines of the Believers' Congregation, and the even more secretive and unreported discussions between the patriarchs who dominated it. These men were not called *Vermahner*—that is, "those who admonish, warn, rebuke"—for nothing. They had no need for chains or tongue screws; they had rhetoric and the church ban.

"We should have moved to Königsberg," my Grossma Triena said fiercely.

Isaak, Peter and I were lying on top of our big brick centre-oven that heats the whole house. Like my brothers, I was supposed to be sleeping, but I preferred to listen.

"At least there no benighted Mennonite *ohm* would tell us what we can't do."

Königsberg was no farther from Elbing than Danzig, though in the opposite direction. That was where Grosspa's oldest son, our half-uncle Isaak, had gone to work with Grosspa's brother, Abel Seemann, who made an excellent living painting gory, larger-than-life murals of land and sea battles on the walls of civic buildings and the castles of noblemen. The Königsberg Painters' Guild had allowed him to join it and so, my father said, he could hire all the apprentices he needed to fill in the huge background spaces.

My father's growing problem in Danzig was the cobbler Georg Hansen. Cobblers were always known as independent thinkers—maybe helping people to walk gives them long thoughts—and even Father admitted Hansen was a very learned, if self-taught, man. Recently elected Elder of the Danzig Flemish Mennonite Church, he had been a *Vermahner* in the church for twenty-five years, and had already published both a lengthy "Confession of Faith" and an exhaustive catechism for the instruction of baptismal candidates.

"Huh!" Grossma snorted, never impressed by *dem Aula*, "That Old One." "The saying is, 'Whoever says cobbler says revolutionary,' but now when Danzig Mennonites say 'cobbler,' they're saying 'older than the Old Testament.'"

I was peering low over the edge of our centre-oven, down along our family kitchen table. Grosspa Isaak sat with his head in his hands, his hair braided in a heavy, tapering rope down his back. He said nothing, but I knew he would not agree to joining his oldest son and brother in Königsberg. He hated the slaughter of war; to use God-given talent to glorify it—even to make a living—was a denial of every Christian feeling he lived by.

"But he is the Elder," my mother said softly. "He leads the church."

In the lamplight my father was staring at her nursing our baby Elizabeth. His long face seemed carved into hard, sharp edges.

"The Guild forbids me landscapes," he said, "and now our Elder has decided to forbid portraits. What can I paint?"

Abruptly he leaned forward and with his gaunt fingers outlined the top of my mother's breast, as though he were brushing its full curve onto canvas.

"Enoch," my mother said, so quietly.

He leaned away from her, back, and suddenly I was looking down into his mouth, right to the bits of that red flesh that stands up at the bottom of the tongue, he was laughing so hard. The room rang, and baby Elizabeth twisted away with a frightened cry, leaving my mother's dark nipple glistening. A bluish bubble of milk grew at its centre, dripped, and grew again, then my mother clasped the baby tight to her.

"*Na*, Enoch!" Grossma said. "Scare her then!"

"If I painted that," my father gestured, and his voice was seething rage, "the most beautiful act in the world, a mother feeding her tiny child, Hansen would call me a sex fiend. Did Mary never suckle Jesus? Oh, what the Italian painters do with that scene, it breaks your heart with tenderness. But in our church there's just Paul laying down law and Big Jesus pointing his finger, 'You sheep right, you goat left!' Judge, judge, no human feeling, just Almighty Judge, right! left!"

"Huh!" Grossma snorted. "I've been a left-handed goat all my life!"

Grosspa Isaak hesitated, then said gently, as if he had not

heard her, "Elder Hansen has studied the Bible, he says it's the Second Commandment, 'Make no graven image,' that's how he—"

"You can bless anything with a text," Grossma said.

"I'm not making a graven image," Father insisted, "a *god*, when I paint a human face! I'm painting a man, a woman, like we all are, maybe looking with love at a child. Any fool can understand that, all you need is eyes and feeling, so why can't our brilliant thinker and writer and warning admonisher, the Most Highly Venerated Church Elder and oh-so-humble leather-stitcher, our Highest Brother-so-beloved-by-all Georg Hansen understand? He can argue a Jesuit into the ground, he's so smart, why can't—I'll tell you why," my father changed direction before even Grossma could pry in a word, "he doesn't look because he doesn't want to see, because if he did he might understand something different, and feel! And then he'd have to admit that he could make a mistake, that portrait painting has nothing logical to do with his argument about 'making God's image' because I can read too and I know the whole Second Commandment says 'Thou shalt not make any likeness of *anything* that is in heaven above, *anything* in the earth beneath, *anything* in the waters under the earth'—then logically painting landscapes must be wrong—they are the earth!—though he says that's okay, but no believer can ever draw a human face. I say he's drunk too much theological Calvinism, I say the Second Commandment is about worshipping, not about sculpture or drawing at all, and any good Dutch Mennonite theologian could have told him that for a hundred years if he'd only read them properly. Lambert Jacobsz was the Mennonite elder in Leeuwarden who brought unbelievers to tears with his paintings of people and stories in the Bible, he—"

"Enoch, Enoch." My mother was rocking Elizabeth on her breast and weeping.

Grossma said sharply, "What is this? Enoch? What happened to you?"

My father was tilted so far back, he had been talking so fast and loud and glaring straight up at me on the edge of the oven; now it seemed he actually saw me, saw what I know was my terrified face. I was seven then, and I had never heard or seen him like this.

Looking steadily at me, he said with his usual controlled calm: "I have destroyed all the portraits."

"What..." My mother, like a sigh.

"They told me this afternoon that if I did not I would be placed under formal church ban, and every church member must shun me. No church member would be permitted to say so much as a word to me. Including you, Susanna, who would have to deny me both table and bed. And even..." and he gestured at me, quickly, but was looking past me, somewhere blank, "even the children, for the good of their souls. So, in the presence of Elder Hansen and *Vermahner* Sawatsky and van Steen and the three who spoke against me, the shopkeepers Daniel Kurtz and Dirck Cowent and Berend Kauenhowen, I cut up thirty-seven paintings, including the portraits I did of you, Susanna, and our boys, and you too," he nodded to my grandparents, "and myself, I slashed them to pieces. And then..."

My father stopped. By now Isaak and little Peter were awake beside me on the oven, and we and everyone below us around our family table were staring at him.

Father took a deep breath and continued, "Then they burned them. Behind the church, where no one could see the fire from the street.

"And," he was talking faster and faster, "I told those three little envious shopkeepers, 'Now,' I said, 'you will obey the Elder's "Second Commandment" too. You will take down the signs above your shops and you will break them in pieces, and burn them. Because they have "graven images" of people on them too!'"

I saw my father then hard and grey, and as sharply danger-ous as any rock cracked by fire.

After some time Grossma Triena said, "They won't do it."

And she was right. Father's portraits of the Council belonged, of course, to Danzig and so they remained on the walls in City Hall, but he had to work to feed us, he said, and the Elder Hansen did nothing about the three shopkeepers, and so he sent them a letter, saying "I see you hold with your picture signs, you continue to worship these graven images because they attract customers, well, as I told you all, I believe I have as much freedom as you."

In the next six months my father painted two more por-traits, of city bankers who were not Mennonites, and he wrote a book. With paint my father was skilled and allusive—a shade of paint on a lip could say more than a whole suit of clothes—but when he handled words he demanded they say precisely what he meant, so his title stated his intention without a hint of ambigu-ity either artistic or theological:

Revelation and Punishment of Georg Hansen's Folly:
For everyone's Brotherly Admonition and Faithful Warning
brought to Light with the best Intentions by a Lover of the
Truth,
Enoch Seemann, Painter.

Stolzenberg, Printed by Christian Philip Goltzen.
In the year 1697.

He wrote in German, and the word he used, *Torheit*, is really stronger than "folly"; it leans towards "stupidity." "Brotherly admonition" and "faithful warning" were words the Mennonite ministers emphasized in their role as church *Vermahner*, and it was obvious that by publishing this pamphlet in German rather than Mennonite Dutch, my father intended everyone in Danzig to be informed of the exact *Torheit* perpetrated by this widely read and highly respected church leader and independent businessman.

Grossma Triena always said that if Enoch wanted to expose That Old One's stupidity, he should have done it with his greatest strength, painting, and not tried to use Hansen's great strength: words. Perhaps, if my father and grandmother had worked together, using his skill with the human figure and her incisive verbal ironies, they could between them have invented the satirical cartoon, even as my great-great-grandfather invented the cable car. As it was, at first my father's "hateful, spiteful, venomous book," as many Mennonites called it, achieved a good deal. The Danzig City Council called Elder Hansen to appear before it, and he had to admit that he had no civic or legal authority to interfere with the conjugal family rights of a properly married couple. The Council then invited my father to accept a new position they created specifically for him, namely to become the official "Danzig City Artist." As far as the City was concerned, he could paint what he pleased, portraits, landscapes, murals—anything anyone wished to commission.

"It is too much," Grossma said.

She was right again. My father now came to be seen as a high-handed man who used his great gifts, and more particularly his political influence with the City Council, to dominate both the members of the church to which he insisted he remained faithful, and the citizens of the city he insisted he loved. The more liberal Frisian Mennonite Church in nearby Neugarten—where since Adam the Wiebes had always been members—would not have banned Father for his portraits, but now their elder had to agree with the more conservative Flemish Church that the Danzig City Council could not decide on a fundamental matter of church discipline. And the lucrative City Artist appointment made the Painters' Guild more envious than ever. Mennonite church members and Danzig citizens: between them our Seemann family lost all community. Because of my father, we were Stolzenberg pariahs.

When Elder Hansen read out the ban against my father, the whole congregation of the Danzig Flemish Mennonite Church at the Petershagen Gate was present. Two hundred and thirty families, over a thousand people including unbaptized children. I was eight, and I remember the Elder's powerful hands lifting the black leather Bible folded open, and his voice like a trumpet:

"Thus doth our Lord command: 'And I will give unto thee the keys of the Kingdom of Heaven: and whatsoever thou shalt bind on earth shall be bound in heaven: and whatsoever thou shalt loose on earth shall be loosed in heaven.'"

And then he turned some pages and looked up. He didn't have to read the words, he knew them:

"Thus saith the Lord: 'It is a fearful thing to fall into the hands of the living God.'"

My father, standing alone before him, turned and walked past us in the pews down the centre aisle; out of the church. Grossma Triena stepped around my grandfather into the aisle and followed him.

"Let That Old One ban me too," she said to my father.

But my mother and grandfather did not know what to do. Night after night our family sat around the table, talking. My father obeyed the letter of the law: he ate separate food and did not speak to us, but wrote short notes, which Grossma read aloud. But soon he stopped writing: it was clear Grosspa and my mother could not defy the Elder.

"God gave Enoch a great talent, to paint," Grossma Triena argued. "Why should he bury it now? If he can't paint here, there are other cities."

Father agreed with her. He decided to leave Danzig and accept an invitation to the court of Augustus II Duke of Saxony, who was now, after innumerable wars, also King of Poland. Father travelled to Warsaw to design and decorate the new palaces Augustus was building himself there, and he took Isaak and me with him to begin our apprenticeships.

Protected child that I had been, I could scarcely believe what I saw in Warsaw; often out of the corner of my eye, it was so shocking. Augustus was barely twenty-seven, and not yet as debauched as he would be when he created at Dresden the wealthiest and most dissolute court in Europe. But, as the dazzling architecture of the Zwinger Palace proves to this day, his obsession with every imaginable human experience of beauty and vice was lifelong and unquenchable. My father was painting an immense wall mural of large figures draped to their feet—though sometimes the drapery fell aside for thigh or breast—he painted the flesh, folds and edges of the figures, while Isaak and I filled in the solid colours of cloth as he instructed us. But the way we did even that seemingly elementary work did not satisfy him.

"It's cloth, yes, but there's a human body under it. Even when it drapes down, straight, you have to see the body!"

Isaak and I could only hang our heads. We tediously brushed endless paint on plaster; for us there could be no bodies, certainly none like those we pretended not to glimpse in a split-second shriek of flight and pursuit flitting through the lantern-light of the magnificent gardens below the royal servants' quarters, where we lived.

"Take off your clothes," our father ordered. "Every piece."

We stared at him. At home in Stolzenberg we three brothers slept in a room separate from our little sisters, but even so we undressed quickly as our mother taught us, without a candle and with our backs turned. We knew perfectly well the shameful, naked story of Eve and of Adam.

"I will too." Father was unbuttoning his shirt. "Take them off."

And when we had, he raised our heads so we had to see him first. All that bare, broad flesh, and so much hair. Isaak...I... hairless, small...but we were shaped exactly like him. Isaak already had a bit of hair darkening there, in the triangle of his little front tail. It was no more pointed than mine, and just as fleshily pink.

"Your bodies, look, look at them. Given you by God." Father's voice was getting louder. "Every part as perfect and honourable as any other, you see? Whoever you paint, whatever covers them, this body is always here!"

He jerked up a bedsheet, draped it over his shoulder so that it covered half of him, even half of his large "member" as our mother never dared name it. He moved his shoulders, his legs, it seemed he might twist into dance.

"See how the sheet moves on this side, and the muscles here, at the same time, see? A beautiful physical machine, each body is different and each is also the same. The best painters always see that difference within the sameness. In Italy, in the studios, they work at that, they practise painting the nude body."

He was putting on his clothes again, but I didn't want to. I had never before felt air all over my skin.

"When I came back from Italy I was baptized in Elbing, and I wanted to paint anyone who would sit for me, not nude of course, men and women in their ordinary clothes sitting, standing, at a window. And I did that for a little while, and one day the *Vermahner* came to me and said it was going around that I had painted a woman lying down. I told him she was leaning on her elbow, stretched out on a couch with her dress draped over her boots...but she was stretched out, *lying down?*"

There was something in the way he said that, the tone of the words, "lying down." I felt cold; as if I'd been dropped into ice.

"Even in Elbing the *Vermahner* asked me about that," my father told us. "Before you were born. Long before the Danzig second commandment."

After two years in Warsaw, Father was bidden to Augustus's court in Dresden. Danzig was now so far away, we could visit our family only once a year; being a court painter, Father said, was little better than being a slave. I was becoming a pretty boy, the King's women living in the Zwinger told me that often enough. There were fifty or sixty of them at one time (Augustus was nicknamed "the Strong," because, it was said, he fathered over three hundred children), and they never had enough to do, so they became very playful. Father watched Isaak and me carefully, but one night after Isaak had turned seventeen—he was more than "pretty" by then—he did not return to our sumptuous apartments behind the Palace until dawn.

Father did not ask him what he had done. All he said was, "This will not happen again," and then Isaak bent over our salon settee and took his punishment on his bare flesh. I had to watch, and I thought I could certainly mix the colours correctly to paint a series of his buttocks as they changed. But I was also weeping with my brother. Within the week Father resigned his position.

The Court High Chamberlain would not accept his resignation, but Augustus did. Isaak and I had already noticed that he was looking at us very closely, and we were becoming apprehensive about it, but the King respected our father and he would not force us to stay, as he easily might have. We returned to Danzig, in one of the King's coaches piled high with gifts.

There came the day when, in a tall ship, our family sailed past the high warehouses of Motlawa harbour. Beyond them, through the wide streets of the Granaries district, we could see the narrow Dutch façades of houses towering over the docks and bridges of the inner channel, the spires of the churches and the Danzig city hall thrust up behind them, the Green Gate entrance of the Royal Route leading into the Long Market and the heart of the city. On the right, out of the Lower City, appeared the orchards of the Roehfer Roads and the walks and green plots of the Long Gardens that Adam Wiebe had enclosed inside the city walls. We were moving slowly, all so slowly. People stood to watch us pass, it seemed perhaps the ship was standing, would we ever get away, out to the river and on towards the open sea?

"Oh, the sea…the sea," our little sister Katerina sang in Highgerman, anticipating. She was less than three, but she loved the sounds of words and could already sigh many of them as long and softly as our mother.

Mother and Father and Grosspa Isaak were in our cabins below; they could not endure this endless leaving. But Grossma Triena was on deck, holding Katerina on her arm, with the rest of us children—Peter, Elizabeth, Abel, me, tall Isaak holding little Johann—huddled around her at the rail.

"Remember this," Grossma said in Lowgerman. "Who will see it again?"

It seemed then the ship would sail inevitably into the giant shipping crane of the Krahnstor directly before us, the immense square tower of St. Mary's Cathedral on the left and on the right, far over the houses, the needle spire of St. Catherine's. We were pressed so close together I could feel all our breathing heave in one gasp and stagger, we would certainly drive into the crane and sheer onto the street! But slowly, slowly, the ship tilted right and there over the narrow, muddy water came the high Church of St. John bending towards us, we were leaning into the east turn of the harbour towards the city walls and the Vistula River.

"Remember," Grossma Triena said. "In 1635 your great-great-grandfather Adam was granted the right to live inside Danzig. There, past St. Catherine's, by the Wagon Gate he himself had built, and the Council gave him, the only Mennonite then, the right to buy land inside the walls and he built three tall houses. You've seen them."

My brother Peter said, "I'm coming back, I'm going to buy them again."

He wasn't thirteen when he said that, the day we were barely moving down the Motlawa River, past the high stone of the Old Castle and all the ships tied to the wharves and anchored out towards the eastern ring of deep-moated walls, leaving Danzig. I did not believe Peter then, and I didn't know if my grandmother did; I could not look at her, we were passing too much. But she did; I think now that not only her left-handed faith but also her left-handed spirit helped her to understand more than we were able to think or imagine, painters or not.

Peter returned to Danzig after baptism, with good Dutch connections in the East Indies, to become an importer of spices and coffee. By 1722 he had bought the most neglected of Adam Wiebe's houses, and a year later Grossma Triena sailed from London to celebrate his marriage in the restored house. Katerina and Johann travelled with her; at the wedding Katerina met Anthoni Momber, a Mennonite who wanted to start a coffee house. Two years later he came to London to marry her, and together they returned to Danzig to build their coffee house beside the Market, near the beautiful Renaissance Artushof where the bankers counted their money. Within a few years, because of its splendid gardens, its poetry and drama readings, its superb beverage, the "world-renowned Momber Coffee-house in Danzig," as Professor Hans Meyer of Hamburg wrote, "invites all the peoples of the earth, even the Poles, Moscovites and Cossacks, to partake of its aromatic beverages, which rival anything London or Paris has to offer the most discriminating connoisseur."

Johann did not return to London; he settled in Danzig because artists were in great demand there, again. He named himself Johann Leonhard Seemann and a decade later painted the portrait of the Danzig Flemish Mennonite *Vermahner* Hans van Steen, whose wife was our second cousin Sara Siemens. Grosspa Isaak, my father and my mother were no longer alive, but Grossma Triena was. She was ninety-one, and laughed out loud when I told her.

"You wait," she said in Lowgerman; between us we never spoke anything else. "He'll be ordained Elder too."

She was right of course, though she could not wait until that happened to laugh with me again. Shortly after her death I married a young woman of good family, who taught me how to behave properly English in high society. When I died in 1744, our only child, Paul, was ten and already away in public school; the last time I saw him, he came into my studio and told me he wanted to be a painter like me and Uncle Isaak. I was then completing my last, and largest, group portrait for Sir John Cust, Belton House, *Lady Cust and Her Nine Children*.

What remains of my life's work is scattered. The portrait of Elihu Yale is in the United States and the much earlier *Colonel Andrew Bisset...*, which I now concede is of more than "somewhat" uneven quality, in Scotland. *The Lapland Giant Gaianus*, painted in 1734, the year Grossma Triena died, is in Dalkeith Palace; *Sir James Dashwood* (1738) at the Metropolitan Museum in New York. My one self-portrait, which Augustus II liked so much, I painted in 1716, rather too young. Seen from the left, I have my hand folded up long and thin towards my chin, a lock of hair too abandoned on my wide forehead, full lips and my eyes soulfully large.

When my grandmother saw it, she considered it for some time before she said:

"Slanted to the light, you look almost, as the English would say, sinister." She was smiling, and I did not need to tell her "sinister" in Latin means "left." She continued:

"You always say you don't want to be a Mennonite, and you've certainly painted yourself as if you weren't."

"Well," I said, "then I suppose I'm a really good painter."

"But you talk about Mennonites so often, you insist too much on not being one."

"Must a person be forever what he's born, only one thing?"

That was not quite what she meant, of course, as with time I understood. During the last two years of her life, when we lived alone together in London, we talked much; sometimes, I like to think, for days without stopping. Grossma could no longer knit, her right fingers were swollen large at every joint, but she could wind thread around them and hold the tension for crocheting with her left hand. Our chairs and settees were covered two and three deep with her delicate doilies, her crochet hook flying. She laughed at her hands, the right so thick and painful and the left so amazingly strong.

"You see," she said, "the left is the side of the heart."

She told me whatever she wanted to remember of her long, long life, and her memory about certain events was astounding. For she of all people understood the continuous contradictions, the unperceived endings that our lives contained. "We are *Himmels Flijchtlinje*," she said—people fleeing to heaven, or spiritual refugees might be the English for it—though at the end of the twentieth century it would be something clumsier, like "psychically displaced." People more devout than I ever permitted myself to appear might say she simply meant "a stranger here," or even "pilgrim."

In any case, during the night of February 13, 1945, that studied self-portrait was destroyed in the firebombing of Dresden. My portraits of the first two Georges lasted a little longer, until they too were transformed into soot and air by the flames of the Windsor Castle fire.

Of my grandfather's work nothing at all remains, and of my father's only a few copies of engravings, one of which is Adam Wiebe's cable car. The copper plates of it were, of course, melted long ago for bullets in some war.

My brother Isaak sailed from Rome to visit me the year before I died, and together he and I attended the first London performance of George Frederick Handel's *Messiah*, at the Theatre Royal in Covent Garden on Wednesday Lent, March 23, 1743. My wife deeply regretted not coming with us when we told her of the magnificence of the performance, with Mr. Handel conducting from the harpsichord, and even more so when a controversy grew in the press about the words of the New Testament and the name of Jesus being sung in a theatre by stage actors of "loose morals" and well-known "dubious sexual habits." The *Universal Spectator* demanded, "Is a playhouse a fit temple for God's Word? Is the New Testament to be a text of Diversion and Amusement? What a Profanation of God's Name, in diverting themselves are they not accessory to the breaking of the Third Commandment?"

Isaak laughed. "Shades of our Danzig Commandment," he said. "What is the third?"

I had no idea, but my wife knew her Anglican past. "Isn't it the 'shalt not' where you're not to take the name of the Lord your God in vain?"

We three laughed a little, together, as people who love each other do when they grow older. We talked about our Seeman family that had once been so close, and was now dispersed so utterly.

I died a year later, to the day. *Messiah* was not performed again for many years, but for me the music and words of one particular song have always burned like driven fire. Bass voice and trumpet:

> Behold, I tell you a Mystery.
> We shall not all sleep,
>   but we shall all be changed
>   in a Moment, in the twinkling of an Eye,
>   at the last Trumpet.
> The Trumpet shall sound,
>   and the Dead shall be raised incorruptible,
>   and we shall be changed.

Changed. No more end. Grossma Triena understood that. On earth she was a left-handed woman.

NINE

TABLE SETTING

Edmonton

1987

THEY ARE SEATED AROUND THE DINING-ROOM TABLE for their Saturday morning ritual, the first since Susannah has returned from Italy. The cinnamon rolls, which Adam as usual brought from the bakery on his way home from his hospital rounds, have been eaten, and Susannah is moving the cutlery around on the table as if a visual model were necessary.

"It's simple," she says. "I go to Calgary," one coffee spoon moves to the left, "your father stays in Edmonton," a fork to the right, "Trish, you're in university residence in Edmonton," a knife to the right in parallel, "and Joel..."

Her long fingers are on another spoon; her hand hesitates, but then she moves the spoon firmly to nudge the fork.

"Little Joel," she reaches up to fondle his tall head bent above her. "You stay in Edmonton, and finish grade twelve."

Joel mutters, "I already had four months alone with Dad."

Susannah's arm drops around his broad shoulders and for a

moment, football tackle though he is, Joel is simply her boy, resting his head on her shoulder.

"You know it's not good to break up your last year so late."

"What's the matter with a Calgary high school?"

"Sweetheart, not the last three months."

"It's just cramming for provincial finals, I can do them anywhere, easy."

Trish asks, "Why are you moving to Calgary now? You said the job starts in September."

Adam is staring out the floor-to-ceiling glass of the dining-room window. The North Saskatchewan valley covered in snow falls away deep and wide to the frozen river, and every tree, bush, park-path, bench and shelter is primed with hoar frost. The distant streets and bridges far below with the small cars edging along them and the glass and concrete highrises on the far bank, bristle, blaze thick silver and white in the morning sun against a cobalt sky. Every crystal of snow and ice is unique, every day the world he sees from his house—when he has time to glance at it— is different, changed superbly by changing cold.

And Susannah's calm voice. She has thought through every detail, it all sounds so practical, sensible, obvious, most reasonable, rational and so painlessly practical...he ran out the words until she told him to stop it, he knew exactly what she was doing so just stop talking and face it, for once.

"The dean of arts called me," she now explains to Trish, "he wants me to teach both spring and summer terms, spring term starts in May and I have to find a house."

"I thought you were going to commute."

"Three hundred kilometres one way? I'd still need at least an apartment there...."

"It's a lot simpler," Adam says, to lay the facts on the table, though he keeps his voice absolutely reasonable. "It's a permanent job and if she can find a house she likes right away, and we buy it, it's an investment. Why pay unnecessary rent?"

"I pay rent," Trish says. "Four hundred a month."

"You want a house?"

"No, I don't want a house."

"If you want, I can buy a house near the university, and you can live in it and pay me the rent, it'd be simple as—"

"I don't want to be a simple investment," Trish says flatly. "I just want to graduate this spring and get out of here."

"What happened to the tightwad?" Joel asks Adam. "You wouldn't even get me a second-hand Datsun when I got my driver's licence and now you're buying everybody houses?"

"Listen," Adam says, holding tight to the voice of calm reason. "Our family is changing. You're both grown up and graduating this spring, your mother has a tenure-track position at the University of Calgary, the kind of job she's so qualified for, after two books and fifteen years of sessionals here she should be the senior professor in that department—so, we're changing, if you're alive you change, and I want to explain something, that we can make good, reasonable decisions about what each of us does, and we don't have to concern ourselves about money. There's enough, I know, for all of us."

Trish says, "What do you mean?"

"I mean..." Adam stops. He hears she is not asking about money, but he continues, "My father told me, if you ever have any money, buy land, land is good, it never goes away. But we both," he gestures to Susannah, who is now in turn studying the glistening hoar frost outside, "both had lots of university bills to pay, we could only start with a small house for which Grandpa Lyons lent us the down payment, but when you were born, Trish, an old patient in the hospital told me, 'If you can scare up a hundred dollars, put it into Xerox shares for your baby girl.' So I did that, and when you were born, Joel—I could scare up a little better then—I bought five hundred dollars' worth of IBM stock. By 1977 we had this house, and more. Plenty more, now."

"You've got land too?" Joel asks, astonished.

"No, not land, and that's lucky because the bottom fell out of Alberta land in 1981, but shares, especially technology... okay, there's enough now for both your educations, including living costs, and a few long trips too, education as far as you want to go."

"I want to finish high school," Joel says. "In Calgary if Mom's gonna work there all the time."

Susannah does not look at Adam, but they agreed, it was part of their understanding.

"That's okay with me," Adam says. "And when you graduate, you pick out a new car."

"What's the max?"

"Depends on your marks. I'd say, first-class marks, first-class car."

"All right! Okay, Mom?"

"I want you with me, but it will take more than a month to get a house."

"But you have to be in Calgary to find it. And I can get a summer job in Banff. With a car I can commute there."

"Washing dishes," Trish says quietly.

"So what? I'll be in the mountains every day."

Adam says, "You don't have to work. You can help your

mother find a really good house, where you can see the mountains, every day."

Joel is laughing. "What are you, a millionaire?"

Susannah says, "Your father and I have agreed, whatever we do, we all share and share alike, equally. But the money has to be used sensibly, and we don't have to arrange everything this morning."

Trish is staring at the cutlery; she says, still more quietly, "I'm beginning to wonder. What all are we arranging, so out-of-the-blue this morning?"

Susannah says, straight and calm, "I've had a very successful time in Europe, now I have to start work in Calgary."

Trish says quickly, "I'm glad, Mom, you deserve a really good job, finally. But you both seem to..."

Adam says, into the intent, lengthening silence of both their children, "I'd like to take a long break this summer. Maybe Japan or Korea."

He touches Trish's left hand. "You want to come with me?"

Her fingers curl, and drift along his. Then she reaches across his arm and draws the two coffee spoons, the knife and the fork together and moves them around on the table, this way and that. Sometimes it seems she is shaping a circle, sometimes as if the cutlery radiated from a centre, were splayed out and flying away in the four cardinal directions.

TEN

CROSSING THE VOLGA

Herrenhagen, Prussia
Alexandertal, Russia
1863

I WAS BORN ANNA WIEBE on June 13, 1842, in the village of
Herrenhagen, West Prussia. I know God has a particular call for
an oldest daughter, but I never thought my hopes would turn to
dust and water just before I was twenty-one. What will happen
now? God knows. If I write down what I can, perhaps the thorns
of separation will be softened.

Our mother died last year. I am her oldest daughter. Our
family made the dikes to build Herrenhagen over 150 years ago,
four Wiebe brothers moving up the delta from the villages near
Elbing. But now Father says wars and kings change laws, no
matter what their forefathers have sworn is forever. King
Wilhelm has made Otto Bismarck his Chancellor in Berlin and
there will be war, he says, more and more war. And our family
has three tall sons.

Which is not many for Mennonites. But there is nowhere

on the Vistula delta to make more land now, and if a man has no land he is drafted into the Prussian Army, Mennonite or no Mennonite.

"Let Heinrich have the farm," said Johannes, the oldest. I'm second, two years before Heinrich, and then Franz, and Käthe, only twelve, and small Margaret. "I'll go to school in Berlin."

"If they see you there, they'll just grab you and shove a bear hat down on your face in the King's Guard."

Johannes said, "Not if I'm smart enough. Smart in university like Eduard Friedrich Salomon Wiebe."

"So smart," Father said. "And what about Franz?"

They were both too tall for the Prussian generals not to take them, both too strong. No Wiebes, Father said, have ever been lost in an army, not even when Napoleon made killers out of the whole world. We had to find new land, as Mennonites always have, for our faith.

So Father has sold our farmstead to young Hans Claassen with only one boy living and three girls. He sent 350 taler to the Russian embassy as a guarantee we will not starve on the road, and bought long wagons and bigger horses. We will leave with a trek for Russia. Elder Claus Epp is the leader and Aaron Ewert the wagon master.

I felt Frederich Ratzlaff of Heubuden was going to speak to Father about me, and I had hopes. But Father said, "Dearest Anna, you are the oldest daughter. If you don't come and cook, how will we eat?"

June 3, 1862: The last night in our home. Lord, abide with us. A huge fire in our kitchen stove, burning, burning. Before bed

I draw my "Daily Watchword" from its small box. The card gives me the First Commandment: Exodus 20:2—"I am the Lord, your God. You shall have no other gods before me."

I memorized the verse in catechism, did it always say that? There are other gods?

June 4: Watchword, Galatians 5:16—"Walk in the Spirit, do not satisfy the lusts of the flesh."

Käthe and I laid our last flower bouquet on our mother's grave. Aunt Anna and I cried together saying goodbye. It is all too much, my heart feels so heavy. My only hope is to leave all hopes behind and carry my duty. The wagons were ready, the drivers too. Käthe and Margaret and I walked around the yard. The flowers bloomed bright like stars in heaven. But brother Heinrich was hard. "Time to go, silly girls, come, come!" We drove along the dike roads under the trees of the green Werder, all the villages and the people we know coming to their gates. Down the street of Heubuden too, but only little Liesjki waved at the Ratzlaffs.

Thorns and tears. Goodbye forever in this world.

June 6: Watchword, Romans 8:23—"All creation groans with us for the redemption of our bodies."

Morning. Our wagons drove over the Nogat River towards the Castle at Marienburg on the railroad bridge. Horribly frightening, but solid. The wood and iron was black, with boards for horses. The horses had to be blindfolded and led. The castle like a black mountain over the grey water.

Johannes said our relative Eduard Frederich Salomon Wiebe designed and built that bridge. The whole railroad too, from Berlin six hundred kilometres to Eydtkuhnen on the eastern border. This Wiebe is now minister of public works for the Kingdom of Prussia in Berlin. Käthe said, "We've never seen him," and that's true.

I could not look, passing the castle. Over a year ago, a Sunday afternoon in April, I walked there with F.R. Never again. I want to remember only the rusting bars across every stone slit, for shooting people. Johannes crawled into the wagon and told us about Josef von Eichendorf who visited Marienburg Castle sixty years ago. It was leased by a Mennonite then. "The great hall," he wrote, "where the Teutonic Knights held their Round Tables for three hundred years now clatters and screeches with Mennonite looms weaving cotton."

My little sisters laughed. It was not funny for me. Johannes tells wonderful stories, but I hear only: You Must.

June 7: Watchword, Galatians 6:8—"He who sows to his flesh will of his flesh reap corruption."

A good Prussian road. Over big fields near Elbing we saw the roofs of the Einlage villages among the trees across the river. Hundreds of our Wiebes, Johannes said, still live there, though many more have moved to Russia. Their dikes were built by Adam Wiebe and his sons over two hundred years ago. They have been opened only once, to see if Napoleon had taught his soldiers how to swim. He hadn't.

June 8: Watchword, I Cor. 2:10—"But the Spirit searches everything, even the depths of God."

I made breakfast coffee with hot water from the guest house

where we stayed. This place was so dirty, worse than yesterday. I could hardly cook our beer-soup on their dirty stove. I slept alone in the wagon, they are guarded all night. Never seen such filth in a kitchen. The woman of the house, really a servant herself, screaming all the time at her sour-faced maid. Today the sun shone, black clouds along the horizon with lightning.

We passed Elbing early. Such church spires, like a city praying always. At night I cooked sweet plums for Pentecost and Elder Epp preached. He sits on a chair that folds flat.

Auguste Ewert sat on the ground with her two little children. We were closest friends before she married the Widower Ewert, his wife dead three weeks. She has four stepsons, the oldest a year younger than she or I. I stood near her. She looked up and smiled. Her Agnes has such beautiful golden hair.

June 12: Rain and mud. This guest house was quite clean. Father let the woman make breakfast. Someone was rude to me, but I feel safer and I told him what I thought.

We stopped in Eydtkuhnen, the last night in our homeland. I wrote a long letter I did not send. My sisters went with Johannes to the railroad station, which is very big but not yet finished. Käthe said, "That's the last we'll see of Eduard Frederich Salomon Wiebe." Small Margaret said, "I've never seen him yet," and they laughed.

Johannes looks sad. Not even eldest sons can do what they most want.

June 13: Watchword, Hebrews 12:1—"Seeing we are surrounded by so great a cloud of witnesses, let us run with patience the race set before us."

A year ago today our loving mother's eyes closed forever.

And we crossed the border, the last Prussian eagle, on my birthday. The border search was short, but made me angry. Such dirty hands digging in our things. Auguste Ewert let them, as if she didn't care. All her careful bundles pulled open.

The hills shone in the distance yesterday, today the high churches shine over village roofs in the sun. Beautiful. But no good houses, everything is ugly, dirty, horrible disorder. Most of the people seem to be Jews. They swarm around us yelling we have to pay them border fees. Father threatened to call the guard and they disappeared fast as rats. Käthe sang a song from school, "All that is good, all that is beautiful, is in our Fatherland."

I have had no time to go into any cemetery. But Johannes went to one we passed and brought me small red flowers. I pressed one between my Watchwords. I have our portable iron oven, I can cook better beside the road even in evening rain. No stinking kitchens.

June 14: Watchword, Galations 6:8—"He who sows to the Spirit will reap life everlasting."

Rain on rain. From far away, towns shine with the pointed onion domes of Russian churches, but driving into them they are so ugly. I feel unwell. I cannot even walk into a cemetery we pass, though there is time. Streets full of mud and Jews yelling. We escaped around Marienpol without being robbed. Such filth, all so poor. Men scream to sell anything, young Jewesses run around in rags with nets over their bound heads. "O Israel, you foolish people of God," as Jeremiah prophesied. We never saw so many on the Werder. They have rejected their Messiah, what else can they expect but poverty?

Father bought oats from a Jew. The road becomes sand
and hilly, the horses labour. I walk behind in the rain. O Lord
have mercy on us and our cattle.

June 15: Watchword, Psalm 9:20—"Arise, O Lord, put them in
fear, that the nations know they are only men."
    Sabbath. I laid out our wet wash behind bushes to dry in
the sun. Sat on a rock to write. My Watchword for today leaves
no room for my thoughts, though they never leave me. Only
men. Elder Claus Epp preached sitting under birch trees and
we on the ground. I thought of Jesus and his disciples. Only
men—did women listen?
    In the evening we sisters sat with Auguste in a meadow
and sang songs. Then all the Ewert and Epp and Wiebe children came, Auguste's little Benjamin and Agnes too, and it was
noisy. They played, running, their voices calling each other.
High and sweet as if they were at home.
    "Now rejoice, poor, sighing creation. Soon your eternal
Sabbath will dawn which no day of labour will follow."

June 18: Watchword, II Corinthians 13:13—"The grace of
Christ, the love of God, the communion of the Spirit be with
you."
    Rose very early today. The wagons drove long before
breakfast. I felt so unwell, but tried to walk to spare the horses.
We want to reach Vilna. Very stony land and the sun hot.
    Today I did walk in a cemetery. There were no grave-
stones, only wooden crosses rotting on the ground. Weeds,
every grave sunken and deep, a picture of life collapsing. I
wanted to write letters, but too many mosquitoes. Little Agnes

Ewert leaned against me after I finished cooking and we ate. Her bright hair.

June 19: Heart, how long will be your longing?

Vilna rises so high on a cliff above the river, it frightens me. Always farther away. A Jew gave us directions, but his road turned to sand through a valley, our men furious. Lucky he was gone or Heinrich would have beat him and got us in trouble. But Father said the Jew sold us a good horse, which helped pull us through.

Father walked in to mail letters, Johannes and we sisters went to see the railroad station. High cut stone. Many oak trees, and fine, white Russian church towers with red and running green cupolas. Beauty without true faith. The cult of priests who stare at us as long and black as their clothes. We bought bread and two more good horses from Jews and drove on.

Toward evening Father pointed out a high, ruined castle. We sisters and brothers, except Heinrich, climbed up. No building, rough stones everywhere as if thrown by giant children. A ruin. There was no time, we had to run down and catch up with the wagons.

Within me I feel dry as sand in a ruin.

June 23: Watchword, Zinzendorf: "O Saviour! Weave your holy flames of love through my frozen heart."

Rain upon rain. A Russian postal road only, sand and long hills. Our poor Fox can no longer pull, he can hardly walk tied behind the wagon. My sisters and brothers, not Johannes, scolded me. They say I am unwell because I eat too much. But I think it is because I always have to walk in wet shoes.

And thoughts, too many to carry. All hopes and plans of
Heubuden hang so heavy. They must be thrown away. Oh, for
the strength. And still they sit like crows. Black and waiting.

June 25: A tiny stream in a deep valley. Johannes and Käthe
climbed down to see it. The narrow road hangs on the edge,
leading forever up and down. The sun set behind a distant
shower, like light through tears.

June 28: I want peace. To think only of noodles. Minsk is far
behind. Could not walk today. Very stony and rough, but
bumping in the wagon I was able to mix dumplings. Everyone
ate except me. Miserable Russian towns, churches shine in the
rain surrounded by rotten sheds under rotting shingles. Endless
soldiers with guns, nothing to do but hold guns and stare. We
could find no drinking water. Drove very late and stopped in
woods. Beautiful evening light, with many mosquitoes. Double
night watch set, this is deepest Russia, Heinrich said. Franz
laughed. "Wait," he said, "there'll be more, wait."

June 29: Sabbath morning, shining with dew. I slept a little in
the wagon yesterday driving, and still weak. Without Käthe and
Margaret I could not have made coffee for breakfast. Elder Epp
preached from Luke, the lost sheep, the ten lost coins. We
rested. It was good for us and the poor horses. Good sun.

After noon all the men sat around Elder Epp in his folding chair and talked about Mennonite non-resistance, how to
love enemies. I had to laugh. Every day we meet so many dirty,
screaming, stealing people, and the men speak as close to cursing them as they dare. Johannes saw me, and I was ashamed

at what he saw on my face. He knows how close I feel to cursing too.

I showed little Agnes Ewert and her two-year-old brother Benjamin the grand birches, spreading their skirts out wide and gentle like ladies between the stiff, dark pines of men. Käthe came to sit with us. My spring is gone. Why can I not find a soft and submissive spirit?

July 4: Watchword, Luke 24:29—"Abide with us, Lord, for the day is far spent and night is falling."

Road like desert. Poor Fox had to be shot, nothing left to give us but his hide. Waste land. When the sun shines it is desert, then it is dark lightning, rain, mud. Thunder like barrels breaking.

So sick but I cooked. Many children, they say, are sick. Auguste's too.

July 10: The men pushed and shouted with Jews, about horses. We were in the right, but that did not help us. Father bought the horses, and made peace.

Hot sun. I cannot walk. I shake in the wagon, burning. Auguste comes carrying Benjamin, and cries. Her small children are both so very sick with fever.

July 18: Watchword, Psalm 63:1—"O God, my soul thirsts in a dry and tired land."

At last the Dnieper River. A single tree on the bank, a great oak like the one in our yard in Herrenhagen. I tried to walk along the bank behind the wagon. The black sound of water rushed by—would it be deep enough? Johannes says this

river flows past hundreds of rich Mennonite villages sixty and
eighty years old, far south near the hot Black Sea. Where we
are not going. Thousands of our people we will never see. Is it
long enough?

My sisters found wild currant bushes. I ate a few, sweet
and sour as they were, both. White water lilies floated in standing water. A cemetery was hidden among trees but I was too
sick and had to cook. I could not walk there.

July 23: Far beyond the Dnieper River now, but where is
Moscow? Always hills and hills, such terrible sun and sand,
such driving rain and mud. Everything is so hard here, even
weather. The land God gave sinful Cain.

Johannes found blueberries under pine trees. We sick ate
all he had. But it was too late for small Benjamin Ewert, he
died in their wagon after noon. Mr. Ewert bought boards from
a Jew who passed in a high wagon. It is very hot. They say a
body can be carried for only a day.

July 25: We did not have to bury little Benjamin beside the
road. A village near great Moscow had a cemetery.

I was too sick to go, but Elder Epp led the service in our
wagon circle. The coffin open, as always. Isaiah 26:19, "Your
dead shall live, their bodies rise, O dwellers in the dust." A
small black stranger lying there, swollen so thick, no one could
have said they knew him.

July 27: Sabbath, and sick. I lie in the wagon, look between
the canvas at the onion cupolas of Moscow in the distance.
Uncountable. Johannes quietly gave me an apple from the

market. He said the evening sunlight shines true: the domes are pure gold. Golden heaven here in Russia and I cannot walk. No no, he said, not the streets, they're dirty and broken cobblestone. My brothers brought a doctor to our camp, but what can a strange man know? Sabbath service.

July 30: They brought the doctor again before we left Moscow. He was German, talking to everyone, and such kind eyes. Some men have eyes so sharp you feel cut. He asked questions quietly. He did not touch me but gave me several medicines. I felt better. Father had bought fresh meat in Moscow and I wanted to eat. I dragged myself to the stove and ate while sister Käthe and Margaret, just nine but learning, were cooking. The wagon is full, but in it I can sleep alone. Try.

August 1: Watchword, Hebrews 11:3—"By faith we understand that the world was made by the word of God."

I can only cry at my weakness. An understanding look and medicines are useless, I cannot lift my head. It was unbearably hot, my mother's thickest blanket could not save me from the endless stone bumps and bang of the wagon. Towards evening it rained and I was so cold. Oh, miserable body that feels everything and knows nothing. Oh great God, create a new world in me.

August 14: My sisters say we have passed Vladimir and Murom, passed Arzamas. What is that? A small city. We are over halfway from Moscow to Alexandertal. There, across the Volga River, Mennonites and our Elder's son, Claus, and our new land are ready. I say nothing. Pain and wagon days. I remember bumping along with nightmares, night and day.

Of the Marienburg, the castle garden and an arm I leaned on. The words said to me—I want to forget what I heard. What I saw. There were iron bars crossed in the thick slits of the walls where they once shot arrows and guns, but sunlight made beautiful faces on a fountain, then ugly. Stone walls. F.R. who spoke so softly to me, the summer after my mother died, a letter I burned in our kitchen stove on June 3. I will forget, all is ashes, leave them in the Russian dirt in this unending land of dirty travel, away. There is enough nothing here to lose your all in nothing forever.

Little Agnes Ewert is still sick. She sits with me now, on the softest blanket in our wagon. Our shoulders bump together, her thin legs against mine. We try to laugh a little. I draw a stick child on her slate, she tries to write the letters of her name. It is all crooked, lines crossed over with bumps. Impossible to read or see. We try to laugh. My sisters cook at the oven outside, and sing:

> "There is nothing on this earth
> Which my longing satisfies;
> O my Jesus, draw me nearer...."

Agnes's perfect face is dried hollow, almost pointed. Like a little golden mouse, her breath sweet. But I see her eyes are growing wide, always deeper.

August 18: The wagons stopped and I heard Auguste Ewert wailing. We were on a crown of hills. The gleam far ahead of us was the Volga River, Johannes said. He gave me more blueberries. It could be the sad Russian Volga, but to me it looked wider than a sea.

August 19: We buried little Agnes by the side of the road, her name cut into the thickest tree we found. I rode in the Ewert wagon with Auguste. Sun and flying cloud, a broken road and hills. The wagon lurched on stones, we could cry together as loud as we wanted. In the evening one of her big stepsons helped her down. I climbed out too. I sat by our stove and rolled noodles for Käthe.

August 20: Rain and thunder, our poor cattle shiver with cold. Steppe weather, they say, Russia weather knows only extremes.

All day our wagons crossed the Volga River in a leaking ferry under heavy rain. I said to Heinrich on the water, "So, over there is Canaan, the land flowing with milk and honey." Heinrich said nothing, and Father heard me. He walked away to rub his newest, and best, horse between the ears. We still have eight horses for three wagons, but not one that started in Herrenhagen. All Russian, bought from Jews.

Johannes was at the edge of the ferry, singing, "Volga, Volga...." and rumbling along in a bass lower than any Russian. We seemed to be down in the river, standing still, the overloaded ferry sunk so deep we could look out level over the immense water splashing in rain. It sloshed cold as winter around our boots.

"This time," I said to him, "we won't get over. We'll sink."

Johannes said, "Anna, this is not the holy Jordan. This is Mother Volga, the land of Stanka Razin. Two hundred years ago he threw his dearest possession into the river, as the ultimate gift."

I asked him who Stanka Razin was, what was his gift? He told me I was already sad enough, I should not ask for more.

I told him, yes, I did not want a horrible Russian story. What I wanted was to see our mother again.

"Have faith," he said. "By faith the walls of Jericho fell down."

I told him the walls fell only after the Israelites had marched around them for seven days, and he said, Well, how long have we been marching?

August 25: Always the steppes now, long, long with grass and not a bush higher than your knee. Sky. Lightning. A cloud rises black anywhere beyond us and for a minute it pours. In our cookstove the fire spits. It cracks aloud with the grass we twist together to burn. Sky. Then far in the west a line of light and a perfect rainbow. The bow of promise, Father said. Johannes said, "It's behind us, in the wrong place." And laughed when Father and Heinrich looked at him. As if he didn't mean it.

We sisters and Franz laughed with him. Tomorrow, they say, we may reach Alexandertal.

August 27: The fifth day with not a tree, only the bends of the steppe, like a hand held flat and always reaching away. We found Alexandertal in a small, dinted valley with little bushes. Young Preacher Claus Epp came out of his simlinka to greet us. A thin, dark man with tears running into his beard. Very good groundwater here, he told us, not deep. A simlinka is a Russian house dug two steps into the ground with walls and roof of sod, see, they used the boards from their wagons to make a triangle roof, which made it better than the Russians' because the rain ran off the roof sods and away very quickly. Inside, he said, they were always warm and dry.

Young Claus Epp was so happy to see us, he talked and talked. But he looked past us when he did it, or over us, as if he could see something far beyond our heads, in the clouds.

Above the narrow valley there was only steppe. Open sky and fresh green land completely empty around us, a line cut sharp as a Cossack sword. Johannes put his hand on my shoulder. He told me there would be hundreds of Mennonites here, just wait a little, young men and women digging into the ground, growing out of it like grass.

I said I had been trying to find a university for him, but I couldn't seem to see far enough on this steppe.

He smiled, his lean face burned so dark and clean by the sun. Long ago on the coast of Friesland, he said, and for two and a half centuries in the Vistula delta, our people learned at the University of Water. Now Russia offered us the hard University of Grass.

ELEVEN

SLEEPING WITH FRANZ KAFKA

Cloister, Passau, Bavaria
Prague
1988

THE MORNING LIGHT SLANTS UPWARDS in the bathroom mirror into high, vanishing emptiness. Like a classic Dutch painting of perspective, Adam thinks: the flat spaces of a door opening and the door itself, the bare floor planks focusing back towards a medieval window, and to one side the corner of a bed with a woman's bare knees bent off the edge, her brown legs down to her relaxed toes. No one in the world knows where they are or that they are together; he feels a lurch of joy at last. An empty day in a forest.

And in this converted cloister—hidden for centuries in this German forest near the Czech border north of the Danube—the hotel rooms are deserted at this time of year. Adam will think, later: It was in that huge nunnish space that I first recognized Karen clearly, beyond infatuation—perhaps because she was replicated, reversed into distance by a mirror.

Now, studying his own razored Wiebe face he calls to her, "Would it help"—trying in the mirror to recall all the pictures she has of her obsession's deep male eyes, the long, bumpy nose—"say, if I parted my hair in the middle? Trimmed it up sort of high, sort of shaggy, like a fur cap?"

Karen's legs swing out of sight; she is laughing aloud about the vegetarians fussing in the restaurant the night before. "Those effete English," she exclaims, "they play with their health as if it were a sickness!"

"You're quoting again," he says.

Perhaps she hasn't heard him. She is still laughing.

"I can't change my jaw," he calls louder. "But how about if I prop my ears out like his, sort of these big scoops catching the breeze?"

"Oh stop it, get back here."

Her brilliant head and body waiting. The ancient, noisy bed too tiny in the huge room, under the ceilings that vanish somewhere above them; her naked body forgetful of any nunnery purpose this vacant building once had. A microscopic image of his face shines in her black eyes.

In the tent of sheets they are hidden from the room's echoing space. Skin along skin, bodies open to enter and leave, caress and re-enter.

"Why do you always want me?"

"An unfortunate state of mind. For me."

"Don't you mean 'body'?"

"Not at all."

"The body is a state of mind?"

"Absolutely."

"'The applicant,'" Adam quotes in German between her

breasts, from one of Franz Kafka's job applications, "'is fluent in the German and Bohemian languages, in speech and writing, and further he commands the French, partly the English—'"

She thumps his head on the pillow. "Stop it! It's hopeless, you never had a classic Freudian father to hate."

He wants to say How would you know? but tight on her moist skin he is instead already translating, against her heartbeat:

"'"It's a unique apparatus," said the officer to the research traveller and considered, with a certain look of wondering admiration, the to him very familiar'—hey, that hurt!—should one translate 'Apparat' as 'execution machine' or—"

Karen is on top of him, his arms pinioned back, her knee thrust between his legs and threatening.

"I'll kick you out," she pronounces through clenched teeth.

"Okay, okay, but please!"

Adam is trying to laugh. But sad words suddenly drift in his head: his mother singing the longing of her endless *Heimatleeda* and he rumbles into one in his monotone:

"Your Bride has waited, oh so long,
O Lord, for your—"

and then he can only gasp as she moves them deeper into each other.

They are in a tight street in the Josefstadt corner of Old Prague, where Karen has found a tiny, crusted keyhole. As she had also found Kafka's air-blackened bust with its unreadable Czech plaque on the wall of a building at what was once, she informed him, the corner of Karpfen and Enge Streets. Everything of the building, she explained, had been torn down and rebuilt except for the original entrance, and even that is now veiled by scaffolding that might have been clamped there since his birth in 1883, bleeding contemporary socialist rust. Appropriately enough, no Intourist official in Wenceslas Square who could speak either English or German or French would admit knowing the least thing about that Kafka corner, that building now incorporated into the baroque profusion of the St. Niklaskirche behind blue hoardings, the nine-spired towers of the Tienkirche poking above roofs shrouded in iron. However, the youngest female guide acknowledged *sotto voce* as the three of them bent together around the map, tracing the curve of the river that pulled the old city together, that, of course, Franz Kafka was born and lived his life in the Jewish ghetto of Prague—yes, right here in this bend—but the ghetto had been entirely rebuilt, after the war, *restored*, "The Memorial of All the People" to the horrible Nazi elimination of every living Jew in Prague, and for those people, she said, one Jew safely dead and buried in 1924 could not be as important as the rabid, genocidal destruction of an entire race, though Prague itself had not been as badly bombed by the West as all those other defenceless European cities, and of course the Grand Soviet Army had not fired one single shot more than necessary to wrest it from the last Nazi gauleiter, shooting him down in this very street, she said, pointing. And...what were they looking for, exactly?

Karen is silent as Adam bends to the keyhole. On the other side of the bolted planks of the door he half expects an insect's legs to waver in unresisting air. The door is at street level, and the long brick cemetery wall in which it is set stretches a metre above his head, but farther along, gravestones abruptly thrust out above it almost to the height of the eavestroughs of buildings at the far end of the wall, gravestones blurred by the moving branches of trees. With stones up there so high, was the city sinking even as it was being torn apart, levelled and rebuilt, the remains of the sinking dead rising up slowly from their centuries? A cemetery rising out of decrepitude and bordellos into tourism, a happening worthy of Kafka himself.

Just inside the ancient plank door—it can't be that old, the wood would be more rotten—the cemetery appears to drop down to the level of the cobbled street they are standing on; no huge insects anywhere. Gravestones only, thick as files in a cabinet, blundered over with moss, engraved with what may be Hebrew, or German, or perhaps Bohemian, every body pulling its slab down to its unique angle of decay. Tall sunlight, a mossy garden of stone knives.

"He isn't buried there, never," a woman's voice says behind them. Gravelly, like her desiccated face.

"Who do you mean?" Karen asks in her delicate German.

"They'll charge you five korunas to go in, but you won't find him. In the graveyard in Prague-Straschnitz, there's his stone." A dark, round mound of a woman, her crushed face held together snugly by a cowl. "Though who knows," she continues, "if he has a body."

"We're interested in Franz Kafka," Karen says.

"Who else"—her mouth gums the words—"on this street?" Amusement ripples, a small wind shivering over her. "But I wouldn't bother going to Straschnitz to look either. If he still has a body, it's been dug up seventy times over."

Karen steps close to her. "Dug up? Who dug him up? When?"

They face her together, startled, almost a little frightened at this sibylesque apparition on a sunlit, baroque street in a magnificent city roaring with markets and voices and cars, its historic centre designated "heritage."

"Heh! They were such organized hunters, where is there ever ground enough to hide a Jew, dead or not?"

"Dug up when?" Karen insists. Her hand has lifted, as if to tug out the next word.

"If he was ever there, and his parents lying right there too."

Karen's mouth is open a little, just showing the tips of her teeth. The sunlight is so dazzling Adam understands how Hermann Kafka could once live here in a house called "At the Golden Face."

"Where? Where do they lie?"

"Straschnitz. There you'll see what they did—to the few Jews that ever got rich in Prague."

"We were there, it's just…an ordinary gravestone."

The crumpled face crumples farther, into what must be laughter. Sympathetic perhaps; or ghoulish.

"That poor Franz. Only seven years' peace in the earth, alone, *ach*, and then his heavy papa lies down on him again."

His mama too. That's what the stone they saw there said: *Dr. Franz…. Hermann…. Julie….* Franz, not Frantisek, as the river for him was Moldau, not Vltava. But facing this apparition their quest—or Karen's obsessive quest, so convenient an excuse to travel without her husband—seems even more ridiculous to Adam. To retrace all possible facts about someone, you would have to literally relive their total life, stupidities and all. Thank god this particular life lasted only forty-one years and not, like Goethe's, eighty-three—but whatever their span, time wiped facts away. In any case, what did it matter where Kafka lived, or how, or even why he wrote, or if his body was no longer disintegrating somewhere? Time had not wiped away his stories and novels, though his literary executor Max Brod had famously published the bulk of them after his death in direct contravention of his will that they be, without exception, burned.

"Max Brod!" Adam swore the name when their conversation in the Straschnitz Cemetery stumbled into that will again. "What kind of a shit friend, and executor—executioner?—was he, huh?"

"You're the shit," Karen told him. "You bully people, you see what suits your fixed preconceptions. You don't listen, you remember even less, you're preoccupied with no one but yourself."

"Why attack me? I'm talking about friendship."

"Friends sense what their friends are saying, no matter what their words are."

"Don't ask me about that," he said, turning away from the tombstone. He had almost added, How would I know, I have no friends—but that would have simply proven her point.

Now he is tilted against the cemetery door in old Prague, and he thinks: I should walk away. I will anyway, better for me to leave her here in Josefstadt with this old sibyl and go away alone, past that parked yellow Skoda to the stone building at the corner and pay the five korunas and pass the weathered doorkeeper who'll be asleep at the entrance, her hand open for a ticket, and in my ignorance search among those crusted gravestones behind the wall. Maybe alone he would find something he could not misconstrue, or forget: an entrance opening down and bottomless, a helpless beetle on its back, a printing machine ripping its bloody text back and forth across the page of a living body—maybe even find a Mennonite there, suffering of course. As Karen had explained to him, over and over, Kafka was like the writers of the Old Testament: he anticipated everything conceivable by humanity and so all his horrors already existed as facts, were already taking place, somewhere. And would in the future; especially, Adam thinks, if you were a good Christian and did unto others as you did unto yourself.

The old sibyl faces Karen chuckling, oddly, without amusement. "And his three younger sisters," she says, "they were so close, those four Kafka children—Elli who travelled with him to Hungary and at last to Müritz on the Baltic, and good little Valli, and Ottla the youngest, she gave him his last summer cottage when he almost couldn't eat any more. Ottla he loved best, but he died in the arms of Dora Diamant."

"So"—he finds his German voice—"where do you say his three sisters are buried?"

Karen turns to him, staring.

"You can look in the air," the old woman croaks. "Gone in smoke, Auschwitz garbage."

"The Kafka word would be *Assanierung*," Karen tells him in English. "You know what happened, why ask?"

"I know, but ..." Such a long list of women Kafka loved, as much or as little as he could, who within twenty years were grotesquely annihilated one way or another. "Only Felice Bauer survived, whom he refused to marry every five years, and—"

"Only refused twice."

"All the fives he had time for."

"And Dora Diamant. Dead in London, 1952. 'The Human *Assanierung*' of Franz Kafka."

"What does it mean?"

"The word they used in Prague then for architectural clearance—'cleansing' is the word today. They razed every house in Josefstadt, after 1893, and built this quick imitation Vienna. Kafka wrote, 'Our heart still doesn't know anything about this completed "*Assanierung*." The sickly old Jewish town is much more real to us than this hygienic new city.'"

Hygienic cleansing. Her calm, straightforward explanation twists rage in him. "God! You know every word he scribbled, down to his casual letters."

"Why should that bother you?"

"Why clutter your mind? Even he wanted them destroyed."

Her tone shifts, acid. "Well, I study them. That's my job. But I don't think Kafka's words are the Eternal Word of God."

"Hell no!" Furious irrationality bursts out of him, surprising him. "*You* never have to 'think,' you just *know* everything, and declare it to the world!"

"And I also 'just know' you'll never divorce your wife."

"No more than you will your husband!"

"You're ready to decide?"

"You don't want to either."

"Why in hell should I? So you and I can kill each other the first time we're not making love?"

"Sweet holy shit!"

The jumble of Friday market in the Great Ring he is now striding through is so much the imploded mess of his feelings when she slices him like that, the perfect angling of her polished words, that he can only long to smash, throw, crash into—something physical, violent, break this relationship forever and absolutely—his mind, legs, feet, arms cramp and hands clamp empty, heave up—a pile of cobblestones slams against his toes.

The mason looks up at him calmly from his padded knees, his hammer poised for another tap on the last stone he has placed in its necessary curve. Wearing a bruised leather apron. Speaking some word in Czech, could it be *comrade?* Adam discovers his arm is raised, a stone clutched high in his hand.

The great clock in the City Hall Tower faces him. Such an amazing clock of interlaced faces. Emperor Franz—Franz's namesake indeed!—Josef I should be riding by with his splayed white whiskers and inbred Hapsburg chin, in medals and fourteenth-century uniform, on a perfect black horse. Riding, riding, nowhere.

From behind him Karen lifts the stone away, his hand left up and foolishly empty. She hands the stone to the mason, who places it in the sand at his knee, then reaches to choose a black one. He is talking to her, Czech perhaps or a dialect of it, and she nods, answers in a perfect accent with the few words Adam knows she knows, "Yes," "Why?" "Thank you," as if she understands every word the man is, at length, uttering. "Goodbye."

"This," she says at Adam's ear, "is the Clock of the Apostles—all of them except Judas. And that"—her warm arm turns him slightly, pointing across the encircling stones set ready for the mason's thick hands—"that is the one Kafka house still standing. That's his 'Minuta.' You ran right to it."

Their mutual, inevitable rage. *You ran right to it.*

Karen continues, so calmly. "His three sisters were born in this house, the family lived here seven years. They moved away to Zeltnergasse just before his bar-mitzvah in the Zigeuner Synagogue."

"'Gypsy,' oh, gypsy," he mutters. "When?"

"June 13, 1896, 10:30 in the morning."

A Sabbath in a leap year. He knows Kafka lived in the house called Minuta between the ages of six and thirteen: when everything new and growing in a life has already happened, when it is all over but the variations, the repetitions, the occasional understanding. Minuta stood attached to all the other houses, three storeys above arches and below a steep tile roof. Blank as a stupid cobblestone. The attempt to reassemble even the tiniest life out of the minutiae of accidental survivals overwhelms him with futility. And this life was not tiny.

"Come," she says. Kissing him with her particular softness among the rushing comrades and anti-comrades of the Great Ring of Prague. "We'll go to Ottla's rented house in the Street of the Alchemists—his most beloved sister. It's over the Charles Bridge."

Ottla's tiny house: two odd windows, a chimney, a door, below the immense Gothic castellated cathedral on the hill where the queens and kings of Bohemia were crowned; when they still had bodies to bury.

"I told you and told you," she explains, papers and books circling her on the cloister bed. "He lived his whole life in that ghetto, within two hundred metres of where he was born. Born, grew up, was sent to a Hapsburg dying Empire German school, to Charles University eventually, graduated a doctor of laws, went into business right there, recommended by his business uncles, but didn't stay. His father moved the family incessantly from one house to the next, upwardly mobile in that cramped Jewish corner—and when he was twenty-five only one of the fourteen buildings in which he had lived—the Minuta—remained standing."

"Yes. So, what's the problem?"

"I'm talking about his past literally being razed behind him, immediately after he's lived it, vanishment."

"My parents homesteaded in Alberta. If I went back I wouldn't find even a cellar depression."

"Jesus, you're a self-important bastard."

"If you're talking vani—"

"You travel the world and see nothing but your past, your ancestors, your self."

"And you've got keyhole vision. Franz-endless-bleeding-Kafka, middle-class, super-educated, super-achieving Sufferer on a huge and absolutely—as you would say—permanent disability pension!"

"You're being an ass."

"Who the hell hasn't suffered? See anybody? Wars, massacres, extermination camps happen to people, right here in his Prague!"

Very quietly: "I know your people suffered, but I'm talking about the writer of *The Metamorphosis*."

"Franz Kafka is an opera, forever dying with gorgeous women in every spa in cultured Europe wiping the sweat off his suffering brow."

"Did you hear what I said?"

"Yes. And he also wrote "The Great Wall of China" and *The Castle* and *Amerika* and *In the Penal Colony* and whatever else he scribbled all his life, thousands of pages. Which he ordered burned."

"How do you know what Kafka ordered?"

"Whatever he wrote—why shouldn't he ash it if he wanted to? You showed me his will. But considerate Max Brod and dear

Momma decided his *Nachlass* was worth much too much for burning."

"Worth. Money." She makes a disgusted sound. "You still have no clue, do you? Kafka's problem of being a Jew but having to write in German, while living in the massively German, oppressively Christian society of the Austro-Hungarian Empire."

He says, "A problem like being a semi-demi-secular Lowgerman Mennonite in a massively Nothing society?"

"I'd prefer not to talk about that, about you, just now. But you can't possibly imagine anything Kafka wrote was that simple—do this, don't do this—even in his will."

"Okay, maybe he was too depressed to write it, maybe he just signed it."

"What difference would that make?"

"Karen, he had a Ph.D. in law. His will—"

"And however he wrote this very personal document, his will, did he mean it literally, word for dictionary word?"

Adam groans. "I'll tell you what I know," he says, "because he published it while he was alive, he didn't burn it: *A Country Doctor*, Kurt Wolff Verlag, 1919. And in it a postage stamp story, 'The Next Village.' I quote the 1933 Muir translation:

> "My grandfather used to say: 'Life is astoundingly short. To me, looking back over it, life seems so foreshortened that I scarcely understand, for instance, how a young man can decide to ride over to the next village without being afraid that—not to mention accidents—even the span of a normal happy life may fall far short of the time needed for such a journey.'"

He stops. Her face is as expressionless as only perfect concentration can be. He thinks, For a woman to be so physically stunning is sinful. And mutters, "Facts enough?"

"You must have been a superb doctor, such a fast, incredible memory. Okay"—and her tone shifts—"why, of all things, did you memorize that?"

"Because—" He stops before her steady black eyes. "I wanted to. I like it."

"Because it has everything you avoid? Life in a claustrophobic village where everyone would know everything, and you couldn't even get away to the next village? What would you do without cities? If you couldn't disappear instantly from one faraway place to another?"

"Do we need this amateur psychology?"

But she reaches to touch his arm, suddenly gentle. "The root of 'amateur,'" she says, "is Latin for 'lover.'"

"That's much better." He lays his open hand on her leg folded under the other. "Lover talk."

"You know all about mine, now, tell me yours."

"My what?"

"Obsession."

"What, my obsession?"

"Or whatever you call it: your thick 'Bloody Theatre' book. Torture as public spectacle, those overwhelming stories."

"You like that title, don't you, *The Bloody Theatre or Martyrs Mirror of the Defenseless Christians Who Baptized Only Upon Confession of—*"

"Hush, I know that, it's magnificent—now, quote me a story from it, word for word."

"It's all Dutch, I only know the translation."

"Okay, you're a lousy scholar, but you're soaked in it, c'mon."

"Which one...you want the Kafka parallel, a sentence being printed in blood into a prisoner's skin? The cry of tender Eulalia when the iron 'claws cut her sides to her very ribs, "Behold Lord Jesus Christ, thy name is being written on my body! With great delight I read these letters—"'"

"No no. One you haven't told me before."

"Well," he says, abruptly calmed, thinking. "How about a martyr song? From the oldest Christian hymnal still in use, the *Auss-Bundt*, a song composed just south of here, in the castle of Passau?"

"There were 'defenceless Christians' on the Danube?"

"All over Europe. About sixty of them were imprisoned in Passau in the 1530s, but before they died they wrote songs so people could sing their stories, remember them. This is song number 17, its title—I translate freely—'Another beautiful song and marvellous story of two women in whom God's love over all things proved to be stronger than death. To be sung to the melody one sings to the King of Hungary.'"

"What does that mean?"

"Each song was composed to a well-known tune, a folk song or ditty, even dance melodies, so when people sang these death stories they could still feel happy, in a way."

"They sang their death—that's profound."

"I don't know the 'King of Hungary' tune, and I couldn't sing a note anyway...well, it begins:

"Sorrow I will leave behind,
And sing with happiness....

"and tells in nine-line rhyme the long, tortured story of Maria and Ursella van Bechum. Two Dutch sisters, I'll save you the communion theology, skip about forty verses:

"The priest led her to the fire.
'Say God is in it,' he said.
But Ursel answered clearly,
'My God is not found in bread.
No bread has ever helped me when
In deepest need I stood.'
And after she had answered thus,
She climbed up on the wood.
To God eternal praise. Amen.""

Even as he recites his translation, Adam sees the aged-oak pages blotched with ink and mould of the *Auss-Bundt* he discovered on an Amish Mennonite flea-market table in Mifflin County, Pennsylvania, bound hard in leather and signed in Gothic German: "This book belongs to me Amos M Yoder." And he reaches up for the warmth of Karen's shoulder. Which for a moment isn't there, but then comes.

"They call that 'singing with happiness'?"

"Both women 'remained steadfast,' so they went straight to God, in heaven."

Her kiss nuzzles him, tongue and lips at his nose. "What would it be like, to live such a life beyond doubt?"

He cannot imagine. The words of the song, such direct, ordinary words—they came to him out of their archaic German into English as quick as stretched string—but somehow he cannot feel them. What if he could sing?

She says, "My all-knowing off-by-heart lover."

Off his heart indeed. She runs ahead of him, along the wall of that neglected nunnery, past the locked and boarded chapel doors, past the square bell-tower towards the great trees of the woods singing to a much different tune.

"Come run in the woods, come run in the woods…come, come."

Running away along the cloister wall. He needed a long mirror to see everyone in his life as they ran away. More often, as he himself ran. Only his mother remained fixed: on her knees singing her living prayer.

He finally catches Karen. She has stopped under the beech branches where they spread over space falling away into the wide, wooded valley. He is gasping.

"And there in the wood," Karen sings, dancing before him, "a piggywig stood, With a ring at the end of her nose, her nose, With a ring at the end of her—"

"Toes, her toes, come toes or come nose, we will come to blows."

"You blow or I blow?"

"We'll blow together."

"And come together."

"Can't—it won't rhyme."

"Rhyme schmyme." She swirls that away with one naked arm flung over the earth. "Flow together, grow together, stagger to and fro together.…"

The branches with their perfectly pointed leaves spin beyond her black hair against the sky, bits of light opening in his eyes like the elliptical movements of a starry night. There is a jagged branch thrust under him, he knows it with a quick stab of

pain and he thinks, I'll carry a scar on my ass for life. But he for-
gets that completely, in her marvellous, ineffably sensual movement coming over and down around him.

It is visible in the bathroom mirror; he bends lower, backs up,
looking ridiculously between his spread legs. Self-examination, a
sharp red depression.

"New angle on yourself?" she asks, suddenly there.
"Physician, cure the pucker of your piles."

"I don't have any." Going to her.

"I know that perfectly well. I've kissed your every pain
away, all week."

"Not every pain."

"Oh, you poor darling." She knuckles his head.

"Yes, kissing should make me feel all better."

And she turns tables on him again.

"Our kisses never will, will they?"

She folds herself into the stuffed chair in that cavernous
room and he kneels against her knees. He thinks later that if he
had glanced back at the open bathroom door and the mirror, he
could have seen them together and reversed, and for a short time
longer they might have escaped together. But his face was in the
fold of her thighs. Only she could have seen that mirror.

Strangely, the double doors set in the cloister bell-tower open
when he pulls at them. Open out together, like the library doors
of his childhood.

But there are no shallow shelves here. Rather a compact,
dusty square scattered with straw, mouse and rat leavings, bird
splatter. Pigeons, their beaks bobbing out from the high beams;

brooding up there in the lengthening summer. Higher still in the cross-light they thump and scrabble inside the upper dome of the tower, where level light dusts more beams into existence.

He climbs the ladder fastened onto the wall rung by rung; and rests, leaning on a dust beam as if it were oak, holding tight an iridescence of air. Kafkaesque indeed. At the thought, the white spot of Karen's face appears far below him, rests on the roundness of her bare shoulders. As unrecognizable as his own face would be upside down.

"Adam, don't."

Her long call climbs the wooden ladder thinly; it reaches him, stretched into one transparent word:

"…d-o-o-o-n't."

In his examination room his medical decisions were once sharp and instantaneous, but for himself he can never decide to go, break and be gone. That first turning away, others always had to do it. And did.

He longs, overwhelmingly, to climb even higher, to see only the backs of the pigeons as they lift their dappled wings wide to escape. He wants her to be terrified with him.

He climbs, hand and foot. Through the arched windows he sees he is lifting himself above the crests of the forest. There is no iron bell above him, only mortared stone and the wooden bell-beam. When the steps of the ladder reach the last oak beam in the empty dome of the cupola, he plants his feet on it and without a thought lunges up towards the higher centre bell-beam, flings himself out into air, grabs it and holds tight, body swinging like a wild clapper. But when he tries to lift his legs, curl up and hook his feet up over the beam, he discovers he can't do it; his feet are too distant at the end of his suddenly too heavy body, the oak beam is now too far away below him. Hand-width by hand-width, the square beam cutting into his wrists, he pulls himself along it nearer the wall, then walks his feet up the wall until they climb onto either side of the beam and he can hang, fastened hand and foot like a sloth, over the deep column of space below him. He has climbed as high as it is possible.

And realizes, with a jolt of supreme terror, That was my last move. My body will never pull itself up, it cannot lever itself over onto the top of this beam. I can only hold on till I fall.

The stupidity of what he has done wraps him in a wondrous calm. He once lifted himself so easily, walked on two-by-four rafters of houses in the southern Alberta wind, or swung between the parallel pillars of scaffolds. This beam is straight rock between his straight arms. He does not dare look down. He will listen to the beat of birds returning below him, the air now a bed of needles; his clenched stomach and hooked feet and hands are locked on something, somewhere, but already they feel nothing, certainly not the edges of a beam older than Gothic, nothing. He is resting in freefall. Or possibly prayer.

> Your Bride has waited, oh so long,
> O Lord, for your appearing;
> When will you come, O Son of God,
> To wipe away her weeping?

The Gothic arches of the bell-tower windows surround Adam. He hangs above the beech forest and the far clearings of German fields, bent roads, villages, the perpetual distant drone of the Autobahn. Beech is *Buche*, he is beamed like a bat above a *Buchenwald*. He knows he cannot get back to the oak beam beside the ladder, and it crosses his mind, suddenly, that rather than the *Heimatleeda* of Mennonites, it would be lovely to hear the cantor at a bar-mitzvah sing those much stranger songs of sorrow and dedication, of lament clear as human mystery. The words between Karen and himself, even the simplest like *go* or *abh*, *god* or *again* or *no* never quite find them home. Not as completely as they desire, search as deep as they may.

Or to hear the delicate medieval angels that sang for his one and only bride at his one and only wedding. The wordless memory of Susannah moves through Adam like ancient air. Perhaps that bridal song has been waiting here for him to climb into, floating here slender as the spin of spiders beyond the tips of the tallest trees, song without body, there will be no body at last, only tips of flame.

"Adam."

Karen. On the oak beam just below him. One hand clutching the top rung of the ladder, her body stretched up as if groping blind to reach him. Her fingers point, they cannot quite touch him, but his one hand lets go and they grip each other and instantly his feet let go too, the maw of space swings up from under him and his heart lurches wauggh! as he thrusts himself towards her and he lets go of his beam completely as she hauls him across air and into her strong as steel.

"You ass," she gasps in his ear. "You-god-damn-ass."

His hand too grasps the rung of the ladder. The air, swaying, wraps them around one another, their brief summer clothes, skin, bones, hair.

"You can't run away *up*."

They are held on the beam by nothing but air and the wall ladder. They fold each other into each other's fear, but their hands and arms, their implacable bodies tighten in the movements of love; imperceptibly she opens her thighs, imperceptibly he pulls her harder against himself.

"Why Kafka, why not Rilke?" he whispers.

"Too much Catholic misery."

"At least Catholics have the Virgin and Child."

"True. More merciful than Moses."

Air the sheet that hides them, for the moment, from the reversals of necessarily being alive.

"We could look for Rilke," Karen breathes against Adam's cheek. "For Rilke too. Their lives overlapped, they lived in Prague, they never met."

"But Rilke wasn't a Jew."

She is pulling him tighter towards the wall. "He didn't have to be. Maybe he was a 'defenceless Christian.'"

"You think maybe Kafka was that too?"

They sway gently, like the clapper of a bell, a memory too light to strike sound. Hold tight on the edge of falling, the lip of terror and ecstasy.

TWELVE

THE HOLY COMMUNITY OF THE BRIDE

Pocatello, Idaho
1941
Samarkand
1881

"I KNOW YOU," MY GRANDFATHER SAYS. His hair is as white as the hospital pillow on which his head lies, but bristly, thick; he has not lost a strand in seventy-three years. He peers up at me as I bend over, expecting an answer to what? Of course he knows me, I want to cry out, he and my grandmother Mamme raised me, over twenty years.

"You have my name," he adds, as if making a pleasant discovery. "Abraham Loewen, you were born April 4, 1914, in Bessie, Oklahoma. But you didn't grow up there."

Mamme said to me, You have to go see him, the stroke mixed him up and his mind wanders, but he talks and talks so gentle now, you can just listen. You have to see him too.

"Paupe," I say, using the word he once liked, when I was

little, "you live in Aberdeen, Idaho, you're here in the Pocatello Hospital."

"Idaho"—his intense eyes sink from their study of my face into a distant bemusement—"but when we first came to the States we went to Oklahoma, the Herald Mennonite Church, all of us from Turkestan, Central Asia...yes, from Kaplan Bek and Aulie Ata too, Khiva...Khiva." His eyes dart open at me. "We tried to build a village Gnadenthal in the mountains south of Aulie Ata, but we couldn't really give those places our names," he says. "When a place already has a name, you can't change it, even if you don't know what it is and think you can."

I can only mutter, "I was two when we moved, I don't remember Oklahoma."

"We moved to Idaho, eleven families, to avoid the army"— his voice is different, but his mind seems to be gathering its old force—"we knew the States was going to war. The Great War they called it, huh! as if war could be great. The Worst War they should say. We were eleven families, there were even less, only ten families in the first wagon-train to Central Asia. I was twelve years old, I could drive the quiet horses. They thought then they would protect their sons from war if they moved into the wilderness, the sand wilderness. We Mennonites do that over and over."

"Mennonites move all the time." I have heard this from him forever; it is what I got away from by removing myself—but with him lying in a hospital bed, so flat, "moving" now sounds strangely warm, almost homey.

"Yes, move," he says, "travel because of land, land and armies. You have to find a place where you can live and the Big Men will forget about you. A wilderness no one else wants to live in is best. Do you remember the train?"

"The train...remember?"

"Here in the States we sat so soft, and the Great Plains going past outside." His eyes closed as if talking in his sleep. "They are great, such good land brushed green and flat by the hand of God." He laughs slightly, only half his face moving. "No wagons or camels needed on these plains, brown rivers and trees leaning, going past outside the window."

My grandfather sounds not at all like he used to, factual, logical, demanding immediate and exact answers. Half paralysed on a hospital bed, he may be freed from farm drudgery and the rigid absoluteness of always "being the preacher." Free perhaps to wander anywhere in his past.

I bend over him; he can only move his right arm and leg a little, his heavy body so pathetically rigid under the sheet. But I want him to look steadily at me if he now feels easier somehow. And he does look, his bright eyes slowly consider every inch of my face. He tries to chuckle, and a bit more of his face moves.

"Where have you been?" he asks, no accusation in his voice.

I've been gone four years, I left him and Mamme with a long, accumulated anger that I certainly let them know about as I went, and now he is trying to chuckle. So helpless, so changed from my long memory of him, perhaps it's more than just the stroke, perhaps he's not so "mixed up" either, would he be completely different—warm, gentle, loving—if he were completely paralysed?

"I didn't go far," I can tell him honestly. "Portland."

"Wandering?"

"I worked there, in a garage." No need to bother him with the "Bud Lyons" I've become, with the year of the Depression in California in hobo villages, or picking cotton and grapes. "I came back to see Mamme, and you too," I tell him. "I didn't know you had…this had happened."

"A man hides, but God guides," he says into my face. Who is he saying this to, me or himself? It's one of his favourite Mennonite preacher "Watchwords for Life," a convenient "sermon in a second" and easily twisted to suit whatever purpose he had at that moment. Abruptly it sounds so much like what I once hated, and still hate, that I jerk away from him rigid as half a log, I'm outta here!

But I glimpse his motionless head, his eyes rolled to their corners to see me, and his face twitching; amazingly, he is still trying to chuckle, right hand gesturing for me. And I take it.

"All good Mennonites wander," he says. "Not hunters following animals, no, we're like God told Abraham, 'Go to a land I will show you' and we go, it's usually because of armies, to stay away from them."

"I don't want land, I'm a mechanic. I can fix any motor." There is no need to mention Pearl Harbor, that the United States is now in all-out war and I've joined the Air Force and I have seven days' leave before I'm gone, maybe forever. At least as far as he's concerned, he's wandering in his paralysed memory, wherever it leads him, let him go.

But he says nothing, and I lean closer to him. "I even flew in a plane," I say. "Whose motor I fixed. You see the whole world under you."

He breathes, rattling a little. "I've never been in the sky. The desert can be like sky, sometimes only two colours and sometimes you're in it you can't tell, they're the same."

His eyes are adrift and his voice so thin he has no echo of the stubborn man I left, not at all. I can just touch him, and listen.

"When you cross the Ural River at Orenburg," he says, "you leave Europe. There the world changes. You see camel caravans, the Kirghiz nomads with their sheep and long-haired goats on the black sand of Kara Kum Desert around the Aral Sea, the water salt and blue as heaven. Three weeks we were among those sand hills so bright black the sun blinded us, heat like walking through melting iron, we had camels to carry most of our food and relays of horses to pull our wagons, if the Kirghiz people hadn't guided us to their deep wells we would never have got across. Eleven children died, every child under four died, they could not drink the water. But I was twelve and strong, the Kirghiz showed me how to ride with my head wrapped in cloth on a camel."

This strange world, numbers, names rise from his dry lips into the warm hospital air. Against the winter darkening beyond the window, his memory burns; as if the city around us were on fire.

"We ten families, we travelled together," he says, "we buried eleven children. Thirty-eight pilgrims came to the fresh springs beside the Aral Sea, praising God."

"Praising God!" I burst out.

His right hand tightens a little around mine. "Bigger treks came after us," he says. "Over four hundred people, we were the first. My friend David Toews came with his family when the weather was better, but all our small children died in the loving arms of their family, we understood it was God's will, dying then, and two were born by the Syr Darya River under the trees."

His story, the only story of his childhood, about that enormous, stupid madness of a trek of Jesus-Second-Coming-crazy Mennonites to the Turkestan Desert in 1880 has lain over my life like a blanket, trying to smother me. In his sermons he used heavy examples from it all the time, how to be faithful, obedient and perfect, how to avoid endless sins. Maybe here, at last, half dead now himself, mind wandering, he will have a plain, human answer for me.

"So why?" I insist, but more quietly. "Why did they really do it? Sell their great estates in the beautiful colonies on the Dnieper and Volga Rivers and drag themselves into Asia, into Muslim deserts they knew nothing about, parents with helpless children, hauling wagons in sand—why?"

His right hand is becoming a vise, but I won't let it go so he can turn his head to look me in the eye. Anyway, he doesn't need to do that. He can still, with the same calm, precise deliberation he gave me before I left—I can feel it coming—declare up into the stale hospital air:

"Didn't you listen? I told you and told you. 'The Revelation of Jesus Christ, the vision which God gave to his servant John, for him to bear witness, as the time is near: And there appeared a great wonder in heaven, a woman clothed with the sun, and the moon under her feet, and upon her head a crown of twelve stars. And she being with child cried out, travailing in birth, and pained to be delivered.'"

The words I certainly know, yes, I know them in the full majesty of the most incomprehensible book in the Bible. The Church as the Bride awaiting her Bridegroom, who will take her to Heaven. The Mennonites as the chosen Community of the Bride to follow their prophet, Claus Epp, who all by himself had made this amazing discovery and connection between Revelations and Mennonites, that the purest Mennonites must leave everything they had behind, "lay aside every weight of sin which does so easily beset us," and go, go farther than they could think, search by faith for months stretching into years to find a desert in Asia where the Beast of Satan would be revealed and they could Await the Actual, Physical Second Coming of their Holy Bridegroom Jesus Christ to Lift them All into Heaven. Everything in capitals. My grandfather was a child then, but even as an old man on the other side of the world in Idaho he remained rigid as iron: a true believer is "married to Jesus"—say that around a hobo fire and you'd get more than you could handle, "Oh-ho, Bud, you're sleepin' with Jesus, hey, is he any good?" That's why I love motors, anything you do either works or it doesn't, and there's always a solution you can figure out, exactly. None of these "Brides," sun women in the heavens, grooms, love feasts—not even a stroke can hammer them into reason in my grandfather's not-so-wandering mind.

Both my square hands are clenched on his single one; I get them unlocked but I can't look into his eyes.

"Paupe," I say, quietly, across his body, "I have to leave for a long time. I came back, just a few days, to see Mamme and you."

He is silent, breathing drily. I lift the glass of water and he swallows as I pour, carefully, a little, into his open, slanted mouth.

"Mamme and you cared for me, brought me up...."

"When Heinrich and Esther were killed, you were a miracle."

"You told me. Their horrible accident."

"The miracle was you, that you weren't killed with them."

"You told me I was wrapped tight, and so little, when they were hit I just flew. It was just an accident."

"There was an accident, but you're not a miracle?"

"In the last second my mother probably threw me away."

His eyes are like bits of steel, so deep if his head was a motor I would have to drill them out to fix it.

"They were driving their buggy," I remind him. "Going home, and for less than a minute they happened to be in the wrong place." His jagged face, that irrational trek. "They didn't deliberately drive along the track for days until a train finally came along and ran over them."

And he understands I am talking about his childhood and mine. "You have thought about this," he says softly.

"Well, a wandering bum has plenty of time—I wanted to thank you. You cared for me."

"You must think rightly, understand. No one loves their children more than people on the way, travellers. When you leave your place and everything you own and every day you have to leave behind even more of what little you thought you couldn't do without, but you have to, then children in your arms are your all in all."

"So . . . why did they go where so many died?"

"Our fathers said it was for our children: we were going to save our grown young men from the Czar's armies."

"Other Mennonites went to Canada and the United States, why didn't you?"

"We were also obedient to the desert vision of the Bride of Christ, the return of Jesus for His own."

And for that vision, I want to tell him again, you saved your young men and killed your small children. But he is lying so still, how can I assault him with that?

"Children," he says, as if he heard my thought. "God gives them, God takes them. Like your parents, given and taken, and we must still believe in Him."

No such "must" for me. But I don't need to say it; even with one ear he would hear me no more than he ever did with two.

"Dust and heat and the track goes on," he murmurs, far away. "It led into earth villages, one after another and out again, we travelled all together, the first year we travelled six months. We stopped in Tashkent and wintered there and tried to grow gardens, but we had to go on next summer, 1881, to Samarkand and Bukhara, to Lausan, Khiva—three years trying to find the exact place, travelling on the way. And always we had our love feasts around the fire and Bible reading and sermons explaining what was happening to us, and sang *Heimatleeda*. We shared all our food, and when we stopped in a circle and the chores were done, David Toews and I played. Such wild land, mountains sometimes and rivers and a sea too, we had never seen anything but a fenced Mennonite street, he said my name was Loewen, which is German for 'Lion,' this desert was the place for me, and I said, Good, I'm Lion, you're Toews, what is that? He said Toews means nothing, so he could be 'Tiger' and we played that in the sand or under the crooked, black trees beside the rivers. Tiger and Lion."

His right hand gestures towards the waterglass. I put it between his fingers and he takes it, lifts it towards his mouth. He doesn't need me to drink: he tilts it into his mouth, holding a little before he swallows, and gives it back. His voice is stronger, with an edge, as if he was again in the pulpit of our small Idaho church.

"Playing," he says, in a tone of wonder; as if he liked the word, as if the memory of it made him, for the first time in his rigid life, happy. "Such strange things beside the road, animals, places. Every wagon was still Mennonite, dragging along so heavy, but in a street turbaned people would kneel and pray when the muezzin called on his minaret. They were very high, always leaning, as if about to fall but they never did—a world so strange you rubbed your eyes and thought it would be gone, but no, it was there. Even their holy Samarkand rising wide out of the brown sand, the Pearl of the Orient with marble stone walls and adobe houses, there were peaches and clear water running in little streams along the street and lamb shashlik and cucumbers and apricots. We heard say Alexander the Great and Genghis Khan rode there, all those unforgettable killers Claus Epp warned us, and Tamerlane was buried under the blue domes of a mosque, a huge slab of black jade over him. There we met the Chinese girl."

"A Chinese?"

"Give me your hand," he says. I give him both, and he moves them close to his eyes. Perhaps the stroke affected his sight as well, I may be a blessed blur to him. My hands lie in his pale bluish one; ingrained with endless grease.

"You always had good worker hands, to hold and fix things," he says. He turns his head away, but he does not let my hands go. He cradles them tight in his wide one, so thick and scarred by farm work, but the back soft, mottled as any old man's must be. His touch seems thin and, I feel it, sad.

"Maybe the Chinese were in Tashkent," he says. "Maybe I remember it was Samarkand because of the mosque Tamerlane built to bury his Chinese wife. They say the builder fell in love with her embalmed body and Tamerlane sent his soldiers to kill him, but he climbed the minaret and flew away to Persia with the wings of an eagle, maybe Samarkand is where the Chinese should be. Anyway, we saw them because my sister Susannah begged your great-grandfather to let her walk and look a little, just see something, she was almost fourteen and without a face covering she would have disappeared without a whisper into a Muslim doorway forever, but my father finally gave in and told me and David Toews to walk on either side of her, we were both tall and twelve."

"Your father let you go?"

"When our mother wasn't there, Susannah and I could persuade him. It was such a beautiful city, clean, trees and clear running water, every day we drove in dust and heat—he wanted us to be a little happy.

"We saw the Chinese shop, after we stood by the ruins of Tamerlane's wife's mosque. Yellow flowers sprouted between the blue and white tiles, everything was so bright, and on the street a Chinese girl sat in front of a shop. At first I didn't know what she was, she was covered in swaths of silk, the colours burned our eyes, gold and blood-red and green like cobwebs and purple. We had nothing but dirty clothes and grey blankets that got dirtier on the sand every night. When I saw this was a girl, all colours, I thought she had descended from heaven with a shout, at the sound of trumpets and archangels. Susannah stopped too, we all stared, but the girl's eyes and small nose widened as she smiled at us. She said in Kirghiz:

"'You like?'

"She passed her hands over the silks on her shoulders and her folded legs, and under her hands the silk changed colour, like flames in a leaping fire. Susannah gave a little scream, it was so sudden and beautiful we were frightened.

"'Feel,' the girl said. She lifted a deep purple that moved the other colours like feathers floating around her, it drifted around my fingers thick from pulling camel ropes and I couldn't feel anything though it lay on my hand, I could see my hand dusted purple.

"But Susannah took the silk from me, she raised her hands

high above her head and began twirling herself into it—what had she ever seen that she could spin on her toes like that? She turned completely inside the silk, as if pointed at both ends, and still there was no end to it; we were laughing in amazement as my sister turned into a pointed, purple flame. If we blinked she would vanish into air.

"And then I saw. It struck me like lightning: if the Chinese girl had lifted the golden silk instead of the purple, my sister on this stone street in Samarkand would be the Revelation woman clothed with the sun.

"I had to hunch down on the stones, I was so afraid. What would I tell Father who prayed and lived and preached Revelations every day, what could I say happened to Susannah? But David just laughed, completely happy, and he reached for Susannah to help unwind her. The long silk never touched the dusty stones, they folded it back in the Chinese girl's lap. She was laughing too, urging them to buy, but all she could say in Russian was 'Good! Good!' and 'Rubles twenty, rubles twenty,' which was a quarter the price of a horse, and we had not even a kopeck between us.

"Susannah lifted her feet out of the last purple silk, and the girl stopped smiling. Her face opened, I was hunched low, so close to her I could feel her eyes widen. And I saw she might be the Great Deception of the Evil One, her frightening beauty covered in flowing silk and strange folded eyes burning now, perhaps this was the Woman arrayed in Purple and Scarlet who sat on the Scarlet Beast in the Revelation of John the Apostle! 'Long!' she hissed in Russian, pointing at Susannah's feet, staring, 'long, long!'

"But Susannah was happy, she sensed no possible Evil, she folded the end of the silk into the girl's lap and lifted herself on her strong toes again and twirled another circle in her worn cotton dress, laughing. 'Good, good,' she said in Russian, 'long feet, dance, come, dance me!' She reached down for the girl's hand, her fingers touched the girl's pale skin, perfect skin so close to my eyes—how could she ever be Babylon, the Mother of all Harlots?—and the girl's face broke, she shuddered and gave a little cry.

"Susannah bent to her. 'What?' she said. 'What?'

"The girl did not answer. They were face to face, and slowly the girl's hand moved down across the bright silk and touched my sister's dirty *Schlorre*, the shapeless, worn cowhide that was all we had to save our feet from rocks and scorpions. Her hand reached out, David's face came between the two girls facing each other and so very different, their skin and cheeks and hair. Then Susannah shifted, she raised both her hands to the girl's shoulder and balanced, she moved her left leg forward so her weight leaned on her right leg only and I looked down, and I saw the girl's right hand rise from her lap of crumpled silk, I saw Susannah's foot lift and the girl pull the worn *Schlorr* off, and then she touched Susannah's naked foot. Her fingertips moved along the sweaty straggle of dust, each finger tracing the arch and instep and toes as though drawing the veins, and Susannah's long foot came up into her palm; the girl's hand bent to cradle it, felt the whole length from the heel to the five toes in the slow, warm curl of her hand.

"When I opened my eyes, Susannah's hand was holding the Chinese girl's foot. But there was no foot. Below her folded knee, at her ankle, her leg ended in layers of wound cloth coiled and tied tight around a square stub. I couldn't understand: where was her foot? I looked at her face: her eyes were stretched shut now in a tight line clenched across her face, a slit where pain shrieked, where it would never be let out."

I am so hypnotized by my grandfather's story that it is some time before I realize he is no longer speaking.

"What was that, about her feet? What?"

"Foot-binding. Chinese men believe the smaller a woman's feet, the more beautiful she is."

"So they tie up her feet, to keep them small?"

"No, they can't tie it small, the foot has to grow, if the girl lives growing feet can't be stopped, so at five or six years the toes are doubled under, the foot bones bent back, bent under towards the heel with tighter and tighter binding until the foot bones break and the toes and heel are forced to meet, folded back together into what they call the 'lotus hook.' It doesn't look like a foot at all."

"They break the foot?"

"The woman sit with their legs folded, that's all they can do, some can hardly walk a step."

"Why?"

"For a thousand years Chinese men have believed this is necessary for beauty. Wrapped stubs."

"Beauty? That's torture."

"It is what it is. They say, for a husband to hold the lotus hook in one palm of his hand is his wife's greatest beauty."

Beauty is a life of pain.

The afternoon light has faded outside into December darkness. Abruptly a starched nurse rustles in beside us with a tiny glass of water. My grandfather releases my hand, reaches for the glass.

"Careful now," she says. "You remember, Reverend Loewen, we must be very careful about our drinking. We don't want to have another little accident, now do we."

"We" indeed! I feel an urge to boot her directly through the window. While Grandfather silently drinks a little, lopsided, she reminds me, twice, that it is well after five o'clock and visiting hours are definitely over. I nod; if I open my mouth I'll curse this harmless woman. She leaves at last and I get up.

My grandfather looks very tired now; but he is open-eyed, staring up into the empty hospital air. "If there can be accidents," he says, "there can also be miracles. Some people look for them all their lives."

The hundreds of stories about the Asia trek he used in years of sermons, but never a hint of Tamerlane's tomb, of silk, of a tortured Chinese girl.

I say, "You still wish Idaho was a desert, don't you. You're still waiting for Jesus to come out of the clouds."

"When you've left everything once, it's not hard to leave it all again."

I want to yell at him. Even if you were only twelve? Even though so many died and Claus Epp went more and more nuts, and Jesus never came when Epp predicted he would, when you all went out to sit praying and waiting on the hill and Jesus never came? Even though your relatives in the United States per-suaded you to come back at last, and paid for the tickets to haul you out of that desert, away from that madman—even after a lifetime you still think you want to leave everything?

"We are still the Bride of Christ," he murmurs.

I want to tell him: And for that you need a desert, you need dead children. But I can't shout at him as I once did. Not in this hospital. And I have no facts beyond what he has told me, no more facts than I ever had. Only anger, which after four years I know is no more useful than ignorance.

But now he has told me this strange story, beauty and

ugliness tangled together. His past, he has lived his life; for me the world is exploding into war.

His right hand gestures, I give him mine to hold. His face half-hunches into what I know is a smile; his hand is amazingly soft. He always worked, farming or preaching, with the relentless, obsessed energy of a driven man who always knew he was absolutely right, and here he lies, so still and talking so quietly. I lean close to him.

"I'll come back tomorrow. I have to go away for a long time but I'll come, with Mamme, tomorrow."

"You going away, to the war?"

"Not the army, the Air Force. To fix motors."

"Ahhh," he sighs.

"Airplane motors," I try to reassure him. "So when the pilots take off, everything is working perfectly and they can fly and nothing will break down, everything will work perfectly."

He appears to nod. He seems suddenly exhausted, almost asleep, or unconscious. I had better warn the nurse.

I can ask Mamme, who is David Toews? Is he still alive, where does he live? And Susannah, Paupe's sister Susannah, my great-aunt wrapped in purple silk, what happened to her? Why have I never heard a word about her, not even her name? Mamme wasn't on that desert trek but surely she knows something.

Did Claus Epp ever fly up to heaven? When?

I am holding my grandfather's hand between mine. He lies flat and motionless, but breathing. He must be asleep. What more can you want?

He has told me what he wanted me to hear. I should just get outta here, go get my head inside an airplane motor. Leave him in peace.

THIRTEEN

EXCEPT GOD WHO ALREADY KNOWS

Little Marten Lake, Northwest Territories
1990

ADAM IS WRITING IN HIS JOURNAL:

The erratics wait on the skyline of eskers like memorial stones, in this land I've remembered nearly thirty years but can hardly believe. From the water you sometimes see sky under the stones, they balance on three or four others like a massive altar, the glaciers melted 12,000 years ago and they still wait there, as if for prayer—"The fervent prayer of a righteous man availeth much"—rest in peace, Mother, I remember. The words at least. Now, through tent mesh I see only white water, this unnamed river grumbling along the Arctic Circle. We have rubbed out every mosquito inside the tent. We will sleep well.

But suddenly Adam jerks erect—"Gronk!"—is that Eric's grizzly noise-maker groaning, failing to work at the instant it should to protect them? He cranes at the tent screen away from the river—danger will come from there, not the water—the white sky shimmers in night brightness—"Gronk!"—certainly not the bear-horn, certainly animal, and so close outside the tent that he shudders despite the warmth of his sleeping bag hooked on his shoulders. He stares at the nylon beyond Joel's sleeping body: claws will slash through there, a snaking head—

Motion, and a magnificent ptarmigan struts regally past the screen door of the tent. The bird's pert head cocked, brown, its lower body and legs mottled white, it seems to float on the misty lichen where their packs lie in the sun lining the northern horizon. "*Gronk!*" it declares again from beyond the boulders.

"Ptarmigans are slow as barnyard chickens," Eric had told them earlier that day, their canoes floating together as they rested, "and as sure to walk their own trails as cows or caribou, but don't knock them, they're beautiful. The Dene story of the creation of woman turns on the good deed of a ptarmigan."

Joel laughed. "Good as Adam's rib?"

"Better! When the bird turns into a woman, she helps the man!"

Christina pushed their canoe into the current. "That's all men want of women," she said, "work, more work."

"Only the one ptarmigan." Adam heard Eric's usual irony as they drifted apart. "They don't say any other bird ever did anything."

"Why would they? One's enough."

Eric's third wife; about half his age, with a perfect J-stroke. Like the quick doctor he was, Eric made absolute personal decisions, no looking back at possible wreckage left behind. Patients loved him: no waffle, no bullshit. Professor and Head of Surgery at the University Hospital. Any time you want, he kept saying to Adam, I'll get you back on staff. Not yet, if ever.

Through waterproof nylon the polar night of summer

glows lemon yellow. Almost thirty years ago, a few lakes south of here, with Eric and Napoleon, and Kathy bending over a three-stone fire. In the days when he fell asleep instantly. Caribou walking the skyline.

Adam feels his body shrink, as if he were smothered by ice; by the deep voice of the river here among stones and light since the slow melting of the continental glaciers spread out the global sea. He feels his own hand, he also is here, and there is his son, sleeping. In the other tent Christina and Eric will have their sleeping bags zipped together, perhaps they are naked. He lengthens out, on his back and staring up. If this were four years ago Susannah would be here lying along him, but she is gone, as he is gone, they continue to agree on that while still looking back at each other, stay away. And Jean gone, easier and quicker than saying "so long." He will not think of Karen and her wide mouth, her subtle and matching obsession of mind; let her be with her uxorious husband, let this be, without ache of mind and heart. Ribbed between stones too deep to clear for their tent floor, indelible as a requiem by Rilke:

So will ich dich behalten, wie du dich
hinstellest in den Spiegel, tief hinein
und fort von allem. Warum kommst du anders?

"This is how I want to keep/remember you, the way you stood/placed yourself in the mirror, deep inside it and away from everything. Why do you come different?" His own life a continual movement of looking back, of looking into mirrors and never coming different.

Warum kommst du nicht anders? That is his line.

His weight, he feels it, is softening the permafrost. When he and Joel fold the tent they will see their shapes side by side between the stones, momentary body prints steaming a little, rising from the tundra. Beside a nameless river somewhere between lakes labelled Starvation and Winter. Not even Eric can say what their Dene names are. His sleeping bag is warm and tight around his shoulders, like a zipped body bag coming home for burial, though he has never seen a body in war, much less felt it. Good sound, "body bag."

Is he north of the Arctic Circle? The creaking globe he memorized in Waskahikan School turns its Arctic face to him and he follows those straight lines that appear to organize and control what, looking down from a Twin Otter, is a simple chaos of lakes, rivers, white flowing eskers. He traces the globe lines revolving and recognizes he is lying on the parallel of the Magadan Gulag just above Kamchatka, USSR. There, beyond the Kolyma Mountain Ranges, somewhere in that desolation of volcanoes between the Yukagir Plateau and the swamps of the Omolon and Kolyma Rivers, they say two of his father's brothers were destroyed digging gold for Stalin. And his mother's brother Peter Loewen on Sakhalin Island in the Okhotsk Sea, north of Japan—but most of it stretches south beyond the latitude of Regina or Vancouver. Why does he always think Sakhalin is north? Because exile, in Canada or Russia, can only be north, frozen extermination.

In the desert of Outer Mongolia, they say, permafrost lives in the ground as far south as the 48th parallel.

"You paddle this nice empty tundra," Joel says to him next day in the canoe, "and you still just think about all your lost uncles."

"Not just," Adam says. Susannah, he thinks, would be taking pictures; hours of stalking, to find a loving partner in a bird, one that rarely flew, and then only a few blustering metres.

They are paddling parallel to a flat esker along a placid lake. That morning they negotiated a series of runnable rapids, then a long rock garden where wading with the canoes in hand was barely possible, and finally a steep boulder-trap of shallow fall in the middle of which Eric stood immovable as any erratic, handing the loaded canoes through with water smashing up into spray against him and the boulders and the leaping canoes all at once, while the rest of them scrambled over shore rocks trying to control the canoe painters.

"This land makes you think." Adam looks back at his son.

"I wish we'd see a caribou."

"Gone north to the ocean for calving."

"So we get mosquitoes. Look at the bastards." Joel lifts his dripping paddle and smacks the roped packs in front of him. "They ride along out into the lake, then drill you, even out here."

"Keep your head-net down, your paddle in the lake. I'm doing all the work!"

"You're just muscle, I keep us on course."

"You still have to think to J-stroke?"

"Ha!" Joel laughs, abrupt, explosive. "Just don't stop pulling when you think Siberia. I see it every time."

The lake is sheet steel; ahead of them Eric and Christina's canoe slides through the long ramp of the exact, inverted esker. No sky or water, a double of horizontals forged by relentless ice.

Joel says out of nowhere, the way canoeists talk, "What did Onkel David Loewen say, about your uncles in Siberia?"

"He talked about Sakhalin Island, not Siberia."

"What's the diff."

"Nothing, in misery. They were his uncles too, Grandma's two brothers."

"How come he knows more in Paraguay than you in Canada?"

"I think they tell more stories, no TV or malls."

The year before, Adam and Joel had landed in Asunción barely a week after Alfredo Stroessner was toppled in a coup by his own officers, but a flip of army dictators was irrelevant to Adam's cousin David Loewen in the distant Chaco. The old man and his circle of six sons sat under their giant paratodo tree, passing a maté cup back and forth. The Paraguayan night, cooling slightly so that Adam's evaporating sweat became a desert comfort, sang with insects and frogs as one by one the men were satisfied, drinking around and then drifting away. Joel had no language to speak with any of them, but the youngest, both mute and simple, offered an eloquence of gesture that made some facts as comprehensible as speech; he beckoned Joel away, past the darkness into the moonlit fields to look at the Southern Cross.

"It wasn't Onkel David who told me," Adam says over his shoulder between the grunt and rhythm of paddling. "It was Taunte Anna."

"I thought she went in the house?"

"She came back. The women don't drink maté, but she sat under the tree, then."

"She's the nicest little old mama." Joel's chuckle is like the sound of the lake along the canoe.

"She's sixty-five."

"So small and brown and wrinkled, Chaco sun, I guess."

"All her life. She said it, Onkel David never would have."

"What?"

"Fifty-nine years in Paraguay, and the Russian Mennonite villages are still so real to them. And all the relatives…lost or not, every one of hundreds of relatives."

Joel says, "Maybe she thinks about it more."

"What, thinks? Old David's the one who knows everything, talks all the time. You saw him, he never stopped while we were there."

"I mean, I couldn't understand them but she always does the same things, clean up, cook, and he's always running around. Maybe she dares to think."

Adam stops paddling and glances back at his son, broad and solid as any Loewen. The lake opens beyond him without edges; his head is down, his paddle driving through the water with a relentless rhythm that surges the canoe straight ahead with a tight, curved stroke. Before he had seen him heave up and invert the canoe on his shoulders and begin that first carry across the tundra, Adam had not imagined him so resiliently strong.

"Dare?"

"It's hard to think sometimes," Joel says, "some things. What'd she say?"

Not a story to be told over a shoulder in quick phrases between breaths, kneeling in a shifty canoe where his knees again alternate between groan and spasm. Sixteen months ago in the insect-singing heat of the reversed southern hemisphere, and now here in their own country's arctic desert. Adam thinks suddenly, My son could become a relentless wanderer like me.

"Dad. What did she say?"

Hard to say on water. But no easier to utter flat on his back later in their shuddering tent. His words bunch into the angles of taut nylon, he can barely speak, words could coil their ancestral past into a winding sheet for him and his son stretched out under the ceaseless wind of the tundra. Perhaps if he spoke to the open, quiet sky...where on earth could you say this?

"Exile...well, they were always being forced into exile. The Loewens leaving Antwerp in the 1580s, the Frisians earlier, even Adam Wiebe when he maybe got lured to Danzig, his travel from Harlingen became exile, I don't think he ever went back. He drained the Vistula delta to build farms, sure, and when he invented the cable car to rebuild the walls...actually, it's like he made land, the way our ancestors in Friesland made land from the sea. I think he probably would have taken it out of the sea too, and deepened the harbour, but the Swedish army was already all around them."

Joel says flatly, "Dad. You said he built twenty military bastions. A bastion is no wheat field."

This is easier, this usual repartee, these genial reacquaintances after months apart; father and son working together and talking easily. Adam concedes:

"Sure. But you can graze sheep on bastion curtain walls if they're made of earth. You saw the sheep on the Dutch dikes. The new land made by the sea, the *watte*, isn't just a field. At a certain point, when the watte's built up high enough they have to make more dikes anyway to protect it from the sea, and that's all a city wall is, a dam of protection. In Danzig Adam built earth dams not to hold back the violent sea, but to hold back the brutal people coming over it. But he was still doing what he'd always done: if he didn't protect the city, even his place of exile would be destroyed, and what new exile would they find then? If they survived at all."

"Dad!" Joel shouts above the tremendous wind that is pounding their tent like a spastic drummer. "Taunte Anna was not talking about Adam Wiebe and his damn cable car!"

Adam continues to evade him. "Our family's had all kinds of exiles," he says. "Hundreds, and sometimes the Mennonites themselves did it to each other. Did I tell you about our relative who got exiled for painting portraits? Mennonites did it to him."

"A Wiebe was a painter?"

"He was both Loewen and Wiebe. The seventeenth century was full of great Flemish painters, so you'd expect some in Danzig, where so many fled. This one's name was Enoch Seemann the Elder, and his mother was Adam Wiebe's granddaughter. He painted all the portraits of the councilmen to hang in the Danzig city hall. But the Mennonite Elder decided painting portraits was wrong, after all, there is the Second Commandment, and so he excommunicated him, banned him from the Church. That meant Enoch had no community— Mennonites were strict with the ban, as they called it, in Danzig. Enoch's family wasn't supposed to even talk to him, or so much as eat with him, because he was banished from the fellowship to hell. But Enoch was too good a painter, he found a royal exile with Augustus II of Saxony, and then a permanent refuge in England, where his son Enoch the Younger later painted portraits of George II and Queen Caroline, and his own self-portrait, which Augustus hung in his magnificent Zwinger in Dresden until—"

"Dad!"

"—until the Dresden firebombing in 1945," Adam concludes gently, the wind catching its breath over the tent. "You're right. Taunte Anna in Paraguay knows nothing about Adam Wiebe, or painters."

"Mom said her father, Grandpa Lyons, was in Dresden."

"I don't think so. He was in France, he serviced the Flying Fortresses that flew there."

Joel says, "So he was there."

"Why do you say that?"

"You pull the trigger, but I loaded the gun and gave it to you, so, who's responsible?"

The categorical logic of youth. "Okay," Adam says, "or I made the gun in a factory, you ordered me to make it…okay."

Nothing to argue there, lying side by side in a shuddering tent on the rocky permafrost of an island barely fifty strides long in Little Marten Lake in the Mackenzie District, the Northwest Territories of Canada. Adam thinks: If I was an Ojibwa shaman, this would be the shaking-tent where the Spirits come to answer my most heartfelt prayer. What would I pray, if I could? For whom?—but his son is lying there, waiting for him.

So, what can he tell Joel of Taunte Anna's prayer-and-spirit story of Sakhalin Island? Taunte Anna knows only one thing about Sakhalin, certainly not the double-dagger map shape of it, as if roughly chipped from stone in the Sea of Okhotsk, because she has no atlas, in fifty-nine years will not have seen one except perhaps in Spanish, which she cannot read. Besides, Sakhalin Island is not Taunte Anna's story. She is a Wiebe, daughter of Adam's father's third brother. Her husband Onkel David is the Loewen, and it was he who took the story of the two Loewen brothers from Canada to Paraguay because Adam's mother told it to him when he visited her in Alberta just before she died; Adam's mother, who was born Katerina Loewen, Onkel David's half-aunt because she was David's father's half-sister. Can you keep that straight without a chart, of family roots and branches intersecting?

"I know we're blood related," Joel says impatiently. "So get on with it."

But Onkel David could not bring himself to tell that small, brutal story under the dazzling night flowers of the beautiful paratodo tree. It was Taunte Anna who had to say it aloud in Lowgerman, quick and flat as if she were telling him her recipe for borscht, something every Mennonite in the world already knew except perhaps one overwhelmed by the stupefying comfort of Canada. She told Adam:

"When my David visited in Canada, the year your mother died, she told him that in the thirties the Communists sent her brother Peter Loewen to jail on Sakhalin Island, and then their half-brother Heinrich, Heinrich Loewen the Communist, he travelled to that place and killed him."

Adam could not see the bright flowers above her or her dark, worn face, could barely see her cotton dress in the light reflected from the kitchen where daughters were clattering dishes, their husbands peering over their shoulders.

Taunte Anna spoke as neutrally as possible, used four little words twisted into idiom: *Hee brocht ahm omm.* Literally "he brought him around," like the colloquial English "he did him in."

She added abruptly, over Onkel David's head clutched between his massive hands, "They say he just brought a knife., And stabbed his brother."

Spetje: pricked. Like a possible needle wandering through wool.

His name only "Heinrich Loewen the Communist." His photograph was in the album Adam's mother left him when she died—head and shoulders, a morose, very handsome young man with a shadow of moustache, wearing a flapped woollen cap ris-

ing to a peak over his forehead and fronted with a star, undoubt-
edly red, and a bar on his erect collar. Was that the uniform of
Trotsky's Red Army, or Stalin's? The cardboard picture was
pasted onto the black page of the album with flour. When Adam
finally got it separated from the album, between blotches he discovered a message angled across the top left corner in a beautiful German Gothic script, which he slowly puzzled into
translation: "With artelistic greetings from your brother,
brother-in-law and uncle, Nove—" the date and place ("—
ovka"…could be "Romanovka," but would he use such a
Czarist name in the 1930s, when his sister was already in
Canada?) torn out forever by paste and black paper. That
Heinrich who it seemed never married, except perhaps the
Communist Party, rubbing it in with a Party word they must
have instantly hated without ever quite understanding. What
happened to him? "*Artel*: a cooperative organization of produc-
ers." Producing what?

His mother Katerina's full brother Peter Loewen was
nowhere in the album, but her father, David Loewen, was there,
stern and bald, a white goatee, thick legs sheathed in gleaming
knee boots stretched out black before him, and his fourth and
last wife (no older than Adam's mother, whose best friend she
, was before, to Katerina's shock, she married him) standing
slightly tilted and unsmiling behind him. Nothing written on the
back of that.

Pricked…they say…half-brother…the Communist.
Nothing on paper, just a few words left in air.

If Adam's father had been alive when his mother told Onkel
David that, his father would have murmured, "They're all dead
now, so long."

And his mother would have answered, "Thank God. The Communists can do nothing terrible to them any more."

And all three of them would have been weeping. Their minds unable to imagine a Sakhalin, but knowing enough of pain for it to suffice; their bodies dragged around the world and destroyed by labour and poor food and care and ultimately cancer, hunched together in prayer, may they rest at last, precious God have mercy. The Alberta sunlight caressing them with gentle, bitter mockery.

But his father was dead when his mother told David from Paraguay that story. And Adam thinks again: my mother named me Peter after her dead brother, but my father once named me officially "Heinrich." After her half-brother, the Communist? Why?

How long had his parents known of that fratricide? Did his mother know when she named him? And his father? Why would he do that? His father died without a word, his mother told only a cousin whom she saw once, for a day, fifty years after they left Russia: why him? To bury it as far away on the earth as she could imagine, in the sand of the Paraguayan Chaco?

"Listen..." The Arctic wind catches its breath again over the tent and suddenly Adam longs to tell the story he has never told anyone about his names—he need tell only the simplest, clearest strand of it to his son who lies so motionless on the permafrost. "Your Grandma told me my second name Peter was for that brother, because I was born just after they heard he died in exile. In the Sakhalin prison camp. But she never explained anything else, not even when we looked through the albums when she was last in the hospital. After Grandpa died she hardly spoke, when we'd drive somewhere in the car, you remember, she just sang a little, off key because she was deaf, or recited words from the Psalms—'the cattle on a thousand hills' driving into the foothills in summer, 'the heavens declare the glory'—she never even cried again, and then in the hospital she smiled, just said everything was fine, don't bother. She never said a word about this fratricide, not one word to me."

Joel stirs, sits up. "Where'd you put the blue bottle?" he asks, so quietly Adam can barely understand.

"There," he gestures. "You piled your clothes on it."

They laughed when Eric first told them the use of the blue bottle, but they discovered that no matter how fast one drew the tent zipper closed around the other's body, they could not get out or in without mosquitoes somehow whining in with them, a horde that must be squashed before they could expect to sleep.

"Shit," Joel mutters.

"Spill?"

"A bit...how do you...?"

"It's better on your knees I think, keep it upright." Adam shifts himself noisily. "Hey, leave some space for me before morning."

Joel snorts. "Good luck!"

"You filled it?"

"It's just a litre."

They are both laughing a little then. Joel reaches to the screen at his feet and stretches back. It is almost two a.m. There is a warm trace of urine, a whiff of body intimacy in the cool, bright air of the tent. Adam cannot remember when the wind stopped abusing them, but if it remains quiet he knows Eric may be up at three-thirty and they will be paddling Little Marten Lake before five, along the shore headland to headland, in all possible calm. If the whitecaps stop running, crashing on the rocks.

"The czars," Adam says, "already used Sakhalin Island as a penal colony. Mostly for murderers and political prisoners."

"Like Britain used Australia?"

"Exactly, but this is an island off the Russian coast, a strait just wide enough not to swim. Anton Chekhov went there in 1890, and wrote that when he first looked across the strait, he saw a horrifying scene, the silhouettes of mountains, and smoke, flames and fiery sparks, so fantastic. Monstrous fires were burning, and above them a red glow rose over the mountains. It seemed to Chekhov all Sakhalin was on fire."

Joel does not move. Adam continues, slowly, "I sometimes think maybe our uncle Peter saw such fires."

Joel says, "Maybe our uncle the Communist wanted to end his brother's suffering."

"Yeah. But he would have to get past the guards of that camp—very dangerous."

"Well...maybe he had to, Stalin's orders."

"That's possible, but...Peter Loewen was just a statistic, being killed by work anyway. Why bother?"

"Hell, I don't know." Joel is suddenly loud. "I'm just a Canadian city kid driven to school and hockey and piano lessons his whole mixed-up life living with his single-parent mother, and his dad travels all over the world to find relatives and all he ever talks about is suffering when he does none himself, what the hell would I know about suffering!"

Adam tries to skate over that with a quick joke: "Just a bit of tundra suffering, two-kilometre portages, sixty-kilo canoe?"

"Oh, yeah, and you pay thousands so I will. Scheduled,

three weeks of summer suffering, complete with freeze-dried food."

"Don't knock who you are."

"Why not? Dad"—Joel is suddenly up on his elbow, looking at Adam in the green night light of the tent—"we sit in airplanes, fly over everything, you have so much time and money you take Trish and me wherever we want, or take anyone else you want... but Grandma and Grandpa, your relatives in the Soviet Union, they suffered, they really did. And still do I bet, the ones who got out to Germany. Remembering their bodies and heartache. So *why* were they tortured?"

"Your Grandma would say, there's suffering and death in the world because of evil. Sin, and its punishments."

"Okay, but there's evil in Canada—according to Grandma you and I sure sin, did your relatives sin so much more than us they have to be punished so much more?"

"Life isn't a system of equitable justice, I mean, how many lifetimes would a Stalin have to live to—" Adam hesitates, confronted by the obvious necessity of his mother's everlasting hell and heaven.

But Joel pushes on: "Why isn't it equitable? Grandma always kissed me and whispered, 'God loves you, Joel, remember.' Doesn't He love everybody? If He did, He would be fair."

"Life isn't fair." Adam can say it again, knowing with a jolt that he is exploiting his own unfairness with every breath he takes. And adds, evading the issue, "We both can thank God it is unfair."

"Yeah, that's easy. So what do you say to your relatives, you so rich and *hüach jeleat?*"

"You remember that, and the tone of it, 'learned so high'?"

"Onkel David made you translate it for me."

"He was laughing."

"Sure he was, but he meant it too. Why didn't I meet him when he came to Canada?"

"He was in Alberta only three days, and I drove him to Coaldale. You were at summer camp."

"Summer camp, trying to ride some stupid horse!" And Joel, in his usual way, reverts two subjects back. "Doesn't your Wiebe cousin 'Young Peter' in Germany know about these Loewen brothers?"

"I didn't know the knife story at first, to ask him. I'll ask. I'm trying to persuade him to take me to Russia, but he's still afraid, if he goes back, they'll keep him."

"The Soviet system has collapsed now."

"I know, but he still doesn't trust them. But he did say once that Peter Loewen was the schoolteacher in Number Eight Romanovka...so maybe he was a Communist too."

"What?" Joel says, startled.

"To be a teacher in the thirties you probably had to be a member of the Party, or at least a sworn atheist."

"Would they arrest a Party member?"

"All the more. Stalin wiped out his closest friends. But how would they accept Peter Loewen as a Party member? He was a Mennonite, spoke German; to prove himself reliable he'd have to do so much dirty work for the Party, otherwise how would he convince them?"

Joel says slowly, up into the tent, which is shuddering again under the wind, "His half-brother Heinrich Loewen the Communist was a Mennonite too. Maybe that's why he travelled to Sakhalin. To prove himself."

Oddly, Adam had not thought of that.

A long island shaped like a knife. Which end was the haft? What did it matter, throughout Russia's bloody history a Russian hand was always closed on some blade aimed at its own heart or throat. As perhaps Peter's hand momentarily closed on his brother's blade also, when he understood why Heinrich had brought it. On that double-pointed stone dagger of an island, barely separated from the Soviet coast by the glacial sea.

In the bow of the canoe Adam digs his paddle steadily into the white bronze of Little Marten Lake. His banned uncles would not have understood this unrequired labour, would have found such travel, forced by nothing but personal whim and weather, insane. However, that their own labours were decided by the infinitely blacker, ideological madness of a dictator could not have escaped either the Wiebe brothers, somewhere in the Kolyma mines, or the Loewens on Sakhalin. But gold, coal, timber, asbestos—whatever technicality together with cold or starvation killed them—perhaps in the end they felt it did so with the massive impersonality of weather; even Heinrich Loewen, travelling for weeks with a knife to reach a brother who perhaps had once pretended to be a Communist in order to stay alive and keep his job, to feed his family, a brother whose bed he had shared in childhood—even Heinrich became merely inevitable. The way Young Peter Wiebe in Germany talked, after ten years of Stalin it was no longer possible to say "I will do this" or "I will not do that" or ask "Why?" any more than, once you had been pushed off a bridge, you could at some point decide to stop falling.

Thunder rumbles over Little Marten Lake; their bodies,

Adam's and Joel's, grind on in the implacable rhythm of driving their canoe.

Before them, south over the bronze water, Dogrib Rock humps like a granite loaf between the angles of two eskers spaced by distance. For two days they have lain in the lee of the tiny island, hammered by the wind that bent and finally split their nylon tentpoles before they realized they would have to take the tents down to save them. But the second night brought a sudden quiet, an eerie calm, to the breakers as if a hand had been laid over them, and they packed and started to paddle south quickly across the waveless lake, over the long, unbreaking swells that now gleam under the level sun resting directly north behind them on the horizon. Here the lake narrows between rocks, darkens imperceptibly into the base of high cliffs. Adam recognizes, as if it were framed, the picture young Robert Hood sketched, with John Franklin on his first disastrous expedition to the Polar Sea: *An Evening View of Marten Lake, 29–30 August 1820.* That strange tumble of rocks on the right like an immense temple toppled by giants against a pyramid: Hood painted that. But in the painting the cliffs were also crowned everywhere by erratics and artistically spaced caribou, their antlers like lyred fronds, animals contemplating the great voyageur canoes passing.

Adam feels the narrow canoe surge beneath his knees, driven by his son's powerful stroke. He thinks, We are travelling, together.

Travel, travail. Really the same word: a journey; a laborious torment, suffering or painful effort. Adam knows that this Arctic journey he and his son have chosen for their time together is both. So why did they choose it? Their journey lies over one of the enormous remnants of prehistoric Lake McConnell, formed from the melting of the Wisconsin Laurentide ice sheet which for millennia covered the eastern half of North America; the eskers they pass mark the leavings of its sub-glacial rivers. Sometime, somewhere to the north and west, when the ice lay here kilometres thick, Asiatic peoples traversed Beringia and travelled south along the narrow corridor of glacial drift between the eastern and western continental ice sheets. What Moses with what rod parted those frozen waters for them, piled mountain oceans of ice into walls on either side so that they could walk safely through the midst of that sea on dry ground? What Yahweh, what God of Wandering and the Journey, of Unending Travel/Travail, His habitation a movable tent, His altar a rock in any barren valley, always promising meat, water, quiet and safety for their children, and yet always leading deeper into some holy desert. This arctic desert, with less rainfall than the Sinai, preserved water in its folds only by the immeasurable blessing of cold, for when the glaciers turned to water and melted back into the oceans, the Plano Indians eight thousand years ago conceived canoes and travelled the streams and lakes of that melting north again. Always with hunger, always with fear, the two poles of all living things; hunger and fear bound together by travel/travail.

Thunder. Thunderbird speaking out of the shadows surrounding Dogrib Rock. The open water before him leads straight to that overwhelming monolith. Which is surely also a Dene story he does not know.

Thunder again, echoing itself. Fear. Can Thunderbird speak to an *aufjefollna Mennist*? He may have fallen off, but he can balance his paddle and look back. Joel raises his wind-darkened face, grins, his nose wrinkles like Susannah's. Behind them Christina and Eric come on in that silent, timeless motion of human beings together in the intimate partnership of a canoe. For a moment there are no mosquitoes.

Carefully, Joel lifts himself from kneeling, sits back onto the thwart to ease his legs. "Over there," he points with his dripping paddle, "left of the rapid, maybe a good campsite."

Adam bends to the aerial picture under plastic in front of him. A detailed photograph exists for every inch of this gigantic country, and the deep roar of this white squiggle on the paper wavers in the bright night air; he feels warmth, then cold move over his face, his aching body.

Joel asks, "Rock garden?"

"Don't think so—steep stone water," Adam says. "Maybe too steep, maybe we can't run it."

"How long a portage?"

"About two, three hundred metres."

Joel laughs, dismissing that. "Just find us a flat place to park the goddamn tent," he says, settling down again, digging in.

Tiny trees bristle here and there, willow, black spruce, a shimmer of birch, at the knotting of lake and river. Adam thinks, We have almost reached the tree line; caribou trails will lead down a possible portage, perhaps past the bleached hair and gnawed, torn bones of a wolf kill. We are almost at Lastfire Lake. There I decided I was not afraid to marry Susannah. I thought I had the power to see my whole life, perfectly completed. How blind I was.

And he still is. At his oblivious, light anticipation of this summer journey with his son who is now twenty-one years old. As if rock gardens and rapids and tundra and standing waves and possibly dangerous animals and food were all one need prepare for; as if words spoken into the wash of thunder, rain and cataracts about the travail of distant blood relations could simply end, far away, with those remembered relatives. All their days together and stupidly he anticipated nothing when, well past the middle of that Dogrib Rock night, after they had together cleared their small site among the stones by the rapids and were once again stretched out inside their tent, Joel asked:

"How many wives did your grandfather have?"

And he in turn asked, too easily, "Which one?"

"Grandma's father, David Loewen. She had all those half-brothers and sisters."

"Four. A lot of women died in childbirth, widowers had to have women to care for the children they already had. An older man usually had property, a young woman might like that. My grandpa David Loewen had four, never widows, Onkel David's father's mother was his first wife, my mom's mother was his second."

"Heinrich?"

"He was from the third."

"Too bad more of the babies didn't die," Joel said, so flatly that Adam did not quite trust his ears. "Save them a murder or two." And then continued, abruptly. "'A woman when she is in travail hath sorrow because her hour is come.'"

"What?" Adam managed finally.

"I read that in a book. Jesus said it. Sorrow probably because of what's been done to her, and all the mess this kid will bring with it, all this travail and sorrow."

Travel/travail; Adam tried to anchor himself, but his mind seemed to be blocked. Then Joel rose beside him, on his elbow in the strangely chiselled Arctic light that can etch faces into skulls.

"So tell me, Father, where's Trish? My gorgeous full sister

Patricia who I suddenly never see or hear from, now our nice little suburban family has been bust up for four years not because anybody died and without any help from the Communists and you stopped being a doctor because you had invested so well in copiers and computers and can run around the world, taking turns, sometimes with me and sometimes Trish, and mostly with serial girlfriends, who knows and I don't care, what I want to know is where's my sister? She doesn't call, why doesn't she even write me any more?"

The spray of the bow smashing into a standing wave in rapids was nothing compared to this drench of words.

"She doesn't write you? I don't know why...she's travelling. You know that."

"Exile travel?" Joel asked. Adam did not try to answer. "Like a woman taken in travail?"

"She's not pregnant," Adam said stupidly.

"Oh? Refugee?"

"She didn't call me for two months either, I told you she called now, just before I flew to Yellowknife, didn't she call your mother?"

"No."

"She didn't say she would, I just assumed...she told me she's fine, she's in Turkey now, going to those buried churches in Goreme, with friends, and then for winter to Greece." Scudding rain ran over their tent, and the wavering roar of the final rapids receded. "She sounded fine. Like usual."

Joel sank back and said something up into the tent which Adam knew he must hear.

"What, what did you say? Joel?"

In the wind's hesitation of quiet, Joel said it again.

"The father"—his voice was as thin and distinct as though he spoke through clenched teeth—"is always a motherfucker."

And then he added, "I read that too, in a book called *The Dead Father*. But I didn't need to read it."

They are almost at the tree line. Even if this beginning rain sharpens, they will carry the portage tomorrow, three trips each as usual on thin caribou trails around the rapids, and travel on in rain if necessary. Joel's J-stroke will hold them steady in the current. And eventually the light will broaden over the open water of Lastfire Lake. It has always been exactly there, he remembers.

And for these moments, before he escapes into exhaustion and sleep, Adam can manage to scrawl on a page in his journal:

It is August ?? 1990—the sun does not yet quite set, tomorrow I will recognize what I have seen before.

And believe it too.

FOURTEEN

A PLAN FOR JEWS AND MENNONITES

Gnadenthal, Ukrainian SSR
1941

TUESDAY, JANUARY 1, 1863:
New Year's Eve in church, Foda preached Ephesians 4:22 and 25. They announced Mrs. Isaak Unruh and baby died after she suffered 22 hours. She was married 14 years and nine children with four living. I knew she died. My friend Anna sat on the front bench by me and cried, she's the oldest.

The first words I wrote in my diary. When you're ninety, your own handwriting is like a story some stranger you once knew made up. Or like looking at an old picture, the only things you remember are what the picture shows, which anyone can see and it isn't really remembering. But then, the longer you look, more begins to come back, until you have lots of bits and scraps and maybes. But they happened when you were a different person.

I was born ninety years ago today, October 4, 1851. Not in

this house of course, or even this village, but not far away. Neuendorf, Chortiza Mennonite Colony, Ukrainian Russia. They named me Katerina. I was the fifth living child and second daughter of Aaron and Esther Loewen.

My father Aaron, Foda we always called him, was born the second son, at last, after one son and eleven daughters. With only seven children living, Grosspa Loewen could have found a full farm for him in Chortiza as easily as he did for my uncle Jakob, but Foda liked reading more than sheep or grain. He became a village teacher.

Then the Czar's government started the Plan for the Jews, the *Judenplan* Mennonites called it. It was to be a model colony of landless Jews settled in villages on government land learning how to farm. And Mennonites, considered such good farmers, were supposed to live and farm with them, to show them how.

Because Foda's brother Jakob Loewen was an exceptional farmer, they appointed him Judenplan administrator. It was he who persuaded Foda to become the village teacher, but also to take a land grant as a model farmer in one of the four new Judenplan villages, Novovitebsk.

So we left Chortiza, and that's when Foda started to keep a diary. Not just of weather and who came to visit, but the colony struggles too because being the teacher means you're always poorer than the large estate landowners. You understand hardship, and you read the life of the village in the faces of children every day on the school benches.

Two years later Foda was elected to be the Mennonite minister too, and then he heard everything else that was happening in the village. He had to settle not only Mennonite school and church problems, but also the quarrels between people—the

Mennonites, the Jews, or both together. Foda heard and knew so much, and he could not lie. He could not stop writing it all down either. Often he had to find words that meant two different things, one good—in case anyone other than he ever read it—and the other at an angle, to help him remember what really happened.

The Judenplan Colony was started in 1852, two days' travel by wagon west of Chortiza. I was less than a year old. We lived in three different Judenplan villages, until it became too difficult and we finally settled in Gnadenthal, a new village for Mennonites only laid out in the new Baratov Colony in 1872. I live here still, in 1941. Live and hope to die here in the house that we, Aaron Loewen's family, built ourselves where its one street crosses the little bridge of the stream that runs in spring.

Foda sat at our big-room table writing, in both Novovitebsk and Gnadenthal, almost every evening. There was no table then in the corner-room where he and Mama, and later Mutta, slept. Too many children, too many chests and too much bedding. He wrote with a long feather he sharpened, dipping into the bottle of ink he made from soot. I liked the paper, folded open, the clean white growing blacker with twists and long strokes of Gothic script. I was learning to write Highgerman words from him in school. I heard Highgerman read aloud in church, but sermons were mostly in Lowgerman and that was all Mennonites spoke at home then, even the preacher's family. With the Jews we used what Russian we had; we children were told the less we spoke to them the better. They were so different, they would only lead us astray.

To write I found bits of paper for myself. The paper felt so fine, so beautifully smooth. In school we wrote on stone slates. I never had a folded book such as Foda would fill, margin to margin, and only a pencil. I started that New Year when Anna cried so much for her mother. Our mother was very sick too but I never cried out loud in church, nor did Foda when he asked them from the pulpit to pray for her. I always wanted to write down more, even when I misspelled most of the words. But I had no paper, and always I knew so little.

Seventy-eight years. I still have that first piece of paper. Like Foda, I wrote the date first. That helps to start: write a fact you know exactly. The piece is with the others in a small box at the bottom of my chest. An old woman doesn't need to hide paper behind a brick in the wall any more, no one now knows about it anyway to want to see it. No one imagines living as long as I have. Nor I think, in Russia since 1917, would anyone want to.

But as the Jews say, Who tells God what to do? In ninety years I've told Him very little, but I've begged Him often enough. And even that...

Many of my diary sentences end like Foda's, with...*ein Gedankenstrich*, he called it. A line sometimes to the edge of the page, a long streak of thought impossible to write out. Or wiser not to.

I find in my Bible what my father preached in 1863 in Novovitebsk. That Judenplan village was thirty kilometres from here, but after pogroms and civil war it's all gone. A ploughed field along the Sheltaia River. Foda was always so sad at the beginning of a year, he warned everyone about sin. But never the Jews. As a child I could not tell whether the Jews actually knew, or cared, what hell was. It seemed to me the Mennonite sin that Foda preached would, if it possibly could, take every person alive down into hell to burn for all eternity but no, Foda said the Jews had to deal with God in their own way. It was not our way, we had the Mennonite duty to be honest and believe as Jesus taught.

There were always some Judenplan Mennonites who thought we should not only teach the Jews how to farm, but also how to be Christians. Foda always said that if we could just live like Jesus, that would teach them enough.

So Jews on the Judenplan came to him only about agreements that they said Mennonites had broken, or money, or property gone. But our people came to him from all four villages carrying their sin, telling him every one of them and going away happy. He grew sadder and sadder, but always asked for more. I read the verses he preached the first of January: "You must give up your old way of life. From now on there must be no more lies: you must speak the truth to one another, for we are all members of one body. Even if you are angry, you must not sin."

I wasn't a "body member." I was barely eleven and not baptized, though I expected to be when I turned seventeen. What "old way of life" could I give up? Surviving childhood, as so many children did not? I wasn't angry. I was a girl, fourth behind men, and boys, and women, and I could cook and milk cows and feed babies—they were sent from God and died according to His Will—the way my friend Anna Unruh, just fourteen, would have to do now, with her mother in her grave. I had never in my life dared to tell a lie. Must I start, so I could then be obedient and stop? What did I know, to lie about it?

Thursday, January 17, 1863:
Diedrich Wiebe came with Deacon Dietrich Franz. I heard Diedrich Wiebe tell Foda he is sick unto death and he dirtied himself with cattle. He was so sorry, for a long time. Foda prayed, Jesus son of David have mercy, cover us with your robe of righteousness so we can stand before you naked.

We were eight Mennonite families living in Novovitebsk with forty Jewish families. I had never heard anything when men came to our door, always two together and sometimes with their sons or even wives but never daughters. I wouldn't have heard what Bigbelly Diedrich Wiebe said either, but I was washing the top of the oven in the big-room when they came in and shut the door. I shrank down still as a mouse. Diedrich Wiebe sat with his stomach spreading rounder than a washtub against the table. A big man crying, after a while he stuttered that. I wrote the words down—it was all so strange—and hid them behind the loose brick below my bed. What did that mean? I dirtied myself with cattle.

But Foda's prayer about standing naked was perfectly clear. In prayer, or preaching, things that were sin if you actually did them were often reversed into wonderful salvation, like being washed clean in the Blood of the Lamb, though the blood spraying from the neck of a chicken whose head I chopped off made me anything but clean. So prayer to be covered with a robe from Jesus to make you both clean and naked was fine. But not Bigbelly's cattle—that I didn't understand then. It was winter, the frozen ground under snow, cows were not muddy. Or smeared with thin shit from spring grass so you got more than dirty when you were milking and they hit you with their tails. Anyways, Bigbelly Wiebe never milked, only Mrs. Wiebe and their girls. What was this?

I sit now with my box of little pencil papers in my lap. I look out of my window at the village street of Gnadenthal, Colony Baratov. Every day, seeing mostly trees. In the evening the glass reflects my old face, folded together by so much to remember, but I can look through it easily. I will not waste oil for a lamp to light up every wrinkle.

The trees are tall again, rows we've planted four times over in my lifetime. During the horrors after 1918 we dug them down to the roots to burn in our stoves. Four armies overran us then, all at the same time, as they pleased. The Czar's White Army, the Communist Reds, the Ukrainians' Independence Army, Nestor Machno with his terrifying Anarchists. After the three united to destroy the Whites, they fought and killed and starved each other until the Reds had slaughtered the other two, and almost all our men, sons and fathers and husbands, including my Benjamin...I will not remember. Trees grow and get chopped down and grow again as they can.

Sixty-nine years in Gnadenthal, this so-called Valley of Grace. My relatives write me that the Mennonites have carried this village name with them hopefully all over the world—Siberia, Canada, the United States, even Mexico, Paraguay, Brazil. I don't know, all the letters stopped when Stalin began dragging our men away in 1937. Over fifty years in this house. And for the twenty years before that in a Judenplan house, built exactly the same way. Foda said most Jews did not like to farm. Mostly they wanted to be pedlars or innkeepers; brandy was so easy to sell. The Mennonites were to teach them farming, but Foda himself had time for almost nothing except teaching and preaching and hearing Mennonite sins.

Poor Bigbelly Wiebe. He could hardly speak, tears running down his cheeks. A big man crying never happened except at funerals, and then at most the husband.

Those tears were strange to me then, overwhelming. Like the shudders you feel walking past the graveyard behind the school at night. In bright sunlight the memory of coffins sinking into opened ground, hell or heaven, feels different. I could not bear his weeping. Hidden on the oven, I wept too.

A man and a cow. Such a simple, you could almost say a "clean and private" sin. In ninety years what haven't I faced, revolution, civil war, anarchists, starvation, Machno murderers, typhus, the God of Fear Stalin and his smiling police. Sometimes your spirit can pray only for swift and final massacre. Eichenfeld-Dubovka, seventy-nine men, three women shot in one night of October, 1919. And how many women and children violated.

The love of God and of family, I have known that too. I must not and will not forget that. So much, flowing even from the other side of the world in letters. Here in my box on my lap. From Saskatchewan, Canada, and once Fernheim, Paraguay.

Now war is come again. German war, like no one on earth, they say, has seen before. Faster than you can think, on the ground and from the sky. Beautiful Kiev is destroyed. Two months ago, on August 16th, I saw the first German tanks come down our street in this lost corner of the world. Into Gnadenthal. Around the clattering tanks, soldiers on motorcyles, one steering, a second in the sidecar holding his machine gun in the air. Hitler's hooked crosses on their round iron helmets. Pouring into Gnadenthal like ants.

Friday, February 1, 1863:
Mama too sick to get out of bed. Diedrich Wiebe died at midnight. Deacon Franz came to attach the Life Awakener to Mama. Its end is a round disc of long needles. I ran away into the barn.

I remember I hid in the dry hay above our cow and few sheep. But even in the darkness I still saw those needles. They used the Brauchscheidt Life Awakener, just brought from Germany, all over the Mennonite colonies. Mama's brother, August Wiebe, had studied in Germany and was a doctor in Chortiza. He called it stupidity, but people used it because so many people of all ages died and sometimes using it seemed to help. Foda agreed they would pray and apply it on Mama's back because she could not breathe. It was a thick cylinder with a spring that you wound up with a handle, then released, and the spring drove the needles on the disc into the skin.

Mama's whole back was needled black in big circles. She could not lie on it. After two days she was covered with yellow pus like a stinking cloth. Deacon Franz said that was very good because that would draw her sickness out. I had to help wrap her with cotton soaked in Brauchscheidt's oil, so the sickness would rise out even faster. But she could sleep. She sounded weaker when she coughed.

Sunday February 17, 1863:
Widow Wiebe will marry Isaak Unruh. Thirteen people, eleven children, brought together. Anna won't have to do all the work in the house any more. Foda preached Isaiah 43: I am the Lord, your Holy One, I make rivers in the desert to give drink to my chosen people. Mennonites are chosen, he said, we must be examples, not drink so much brandy at weddings and funerals. Mama lies under the blanket, she wants to work and she wants to die.

No adult would tell a child such things then, but, besides sickness, our Mama was also pregnant. Foda insisted that all life, in sickness or in health, was a gift from God. Such a great gift.

Friday, March 22, 1863:

We started to seed, our family was first on the land. Uncle Jacob's Jewish workers helped us. At supper Foda said it was seventy-five years today, 1788, when the first Mennonites left Danzig, on the invitation of my namesake Czarina Katerina II. Grosspapa Loewen was eight, he told him many sad wandering stories. Foda said remember 1788, fifty Mennonites by oxcart went to Riga, and then Dubrowna for winter. In spring they and a thousand more from Danzig came down the Dnieper River to Chortiza, and there I was born sixty-three years later.

Uncle Doctor August came this afternoon. Mama's back is a little healed. She moans, she does not move.

Monday, April 1, 1863:

Today Miller Abraham Reimer lay in the ditch. Abel saw him and told Foda. He was drunk, the innkeeper Lippen on Ekaterinoslav Road sells him brandy when he wants it.

Easter Monday, April 8, 1863:

Our Mama died. At last she is with Jesus and his angels. The Abraham Reimer buggy came around our corner fast and tipped and broke, the team ran away with the front end. The family, eight, fell in the ditch, and screamed. Mrs. Reimer hit him on the ground, that's what you get for drinking. Foda said before God's Almighty throne for our Mama there is no sin or death or sadness, only golden light.

Wednesday, April 24, 1863:

Foda sold our last wheat to the Jew Stuppel, Abraham Reimer's partner. He settled a dispute about milling. Greta and I made butter for Gerhard and Foda to sell at the market in Krivoi Rog. A letter came for us with eleven silver rubles in it....

We had almost nothing to eat after Mama died, but Foda said the faithful Lord would provide. As I remember He did that mostly through our relatives, especially Uncle Jacob Loewen and also the Heinrich Heeses of Ekaterinoslav. Tante Anna Heese was Mama's aunt. Onkel Heinrich was called "the Prussian" because he came to Chortiza as a Lutheran to live with the "defenceless" Mennonites, as he said, and escape Napoleon's army. He was a better pacifist than most Mennonites, and a kinder, more gifted teacher too. He built schools to train teachers, but the old *Ohms* thought he taught students too much, it was better Mennonites didn't know all that. So when he was already white-haired he moved his family to Ekaterinoslav. The rich Russian noblemen there paid him a great deal to teach their sons. He loved Russia and wrote poems for children in Russian, he taught us one of them when he visited Novovitebsk. It began with a lilt, we could sing it:

> The proud Queen of Great Britain,
> Consults with frauds and liars....

The first Russian words I knew. I was only six when the Crimean War started, but I remember the proud Queen of Great Britain, so young and already such a liar. "Victoria" Onkel Heinrich Heese called her.

Thursday, May 23, 1863:
Pentecost. Eleven boys and thirteen girls were baptized. We heard Bernard Klassen the widower wants to marry Maria, the

daughter of his second wife, who died. She is sixteen and not even baptized. Gossip is sin, Foda scolded us. The Ministers' Committee will send her to relatives in another village.

Friday, June 21, 1863:
We harvested our oats, again we were the first. Not much, the summer is so dry. Uncle Jacob hired fifteen Jews to cut it in a day. He paid each half a pud of grain and the noon meal. Foda wrote down the names and numbers.

In those years on the Judenplan we harvested oats in June. This year in June we heard Germany had invaded Russia. Adolf Hitler, whom Stalin had praised so loud in every newspaper and radio speech, was now a "fascist bloodsucker." He had broken the "eternal friendship" treaty in less than two years.

"Though we are unprepared," Stalin's voice thundered, "we will never surrender so much as one metre of our homeland! Now every patriot will fulfil double the prescribed work norms."

For Gnadenthal, whose collective farm is a large dairy, this meant delivering double our quota of milk. The patriotic Communist Party overseer, before he fled east, ordered the green-feed for the herd to be doubled, and our Mennonite workers in the barns of course obeyed. What else could they do? In a week, twenty-one of two hundred cows were dead of diarrhoea. The NKVD recognized this as obvious sabotage and the workers who didn't run quick enough disappeared in Black Marias.

Since the Glorious October Revolution, Mennonites had been called racial Germans. "German" is printed on the passport needed to travel inside the Soviet Union; no one travels outside. We can of course have no churches for Highgerman, but

Lowgerman is still how we talk to each other. When we heard of the approaching army, who knew what to think? What would the soldiers do? Would they believe we were Germans? Could it mean we would be delivered from Stalin? From his endless police?

The Jews thought for themselves faster than we. They began to vanish. In every direction, away from the coming German front.

Tuesday, July 2, 1863:
Today Foda came home with his new wife from Neuendorf, Chortiza. Judith Wiebe has not been married, she is three years older than Gerhard. She kissed us all. Now she is a Loewen too, we call her Mutta.

Mutta was the best, most practical and organized mother any orphan family could have had. She bore six children in twelve years, all living, and cared for our father until he died in 1888. A few years later Mutta decided it would be better to immigrate to Canada where so many had already gone. Ten of us children went with her, married or not—all except me. I wanted to go, but my husband Benjamin Wiebe, her nephew, wanted to take over our farm. My sister Justina wrote me in 1919 that Mutta died at the age of seventy-nine years, seven months and twenty-seven days in a place called Saskatchewan. Of the flu spread by the war. War finds you anywhere, Justina wrote, even in the high, stony bush of Canada.

Monday, August 11, 1863:
Dearest God, Foda said, he and Mutta drove to Chortiza Saturday and a village there burned down. Ostwick, houses,

barns, the new school, all the grain and feed. Over seventy buildings. Nobody died. Sunday he preached in an orchard on Peter
2: You are a chosen race, a holy nation, God's own people. Mutta
said everyone cried.

We had such a terror of fires, and there were many. Houses and
barns were built together, straw-thatched roofs and mostly
wooden chimneys. And often great stacks of hay dried in the
yard. But this "Great Fire" was the worst. The land was already
burned by summer drought, and an east wind came up hard at
noon. Mrs. Johann Tillitski was heating lard for pancakes, she
climbed up under the rafters to get more flour and the pan on
the stove caught fire. When she rushed down the room was
already burning. The windstorm did the rest. Burning thatch
flew the whole length of the village.

I look up the verses in Peter 2, and I see the last words are:
"Once you had no grace, but now you are in grace." How like
our innocent Foda, such a text at such a terrible time.

Saturday, August 16, 1863:
Heinrich Penner's cow wandered loose. It was seized by Stuppel
the Jew, then Peter Teichrow bought it from him for the pawn
price. Mrs. Penner was so mad she hit Peter Teichrow with a
whip. Foda settled the money between Penners, Teichrow and
Stuppel. He said they were reconciled, all departed in peace.

On August 16, 1941, the German army thundered into
Gnadenthal. I heard the tanks rumble on the bridge and there
they were, those horrible machines rolling at us on their own
steel. The soldiers on motorcycles around them in strict order,

staring at every yard and house. But the Russian soldiers and all working people were gone, we old German people still left stood in our gates on the street with white flags. An officer had his driver turn towards me; his gun was pointing into the sky and I spoke to him in Highgerman. I asked him please, don't shoot anyone.

"Don't worry, Grossmama," he said. He spoke as if he were a teacher reading from a book in school. "We have more than enough Russians to shoot."

In six weeks they've arrested seventeen people, but German soldiers haven't shot anyone in Gnadenthal. Not yet.

Thursday, October 3, 1863:
Two days on the roads, so much dust, Foda and Mutta and I came to Onkel Heese's house in Ekaterinoslav. The Czarevich Nicholas Alexander, heir to the throne, has come from St. Petersburg in his train. He rode a black horse with an arched neck to Prince Potemkin's palace, thousands of people shouted hurrah. The arch over the street has so many lights it looks like blazing fire.

Friday, October 4, 1863:
Onkel and Tante Heese took us to the Potemkin Palace, all decorated for the Czarevich. I saw my stone Czarina Katerina II where she sits so wide on her stone throne in the park. The Czarevich came riding on a white horse, he looked beautiful. Onkel Heese shook his white head, the Czarevich is too thin, the Romanovs are always too pale and thin. In the park walking he sang the whole song he had written for children during the Crimean War:

But Russia's Czar is faithful,
He fears no dragon's raging.
He draws his shining sword to...

He sang and I did too, and Tante Anna and Mutta laughed. Foda looked only sad.

Oh, my twelfth birthday. Twelve. I was in Ekaterinoslav for the first and last time in my life because of my name and my birthday. Mutta said every child must have one special day in its life, baptism and wedding later didn't count. And that was mine. Within two years the handsome Czarevich had died of poor blood. Perhaps it was a kindness to him in the end—he did not have to see his father Alexander II blown up in St. Petersburg by a bomb. He'd survived nine earlier attempts, and they say a great church was built on the bloody spot where it happened. His brother became Alexander III. They always said those pale Romanovs were good to the Mennonites, but they were all killed, one way after another. Sad Russia.

Today, Saturday, October 4, 1941, I have lived ninety years. Alone so long. Husband Benjamin Wiebe dead since the anarchy, 1919, three sons Aaron, Isaak and Daniel vanished by Stalin in 1937, all other children, grandchildren, great-grandchildren grown and gone. With two Ukrainian families—now fled—I have been allowed to live in a room of this old house we Aaron Loewens built, from parts of barns in other villages, when the Mennonites of Chortiza Colony bought land from Prince Repnin in 1872 and named this village of thirty-five families Gnadenthal, or in Russian Vodyanaya. Valley of Grace. No Canada, or Saskatchewan—whatever they mean in German or

Russian—for me, though not because I once didn't want to. And Eli Stuppel is here.

Eli was the miller in Novovitebsk after his father died and all the drinking Reimers that were left moved to Canada. Village miller until 1928 when Stalin changed the world with his first Five Year Plan. Eli Stuppel is a little older than I—how much I don't know because Jews are even more secretive than Mennonites about so many unnecessary things—and tonight Eli has come to visit me.

As he does once every year, at night. Often we talk a little about our fathers. They respected, maybe even loved each other, and both are dead now over fifty years. I have my box of small papers on my lap, I have been remembering.

But tonight Eli starts nothing about the past. He has no laugh about our childhood when we lived in the same row village but neither of us could know the other existed. Instead he says:

"I have heard, on September 19, two weeks ago, the German army entered the Kreshchatik in Kiev. Their generals immediately moved into the luxury Continental Hotel."

There was no point asking how he knows this. He has always known what is necessary, even when they made him destroy the great stone mill because milk production, not grain, was the Moscow order for Gnadenthal Collective. Starvation or no starvation, those were Moscow orders. In the brutal years of the purges he always knew how never to be at home when the NKVD hammered unexpectedly on his door, front or back or both, day or night. Now German army curfew is at sunset, and he has come in the dark. We drink tea, the windows are shuttered and there is still a little oil in my glass lamp. If a German night patrol bangs on the door, he won't be here.

The Kreshchatik. He is talking about the ancient centre of
Kiev, the most beautiful city on earth, he says. Which I have never
seen, high on the banks above the Dnieper. The village where I
was born, Neuendorf, was twenty kilometres away from where the
Dnieper River flowed, but twice I remember, after we moved to
the Judenplan, our Loewen relations had a picnic under the great
oak on Chortiza Island. Foda said, "The river flows all around us,
it holds us in its arms," and then Mutta fed us her golden zwieback
with butter. Yes, like Eli says, it must be the most beautiful river.

"Last Wednesday," Eli says, "when they were all nicely settled and happy in their looting, the first big bomb went off. The
German command headquarters in the business block on
Proreznaya Street blew up. The second bomb spread the Continental Hotel out in the air like a flower of garbage, the third..."

"The NKVD?" I ask.

"Of course."

"Like burning Moscow for Napoleon?"

"Not quite. The NKVD didn't warn anyone, they killed
more Russians in the Kreshchatik than Germans."

"Well, Stalin would say, if any of us are around there, we're
no patriots. We deserve to be garbage."

"So?" He looks at me while he draws tea through his long
teeth. He still has good gums, at least in front. His gentle tea
hiss. "So what are you doing here? The Germans have been in
Gnadenthal since August 16."

"What are you doing?"

"Aha. And where am I?"

"I don't know. Maybe here. Talking to a very old woman
who still speaks German better than Russian."

"Yes...yes." His lean, ancient face—such good bones and

skin all these years for laughing—folds itself into a sadness deep as my father's long ago. "On September 22 the last Soviet troops left Kiev, many of them running, most of them without weapons, and two days later the Kreshchatik started blowing up. It burned until the heart of the city was gutted, and then, on September 29, last Monday, they started shooting Jews. First they beat them together with clubs and rifles, then they ripped them naked and lined them up in rows of five, and they shot them so they fell back into the huge ravine by the Dnieper. Into Babi Yar."

"Babiyar?" I have not heard of such a place.

"Babi Yar. Remember that name. The first day they shot seven thousand."

An unimaginable number. People falling, piling up.

"Into a ravine, beside the Dnieper?"

He nods. "Every Jew in Kiev. But five at a time takes too long, there are only fourteen hours of daylight. Next day they had three rows of five and three shooting squads relieved every ten minutes. They could average five fives a minute, a row of five every twelve seconds, and seven officers with pistols in the ravine walking on the bodies to make sure. Total, twenty-one thousand."

More maybe than there are Mennonites on earth. I have lived too long, the world is become unthinkable.

After a time he continues, "During the pogroms in Odessa and Kiev, when the Czar was still alive, the Hasidim always had one last prayer. 'Blessed are you, Lord our God, King of the Universe, who has not made me a heathen.' But I don't know, now. Where has it got us, not being heathen? As our rabbi always says, being beloved, 'God's Chosen People'?"

I have to laugh a little. "Huh. Mennonites always want that

too. My Foda, all his life, praying to be forgiven his sin and be chosen, to do exactly what God wants and live in grace, be chosen."

Suddenly, in the quiet house, it makes no sense any more. None whatever.

We are two old, old people drinking tea. Saying a few words but writing nothing down. Written words have become worse than bullets. Everything in the world we know is as quiet as my small lamp on the table, burning. And yet in an instant we could explode, like the Jacob Wielers. One bomb fell here in Gnadenthal, a Russian bomb from a Russian plane in retreat. While trying perhaps to hit the advancing Germans—who knows?—it fell on the Wieler house. Through the roof and onto the table where the family and those in flight they had taken in were eating. It tore them up so small, no one knew how many coffins to make, just gather three baskets full. Or worse than a quick bomb, a knock on the door will start something slow, something very slow and endless.

Eli slurps tea through his teeth from the saucer. And suddenly I feel I should greet him. As he greeted me when he came in, with a full Russian kiss on both cheeks. I get up, shuffle around the table, and do that.

We stand together. I am still holding his face between my hands, and his hands come up to hold my face too. His soft, grainy hands are swollen with arthritis, warm, strong, his black eyes look into mine. Slowly then we begin to laugh. Gently as we always do.

"For me," Eli Stuppel says, "I'd be glad to share God's love with you..." and he hesitates. "But I don't know if you're tough enough. You want at least to share as much of it as you can stand?"

FIFTEEN

THE SHELLS OF THE OCEAN

Sanur, Bali

1991

ALL LIFE, THEY SAY, comes from the sea. It would seem reasonable then that all life must return to it. Reasonable. Adam sits alone under the palm trees, or sometimes on the incandescent sand under one of the tiny frond-thatched roofs. Sometimes he contemplates the two volcanoes floating high, far above the bay; or the sound of bare feet passing. Along the curve of reef paralleling the beach the swells heave, break, smash down in the continuous and interrupted rhythm of a wall toppling from left to right; heave up and smash down again, their beginnings and ends lost beyond light that he cannot distinguish. Sometimes he thinks: We thought we were so reasonable in 1987, when Susannah first moved to Calgary. Sometimes only the shadowed cones of one or the other volcano breaks through the clouds to insist on land somewhere; certain and reasonable there, beyond or above the water.

All seas are the same sea, and Trish is gone. Adam has run away to this sea that surrounds Bali because he and Trish were never here. The creatures appearing on the sea are always different, those in it always strangely the same. The spring and summer their family broke into shifting halves, into quarters—four years, isn't four the natural cycle of return?—that summer the porpoises crossed the wake of their ferry between Honshu and Hokkaido again and again, and Trish saw them playing, as it seemed, beside the ship. Together she and Adam watched those dark shapes torpedo into the ship's wake, back and forth, white bellies arching. The killer whales off Galiano Island revealed their glistening black backs once and then the sea swallowed them, but off Japan the porpoises followed as far as he could see, despite the ship's turbulence perhaps because of it?—that left them behind, while the several hundred Japanese students aboard in their navy-and-white, almost military uniforms gathered around Trish, testing their teen English. "What your name?" "What age you?" "Where you live?" until her blondness swam above their gleam ing black heads. She was a celebrity signing schoolbooks, bits of paper, and he was in an eddy beside her. They were begging her to accept the trinkets they were taking back to their parents from their school outing, and soon the delicate girls reached for her with fingertips like leaves, her pale skin and golden hair, the grey porpoises riding unnoticed far behind in their wake.

Wake—because the sea was also asleep? Did ships, like intruding bodies, wake it? Four years he had been in self-indulgent sleep, thinking—when he did—We are all adults now, we are family, life has changed, we go our separate ways and life continues, IBM and Xerox produce more than enough for us all, stick to your budget and go to school and do what you please, your brother and mother and I will do what we please. Oh, yes, he was pleased now, very pleased—when it was possible to fall momentarily asleep with a pill.

Two summers ago he and Trish travelled the arched coast of Wales. Among the massive ruins of Edward's enslavement of the Welsh in the thirteenth century she had seemed no more preoccupied than he: their mutual melancholy a closer companionship than they had found together since the family separation. He thought then her occasional singing under her breath made her sound almost content; to him the sound of singing had always meant a touch of happiness, and he certainly could have done with a bit of that from her again.

"Oh, just a folk ballad, it's turning circles in my head, you know, just the tune."

But she did know words as well, at least one verse, and her sudden silence when the three young people, like medieval musicians, laid their instrument cases open in the inner ward of what was left of Aberystwyth Castle and piped the melody she had been humming, and the lean girl haltered in a peasant dress sang with aching sweetness:

There is a deep valley, a valley so deep—

"Hey!" he exclaimed, "that's your...now you'll hear the words."

But her face went blank, momentarily it seemed broken like the wall against which they were leaning, a wall blown apart by Cromwell's cannon destroying the last Welsh resistance in the very years when Wiebe Adams was pouring walls of earth to protect Danzig. The falling sunlight glanced up off the St. George

Channel, lit the tiny particularities of the face he had studied, cared for, adored since he held her in his arms within hours of her birth. "Those are different words," was all she said.

"How is this possible!" Susannah cried on the phone.

But in two months, even with all her languages and other private investigators, she found no more than he already had. In essence, nothing.

Wherever he may be looking makes little difference now. There is nothing to see but the inside of eyelids; arid tears finally. The endless roar of the reef has hardened on the wind into moments of crash as the tide falls steadily higher and higher up the beach.

"Another drink, sir?" A soft voice in his ear.

"A mixed juice." Not opening his eyes.

He had grown to detest the very vapour of alcohol during years of smashed weekends on duty in the emergency room. If he pushed through that revulsion now he would never stop, would collapse drooling tears under the table. The waiter is gone without a sound, dark feet bleached in the livid sand. Without opening his eyes he hears his daughter's wordless song float high like the cones of the volcanoes, now this one, now that one faintly visible in its bed of cloud. He should ask the waiter: if destruction comes, as it certainly will, how would you prefer that it come? From the solid flanks of the mountains you know are always there inside that mist, or from the great sea you can never not hear? From the flanks of mountains that sometimes adjust themselves, shrug once or twice in a generation and run fire and molten rock over you? Or from frightful people smashing through the white wash of the sea with no more warning than the volcanoes: a thousand years ago the Hindus from India, then the Chinese, then the Arabs, each bringing in turn slaughter and new overlords and new religions, and then the ultimate invasions of unstoppable Christians: the Portuguese and Roman Catholicism, the Dutch and Calvinism, the English and Anglican capitalism, until finally the Japanese turned annihilation back to Asia again, killing for no apparent reason except power. Each in turn destroying and building, and destroying again in a millennium of invasion from the sea with knives and spears and arrows and cannon and machine guns and grenades and diving planes, until now, when incomprehensible space rockets and bombs hang over the world.

And he sits here day after day remembering one single life, fingers it apart thread by thread. How can you comprehend centuries, and millions of people—or even the branches of a single family—when one day, one vanished life, overwhelms you?

There are infinite ways to be destroyed: sliced, spiked, slit, skewered, decapitated, smashed, shot, earthquaked, buried, drowned, burned, blown to bits, incinerated, run over by flowing molten rock. The irrefutable needle of longing. Also separation. Stupidity.

The sound of Trish's voice, and the song she would not sing aloud:

> I never will marry,
> Nor be no man's wife.
> I expect to live single
> All the days of my...

and never sang word for word; not that he heard. But she hummed it in his mother's high soprano, once even on the northwest tower of Harlech Castle where seven centuries of sand dunes now separated its massive inner wall from the white line of the sea. They were looking across a miniature railway and the golf course and the campground and the trailer park packed tight, window to wall, with holiday tenants. On the tower wall she murmured something about the Carter Family always "hurtin' and hurtin'."

After she was gone, all that rose like flotsam in his memory: the Carter Family was his sad mother humming to the static of battery radio in the low house in Waskahikan, those Carter guitars laying a clanging riff on turn by turn of rhythmic whine until Maybelle alone or Sara alone, or together, or both joined by A.P., droned their flat voices into tragedy, as if gentle knives were sliding flat through their gut and you would discover tomorrow you had been disembowelled, were already eviscerated though still sadly walking about the day after yesterday.

The Carter Family, strangely come again on that summer trip.

There are beautiful palm trees here, but where would you kneel if you wished to pray? Rice fields now rest like stamps brushed on the peaceful mountain...but there is never any warning of destruction, mountain or sea, and you never want to believe it anyway. You always hope—faith and love protect the heart but only hope can bastion the mind—and refuse until facts crush you, and where, when crushed, can you pray? She detested their family separation. Why, Mom? For god's sake, Dad! Susannah had not anticipated such anger either. When they negotiated the spring and summer of their practical working and living arrangement, and it hardened as they both knew it would into a continuing separateness, neither Trish nor Joel could quite understand. Though eventually they had all, he thought, managed to be so logical. They were living more and more independent lives, there was no need for the usual stupid trauma, money problems, whining. Everything could be reasonable, equitable, sufficient for four intelligent adults—highly emotional adults sometimes, yes, there was shouting, the odd explosion and occasional tear, but clearly and adultly reasonable. Not this.

There are no gulls here over the windy sea; there is nothing thrown away to gobble up, no garbage in a Balinese paradise. Above his father's plough, folding back the grey-wooded soil of their homestead, the gulls circled in hundreds for an occasional offering of worms, his parents' bush piety becoming for him such a swamp of sin-soaked boredom that it must be escaped, fled. And having fled, he discovered he could offer his children only folk tales, paintings, classical music, ballet, hockey, his daughter's small sleeping body first in his arms swaying to Brahms and deep, inarticulate (beautifully so to him) Russian harmony. The Cossacks sang their discovery of faith and pain so deep in a land so far from home that he broke the record. But her baby face, her tiny fingers curled against it like his memory of her humming:

I expect to live...
All the days of my life

Maybelle Carter sang those words like a taut string; his mind is avoiding the rest of the song. He found that Carter record under the Coca-Cola sign at Piccadilly Circus, the song Trish hummed at Aberystwyth but not after.

For almost a year he has looked for her, he stares now into every crowd: such masses of people in cities, thousands, millions alive. If he stood at Yonge and Bloor in Toronto or the overpass on Waseda-dori at the Iidabashi Subway Station in Tokyo, or sat at a restaurant window above Leicester Square in London long enough, he must inevitably see her: there were so many people one must be she.

And sometimes he did see her, even among the black heads of Jakarta and Singapore, the incredible complexions of Lima, Kuala Lumpur, São Paulo: a profile, a momentary back, a jacket fold or blond flip of hair and shoulder shift, and his heart would lurch for the certain disappointment. But the first betraying detail always crushed him—the walk wasn't right, the length of leg or nose, the hands too large. Millions had been born on her day, and in grief he feels he would search out every one in every country on earth if only one were she. He had, since she disappeared, never actually seen anyone, he realized at some point, except those who in some detail suggested her; the day he was finally forced to recognize that she had vanished herself, deliberately, he was walking through an Edmonton park where young women were running, playing, field hockey perhaps, and he had to crouch against a tree unable to walk past their bodies—they were running, laughing aloud, he would not have missed a single one if she had not been there, and yet there they all were. And one had come and touched him, with that girlish lightness he knew and he could barely shake his head at her.

But he found the words when he clamped the earphones to his head in the store above Piccadilly Circus. They chiselled themselves into the acoustic tile of his mind, indelible wherever he happened to be:

> The fish in deep water
> Swim over my head.

So he has come to the sea. Again. The Java Sea where he has been with no one, neither family nor lovers. Not Peru, where Susannah and baby Joel once sat safely beside volcanic boulders watching the ocean break like mountains after a run across the whole Pacific, and slice up the beach faster than Trish's baby legs or his adult ones could run; not Copacabana, where the warm hiss of undertow was hedged in by extravagant cliffs of rock and celebrity buildings; not the night surf's crash and hiss below their hotel window in San Juan—he still went to medical conventions then—and Trish so exhausted after the long flight, "I want to sleep, Daddy, sleep." Unlike those beautiful seas, this one at least held no memories of her.

She crawled over him like a rock at every age, he changed her diapers streaked with babyshit and cradled her around the room against his chest to Handel and Vivaldi and Cree drumming and Schubert, and only two summers ago she led him through every clean and messy hall and cranny in Harlech and Caernarvon and Beaumaris and Conwy and Rhuddlan and Flint—and Beaumaris again because it was so symmetrical, so well preserved and historically useless—and ruined Aberystwyth, returning there as if by necessity in daylight after they had walked there in night mist. They would never have heard the musicians that day except for its three centuries of grass and the sudden sunlight on the exploded stones—see, our ancestor Adam could have shown the Welsh how only earth can swallow cannonballs. She must already have been wearing her deepening necessity then, everywhere they went, where were his goddamn eyes?

But among the castles she was brilliant and quick, laughing, dearest Jesus how he had longed for that, for four years, even the faintest trace of it and there it was at last, she was humming a song! And then the medieval musicians at Aberystwyth began that same melody, singing, "There is a deep valley..." and she stopped. "Those are different words," was all she said. The blacker words she had hummed, and never uttered, now spun themselves round and round on the record of his memory.

> The shells of the ocean
> Shall be my deathbed;
> The fish in deep water
> Swim over my head.

The open parkland and prairie where he had lived most of his life was always being compared to the sea; land and sky and sea and song: somewhere the sea must hold her.

On their last journey together, to the Frisian coast of the Netherlands where the Menniste Wiebes began, they saw how for centuries the Lowland people had lured the sea into slowly making land.

"The winter storms are very good, they bring up ground," the young Frisian guiding them said carefully. "The heavy wind piles the muddy water against the coast and—"

"The wind does what?" Trish interrupted.

"The steady winter wind of course, day by day," the guide said into its November bite, his accented words almost lost with all their hair streaming across their eyes. "It is the friction of wind on water, friction piles the water up against the dikes and slopes of the watte, here, we call the whole area outside the dike 'watte,' and the wind dies, then the water has to run back of course and that is why we build low rows of twisted willows, these reeds across the watte, because when it runs back the mud in the water sinks down, catches in the rows and builds up, you see, grain by grain it stays here, land."

Like snow carried by wind, caught in drifts by prairie brush and fences; but here the water was wind and the brush was deliberately laid out to catch it, a thin, slimy ridge and ditch growing imperceptibly out of the frothing sea that continuously played over them.

"So after some twenties or thirties of years the rotting willows are covered like over there, and then there is land enough for sea grass and the grass catches mud out of high tides and storm flooding even better and then soon the sheep, there you see, graze and only the high winter storms, very high, come up here and you see it keeps building. Fresh land of course, the salt leached out."

She was squinting past the young man's pale hair into the sea light. "The rows are all so…straight," she said. "Right angles."

"Engineers say straight catches best."

The sea light was relentless, like her voice. "But if the sea is so muddy here, it must be tearing down land somewhere else."

"Well, of course, the sea is always tearing down somewhere, but also deep from the bot—"

"And there is far more sea than land, eventually there can be nothing but sea, everywhere."

"Well," he laughed, startled, "there are such very big lands, also mountains."

"Some of the highest mountains are closest to the deepest

seas, the Himalayas to the Sanda and Philippine Trench and the Andes to the Chile Trench, the whole earth will be…"

Adam and the pale young man were staring at her; he remembers thinking then, We named her wrong, she's a real *Menniste Suzje*, always so quietly lovely and proper but setting sly traps when you least expect it—oh, Susannah, I can find ancestors anywhere, could we find each other again?—looking at Menniste Suzje Trish bent into the hard sea breeze, there was more than wind starting tears in his eyes. Bad decisions.

Trish said, "It has to be, when the sea has torn down all the land in the world, the entire globe will be two hundred feet under water."

The young man replied, very gently, "But it will take very long. And here"—he was reaching down and he might have taken her arm if she had been the kind of woman a man could touch easily—"here, the land mostly comes deep up, from the sea bottom."

His fingers dug in the muddy slime. They were standing on a buried line of woven willows, the ridged, muddy silt stretching far away to the frothing but mostly indistinguishable edge of the grey sea.

"Many shells, many, many bones. Ground into bits," he said, spreading that mud across his hand like a page.

He has nothing to hold in his hand. The memory of her last voice—"I'm in Patrai, I may take a ship up the Adriatic coast"— and then nothing. Not a penny withdrawn from her account after November 16, 1990. She never wrote to him anyway, not even a postcard, only that occasional beautiful "Hey, Dad" suddenly assuring him she was somewhere on earth; or Susannah's voice telling him what Trish had told her, Susannah still anchored in Calgary, receiving and relaying messages between herself and Adam and Trish and Joel wherever in the world they were. Once, when Adam called from a street phone in Rome, Susannah muttered out of her sleep, "Dear god, I'm becoming a satellite connector, it's four in the morning and Joel phoned an hour ago from Mexico, I'm getting a machine to exchange all your messages for each other!"

But she didn't then, and certainly would not now, after a year of Trish gone.

"'Hello, Central, give me he-e-aven,'" she sang the Carter twang perfectly in Wales:

> For I know my gramma's there;
> With the angels there a-waitin',
> Waitin' on the golden stair!

"It's not 'gramma' in the song," Adam said, "it's 'mother.'"

"I know," she said, "but my mother isn't with the angels yet, is she. Watching us every second from 'up there.'"

"Please," he begged her.

"Please you too," she said, going. "Pretty please with artificial sugar on top."

He had noticed it, finally, the depth of her accumulating sadness. He had not sensed that during their early travels together, and never before their family splintered—but maybe he was just stupid then, and she younger. Tomorrow, October 25th, she should be twenty-six years and three months.

"Eighteen is old enough, girls should be married," his father had always pronounced. The family wisdom of

Mennonite-village Russia, as usual worse than useless in Canada.

Three weeks ago, just before he fled empty Edmonton again, he had recognized, across a crowded concert hall lobby, the back of a business acquaintance whose wife he knew was dying of cancer. He had known for months but easily avoided him, unable to consider the words he must try to say, but suddenly he was beside him, touching him, and Fred turned instantly and they embraced, quickly, between clusters of concert chatter. "I've been thinking about you," Adam murmured against his ear, and Fred murmured back, "I know, I know…I've been thinking about you." They could hear violins tuning in the concert hall, some elementary Mozart delicacy, and Fred was describing a sigmoidoscope, which he explained at length was something like an eye at the end of a hose with which doctors had seen the enormous cancer, and drew a map with his finger on the white shirt of his abdomen, tucked right in there, and they had cut that all out, every bit of that. But the liver was beyond any scalpel. I know, Adam said.

And they had stood there together as if content; they found they could speak this factuality more easily than a hockey score. Crowded together in the noise of the lobby they seemed close and understanding friends. And Adam remembered he had kissed Fred beside his ear; that they had held each other's hand while they were stating those clear facts, things discrete and medical that mirrored nothing else, presumably, if they spoke them fast enough.

And at some point they both said, "Miracle." Almost at the same time, now that he thought about it. Both of them blurted out that aberrant, old-fashioned word as if it had been lurking there all along under the logical science they pronounced in the loud lobby.

He has searched for a miracle. Eventually he knew that he would not find her without one. During that grotesque winter and spring he still cannot avoid remembering, he stacked up note-books and files and police and translators and hired detectives and embassy and government reports, he searched the Adriatic coast from Patrai to Dubrovnik to Split to Trieste, even across to Bari or Ancona, to say nothing of Venice, a gathering confusion in winter rain of uncountable islands and inlets inhabited and killed over since before identifiable history, and harbours of tiered houses climbing up the hills filled with sympathetic or apprehensive, staring people who in two dozen different lan-guages could say nothing more than *no, never saw, no*. The raw limestone cliffs, blazing white in rain or merciless sun, smashed everywhere and crumpling down into the sea.

He remembers the low spring light that evening. Perhaps it was that, and his exhaustion, as he turned his rental car away from the coastal road, up a twisting lane among minuscule fields scraped out flat between spines of rock, and the walled splotch of a village was suddenly there. The sand and blue curve of the deeper blue Mediterranean shone far below, to a horizon washed into sky. He got out, locked the car—which was useless, he knew, he had been stolen clean twice and everything that mattered he carried under his shirt or zipped in various pockets and back-pack—and walked down into the village. The street that opened through its surrounding wall was so narrow between over-whelming whitewashed stone that if someone had been with him they would have had to walk single file.

He met no one. The cobblestones, rough and unworn as if gathered in a field yesterday, led him down into the day's deepen-ing twilight. It must have been the time of the evening meal, he could hear voices, and kettles and pots banging through open windows too high to look into but letting in, at last, the evening coolness. He felt his skin loosen a little after the tremendous sun all day, and then turning a corner he saw what must be momentary people passing far below him, where the narrow street he was walking down crossed another. But when he got there, he was still alone.

A tiny intersection between houses; from five directions streets emerged out of their straight narrowness and circled their cobblestones around themselves. The tops of Adam's feet felt suddenly cold in their sandals: as if along one of the radiating streets a breath had drawn up from the sea.

"May I take your photo?"

It was a moment before he understood that he had been spoken to; in unaccented Canadian English, after months of incomprehensible sound. A stocky man stood in the fold of a wall. Adam realized that must be the person who had spoken to him. A square camera—could it actually be wood?—stared at him, its black cloth partially draped over the man's arm.

Adam said, a reflex brushing him away, "It's too dark here for a picture."

"No."

That word, trailing him along this endless coast, slowing him farther into hopelessness; he jerked erect to glare, perhaps to curse, and he saw the single eye at the centre of the wooden face flicker even as he turned fast to leave.

The man's left hand emerged, offered a piece of paper.

The paper was the picture. Adam saw himself in black and white, framed full-length between the house corners of the street he had just come down, his face unguarded and open: as always, running away. But even as he saw this, something else appeared in the stony street behind his image, level, above his shoulders; he took a step into the low evening circle and clearly there was a shape behind him in the picture, long, stretched out, delicate arms and legs reaching as it seemed into the next stroke of water, and blond hair—certainly long and blond!—he saw that more and more clearly, hair streaming flat behind her, over bare white shoulders and black swimsuit, she is there! swimming down the rock street of the narrow village.

The world crashed so dark the street behind him was hardly discernible, but it was certainly motionless and empty. He could only stand there, barely trying to breathe.

The man was beside him, glancing at the picture in Adam's hand. "No," he said again, crouching back as if he wished to disappear into the wall. "It is not good, no."

As if she swam in a layered sea of rock behind and above him.

"I'm sorry, I'm sorry, I did not really want to take it." The man was contradicting himself in abasing apology, his face hunched with pain and his voice so deeply gentle, almost as though he were praying the Miserere.

The village was like hundreds of others on the cliffs above the Adriatic and Adam had never intended to come here; he had to get to Trieste, to ports where sea ferries landed, where officials guarding gangplanks had to be questioned, a twist of the key would carry him instantly, permanently to those places for disappointment. But here this picture lay in his hand.

"Where is she?" he demanded. If he had had a knife, it would have found the vein in the man's throat.

He whirled around to stare up the street, then back again, both his hands opening to grab the man, but he was gone and the camera was gone and the picture had fallen away from him, between the white buildings there was only gathering darkness and the empty stones circled under his feet. On his knees in the tiny intersection Adam searched, brushed his hands over every cobblestone and up into one after another of the radiating streets, and finally he scrambled to his feet and hammered on door after door. He had no words to explain himself, he acted out "flashlight," then "camera," leaped about "taking a picture," but it seemed no one could understand the frenzy of his behaviour. He ran up the radiating streets until he found the one that opened to his car, he drove into Rijeka, found a librarian who spoke some English and rushed back. But flashlights revealed nothing on the cobblestones, the villagers insisted they had never seen such a thing as a wooden camera, leave alone a stocky man who spoke English. The librarian who translated this looked at him, as the villagers did, standing in the dim light of their doorways, with a profound and blank compassion.

He is standing on a reef in the Java Sea. Unbelievable coral ebullitions roil everywhere in it, reflect a pink surface scrolled in shimmers about his knees. What may be his own thonged feet ripple there, and a purple starfish inert on the sand. Through the water he sees his toe approach, nudge closer, flip it over. A skiff of drifting sand. It is certainly upside down now but still motionless: long before this sudden inversion it must have already been protecting its central mouth like that with its curling self; probably had done so all its life in hopeless anticipation of this unexpected and merciless Canadian.

The upside-down starfish does not move. Adam stares away over the vacant sea, avoids every faint shadow of wave or mountain and concentrates on the meeting of water and sky. Counts slowly. After the third quick glance down he knows that the top left arm is beginning to curl. Under. At the tenth he sees a tiny ripple of water help bend the second arm. In eleven minutes the starfish has almost folded three of its arms back under itself, and then a sea surge lifts it upright and over, flat.

The water clucks around his hips. One flip is not enough. Another.

He lay on his hotel bed in ancient Husum, the Schleswig-Holstein town where Theodor Storm wrote *Der Schimmelreiter*, reading the novel in the new edition that included pictures of the latest movie made of it. When Trish came through the connecting door and sat on his bed, she barely nodded at the stupendous grey horse he offered her, rearing above a dike ripped through in vicious rain.

"You know I don't like horses," she said. She had not yet cut her hair short for travel.

"Joel doesn't either. What's with you, Albertans and you don't like horses."

"You don't either."

"Those were our homestead plugs, *Schrugge*, that I had to ride to school, but this is a beautiful *Schimmel*."

"If only the sea can make land," she said, "we should have driven along every dike and watte and polder all the way down the North Sea coast."

But his mind was lost in Storm's sonorous German and the great farmsteads they had seen that day on their high, diked islands, coming up like ships out of the midst of the driving sea. It was only when she added, "If you think you can follow all your ancestors backwards through your *Martyrs*

Mirror," that he understood she was talking about something quite different.

"What?" he said, apprehensive.

"You should go to The Hague, to Makkum, and Antwerp, the Frisian Islands too, to the places where the Wiebes started and burned."

"We'll get to Harlingen," he said quickly. "Next time, and Danzig too, I promise."

"And Russia?"

"Of course, I told you I just have to persuade my old cousin to come, show us everything in Orenburg, but he's still afraid."

"There's Gorbachev now, nothing will happen."

"But Young Peter had three arrests, you can't blame him—" He stopped, abruptly happy. "You want to come with me, to Russia?"

"No," she said. She was standing against the sheer curtain at the hotel window, and he could not see her face. "I'm sorry," she said abruptly.

"Why?"

"Oh—" She gestured, tossing aside whatever they had said with a flip of her hand. "You said one ancestor was called Adrian. Where would they get such a name from? The Adriatic?"

"Maybe it's Latin," he said, puzzled. "I don't know what it means."

"It doesn't matter...sorry."

Sorry. Twice in one minute, when she rarely said it at all.

Adam thinks of that pale young Frisian explaining the watte—perhaps his name was Adrian—if he could find him again above the grey sea, they might both be hunched there; together, her fingers accepting the smear of mud and bony bits he offers, they could be holding slippery hands. "In the next century," Adrian would be saying, "we'll grow wheat here where there was only sea. This land will grow everything."

If war doesn't happen, and flight.

But obviously the fire and brimstone of war does not concern her. She is holding specks of molluscs or bone in her hand, is rolling white specks ground roundly into powder between her slim fingers, the North Sea wind whipping her hair, grown long again, across her face.

"That's easiest to do," the young man says, "to try and build it straight. But the sea is always bending everything, of course."

"Trish?" Adam asks. "Trish?"

But she is not listening to him. It may be she is laughing, like a Menniste Suzje.

Adam stands on the reef in the rising tide of the sea. Far behind him the narrow sand on the rim of land shades dark into palm trees, into high towers of hotels white against the magnificent jungle hills singing with insects and parrots and dipsidoodling monkeys; but he faces away from all that, looks ahead over the flat, reflecting surface. When he bows his head slightly, his chin and the tip of his nose are touched by the sea, the columns of his body, legs, his sandal-patterned feet are as precise as cut crystal bent among coral, gesturing fronds, creatures perhaps moving though seeming still as ash, a strange world so brilliant that at this moment he cannot recognize any bit of it, though his eyes are wide open. With time the sea will reveal everything, of course. Adam simply must know at what moment to look down into it like this, and remember.

SIXTEEN

A Tour of Siberia

Marienburg on the Nogat, East Prussia

1945

I WAS BORN ON SUNDAY, JANUARY 28, 1903, in the village then called Gnadenthal, Colony Baratov, in the country whose name Josef Stalin later decided would be Ukrainian Soviet Socialist Republic. Elizabeth Katerina Wiebe. My mother, also Elizabeth, told me I was born long, so long I did not really uncurl, as she said it, until she had survived seven days of blood and fever, but she lived to bear two even longer children, sons Enoch and Abel, before her motherhood bled away into miscarriages.

I remember my mother always slender, and pale, she might have been a morning mist drifting through the house from the autumn orchard. And sometimes when she endured one, or sometimes two, of "my days" as she called them, in bed, when she lay with her head turned to the wall and her breath so low the blankets did not stir over her, the spread of her marvellous hair made me simmer, I felt myself humming with a happiness I could never quite feel looking at her beautiful, gaunt face.

I know my father, Alexander Wiebe, felt both the beauty and the pain from her as well. In the finest portrait he ever took with his large studio camera, she is half turned, half kneeling on a chair, her left leg almost doubling her long skirt under her and her arms crossed on the chairback; strands of her hair stray back down to her waist, and forward over the lace-trimmed blouse on her breast. She is looking right, serene as glass with the painted studio backdrop behind her, her eyes raised as if anticipating a vision from heaven; it is coming, yes. Her lips will open in adoration.

When I became a nurse, I understood she lived with a prolapsed uterus, her inner organs torn by inflammation and miscarriages. Many women suffered that in her time; she was forty-seven when she died. In 1931, just as Stalin's freight trains began hauling "kulaks" and their families north to slave to death in the mines and forests of Vorkuta, a name we had not known before and soon could hardly whisper. Perhaps then my father's missing right arm saved our family from arrest by the State Political Administration, a fancy name for political police, we called them GPU. If it saved him, he always said even a right arm was well worth the price of not having to tour Siberia in a cattle car. But he also insisted our mother's affliction actually spared her life for a time, since it prevented more childbirth, and childbirth, he said, could be as dangerous for a woman as war service for a man. He thanked God that they had been given three strong children and twenty-seven years of love and care together.

"And all her pain?" I asked him.

He was silent, and abruptly wiped my question aside with his single hand as if it were less than a fly. His right arm had been cut off at the shoulder during the Great War, after an exploding bullet crashed through it and destroyed the Russian soldier he was trying to carry to safety on his back.

"'We are born to suffering as sparks fly upward.'" His favourite book of the Bible. "Have you ever heard in Russia of anyone who doesn't suffer?"

I remembered my youth very well. "We never suffered, not before I was fourteen and you had to go to war. Except for her 'days' all our life was wonderful."

"I'm talking lifetimes, and we're no Jobs, we're just Mennonites. We don't argue with God."

Both my mother and father were Wiebes, I was *een Dohbel-Wiebe* as they teased me, double Wiebe, and named after my grandmothers, only one of whom I knew. My second name is, of course, all princess and purity, but the first means "dedicated to God," and I have never married. Since the age of fifteen I have been a nurse, caring for the sick and the elderly; when I began nursing during the Revolution there were more than enough hurt people to care for, and I soon realized that being a nurse would save me from the grinding labour of a collective farm, so all these years I appear to be truly "dedicated to God" in caring for others. As only a single Mennonite woman can be who, for whatever seemingly unfortunate reasons, has not been able to dedicate herself to the highest of all womanly callings, that most dangerous one of wife and mother. At forty-two I still appear to be dedicated, a princess, pure.

In January 1945, appearance is all any German has left in Marienburg, in what was once Poland, or East Prussia, or perhaps it is Poland again—who knows what country we're in or will be in a day or two, in war there is no time for anything but "here." At night the southeastern horizon flashes and screams with an endless, flaming light. One could imagine the rumble was an immense, unnatural summer thunderstorm, but there is snow on the ground tonight, it is twenty-five degrees below zero and we know that the light is the hordes—as the Germans call them—of the Soviet Red Armies approaching. With Siberian cold and American steel they are steadily killing the German Wehrmacht into a devastating retreat over which Hitler's insane orders have no control.

Ancient Marienburg Castle is barricaded, surrounded by anti-tank trenches hand-dug by starving Russian prisoners of war. The SS officers who now speak for the Wehrmacht tell us, who live in the town around the castle, that the Red Armies will never cross into the Fatherland, they will be stopped right here on the eastern bank of the Nogat because our massive fortress, built by the German Order of Knights, has withstood over seven hundred years of siege and has never and will never be taken by subhuman Communist Slavs. I don't remind them of Gustavus of Sweden or Napoleon (they were supposedly Christian and more or less blond), I just fill my two water pails as well as I can where the millrace runs open over the ice-slivered dam, and carry them back between the zigzag tank barriers to Mühlengraben 34. The door opens when I reach the step: Sister Erika is there, smiling as she reaches for one heavy pail, and I am inside the warmth of the Marienburg Mennonite Home for the Elderly.

Our building is outside the dry moats and stone walls of the castle. Whether this is unfortunate or not, time will shortly tell. We have not fled west like the other Germans and Mennonites (and the Poles and Russian prisoners of war working for us, who fear the coming Communists even more than they hate and fear the Nazis) because the local Nazi gauleiter and the Wehrmacht betrayed us.

Three times in the last two days we told the evacuation authorities that we have thirteen aged women and one man in our care, four of them very weak; please, *we beg you*, bring us trucks or wagons and either help us to the train station or to join the road treks so we can escape west, over the distant Oder River and into Germany, before the massive flight of people clogs all transportation. The gauleiter insisted he could never contravene standing orders, screamed at me that the Red Army would be stopped and driven back, what was the matter with us, were we spies, despicable traitors?

Staring, his frightened little eyes; he even affected a small moustache like his deranged Führer. I had not spoken a single word in Russian since November 29, 1943, when, with all the other Mennonites who had fled ahead of the retreating Wehrmacht from the Ukraine, I had been made a German citizen in the re-Germanized Wartegau, and given ethnic German identity papers. Only Sister Erika knew where I came from and she thanked God, she said, in silence.

The next day, January 25, two diving Russian planes fired four cannon-shells into the Marienburg before our anti-aircraft guns drove them off. One shell hit beside the gauleiter's office and he began to scream, "All civilians evacuate!" He got out ahead of them all because, rumour had it, for three weeks he had already had his Daimler and mistress packed. The Wehrmacht officers assured Sister Erika they had never yet left any civilians behind (they certainly had enough experience, with over five years of war and a three-thousand-kilometre retreat from Stalingrad and Moscow), never left any elderly, don't worry. But despite endless vehicles and carts and distraught people streaming past our door west to the river, the officials brought no transport.

The last German soldier we saw was at noon today, January 26, the sky screaming with fighter planes and shells, and high bombers droning west with not an anti-aircraft gun to stop them. Three uniformed youngsters came down the littered, empty street as Sister Erika and I were ripping down our window curtains to prevent them from catching fire.

"You're still here?" one called to us, and gestured with his machine gun. "Get away, hurry, the Reds are on our heels."

"Please!" Sister Erika cried. "Please, as God is good! Find us a truck, a cart, anything—we have fourteen old people here who cannot walk to the end of the street!"

All three looked at us sadly, but they didn't stop or even hesitate. The very youngest raised his right hand as he passed, palm up and wide open; it was no Hitler salute.

"Jesus Christ," he said, and I thought at first he was cursing, but then I understood, "the same yesterday, today, and in all eternity."

"Amen," said Sister Erika. She turned to me. "We must move them. Down into Frau Heinrichs' room, behind the air-raid shelter."

For our evening prayers she has only her pocket Bible: everything else is upstairs in our rooms, where we dare not go. Sixteen of us crowd in a circle around the room, fourteen on chairs with the oldest, ninety-year-old Taunte Gertrude, and the weakest, Onkel Johann, who is seventy-four, propped on the sofa. As the panzer fire on the street thuds and rattles the building above us, the windows shatter, Sister Erika smooths back her black, springy hair and reads:

"When the Lord brought back the captives to Zion,
  we were like them that dream.
Then our mouths were filled with laughter
  like water brooks in the desert,
For those who go out in tears, carrying seeds to sow,
  will return home with songs of joy,
  bringing their sheaves with them."

"Listen!" whispers Frau Heinrichs. "They're upstairs!"

We hear them then, and in our stunned silence I understand their Russian yells, orders, as doors crash open. Before we can move, our door breaks inward off its locks and hinges and men burst in, one and another and another, so enormous with heavy fur hats and quilted uniforms. And the guns in huge, knobby hands. I have had to look at them too often, but now that blue circle like a pursed steel mouth is searching around the room in such hands—the leader glares, his eyes are barely slits in a livid face darker than any winter sun could burn off the snow and if I weren't seated my legs would surely collapse.

It's the surprise, I tell myself. What's the matter with me, I should have expected this, a quiet year caring for old people and you forget that war always returns with more horror, over and over? And then, if his face hadn't told me, the sound of his voice does.

"Germans, hear, you Germans," he stutters each memorized syllable. "We not here for land, we have plenty land. We here for revenge!"

And quick as lightning the gun leaps in his hands and he fires into the ceiling, three shots that explode inside our heads, and screams a command. All the gawking soldiers blunder back out ahead of him; we hear them pounding, yelling up the stairs and through the air-raid shelter. They are gone.

"O dearest, dearest God in heaven," Onkel Johann prays.

Sister Erika gets up slowly and moves to him. "Yes, of course, God will protect us," she says. Her voice tries to find its unshakable calm. "See, shooting is very loud, but doesn't hurt the ceiling, the beams are two hundred years old."

"I'm ninety-one years old," Taunte Gertrude explains again. I am thankful that she doesn't comprehend.

We brace the broken door in place with chairs, spread sheets over the straw we have brought in and bed all our beloved old ones under the quilts and blankets we brought from the rooms upstairs. There is no electricity for light, but we still have a bit of gathered coal for Frau Heinrichs' heater; if you look directly at it you see light flicker in its tiny slate window. The house no longer shakes, the night outside has grown momentarily silent. Sister Erika and I lie down together on the bare floor where the door opens, there is no straw for us but we have two quilts, one wool, one feathers, and one pillow between us. On that warm stone floor, breathing and ancient rustling all around me, I can almost imagine the world a place where one could sleep.

Not an instant! I reach in the darkness, touch Sister Erika's face, her nose, with the tips of my fingers, her temple, and I turn until my lips are against her left ear.

"Tonight we can't sleep," I whisper. "We must tell each other everything."

Her breath runs over my chin and throat. "Yes," she says so low no ear but mine could have heard it. "I saw you. Did you know that Russian?"

"He's not Russian, he's a Tatar, from the Caucasus. They're

Muslims, and if anyone touches a Tatar woman…those dark, slant-eyed women hidden under veils, to the Wehrmacht in Russia they weren't human, they ripped off their veils, used them like whores, like animals, anything they wanted they did."

"Elizabeth!" She twists her head, hisses against my mouth, "What's the matter, what?"

The room is warm but I am shuddering. It is as if the gunfire still hammers in the room; those blue mouths searching, those rifles so smooth and shining as if grown out of those terrible hands like steel trees, they make everything that has been impossible to say until now absolutely necessary. I have to say it:

"Have you ever been violated?"

"No…no."

"Then listen," I say, "may God have mercy but listen, you and I could flee, but our very old people…there are two things we can do. These are blooded soldiers, they've survived and killed, who knows what's happened to them and their women in four years of invasion and counterattack nothing has happened to you till now, but I was two months on the muddy trek, retreating before the Soviet advance from the Ukraine to the Wartegau and I know— these soldiers will take Marienburg building by building and the castle too, they broke in on us, we can't hide and they'll come back whenever they want, there are two things we can do: try to resist, or accept. It will happen so fast, like they broke in and he yells and fires into the ceiling, your mind goes white, gone, so you must think now, before it happens, two things, resist or accept—"

"Elizabeth—"

"Listen! We are women. In war, women are only one thing for soldiers. First try to talk…when he grabs you, talk, talk if you can as long as you can, even if he can't understand you, a human voice and words, with one soldier alone it can be possible, but soldiers in a gang are not men, they're a trained kill machine, they have no head, no conscience, no reason except fear and you can't scare them. Listen. For a front-line soldier any woman is a hole to be fucked. When they knock you down and one is on top of you, and you're still conscious, resist only if you can grab something you can kill him with, grab a gun or a knife or club and use it instantly, don't hesitate, don't think, grab it and hit the body, the head's too small and hard, always the body, the best is the throat or under his arm or in the belly as deep as you can when he's over you, but don't *hesitate*, stab his eyes if you have a chance, that's good...as hard as..."

I'm gagging, I have to stop. She lies against me, her heart beats steadily; doesn't she understand?

I try to whisper more calmly. "Even if you stop one, kill one, alone, or even two, it won't do any good. There are armies of them, they'll only be more enraged and come and they won't waste bullets, whatever they want to do, they'll rip our old ones open with bayonets, fingers, cocks, they'll blow..."

Erika turns completely, pushes her left arm under my neck and with her right pulls me against her. Tight, she is tenderness and warmth, my face held between her breasts—but I have to concentrate, prepare her!

"Shhhh," she whispers, "that's enough now. There're two hundred German Wehrmacht in the Marienburg, if they can fight their way out, they'll take us all west, over the Nogat."

"Fighting for their lives, you think they'd carry fourteen old people four hundred kilometres to the Oder?"

"Danzig," she says. "Ships are evacuating people from Danzig."

The great city I have never seen. Which our ancestor Adam Wiebe once protected with a wall no army broke through in one hundred and fifty years. Our father told me and my brothers that the centre of Danzig is unbelievably beautiful. He said the tall, narrow buildings that line both sides of the Long Market have stepped façades like the houses that tower over the canals of Amsterdam.... Erika holds me, her voice quiet. In my thirteen months at the Home I have known her as a person of calm, superb organization, and unquenchable hope. And no fool.

I shiver. "Yes. You and I could reach Danzig."

Her arms loosen; she whispers, "You could."

She has understood the longing in my voice when I said that name. Long before the Great War, when I was barely a year and the world for Russian Mennonites was always summer and always light, my father travelled through Danzig on his way to Germany to study photography, on railroads, he said, first built by the engineer Eduard Frederich Salomon Wiebe, another possible ancestor. Now war has driven me to Marienburg, less than seventy kilometres from Danzig. I could walk there through the world of villages the Mennonites built after draining the delta marshes, and from which most have already fled. I could walk to Danzig in two nights and a day, with only two rivers to cross.

"The gauleiter," Erika is whispering in my ear, "betrayed us, now you must save yourself."

I could try. But my body lying on these stones seems to know more than I can plan now. My arms are around her strong body and so we hold each other as closely as two women can, breathing together. After a time, the prayers still rustling in the room, she can say to me:

"You were violated."

And I can say it. "Yes." And, saying it, I must go on. "In war men are brave and killed, women are brave and raped and killed, war and rape always slide off the tongue together, but we don't need war to be brutalized, a girl can get beaten and violated and sodomized..."

I get myself stopped because Erika's arms pull tighter around me. "Later," she says in my ear. "Tell me, if I don't resist, what?"

"For war they train soldiers how to kill, how to look at wounds and the dead without feeling, but no one trains women for this."

"Ssshhh," against my mouth, "not that, not now."

And I hear, near us, Frau Heinrichs snoring a little, good, but in half our room the straw stirs with sleeplessness, prayers in various languages for mercy. O beloved Saviour only you can save us.

So I can begin to tell Erika, in my arms, "They will take turns, one after the other. If you struggle, try to resist, some of them will hold you down, sit on your face or break your legs wider apart or bend you over because if they sodomize you they think they...some will bellow like animals, their hands grab you anywhere, there's nothing human about them, especially their laughing, you must pray to go away, go as fast and as far as you can, away.

"You'll see it in their eyes, don't struggle, don't stiffen or brace yourself, it'll hurt you more, make yourself limp, try, and you must do this right away: as soon as they grab you, as soon as it's hopeless, try to pick a place where you can go, go away."

"What...a place, to go?"

"Go away, a nook, a corner, if there's a closet or a space

behind a stove, go there. Not a corner up in the ceiling because from there you'll see. Any place where it's dark, go."

"Like…under berry bushes, in our garden?"

"Yes yes yes, good, under thick bushes, as far away and green as you can, go! You're limp, you go fast, the stabbing pain will try to drag you back but don't let it, concentrate, a name helps, 'Jesus, Jesus, Jesus,' if you can make yourself a little wet before it starts then maybe the pain won't cut so hard."

"Wet?" she whispers.

And I can't stand this, I have to snort against her skin, this is so stupid. Trying to say words about what lives forever inside you like blood, like cancer, whispering as if you could prepare to be smashed by pain, your body left dead except for shame, this could only be your own fault, talking is so uselessly stupid.

"Elizabeth Katerina! Those soldiers were in this room!"

"And we did not bring them here!"

"This is war training, tell me!"

"All right! Where could you get it, wet?"

"Spit?"

"Maybe. But my mouth is so dry then, it's useless."

"Tears?"

"Yes, tears, or sweat, blood. Don't fight, you'll want to, but don't, the faster they'll do it. Remember, to them a woman is three holes, and they'll use every one."

"What?"

"Yes, three. If you have to swallow sperm, or piss, it doesn't matter, vomit if you can but it's not poison. Just go away."

"O Lord"—her voice is suddenly broken—"please."

"Erika." I can only hold her.

"O Lord, Lord our God," she gasps against my neck,

"you have been our refuge forever, before the mountains were born, before you formed the earth, from the ages to all ages you are God."

I cannot join her. I have begun to weep, in the vice of memory, foreboding. Jesus, Jesus.

We awake from exhaustion into a blanket barrage outside. I do not dare venture out for water and, crowded into one room, we have so much we need to clean that the level in our storage barrel drops badly. Our storage room is still locked and filled: bread, dried noodles, canned fruit, a little smoked sausage, we do not talk about how long we can ration ourselves in a siege, we think of that but this is war and we do not think of that either, today is today and hopeless enough unto itself. And in the basement cubicle next to ours we need water to wash our waste into the open sewer; if that is plugged, Erika and I will have to carry everything onto the street by pail as well. The house shudders and creaks, bullets shriek, the world is breaking over us. But we clean, we eat, we pray long prayers, or moan them as we are able. Our shivering people settle closer together in the most protected corner of the room.

"Yes, close together," Erika says, her tone quiet as if she were changing a night sheet, "then they don't have to dig in so many places, to find us if the house collapses."

Frau Heinrichs begins to sing, her voice light as a bird flying:

> "We are on our heavenly journey,
> To our blessed home above..."

When she reaches the chorus, other voices are trying to climb with hers:

"We're travelling home,
we're travelling home,
When our battle has been fought
we'll journey ho-o-ome."

Onkel Johann's lips move, though he makes no sound.

It is early afternoon when we hear the door upstairs crash open, a moment of silence, and then feet pounding in. Shouts, curses, then a barked Russian command and footsteps, bodies are crashing out again. We are so relieved we are almost breathing when, without so much as a step creaking to warn us, a fist pounds on the door and it falls open: an officer.

My heart jolts, for a moment I can only stare at his knee-high, polished boots. It is always the same, any, every Red Army officer could be Abel, the happiness and the horror that would be. But of course it is not, not my lost Communist Party brother.

Two soldiers with automatic pistols close behind him. He bends into the room and stands with feet apart, his uniform clean and smartly creased. In amazement I see him lift his peaked cap in a polite salute from his wide, bald head—does he shave it like Lenin?

"Does anyone speak Russian?"

We have planned this. Only Frau Heinrichs will speak, though half the room could. Sister Erika has rehearsed with each of them my warning not to reveal any knowledge of Russian, because the Soviet military has Stalin's absolute orders: anyone found in Germany who has ever lived in Mother Russia can only be a traitor to the Great Communist ideal and is to be arrested immediately and sent back for punishment. But Frau Heinrichs volunteered. At eighty-seven, she said, what can they do to me?

We pray she is right. She does not hesitate to answer. I watch the astounding officer, with a little hope but no confidence in his apparent momentary decency. In the war business of cleaning German soldiers out of Marienburg house by house, should we be more useful to him dead than alive, we will be dead.

Major Malenkov assures us that they do not hurt old people. If we remain quiet and do not shelter German combatants, we will not be harmed. But Frau Heinrichs cannot help herself, she gestures to our cowering people and begs him— Last night seven soldiers broke in, see, the door, the ceiling—and I have to remind her in German not to ask or offer anything beyond what he said, only short answers.

Malenkov is looking at me too sharply. Both Sister Erika and I have pulled worn shawls tight over our hair, we stand as bent as sticks but we dare not overdo it, we cannot hide our skin or eyes. Then, his Russian so unthreatening and cultured that in civilian life he might well be a professor, he tells us he knows how we are suffering, war is horrible for everyone, and especially for the aged, but the front will have moved past in two days and we will be in the excellent care of the Red Army. They are unstoppable, and he will leave orders we are not to be bothered by anyone, not for food or anything else, nothing. He will post a guard at our door. Frau Heinrichs is overjoyed, she and all the others pour out their thanks as he gestures his two glowering, helmeted louts out ahead of him. When he turns to go, he smiles directly at me, and I'm certain my face betrays to him my knowledge and my great fear.

True, the louts are at the door when I venture out with my shawl and water pails. One even opens the door when I return, but I know their young, starved eyes have followed me every step as if

I, draped as I am, were a recovered memory, a village mirage in this filth and blood—look, a woman walking with water pails!—in the boredom and abrupt brutality they live day after day.

"We thank God, oh, we thank You for this safe day," Sister Erika says at evening devotions, and immediately they all together begin to thank so deeply, so pathetically, even unknowing Taunte Gertrude, their frail voices staggering away into exhausted repetitions most of them have been sighing all day long.

"Our ancient Sisters and Brother of Perpetual Prayer," Erika whispers to me on the floor. "God will answer them, certainly."

We lie warm against each other; I cannot speak for fear. The water barrel is full but my shoulders and arms have lost every sensation except ache. Perhaps, like my father, an arm gone could still save me? Or better, a leg? No, no, a one-legged woman would be worse—no, if I could find words, could somehow explain to my father now, as he once explained to me the immense land of Russia, which since the eighteenth century gave us Mennonites shelter and allowed us to build our colonies into wealth and comfort. Russia, its incomprehensible variety and traditions of peoples, its long, violent history of unimaginable riches and beauty and power for a few and slavery for all the others.

Listen, Papa, a woman with one leg, two legs, no legs, any limb you have or don't have means nothing. With a gun barrel in my ear I have seen babies and grandfathers and great-grandmothers sodomized by a regiment—listen, the brute beasts would not do what I have had to see men do. War drives men together, it drives them into violence beyond themselves. You can be killed in an instant, so when you have the power you carve it into the body of your enemy with every brutality you have learned. Revenge. The Tatar who broke down our door knew that, straight from his Mongol ancestors who rode their horses from China to the walls of Vienna, piling human heads up in pyramids long before we Mennonites existed.

Yes, my father would say. Power forced onto, into your body. This soldier began by assaulting you with surprise, by threat and the explosion of gunshots. He clubbed you with the knowledge, "I will do what I want to do." Then his officer comes in, polite, humane, and you think perhaps...but you know that Tatar learned those German words only because some educated officer like Malenkov taught him. Taught him to say what he has already known for seven hundred years: Violence breeds hate, and hate grinds slowly, but steadily, into fear, and fear driven by time grinds ever finer, into revenge. Do you understand, my dearest Elizabeth Katerina?

Yes, Papa. Now, please, can I see a picture?

Which one?

Of Enoch and Abel, my beautiful brothers. Not where they are four and six and looking from under broad, black-brimmed hats, their small hands clutching the railing of a fake bridge set over a stream that does not exist on your sunny studio floor; not the picture where they sit in a cardboard boat with sailor hats to sail across a paper-painted sea, no, show me the sweetest portrait of all, the one I watched you and mother arrange so carefully, together. There is a background of bushy shadow on the right, and wide scrolled and flowered steps leading upwards, left. Enoch, aged three, stands in his striped summer shirt and shorts looking into the distance while he holds the large china family chamberpot at his side. And just under his gaze, facing into the camera and bare to the waist, beautiful Abel, aged one, sits with

his chubby legs bent, on the smaller, rounder chamberpot that
was first mine, then Enoch's and now his, Abel's eyes so enormous
and his face as blank and perfectly sad as any small animal's—O
my brothers, O Enoch, O Abel, Abel, my lost brother Abel....

The next morning, January 28, there are no guards at the
door and the cloister across the street is on fire. When the elderly
caretaker couple and their lay brother appear at our door with six
girls in nuns' habits huddled between them, Erika just says, "Come
in, quickly quickly," and leads them down into our crowded room.
We have opened the two small windows that face back into the
yard, the outside air is freshening the room a little, though it drives
in the cold as well and our old ones cannot endure that for long.
Erika crowds all nine newcomers into the corner opposite the door,
and then arranges our people in a half-circle close in front of them.

Our dear ones sagging so close together on chairs, their old
bodies swollen, twisted with labour and motherhood and age,
shaking, some so sadly bewildered.

"Good," Erika says to our hidden guests, "I can't see you,
nothing at all. But you must try to stop crying, you cannot make
a sound, if someone comes in you must not cry."

After some time they do. In fact, no one comes down the
stairs all day, and from the sounds outside, the bombardment and
return fire from the castle—even in the cellar I recognize the
sound of each different weapon—the chaos of grinding war
occupies everyone. We eat our small supper of bread and canned
fruit. We light a candle and set it on the table. Sister Erika, our
"dear angel from God" as Taunte Gertrude croons to her, lays
her Bible in the warm yellow light and stoops over it, her hands
folded against her forehead. My father and mother never
designed a picture more moving.

The street door crashes open above us. The couple, the six girls and the lay brother sink to the floor as we shove our chairs closer around to shield them. But we need not have scrambled so fast; whoever has entered, and there are at least ten or twelve of them, they are first destroying what is left of the upper house. They come down the steps and we shrink together in terror, but someone smashes the door to our cellar food storage and we hear them laughing, yelling, glass shatters, shelves crash. Sister Erika looks at me with a little hope; perhaps in stuffing their bellies they will forget us. But I am cursed with Russian, I understand their obscenities.

They are in our room, yelling as if drunk, our food dribbling out of their hands and mouths and drunk on themselves, shoving each other aside with a violence that cannot wait to hit another body. And there is a leader, there always is one who can beat the others into silence. He is the one who first bellows:

"Woman, come here!"

An essential element in Red Army training for invasion: to say those German words. Say them not like sounds that are memorized, but horribly. The way a man who with fists and feet has beaten a woman to the edge of senselessness will lean down and say, "Now I'm gonna fuck you." Trained to say them as often as they can, in any circumstance, until, when the war is finally over, the uncomprehending children of tens of thousands of mothers enduring in refugee camps will play at what they have seen so often, as naturally as they play at washing clothes or making mud pies or church singing. "Woman, come here!"

We had only one mercy: there were no children in our room. But the girls who had once prayed to be nuns were there, and our old ones' desperate attempt to shield them with their ancient bodies did not last through the second night. The next morning at daybreak, the elderly couple led the girls out onto the street as massive air bombardment began smashing the castle. They had come, they had been violated, they were gone in the hopeless ways of war.

But their lay brother, Karel, remains with us. He carries in water and charred wood from ruins for our stove; no soldier accosts him. Our old ones are more loving than ever, though not even Frau Heinrichs has a voice to sing and some can barely murmur prayers. They lie twisted with age and despair on straw beginning to rot, but several are strong enough to help us clean. Those who can do no more than sit form circles of chairs so that Erika and I can wash and wash ourselves behind their backs. Warm, clean water, when a handful of it touches you for an instant you feel and remember nothing, white as snow. Frau Heinrichs untangles our hair, and coils it into clean, tight knots the way Gnadenthal Grandma Katerina always wore hers; I brushed it for her when I was little and when I was grown, she was so patient as I brushed it to the long curls that fell below her waist. Erika and I tie our shawls tighter and work, work. We can no longer fall into the brief oblivion of sleep.

"What is Russian for 'kill me'?"

"*Ubeyte menia.*"

We both say it, but they won't. Every evening and any time in the afternoon the soldiers come with their horrible mouths and raw, pointed bodies. In the cold, early morning darkness of the floor our skin can endure no touch, we can only tell each other everything we promised a lifetime ago, our lives as they reappear to us splintered, remember, we talk and listen at the same time, she about her golden summer life growing on their

Herrenhagen estate which the Wiebes first dammed and built out of the marshes between the Nogat and the Vistula, and I about my family millennia ago in Russia, green Gnadenthal and the bright studio and the terror of the flight to Moscow and the return, the village of Susanovo, Orenburg, and collective farms and purges where not even my father's missing arm could save him, nor Enoch either, and to Gnadenthal again, me alone with Grandma Katerina, alone in devastated Gnadenthal after the Wehrmacht tanks came and the Ukrainians and Russians fled. But we Mennonites were Germans, we welcomed them.

Erika clutches me, beyond terror now.

"Did you have a child?"

"It was dead. It will always be dead."

My grandmother's flowing hair, the stone-and-wood bridge on our village street, over water running clear between tall grass and over stones like glass, there is more than can ever be said. We understand each other's stories, which we have never heard before, as clearly as if we were falling into a lake of warm, clean water, which is all we long for, warm, clean, hidden.

Father, show me a picture.

Which one, sweetheart?

You know, you know.

You made me laugh, he says, laughing. So hard I shook the camera under the hood. You and Greta Isaak were perfect slender young men in trousers and tied cravats, flat-brimmed hats, pince-nez and twirled moustaches, superb, she in black, stood leaning towards you in grey, seated in the round-backed chair with your left leg perched at the ankle on your right knee, each of you with a long cigarette elegantly between your fingers, rolled paper actually, such beautiful young men.

Greta Isaak. If Sister Erika Wiebe, our Herrenhagen cousin seven or eight generations removed, had known of us to visit in Gnadenthal in 1917, she could have been the third, slightly younger young man in the picture.

But this is 1945. I pray that Greta Isaak, now Penner, is somewhere safe in Germany with her four children, but our "dear angel from God" grew too gently into caring middle age on her family's estate; for her to endure, my few whispers of war training could not be enough.

On the fourth night, a man's sudden scream. Twisting into a howl, Russian bellows, a shot. Someone has been stabbed, cut deep. Someone tears himself out of me. Boots pound, blunder away. When I can, I crawl through the destroyed house, feeling through the debris until I find her bloody body. I touch a bullet hole high in her temple, and her face below her eyes crushed as if a tank had ground into it. Or boots.

Frau Heinrichs brings me sheets, still warm, and I wrap her body, and myself. Karel helps me carry her into our room. We huddle against her, weeping. It is some time before we realize Major Malenkov is watching us from the doorway.

I tell him in exact Russian that we need none of his soldiers to dig her grave. But the ground of the convent churchyard is frozen too hard for us: Karel and I can only cover her shroud with rubble in a corner of the burned ruins.

The next day two carts pulled by six bony horses hitched Russian-style were at our door, with a single driver. It was the young Tatar. He said he had orders to move us, the Red Army front was coming through. In bitter cold we loaded our old people and what food and bedding we could, but two were unconscious even before we crossed the Nogat River in a rowboat. There were no bridges left, and when we reached Damerau on the east bank of the Vistula two days later, four of them had died.

The Tatar drove one team, I the other, and even in the destroyed, flooded and frozen country of the Werder he was very good at keeping starving horses alive. He had Malenkov's orders to take us where we wanted to go, so in Damerau I told him we were turning north to Danzig. He laughed at me, the city was still held by the Wehrmacht!

Exactly, I said. And if you get rid of your uniform, I'll help you disappear among a million refugees, you can leave Stalin's paradise and find a new life, that's what war is for, so young men can see the world and escape to America.

He laughed again, but differently. I knew he could not believe a world existed where no one would order his obedience, but what he said was why would he desert his comrades, with whom he could kill Germans and fuck their women? So I said tomorrow he should help me drive our wagons as near to Danzig as he dared—the city was only thirty kilometres away—and then he could go back to his regiment. In return, he could fuck me all night.

That puzzled him. "Why would I do that?" he said. "I know you."

There were no bridges left undestroyed over the Vistula either, but we found a Pole with a scow and a long oar and we traded him the two best horses for it. As the current caught us, we saw Onkel Johann hunched up high against the top board of the scow and the Tatar and I scrambled to help him. When I took his arm, he said, "No...no." His eyes were shut, he had seen enough of the world, so I touched his soft, wrinkled cheek and we turned away. When I looked down again, he was gone, and in the February light the wide river seemed to be grey ashes, boiling.

Karel disappeared in Danzig, but I and six of the Marienburger women, including Frau Heinrichs and Taunte Gertrude, survived all the "friendly" and "unfriendly" bombing—there was no difference in what they did—until the Soviet army finally overran the city on March 29. By then we were far from the main front and out of the city, behind a disintegrating wall of Wehrmacht backed against the Bay of Danzig where tens of thousands of us refugees were crammed along the sandspits. Ships could still reach the temporary docks and boats there, to try and ferry us to Denmark. On April 16, the *Goya*, the fastest ship on the sea, they said, returned for her fifth evacuation. We watched two Russian planes attack her coming in, and she was hit, but the planes were driven off and the fires put out. Loading began immediately. I got my six dear women hoisted aboard, and within two hours saw the ship cast off with thousands of people packed tight on every level and hunched shoulder to shoulder on the deck. Two minesweepers formed her convoy and we watched as she rounded the peninsula of Hel and disappeared, thousands of us left behind, crying aloud in despair.

For two months I had scrounged for food while Danzig was destroyed. The spring weather had warmed into a fiercer assault of unfound bodies rotting along the footpaths worn between and over the ruins, the collapsed, roofless walls of the Long Market, the Church of St. Catherine, the old docks along the Granaries. Only the massive tower of the Church of St. Mary and the beaked harbour crane at the Krahntor stuck up high into the air, but you dared not walk near them, stones and slabs of brick would unexpectedly come hurtling down. For centuries Danzig's walls had defied attack from land and sea, but attack from the air was too much; the stone ruins stood like broken sticks, crushed paper along the very slopes of the Bishop's Hill. In all my searching I found nothing of Adam Wiebe's original walls. The great city had been smashed, the thousands of dead beneath the rubble drifting away as stench in the spring air.

The ruins of Marienburg Castle on the Nogat were, of course, occupied by the Red Army when I returned, but there were more than enough cellar holes in the town to shelter me. It was after I had uncovered Sister Erika's body and reburied it properly in the earth of the churchyard that I heard the rumour: at midnight on April 16 two Russian submarine torpedoes had hit the *Goya*; it sank in seven minutes. Fewer than two hundred people were recovered alive from the icy Baltic Sea, over seven thousand drowned in the worst marine disaster in history.

I stand at the grave of my friend and speak the names I know aloud over it:

"Gertrude Dyck, ninety-one
Agnes Heinrichs, eighty-seven
Margareta Fast, eighty-one
Johanna Fieguth, seventy-nine
Anna Claassen, seventy-eight
Maria Isaak, seventy-two."

And I remember the Vistula scow. The river will have taken him down to the sea as well, and I say:

"Johann Isaak, seventy-four years."

Tomorrow I will go in search of Herrenhagen, if it can be found on the flooded Werder. If there are dikes visible above the water, it will be no more than twelve kilometres. If the Tatar survives to march through the rubble of Berlin with his comrades, he is certain to be arrested and shot for helping us, briefly, escape. And the implacable Russian comrades will very soon discover me, and I too will be arrested. I may yet, as my father said, make a tour of Siberia in a cattle car. Or of frozen Vorkuta.

Carefully I smooth the surface of Erika's grave out of existence. Under my hands the soft, enduring earth. Then I take out her small Bible, which I took from under her shroud, hold it tight and say aloud, as well I can:

> "When the Lord brings back the captives to Zion,
> we will be like them that dream."

Father, show me a picture.

The summer picnic on the banks of the Dnieper River. Mother, on the right in her broad hat and long white dress, leans back against the cliff; your five friends lounge on the grass and against the rocks between you; and you sit on the left by the basket, the picnic blanket and the samovar. Everyone except you holds a glass, lifting them towards you as if in a toast. Father, why are you holding a guitar, the fingers of your right hand curled as if you were playing it? Did you, could you ever, play the guitar? Sing?

But he does not answer me. Finally I must continue for myself. I tell him: I am in the picture too, even if no one—not you, perhaps not even Mama—knows it. I am there below her heart, hidden, untouchable, safe.

SEVENTEEN

IN THE EAR OF THE BEHOLDER

Toronto

1992

ON THE TELEVISION SCREEN between the opened cupboard doors a gaunt woman and a very stout man are explaining why John F. Kennedy could not have been killed in the way the Warren Commission reported he had been. Adam is, as usual, clicking through the channels to avoid boredom and himself when this passing image—such an amateurish home video, two motionless people pinned behind a table scruffed with papers, talking—stops him in mid-click. He is already three channels past when those two plain faces twitch him back, a memory of a word, their—what is it?—their TV-unnatural normality?

A diagram fills the screen: a side view, a line of dots plotting the flight of Magic Bullet. That is its name now, the man's voice-over explains, "Magic Bullet": it was the first bullet—not the actual killer bullet—fired from Lee Harvey Oswald's rifle, and it must have gone in six different directions, first through Kennedy and then through Texas Governor Connelly, to end up resting in

Connelly's left thigh, though it was not found there. The dotted line shows it caroming about, thud thud thud—off what, political flesh hardened into high-office stone?—and then the camera shifts to an overhead view of the necessary trajectory: the bullet, moving from president to governor, ignoring completely the tender proximity of the presidential lady, must also have hunched itself sideways at least 1.7 feet to orchestrate all those wounds—seven in total, entrance and exit—before bursting from the two men, and gone.

Apparently not quite. The screen cuts to Magic Bullet itself, in extreme close-up, a picture never shown in the *Warren Commission Report*. After smashing through Kennedy's neck and into Connelly—his chest, ribs, arm and finally wrist—this bullet had come to rest in the flesh of Connelly's thigh. Job done. Perhaps because of its miraculous changes in direction, it also revealed itself quite unmarked when it was discovered—the doctors found only its final, and empty, hole in Connelly's thigh—on the Dallas Hospital floor an hour later, fallen from no one knew which, if any, stretcher; perhaps someone had stepped on it.

Quite unmarked. O marvellous Magic Bullet, flying destruction everywhere without killing. Described in the *Report* signed by the Chief Justice of the Supreme Court of the United States of America, Earl Warren himself, and six others as: a bullet. The most venerated of American death-dealers, the perfect solution so every TV crime problem could end on the hour with ads included; but no solution here.

Lovingly the male voice lingers over the image of that bit of lead, a faint gleam along its right side—such blunt photographic silence—framed on blank paper. The voice grows profoundly deep when recalling the entire century now nearly completed, approaching the millennium and every trace of humanity anywhere on the globe: the greatest, the mostest— more than the World Series and Oscars and Super Bowl combined?—this simple made-in-the-USA mail-order lead bullet that has become the unfathomable mystery of the century. Icon forever. And suddenly washed over by a long skiff of laughter.

As if he had laughed himself. Adam has dropped the book he held, though the remote control seems still in his right hand. He can feel it.

The gaunt woman is talking now. Seated with calm, number confidence beside the man who explained the inexplicable bullets, she is listing the names, ages, home addresses of witnesses and ever more volunteer witnesses. The unassailable TV evidence of numbers, running lists like accumulating weather, scrolling too fast to read but most irrefutably there. Five hundred and fifty-two in all, yes, every one of them, the names vanishing as Adam hears them explained: so many hundred-and-something witnesses who had been clustered around that corner of Houston and Elm where the motorcade turned in Dallas on November 22, 1963, and who had declared to someone or other that they wanted to testify to the Warren Commission, but only a small number (how many?) had actually been interviewed, most of them superficially, without tape recorder or even notes being taken; and of the five hundred an amazing percentage (how many?) were in 1992 already dead. More than a statistically probable percentage (how many more?) of these dead had died of non-medical causes: single-car accidents, suicides, fires, lightning or tornadoes; plane crashes, cave-ins; they dropped out and vanished untraceably even to their nearest families. Lloyds of London had calculated the odds of such a series of disappearances happening within thirty years to that number of persons gathered fortuitously in one spot as being in the range of seventeen trillion to one.

Who laughed? A TV audience unrevealed by the camera? Seventeen trillion was laughable, but one was not.

On the hotel bed, staring along his legs stretched towards the TV in its imitation oak cupboard, Adam thinks: vanishment. Also a decision.

No, forget that, shift the camera two inches from those two ordinary people talking and you'll destroy the illusion of what I believe I see, a shift to me sitting here, my possible cock a possible stick in my hand, as easy as the shift to the exact moment, the exact place where I first heard of that disappearance—no—of that shot.

Or three shots, as the Commission claimed. Or more than four, as various people, never officially believed, insisted. Oddly, on November 22, 1963, Adam was in the United States, at the University of Illinois completing a three-week seminar on endocrinology. He was talking to the senior professor in his office—an exchange of calm information between scientists who know everything they need to control their laboratory world, the complexities of hormonal secretions in Native North Americans, or Indians as they were then called, on U.S. reservations—when Adam's freckled lab assistant thrust her red head in at the door and gasped, "They have shot my president!" Just like that: "*They* have shot *my* president," and fled, sobbing.

He smiled then, stupidly, puzzling whether this might be a new student joke; perhaps he even laughed. Though he could not forget his first clear thought: You Americans! You'll try to make an Abraham Lincoln out of a photogenic president even if you have to murder him. His American colleague stared at him; he must have laughed, or worse, spoken aloud. He knows for sure he stood in the crowded residents' lounge watching small-screen history being fumbled about, summary and detail upon inconsequential detail in inconsequential repetition and the grey voice of Walter Cronkite; to see him remove his heavy glasses and glance up at a studio clock offscreen, to hear him say "...thirty-eight minutes ago," was to believe. Women and men and doctors and students alike were weeping aloud.

The ultimate TV murder, with the killer, including full-length and close-up photos, rifle and complete U.S. Marine biography, revealed on the screen within three hours. Not to miss the New York evening news? And formally charged at 1:30 in the morning local time, November 23. Adam's flight home arrived in Edmonton just in time for him and Susannah together to see the show continue, with Lee Harvey Oswald murdered on TV between two policemen. She had bought their first set because, Susannah told him, she didn't want to miss the funeral.

We made naked love that night, Adam remembers suddenly, on the rug in the bathroom with mirrors standing on the floor all around us. As if to replicate at least our bodies into infinity.

Now only a book lies beside him on the hotel bed. Where it fell from his left hand: *A Gun for Sale*. It first appeared that afternoon in a box of books he pulled out from under a rummage sale table in the Bloor Street United Church Hall, still spine-coded G 311 but stamped all over in capitals DISCARDED from the George Brown College of Applied Arts and Technology Library, Casa Loma Campus Library, Toronto, last Date Due Apr 1 1986. Six and a half years gone, a dog-eared orange-and-grey Penguin whose first words emerge out of forgotten distance like an intimate, ghostly voice:

> Murder didn't mean much to Raven. It was just a new job. You had
> to be careful. You had to use your brains. It was not a question of
> hatred. He had only seen the Minister once...an old, rather
> grubby man without any friends, who was said to love humanity.

The voice of a narrator invented by Graham Greene, fifty-six years ago. Speaking the strange enchantment only language can create out of fear and botched murder and luck, harelips and gas masks, a chorus-line dancer (such an un-Canadian Anne with an *e*) tied, gagged, and thrust up to die grotesquely in a fireplace chimney, but she doesn't die, tough chorus-line Anne apparently untraumatized by hours rammed up into sooty claustrophobia; an accumulating double hunt into the black hole of criminal and business and military and individual amorality. Subtitled "An Entertainment."

The short man behind the church hall rummage was labelled "Hello, my name is Arnold." Too close to mine for comfort, Adam thought. He stood holding *A Gun for Sale* against his chest, and it came to him like words in his ear: there will be other books for me here. And discovered his right hand already resting on one: *The Death of ADOLF HITLER / Unknown Documents from Soviet Archives*, by Lev Bezymenski. In perfect hardcover condition complete with somewhat ragged dust jacket, undiscarded and unmarked—no one, not even a library, would acknowledge owning such a book—available for one Canadian dollar. Between his fingers it opened like a trap: a black-and-white picture of a small, ghostly head, eyes shut and bruised mouth, held erect by rubber gloves cupping chin and hair, "Helga Goebbels after autopsy in Berlin-Buch." And on the facing page, "Corpses of Goebbels, his wife, and two of their children," this captioned upside down, so that the charred, horrible remains of the adults were at the bottom, the unburned children with their delicate hands and legs protruding from white nightclothes lay side by side at the top. The smallest was a tiny girl, her head tipped forward to reveal only her nose and dark lashes, her left foot bent shyly over her right.

The hubbub in the crowded church hall shifted like a shudder washing over Adam's body; as if every straggler and book lover stood motionless with him, an exploded book in their hands. The human animal run to ground.

"Quite a book, eh, for Wednesday?"

From his open mouth it seemed that Hello-my-name-is-Arnold had spoken. In a voice as small as a Canadian apology, but precise too, in the texture of his lumpy sweater. The small voice nagged at Adam along the dusty book spines crammed into boxes, in jumbled heaps on the folding tables more accustomed to serving coffee and day-old doughnuts to people hunching in from sleep somewhere under Toronto cardboard: Adam sensed he was standing on a book. Its edge slipped aside under his foot, and he kicked it away, anywhere.

"Remembrance Day I mean, next Wednesday, that beast"—gestured at the red, squared name.

"Oh...shouldn't insult the beasts." But Adam felt distantly stupid, he closed the book softly on the gruesome pictures as if they might crush. The small men of rummage sales should shut up and shuffle books, who wants to feel observed confessing their ashes there? It was enough to try and walk thoughtfully

down the north side of Bloor with November sunlight almost
warm off the brick and concrete walls with the careful, heaped
trash of transients buried in the corners of cemented parks, and
not be required to make a sound louder than breathing in a char-
ity hall or pretend there is a reason why you are in this enormous
city—where did Hello-Arnold get the gall to utter a word? Had
he made the mistake of catching his eye? Not consciously—
could you catch someone's ear? By the mere pass of hearing?

Adam was at the left corner of the cashier's card table with
his two books, and he laid them down, fumbled as if he were
looking for . . . and discovered himself bent over the wondrous
blank of romances. Tender pastel chapters always ending when
Eric's or whoever's hard but gentle hand just brushed Isabelle,
or whoever, at whatever sensitive place, oh, so gently. Shit—he
turned to see a dark, belted man who might at some point have
been standing beside him hand the Bezymenski book to the
cashier. Were there two? Or had he been spared? His own was
no longer on his small pile, gone, surely he could resist going
back to see if another one—his heart leaped quick as if he had
bolted oxygen. There was cosmic design, *I did not run to it, it
has been taken from me*, and in his hand he found another airbrushed paperback woman, one Regan O'Farrell to be exact,
bosom about to be undraped by Ashley Darlington Crockford
III in *Wildfire Dreams* by one Megan Flanders:

> Last evening, with one incandescent kiss, for one unending
> moment he had pressed her soft skin between his hard hands,
> against his steely body, and she had felt herself melt, spread wide
> and warm like the burning wax of a holy candle.

Good God, Regan, already on page 17? And with "this primal drive to fuse," on page 29, my my, how will you ever ("she knew he would lead the way") reach page 189 ("like the thrust of a glowing steel rod") unpenetrated? Try page 34: "First, we must be careful. Are you safe?" A psychological sheath.

Forever Romance number 5A3Z8. There was no one in front of the utterly young cashier, whose slim hand was pushing *The Death of ADOLF HITLER* aside. The belted man was gone, did not buy it. Perhaps he accidentally picked it up together with his own worn selections and, seeing it when he paid, said, "I don't want *that*." The cashier girl—too young to be tempt-able?—had pushed it behind various plastic containers of paper money rolled on edge, a huge map of coins spread at her fin-gertips. That's the way to treat money: stand it indistinguishably on edge in recycled plastic, dump it in a heap in front of you, all this careful ordering, this dedicated veneration of numbers and penny-counting taxes on every goddamn copper, throw it on a pile, pluck out what you need and finally scrape it all, paper, coins, plastic, dirt, off the table from too many dirty books into a sack—Adam put the books in his hands down, and placed Hitler on top.

"This one too."

"Great!" exclaimed the girl, unmolestably cheerful. She was a counter only, her unlabelled hands flew. "One dollar for the hardback one for two paperbacks two dollars in all thank you have a nice day!"

And no fourteen cents tax. He bobbed his head, trying to focus on her, but his bifocals fuzzed: to see her exactly he would have had to lift his glasses and bend to within eighteen inches of her good, round face, perhaps even take her by the shoulders and lift her firmly so his eyes—you could not touch a woman in public, especially a young woman. She wasn't even looking at him, it seemed her mouth actually meant what he heard. A nice day: I have no idea who you are and I don't want to know, just have one. It was only on the street that he saw the third paperback he had carried away, forgotten in his left hand: a dark, glowering bald face, by Roderick Stewart, *The Mind of Norman Bethune*. A book twice as big as the others, in fact, folio size.

Inadvertent theft, fifty cents; but he did not go back. His recognition of theft happened in the shadow of what was once spaced-out and blissful sixties Rochdale College, so what could one worn paperback matter? He almost laughed aloud: he was politically left correct, stealing Norman Bethune!

Adam sits on the hotel bed with his legs spread and glasses beside him, beside the spot of battered orange Greene, the afternoon light in blotches careening about the room. The steady TV drone of the stout man continues until Adam finds the mute spot at his fingertips and the sound fuzzes away as well. He remembers the venerable brick assemblage of Bloor Street United Church once overflowing in a good memorial service for the novelist Margaret Laurence. Why cannot goodness lurk between rummage books? Behind old brick and cracked concrete, in urine-soaked corners and around peeling trees grown lopsided with survival, why not that, waiting patiently through a January funeral to waylay you into purity and care and enduring compassion and reconciliation with at least the members of your own small family, goodness all humanity prayed for, blossoming inside you like pain before you were aware of it and could set yourself against its wilful seductions? He had always been a coward, always a fucked-up weakling about goodness. Disappearing into work or excuses or—hiding; if not in a blank then among the sadly forgettable dead.

He has already gulped Hitler to page 51, the indigestible brutality of Document 12:

Concerning the forensic examination of a male corpse...The remains...disfigured by fire were delivered in a wooden box... severely charred and smells of burned flesh...Height 165 cm. [5 ft. 4.35 in.]...On face and body the skin is completely missing.... Part of the cranium is missing.... Berlin-Buch, 8. V., 1945...In the upper jaw there are nine teeth connected by a bridge of yellow metal (gold).... The heart muscle is tough and looks like boiled meat.... The lower jaw consists of fifteen teeth, ten of which are artificial.... In the scrotum, which is singed but preserved, only the right testicle was found. The left testicle could not be found.... A smell of bitter almonds...The left foot is missing.

A male so far right as to have no left foot or testicle? Or left cranium? That actually made sense.

There is a knocking at the door. And again, like persisting memory. His door? No one knows he is here. Then the rattle of keys with another gentle knock makes it obvious, and he calls:

"Yes? Come in?"

He hears the door open; the hotel maid. The skin of her bare arms and her face is not quite as black as the stockings on her slender legs; her superb hair, if possible, blacker.

"Oh, I'm sorry. I'm just here to turn down your bed."

She may have said that. He is looking at her and after a moment she comes towards him, very close between the two queen-sized beds, and places a rectangle of silver-wrapped chocolate beside the telephone on the table nearest his elbow: two. Does she think he is expecting someone? She turns her back to him, lifts counterpane and blanket from the bed on which he is not sitting, folds it back triangular with one smooth motion to the white sheet, the white pillow; the pale skin of her inner fingers sharpens that edge straight at herself quick as a gesture.

Such bent textures of slender black; such tightness. There is a seam of her uniform tucked at her waist and he speaks to that.

Would you care to earn some extra money?

Her back straightens into an instant of hesitation, then she turns. The beds are so close he must very nearly touch her. Her right thumb and finger offer between them at the exact point of his shortsighted focus a plastic package. A condom.

You will have to include the 7 per cent Good Service Tax.

He swings his legs towards her and she is standing between his knees, so close his nose edges a button of her uniform. The uniform is buttoned grey up between her breasts to the dark vee of her neck, down the middle between her thighs, one straight line up and down, five buttons only for easy egress, ingress, aggress, under her fingers they are slipping open, top to bottom, he does not need to move his head, he can hear it, and she wears nothing underneath, he can hear it, only the pantyhose, black textures changing in the light tighter than glistening skin; her body absolutely there. As it of course always has been, somewhere.

We carry within us the wonders we seek without us: there is all
Africa and her prodigies in us.

The full white goodness of Sir Thomas theological Browne. Adam sees his own pale hand gesture and she shifts slightly, aside, and with long fingers (the plastic still gripped between the thumb and finger of the right) widens the pantyhose elastic out at her waist, slides them down over her hips, down her long legs, together with the shoes off her feet, first left then right.

Is there anything else?

Her endless skin laid it seems against his very eyes. He tries to tilt back, to see her face and she is towering so valley and hill over him that he cannot decipher his thoughts—nor does it matter since she is already doing what he would want to imagine were he capable of it: an ineffable movement of her arms lifts both her hands to her breasts, pushes them up so that the nipples beak forward, and her breasts are so full and her neck so long that if she bowed her head over him she could curl her moist tongue around either nipple, whichever she chose, it is as if she spoke these impossible possibilities into his very eyes, numbered them in his ears.

Everything else?

His senses stagger, perhaps he is tilting, but her hands continue to push her breasts up, and they are completely distorted now, they are being lifted from her ribs, she is slipping them up past her face like a knitted sweater, over her head and she drops them behind her without a sound, her hands quick as water flowing down her skin and stripping off her hips and buttocks, the hollow between her thighs, the backs of her legs (that little safety plastic flickering) and her hands rise to her belly, her groin, the black centre of her curled mons, which ever since she turned to him has always been there and a tongue-length from his face, and it is gone: she is become the thing itself. And once her dreadful hands reach her exquisite face, who could say she is there at all. This poor, bare, forked animal.

"Anything else I can do for you, sir?"

She stands at the door. It may be that Adam shakes his head. When the door sighs and clicks shut he glances at the bed for whatever she has stripped off and left behind. Nothing.

On the screen of the cupboard TV the woman and the man still sit motionless and silent, though talking. The electrical box can offer Adam any number of backs, faces, breasts, hands, bunched buttocks, nipples, knees, cunts, elbows, hair, thighs—in Canadian hotels all possible human parts are now available except entering cocks and assholes—bodies in whole or in part moaning with relentless endurance hour after hour, airbrushed colour nothing at all like these patterns of shade and density that solidify Blondi's German shepherd corpse, the dog that belonged to the German Shepherd, their leader, guide, chief, commander—god. Following the six white and grey and black Goebbels' children: Hilde, Helmut, Holde, Hedda, Heide, Helga, all H in honour of His Inexpressible H-ness and falling into their last sleep with the Third Reich prayer caught in their teeth:

Händchen falten,
Köpfchen senken,
Und an Adolf Hitler denken.

Fold your little hands, Bow your little heads, And think of Adolf Hitler. No rhyme or reason in English. All the parts of the children so carefully dissected by Soviet forensic officers, two lieutenant-colonels and three majors: each child brain, tongue, lungs, heart offering up the smell of bitter almonds.

And glass splinters in every small mouth. A few corpses among those European mountain millions, the few he has himself held living and dying; his own. These six so harmless, and with four inexpressibly harmful adults proving what everyone already knows: that a human body will burn only badly and in part, unless placed, or piled if necessary, inside a scientifically designed and properly fuelled oven. Or chained individually over or inside carefully stacked, carefully split and tended wood.

Adam's stomach heaves, a pathetic exorcism of bile and revulsion. He is staring at the other bed, folded triangular and crisp to its white sheet.

Under the other books, beside him, lies the biggest: the one he inadvertently carried away from the church hall. Susannah would say, That's you, your subconscious would pick up the glowering, almost devilish book-face of Norman Bethune: a man vaguely known to some as good, though continually and throughout his life an egotistical bastard. Well, Adam would respond, not according to Chairman Mao. What did Mao know, he only met Bethune once and never answered a single letter he wrote. Okay, but he did sacrifice himself when no one, not even a state, demanded it of him, rich as he could have been. Maybe because he knew he was dying. We all know that. I mean, he was sick. Maybe, but that's better than becoming worse, the way men usually do when they face death, apparently he became better and better as his blood circulated rot through his body from the gangrene that entered at the bare tip of his finger. That's the official record, it could as easily have been the bare tip of his cock, would you say if a man is in pain and dying at his farthest extremities long enough, slowly enough, does gathering goodness at last become a possibility, mould you eventually into a good wholeness? Not a Hitler, he came apart piece by piece, hair, teeth, brain, and he just got worse. All that, with only one testicle to begin with, are you having death pains?

Stretched on the bed, Adam has to laugh; he could tell her no, not in his testicles. Nor anywhere else, not yet, though it's inevitable. Pain, in the enervating comfort of a Toronto hotel where a tall woman has just turned down his bedding and left him two exquisite chocolates: he feels blank and alone, but—unfortunately—he knows from long experience this is no pain unto death. Nothing possible at his fingertips in this oblivious room will make him, or anyone anywhere, any better. But if Susannah were actually here, stretched on this bed with him, or humming in the bathroom—or Trish in the connecting room, or Joel—there are people he knows in Toronto, women and men, but this trip, however many days it may be, is simply one of his *blank moves*, to keep it that way he should have gone to a musical, or a comedy. A ridiculous movie with John Candy. Or run to China.

He could have, he should have run to China himself for the Great Leap Forward, and shown Chairman Mao what another dedicated Canadian doctor could do in a Revolution, cultural this time, summer 1965. He was exactly the right age for the sixties, not yet thirty, he could have been politically and medically ready—but he was married, Susannah was about to give birth to Trish, he was creating a life's career out of medicare. A liberated Mennonite choosing culture and revolution when he might be working like a dog to make himself rich? Trish once asked that, almost.

Lucky Bethune. Inheriting class and wealth, plenty of lovers, smart, a failed marriage quickly over, no children, three highly acceptable revolutions to escape to in a decade, Russia, Spain, China, all of them marvellously far from home and family, on opposite turns of the globe actually, and in languages you fortunately cannot speak: you feel good about "saving lives," so called, treat as many wounded soldiers as possible and send them off healthy enough to kill again. Then from the isolated Wu T'ai Mountains of China, August 21, 1938, you can write at last:

> I don't think I have been so happy for a long time. I am content. I am doing what I want to do. Why shouldn't I be happy—see what my riches consist of.... Here are found those comrades whom one recognizes as belonging to the hierarchy of Communism—the Bolshevists. Quiet, steady, wise, patient; with an unshakeable optimism; gentle and cruel; sweet and bitter; unselfish, determined; implacable in their hate; world-embracing in their love.

Write so peacefully about trained and blooded killers; whose hatred and love, gentleness and cruelty conceived dreams to rule the world and all the people in it. Chairman Mao at their head, with no more discernible a trace of conscience than Genghis Khan. Abruptly the deftness of Bethune's scalpel is so temporary, his disordering of the alphabet too masterfully contrived, as any doctor would recognize: "How beautiful the body is; how perfect its parts; with what precision it moves; how obedient; proud and strong. How terrible when torn." When burned, beautiful? "The little flame [!] of life sinks lower and lower, and, with a flicker, goes out.... Like a candle goes out. Quietly and gently. It makes its protest and extinction, then submits." Huh!

...Four Japanese prisoners. Bring them in. In this community of pain, there are no enemies. Cut away that blood-stained
uniform. Lay them beside the others. Why, they're as alike as
brothers!...

What is the cause of this cruelty, this stupidity? A million
workmen come from Japan to kill or mutilate a million Chinese
workmen...Will the Japanese worker benefit by the death of the
Chinese? No, how can he gain?... Then, in God's name, who will
gain? Who will profit from it? How is it possible to persuade the
Japanese workman to attack...his brother in poverty; his compan-
ion in misery?

God, gain, profit. Even Bethune dying could not escape
that prayer of excuses. As if Bethune already anticipated Mao's
coming manias when he at last totally controlled the Chinese, his
behaviour thirty years later indistinguishable from any horror
the Japanese perpetrated. Well, distinguishable perhaps because
it was worse, since no stranger, no matter how sadistic, can ever
hurt a race—or a family—as deeply as one of its own members.

But of course in spirit Bethune can insist all men are brothers, so he can go to China and be good enough to die, can go
there and be good enough to watch: what is happening there is
not happening to him though of course he understands and sym-
pathizes so deeply—Adam sees himself briefly in Illinois that
convulsive November, 1963, and knows in a rasp of sarcasm he
is rethinking himself—from far away I can always write lone-
somely home even though when I am home I cannot endure half
the silly bastards who imagine they are my friends simply because
they knew me once, but cannot imagine what I am become. If,
now, I am any more than bits and pieces of something at any

given time. And I can run anywhere I choose in the world, to the Wu T'ai Mountains of China, now that I have heard of them, but I can't drive down the highway from Edmonton to Calgary and knock on the house door of the woman to whom I am still legally married, and when she opens it, touch her, with either a word or a gesture.

The electronic shimmer of her voice, my voice, occasionally meeting. No touch. Our son left, our daughter gone; the mirrors of the past refuse to break.

What is the matter with me?

The TV mouths move without visible emotion, still presumably explaining why a weak-minded man like Lee Harvey Oswald, who in a short life had been used by everyone he ever met—and by so many organizations, both illegal and official, both in the United States and in the Soviet Union and perhaps even in Cuba and Mexico—how such a slight man, acting alone, could not possibly have conceived and carried out the assassination of the most carefully guarded man in the world with such brilliant and untrackable success. The fact that he happened to be working, temporarily, on the sixth floor of the Texas Book Depository was as unlikely as his being able to fire three shots, or four, with such accuracy at a target moving away from him, from a bolt-action rifle in less than six seconds, the last shot blowing John Kennedy's head apart so that Jacqueline Kennedy's first instinctive reaction, her mouth open in unutterable scream, was to scramble onto the trunk of the Cadillac and gather up the bloody pieces. The scientific question was: would those skull pieces land on the trunk *behind* them if the killer bullet came from *behind* the car?

The stout man and the gaunt woman behind their table are

saying this. In a thousand repetitious ways. Adam does not need to hear them, their motionless bodies a cipher of invisible words. The room he sits in is as blank as a room in any enormous city can be: a faint utterance of traffic, of plumbing, of heating: the white noise of twentieth-century indolence ending. Nothing is here for tears, nothing to wail, nothing but tremors of sad memory. Avoid the worst, as always, as you can; find void.

Television lumbers on in its unstoppable chronology of bits and pieces. That is what Adam has always loved about books, their singular and un-timebound discreteness. Lovely to hold complete in your hand: beginning, middle, end, and return to any one, any time, anywhere, as you please. Totally here now, no mirrors necessary. Adam holds them, thus:

The Death of ADOLF HITLER:
The corpse is that of a girl appearing to be about 15 years old, well nourished, dressed in a light-blue nightgown trimmed with lace. Height: 1 m. 58 cm. [5 ft., 1.6 in.] Chest measurements on the nipple line—65 cm. [25.4 in.].... No signs of use of violence on the body surface.... In the mouth... glass splinters.

The Mind of Norman Bethune:
Comrade Bethune's spirit, his utter devotion to others without any thought of self, was shown in his great sense of responsibility in his work and his great warm-heartedness towards all comrades and the people.... I am deeply grieved over his death. Now we are all commemorating him, which shows how profoundly his spirit inspires everyone. We must all learn the spirit of absolute selflessness from him. (Mao Tse-tung, Yenan, December 21, 1939)

Wildfire Dreams:...what does an idiot romance know of fire? Not the cliché love image—the sheer fact of flame, a body searing into smoke and scream. Adam drops the book to the floor.

> *A Gun for Sale*:
> "Oh, I'm sorry," she said. "I've said it before, haven't I? I'd say it if I'd spilt your coffee, and I've got to say it after all these people are killed...." She began to cry without tears; it was as if those ducts were frozen....
> "All the same," Anne said, as Raven covered her with his sack: Raven touched her icy hand: "I failed."
> "Failed?" Mather said. "You've been the biggest success," and it seemed to Anne for a few moments that this sense of failure would never die from her brain, that it would cloud a little every happiness; it was something she could never explain: her lover would never understand it. But already as his face lost its gloom, she was failing again. ...

Adam places the "entertainment"—only in Greene-land would this book be called that—on the bed. He gets himself stiffly up from the rumpled counterpane and walks past the black, silent TV with all its trapped, unnecessary pictures—in which you can, nevertheless, still occasionally discover individuals who believe in planning their lives; who believe in responsible actions; who actually believe there are some decent people with some control of the world who know what they are doing and can make decisions. Who can somehow believe with their wavering Greek minds in a vaguely Hebrew god and hope for him too; hope he can help them decide for goodness.

The bathroom door, angled open, is all mirror. A man fills

it: the greyish tousled head, a white hotel dressing gown belted, two legs with feet slightly turned out.

Adam turns to the window behind him, and his hands—he knows them for certain—pull the curtains aside. All around him the stacked city burns in an unending light.

He thinks, This is safe. Like Greene's Anne, he thinks, Oh, I'm home. He should have left the books in Bloor Street United Hall, should have walked up the steps into the church nave of high windows and wooden balconies curved all around, where he could have heard the bagpipes enter wailing the pibroch, heard a low voice read what should have been said over the flowers of Margaret Laurence's memory: *How blessed are those who know their need for God, the kingdom of heaven is theirs*; heard the strange community of the tribe she drew together in her death sing "Come ye before him and rejoice." Like Laurence's Hagar he thinks:

Someone really ought to know these things.

Twenty-seven storeys below him a shadow moves along the base of the building. I failed. It seems he can hear footsteps; there may be a knocking at the door. Oh, I'm so sorry.

He touches the window with the coiled surface of his ear. It is there, it is cool.

EIGHTEEN

My Brother Vanya

Number Four Friedensheim,
Fernheim Colony, Paraguay
1980

ADAM WIEBE FROM CANADA is, as I tell him, my sort of lopsided double cousin: third cousin on the Loewen side, second cousin on the Wiebe. We laugh at that, and he tells me again he's a good listener, he didn't fly almost to the bottom of the world to hear himself talk. I tell him I've heard the world is round, and I think he's farther north than I am south, maybe it's he who lives at the bottom. We laugh again, there's so much to tell, ten days will hardly get us started.

"I was named David for my Grandpa Loewen when I was born on November 25, 1925. A Sunday, my mother said, in the Mennonite settlement north of the Russian city of Orenburg, the Communists changed that to Chaklov. In the village we called Number Eight Romanovka in honour of the Czar, long before Stalin murdered his way to power and tried to rename the whole world. Stalin had changed his own name. He was a

Georgian called Iosif Vissarionovich Dzhugashvili, and with a name like that maybe he would have lived as long as Georgians do, sometimes they say over a hundred years, but with the revolution and Moscow and power he only lasted seventy-three, not nearly long enough to murder and wreck everything he wanted, thank God; the air must be a lot worse in the Kremlin than in the Georgian mountain valleys. My mother, Maria, told me I was born so quick in the early morning my father would have had time to drive her and me to church in Number Five if they had still had a horse and wagon. Really, it was no wonder I came easy, she said, I was the last of eleven, though only six were living, including me.

"Orenburg Colony was once well-to-do, but after revolution and civil war, by the winter of 1925–26 no one in our villages had anything, my mother said, except empty bellies and dying children. There were too many of both, no one could have dreamed what the date of my birth would become for us in Paraguay. I don't know if Orenburg Mennonites had ever heard of Paraguay then, maybe not even of South America, but here the Mennonites have made November 25 the anniversary for all we have been forced to flee, and we celebrate it as the Thanksgiving Festival of our escape from Stalin in 1929 and a memorial to the thousands we had to leave behind, like her *Jahonn*, our father John Loewen warm in our hearts forever, with deep sorrow and sudden tears.

"I have no memory of seeing my father. None. Though I have tried, staring at the one picture we have of him. My first memory of anything is so clear it must be from before he disappeared, and so strange too I wondered about it for years and could never say a word, not even to my Leinchi when she held me in her arms, and still I thought about it. I finally recognized it when I sat at my mother's bedside when she was dying. That first memory came together with a second memory, where I'm very little and I'm in front of a woman in a dark dress sitting in a chair. She is holding a baby, and it's pressing its face against what I think is a smooth white melon that sticks half out of her open dress, and I ask her what the baby is doing and she says it's eating like babies do and I wonder, how can a baby eat a hard melon that way, and in winter, I have never seen this before though I have seen many babies. We're in the bedroom of our house with the winter coats of visitors piled on the bed, and I reach up and touch the top of the melon and it's not hard like a melon would be, but soft, warm like the porridge I touch with my fingers, skimmed over and waiting for me in a bowl sometimes in the morning, oh, I thought then, if only we could have porridge every day! And I say to her, it's you, the baby eats you! But she laughs, no, no, see, it drinks my milk, and she leans the baby's shiny head away and I see her dark nipple, a drop of white on the centre growing pale blue as the baby bursts out a roar, its hands clawing frantically and she clasps it against her again and its cries choke, it gurgles, I see its mouth clamped there into fast sucking. And I recognized my first memory only when it and the 'melon' came together—why could I never see that before? Isn't that crazy? My first memory was of my mother's breast?"

Adam Wiebe, my cousin but a stranger from so far away, has a quiet, listening, doctor's face. How can it be I have told him this, things no man would want to admit he could even think? But his expression, his eyes do not change, as if he understands there is more, and there is.

"Her breast, I mean my mother's, was not full like the

young woman I saw, I remembered only the fold of her skin moving under my eyes and my fist, and the thump of my face against the fold of it bumping on her ribs, memories so sudden as she lay there. I held her hand and cried, I couldn't explain myself with her on her last bed. You can't say that, to your own mother."

"Strange things," Adam says, "people think of beside deathbeds. Often wonderful things that comfort us."

His Lowgerman is all *n* endings like mine, a good Chortizer inheritance, but it sounds a little different, maybe that's why—Lowgerman brushed with stranger English—we feel easy together.

"My old mother," I say, "then talked mostly to me about their first year in Paraguay. She talked so much in the hospital, she never had before. But she wanted to tell me more, day after day, it was the heavy heat of January summer, 1967, but January in Orenburg was always cold, no one can imagine it living in Paraguay, with all the rivers ice and the ground hard as rock, and they were always hungry, those Soviet years before our father was gone. It was very heavy, what my mother had to carry over forty years and only silence could do it, she said. She tried to nurse me in Russia until I was almost two, tried with the little she had. The children before me, Peter and Anna, died before they were a year old during the civil war, and in summer 1925 our last cow died too and they had no money for another one, they could not even eat the meat, the cow was sick, so they gave it to the people who still had a pig to feed, and they had the last manure to dry and burn in the stove, and the cow leather that *mien* Jahonn as she always called him, 'my John,' and my oldest brother Vanya tanned and traded for grain they could grind into

porridge. That was what we ate that winter, oat and barley porridge and sometimes small cakes of it fried with a little fat.

"'You would be the last one, I always knew,' my mother said,
touching my head, her hand so twisted by arthritis and endless
work, and I, alone with her, strong and forty-two years old and
married with healthy children and usually enough to eat here
now, sometimes I couldn't stand the thought of her leaving us—
gone—I hid my face in her thin sheet so no one outside would
hear me cry. 'David, David, you were such a nice, heavy boy like
all the biggest Wiebes and thick Loewens, when we married we
trusted God would give us a strong family, and I told God He had
to let you live, grow up like Vanya, our strong Vanya.'

"My oldest brother was, as they said, such a 'Jahonn' he was
too much for a Mennonite name only, they had to call him something Russian too, happy and short. Vanya here, Vanya there, my
mother said; nothing on earth could discourage him, he was so
strong at fourteen. He and our father tanned cowhide for shoes
and then for several winters they steamed and pounded old cloth
and wool together into felt for boots and the summer before I
was born they set up a press to make sunflower oil, first on a
treadmill with neighbour horses walking and next spring Vanya
drove a wagon to Orenburg and brought back a small steam
engine press, and the summer after that they bought a threshing
machine and then people planted more sunflowers and grain for
our own food. The village and the whole colony too were slowly
living a little better after years of barely starving, but Lenin was
dead and then the collectivization planners came to Orenburg in
1928 with Stalin's first Five Year Plan disaster. Well, by seeding
time next year our father was gone, my twenty-one-year-old
brother was left the man in the family and he came to her quietly

and said, 'Mama, what do you think? Do we have to get out, try to go to Canada? Onkel Nikolai Wiebe thinks we should all try, and Taunte Tien and her Abraham think maybe, too.'"

"Were those my parents?" Adam asks me. "In 1929, they knew when to leave, for Moscow?"

"Oh, they knew, by July '29 everybody knew. Your father Abraham Wiebe, my mother said, heard everything in the village and your mother could think quicker than a Jewish pedlar counting change. 'Vanya! Vanya!' my mother still wailed for her oldest on her last bed, though without a tear. Long ago she had cried enough forever in Paraguay, that was a knife through the heart, she said, but in '29 there was nothing left to do but try to leave, escape if they could. But how could she leave and not know to remember the place where her Jahonn was thrown away in a grave, to pray there and weep?

"Stalin's political police—the GPU—had come the night of January 3, 1929, and they hauled our father to Orenburg for questioning. And then he disappeared. Why? Even in those early days the Bolsheviks wouldn't explain anything. After bringing the oil press and the threshing machine into our village he could never be anything but a Rich Kulak, but when they took him it saved our family from the worst the Soviet Collectivization Committee could do, they didn't yet blame everyone in a family for what one person in it did, the way they did later. We would never be classified as the best, Poor Citizens, but with him gone and the oil press taken they registered us as Middle Citizens, which was not as bad as Rich Kulaks. But when we knew that's what they had done, my brother Vanya went one fall evening to the head of the local committee and told him we wanted to go to Moscow where over three thousand Mennonites were already trying to get out of the country. Vanya didn't say the word *Moscow*, of course, or that our Anna and her husband with his whole Peter Wiebe family and your parents, Taunte Tien and Onkel Abraham, with their family were in Moscow already. Vanya just said, 'You don't want us here, give us papers and we'll leave.'

"The head of the village *soviet*, the kolkhoz they called it, looked at him across the table, my mother said. Vanya didn't have to tell him anything more. He was our cousin Nikolai Wiebe, the same age as Vanya, twenty-two, we always called him our Kolya. They were friends, they grew up and went to village school together when there was one. Kolya was often a day worker in our oil press. He was as smart as any Wiebe ever was, the second son of the eighth son of old Foda Jakob Wiebe who was for twelve years the elected head of the whole Orenburg Mennonite Colony, and now Kolya was really lucky: his family was so very poor, but under the Communists he was named to a place on the other side of the big table, with all the heavy stamps and papers on it."

"So," Adam says slowly. "In '29 a Kolya Wiebe was head of the Communists in Number Eight Romanovka?"

"Yes, of the kolkhoz. The son of your father's youngest brother, Nikolai. Your first cousin."

"They knew how to break up families, didn't they."

"Better than anyone. They were really smart, like devils."

Adam is squeezing the orange I gave him from the tree under which we are standing in our orchard. At first he couldn't quite believe what he was seeing: a tree with shining new leaves that also had bright flowers and little green oranges and large yellow ones ripe enough to eat growing on it, all at the same time. I told him Paraguay offers very few miracles, but luckily those few have to do with things you can eat. He is quiet so long, I finally ask:

"Did your parents tell you how they went to Moscow? How they got out in '29?"

After a minute Adam says, "I don't remember very much, those stories, I'll talk to my mother again. I know two of my Wiebe uncles and their families were sent back from Moscow, back to Orenburg."

"Yes," I say when he stops. "Peter Wiebe and Nikolai Wiebe."

"Yes, I think so, but my father never spoke about them. He didn't want to. Once he said my older sister, Margaret, she was the baby then when they got out to Germany and the German refugee camp, she was always sick and no one could understand how their family was always stamped 'healthy' every time the Canadian doctors came around...though maybe they told me more, maybe I was too stupid to listen. I'll ask my mother now."

"Sometimes, in their old days, people can talk more."

This Adam Wiebe, only ten years younger than I, was by the grace and mercy of God born in Canada, and became a doctor. He has so much education and is so smart and rich he could probably be president of the whole country someday if he wanted to, they've never had a dictator like Paraguay. We hear Canada is very good for refugees, if you're smart and aren't lazy, they say, it's all easy there, just work.

"Those Canadian doctors must have been in Mölln," I tell him, "the refugee camp where the German and Canadian government people sorted them out, before the ships in Hamburg."

"You were there, you remember that?"

"I was four and always nice and sick for the Canadian

doctors too, my mother said, I..." And I have to laugh. "But no miracle like your sister Margaret! I made it easy for the doctors to say no, not into Canada. If I remembered any of that, fifty years of Chaco sun fried it out of me."

A good Mennonite joke and Adam laughs with me, he sometimes has a warm, even friendly face, if he wants to. He bites a small opening in the top of the orange he has softened and squeezes the juice into his mouth, sucking.

"This is really good," he says, "sweet and sharp. So, David, our cousin Kolya Wiebe was a Communist in '29, and all of a sudden he's the big Soviet boss in Romanovka?"

"I don't know if he was a Communist in his heart, but he worked for them. Lots of people did, what else could they do? Kolya was Nikolai Wiebe's son, and maybe he was the reason the Nikolai family got sent back to Orenburg from Moscow in '29, why they couldn't get away. In the summer when Kolya and my brother Vanya were schoolboys, they often herded the village cows far out on the Number Eight Hills that began south of the cemetery, the open steppe where there's nothing between the grass running in the wind as far as you can see all around you and blue heaven above. Maybe in the clouds they saw ships, or trains, or mills like Mennonites had always built, with giant sails turning in the wind to pump water over dikes or grind grain to feed everyone they knew in the twenty-three Orenburg Colony villages. Maybe they saw double-winged airplanes they thought they'd someday fly like birds in God's free air, but there was nothing Kolya could do about those heavy stamps he had to use. The orders that came with the bosses from Moscow were no better than boulders in the Little Uran River—if you couldn't find a way to flow around or between, you smashed into them.

"'I have no stamp that goes to Moscow,' Kolya told my brother.

"'Then give me a paper to visit our father's grave,' Vanya said, 'for the whole family.'

"My mother had been told that our father had been convicted of being a kulak and sent away. Just wait, Maria Abramovna, you'll hear how you can write to him. But we already knew from the families of two men in prison with him, one from Number Seven and the other Number Five, that they had both recognized our father's bloody face one morning in the Grey House on Kirov Street in Orenburg, where a sheet had fallen off one of the tables. In the cellar, they said, in the morning bodies often lay under sheets soaked with dried blood.

"I was three, and I can't remember him, nothing. We have only one small picture from Number Eight Romanovka. My father sits on the right and Vanya on the left, and between them are Mama and we four younger ones—the oldest, Maria, is not there, she's already married—with me, a little bald-head, sitting on my mother's lap. My father is fifty and almost as bald as I, only a line of hair above his ears, but my big brother has black hair cut so heavy it bristles thick as fur all over his long, gaunt head.

"Over the table Kolya said to Vanya, 'Only the GPU know, and they'll never tell you where the grave is.'

"'Is there one?'

"'My word, Vanya, I don't know. And I can't ask, especially about a relative.'

"'Then give me a paper.'

"'I told you, there is no place I can put on it.'

"'Well,' Vanya said, 'then we can look anywhere for the

grave. Just write, *The John Loewen family, mother Maria Abramovna Loewen née Wiebe, and her five children, six persons in all, has permission to visit the grave of their father, John Loewen.* Just stamp and sign it, that's all, no one can read your signature.'

"'The stamp says Orenburg, and a gun will stop you.'

"'So, the worst a gun can do is shoot us.'

"'No,' Kolya said. 'The worst is shove you all on a train going north to the Mezan River in the Vologda forests. Or worse, Vorkuta.'

"'You maybe too?'

"'Who can say.'

"In September, 1929, young Nikolai 'Kolya' Wiebe already knew so much, too much, and the stories we heard twenty years later from the refugees coming after the Second World War could only be true: before he was twenty-five, he had disappeared too."

"But," Adam says to me in my Paraguay orchard, "he gave your brother the papers to go?"

"He must have, we were in Moscow, and got out to Germany."

"And Kolya's family went too. Was he with them?"

"No, my mother said he wasn't. She never heard how the Nikolai Wiebes got there, but before November 25, the GPU sent them back to Number Eight Romanovka."

"The Peter Wiebes too."

"Yes."

From his face, suddenly, I know Adam knows more than he will tell me about our families. Like every one of us. After a moment he asks:

"And Vanya, how old did he get?"

"Not as old as Kolya. December 24, 1930, twenty-two years, eleven months, one day."

"But then you were already here, except your father, all safe in Paraguay."

"Safe from those Communists, yes, but there is still everything else on earth."

He says, strangely, "Always enough 'everything else' for Mennonites to keep on suffering."

I don't understand his tone. "It was typhus," I tell him. "In our first year in the Chaco fewer than three hundred and fifty families buried ninety-four people, forty-four of them children."

"Ninety-four deaths, in one year?"

"My sister Maria's two children too. Heat and dysentery, and forty-three of typhus. One whole family died out, parents and three small children, and all the orphans...they said the Chaco was too dry for typhus, but we brought it here, with us."

"Ah-h-h," Adam says. He is looking at the empty orange skin between his long fingers, fingers so pale and soft it could be he has never, in his whole life, so much as touched a shovel. Suffer? He looks up and smiles a little, so I tell him:

"There was no doctor in the Chaco. After a month of dying they brought one from Asunción, and he said people on the river-boats coming from Argentina sometimes had it."

Adam nods. "Epidemic typhus, carried by lice, aided by dirt and bad water."

"Our ministers could only pray and read the Bible, my mother said, it was all over again what the conservative Mennonites from Canada found here in 1927. They had come to the Chaco to get away from the big world, and have their own schools for their children and live in villages as they wanted to, but what they got here at first was mostly graves in the bittergrass."

Adam says, "I haven't been to their colony yet, should I visit them?"

I laugh a little. "If you're looking for really faraway relatives, I can take you to a few living there, really stubborn Wiebes and Loewens who already left Russia by the shipload over a hundred years ago."

"No no," he says fast, laughing with me. "But they had typhus too, when they came?"

"Those Mennos call it their 'Great Dying' to this day, in a few months of waiting in grass huts to move here into the Chaco from the Paraguay River, over a hundred died, fifty of them children under two—even more than with us. It all comes from the hand of God, the Canadian Mennonites in the Chaco always say, health or sickness. At our funerals in 1930 our ministers preached that too, though often they broke down crying when they said it. My mother remembered the one verse they always read: 'And King David built an altar to the Lord on the threshing floor, and sacrificed burnt offerings and peace offerings. Then the Lord answered the prayer for the land, and the plague was stopped.' Russian or Canadian Mennonites, we certainly aren't kings, my mother said, but after our long, hard journeys to reach the Gran Chaco, we did sacrifice, all of us, until the plagues finally stopped, they truly did."

Adam says slowly, "I guess it doesn't matter how far you travel, you always carry...things with you. But sacrifice children...such suffering? The ministers said it was from God?"

"All life comes from God, they said, and suffering because of sin."

"But that verse about David, I think he sacrificed animals on an altar for something he had done wrong, I think he made God angry by lying with a woman or counting people, I don't know exactly—but what big sin did you people here do?"

"I don't know. Maybe it was our escape from the Communists, maybe we were supposed to pay here what our relatives were still paying in Russia."

"Pay? My parents escaped too. Pay what?"

"For evil, pay for sin in the world. The sin of Adam."

My cousin Adam from Canada stares at me, almost as if I had meant him! I say, "In the Garden of Eden, the snake and Eve."

"I know," he says. "But some people seem to 'pay' a lot more than others."

"As my mother always said, who can argue with God?"

"If we were Jews we would."

"Who'd want to be a Jew? They don't believe in the New Testament."

He makes a hard sound in his throat. "The New Testament says Jesus paid for all sin on the cross, so why do we still have to pay more?"

I don't know what to say, nor, I think, would my mother, who certainly thought about this longer than I. If she knew, she never told me. I can only ask Adam:

"What do you pay for sin in Canada?"

"Hmm! Not much. Hard work; my family started in a log house no bigger than a granary, they worked like slaves—but no hunger or Communists, certainly not typhus or—" Then he laughs, and I hear his thoughts change in his laughter. "Maybe my debt is piling up interest, who knows how big it'll be when I have to pay!"

We laugh a little, together, as people do when there is nothing to say about something that is not funny.

"But your brother," he says, "that wasn't typhus."

No. Not typhus. In the ten days we are together I tell him our worst and best story, the one that started our life in Paraguay in 1930 when we already had no father. Tell it in pieces, as I can bear it, even while we're grinding along the narrow cactus and sand tracks that connect Menno Colony's eighty villages, making sure, as he says, we don't find any relatives among the six thousand people living there, their families with sometimes fifteen or even eighteen children.

At the water oasis of Boquerón, where two years after we came the Paraguayan and Bolivian armies fought in the terrible desert heat until they were both defeated, over three thousand soldiers dead, we spend a few hours talking about the Chaco Border War that ran over us before we even had our villages built. How our mothers gave bread they baked to soldiers on both sides for Christmas and they thanked them with volleys fired into the air and dancing, and our young men took their dying horses home and fed and watered them back to life so the army officers on either side could commandeer them again. You flee to the ends of the world, my mother said to me, and still the first thing you meet is war, fought over thorns and sand.

But Adam and I come back to my brother's story: he won't let me stay away from it.

I tell him my mother said Vanya's will was unbreakable. He was the head of the family, he must work. Not the heat and bittergrass campos and thornbrush sand flats and mosquitoes or the endless labour of building a village out of nothing in a strange, desert world could stop him, by God's grace we had escaped the

Land of Terror and he would build our home again as our father surely would have if he had lived.

But my own small first Chaco memory is not of him working. I know that even before the paratodo tree in our yard burst all over yellow flowers like the flaming bush of God speaking to Moses, I saw my brother's bandaged head lying on a mat in the terrible heat of our house tent, the strips of my mother's cleanest, whitest sheets soaking blotches of blood around his neck and head crushed by a wagon yoke for oxen, a yoke of red quebracho so hard they called it "axe-breaker," so heavy it sank in water like steel, and our village made a mistake sawing a yoke out of it, but they wanted the strongest, they said, and didn't listen to the Canadian Mennonites in Menno Colony who after three years in the Chaco knew better. And that was what smashed Vanya, beat him to the ground behind the corral where we kept our cow, a Paraguayan beast so wild she had to be roped and tied up, head and foot, her back legs spread wide and tight against two posts to strip a small bottle of bluish milk out of her. Vanya did that twice a day, my mother said, the milk was for me and our third little Frieda, but that day before our first Christmas here, in the terrible summer heat when she heard him, she knew no cow would make him scream like that, she heard the thud! thud! thud! of red quebracho as she ran crying his name from our tent and around the corral.

"What?" Adam asks me, "what happened, what?"

For fifty years I have said nothing to anyone, nor asked, nor has anyone in Fernheim spoken to me of it. Mennonites know, they understand silence. Now this "lopsided double cousin" from Canada, a doctor with soft hands, so rich he can fly around the earth and probably talk to all those big men, too, who control the way the world is and have never heard of us or the miserable Paraguayan Chaco and how you work like an ox to just exist here, decade after decade even after the million-dollar credit from Mennonites in North America bought us machinery for growing cotton, and built a highway to Asunción so we no longer need the wagons and the narrow railroad and the filthy riverboats to take our cotton and peanuts to market, now there's a paved highway straight to the bridge over the Paraguay River and the capital— why don't you leave, they ask, go to Canada, there's no police or Communists to stop you here, leave this Stroessner dictatorship like more people than live in Fernheim Colony have left in the last fifty years, left as soon as they could borrow or beg enough money from anyone. Take a bus and plane and in two days you'll be in God-blessed Canada, or even less than a day in tropical Brazil, or Argentina, or Uruguay, why stay here?

Adam Wiebe comes out of the sky alone. He tells me nothing of his own family, although he has one, he wears a ring and is married but with only two children after almost twenty years, so he won't have any more. He must know more about our families, running to Moscow even if he wasn't born in Russia. He says if I tell him our stories he will remember, but how can he know so little? What did his family talk to each other about, year after year? His father is dead but his mother is still alive, he speaks Lowgerman as easily as I and listens to me, why come to this sand and thorns when he can sit in Canada and talk to enough Mennonites or travel anywhere in the world where it's comfortable, not stand here sweating in our little shade, sucking oranges with his expensive shoes dirty?

In a few days he'll be gone. He laughs a little about his debt to sin growing; children being sacrificed to pay it. Just words to him, I think, words, would he laugh if it was his daughter? Patricia, he calls her, fifteen years old, an English name, his wife is from the States, and a son Joel, a name from the Bible. The way he smiles sometimes, I hope none of them will have to suffer. Like our parents. But I don't think even Canada is the heavenly Canaan yet. It comes when it comes.

Only God and forgiveness can end pain, my mother said on her deathbed. And each one forgives for himself; we cannot forgive for others. Though maybe in heaven we can do that too. There we'll all be perfect, if we get there.

"David, what happened?"

Adam is peering at me so hard and Wiebe grey, as if he intends to find Vanya in my eyes. I could tell him I don't look like my brother at all, that I have the long nose and heavy eyebrows of my Wiebe mother, he should look at my ears. In the one picture of our family in Number Eight Romanovka I know that both Vanya and I had our father's ears, even as a baby on my mother's lap you can see it, ears sticking straight out and so broad, if we were heads only we could fly away.

I tell him, "My brother's neck and shoulder, the left side of his head was smashed. We had no doctor then in the Fernheim Colony, only Heinrich Unruh who had been a hospital orderly in the First World War. He knew how to bandage a wound. Such horrible pain in the heat boiling our tent, I remember his face wrapped up and soaking bloody. He died after three days."

"God. With a wagon yoke?"

Quebracho wood. There were only two wagons then, my mother said, in Number Four Friedensheim, all lotted and planned for twenty-five farms and each farmer agreed upon in Mölln, Germany, when they finally knew which families Canada would not let immigrate there because they had eye trachoma and tuberculosis, one wagon in Friedensheim for those south of the school lot—there was no school yet, they started with houses—and one for those north, and they were still trying to break in the Paraguayan oxen to carry a yoke and pull properly. Vanya had just returned from taking his village turn *tschmaking*, as we called the wagon treks to Endstation on the railroad for freight from the riverboats before we had the Trans-Chaco Highway, two or three weeks' labour on the two hundred kilometres of trail winding through desert and thornbrush and bittergrass—and bottomless mud too if it rained, as it could after months of forty-five-degree heat, rain like buckets pouring, a world always of extremes—and Vanya had finally gotten the oxen yoked under that unbreakable yoke and pulling together, he could quietly talk any animal into doing its proper work except that beast our first cow, my mother said. The yoke was still warm when that man lifted it up.

"Who?"

One of our village. Actually three of them came to argue and yell at Vanya, they were his age but only one stayed longer, he was so strong, to lift that red quebracho high enough. And angry enough to do it. What was the matter between them? I asked my mother as she lay on her last bed, tell me, you have never said anything and I heard the man is maybe dead now, he moved away to Uruguay after it happened and is maybe dead, please tell me. There is no more time left, why did he do it? Why?

She did not open her eyes, and she would not tell me. Perhaps she could not. God had given her the mercy of washing her worst memories clean in forgiveness. Even the name—who can deny their mother on her deathbed, who would force her, draw out what she has already left behind?—she told me only what I myself already knew. My dead brother lying inside the bulge of a bottle-tree log our neighbours had cut and dragged out of the thorn bushes, which is all our forests in the Gran Chaco are, and they had sawn the tree open, dug out with shovels and hoes the pulp in the big bulge of the stem where the tree stores its water, dried it out until the smell of it was almost gone in the sun and then the women laid him wrapped in a sheet down inside it and the men covered him over with the sawn slab so there was only the thorn-studded barrel of the dead tree left. It seemed to her, my mother said, as if they were sinking a piece of the thorny Chaco down, laying it back deep in the Chaco sand, trying to bury this terrible land into itself, but they never would be able to do that, get all the Mennonites quiet and buried and in no more pain, not even if they prayed and shovelled forever. And the poor man who had done it kneeling by the hole, weeping as they broke the edges of the hole in, and the sand flowed down over the bulging tree laid flat, as they filled the hole until it was heaping high on the far edge of the school lot next to our farmyard. She told me how the Paraguayan army captain who had met Vanya on his trip to the railroad came to the funeral with his soldiers and said to her he would deal properly with the killer, as Paraguayans do, but my mother forbade the captain his vengeance, no, she would hear nothing of it. She told him she must forgive the weeping man as Jesus had taught, and she invited the man to our tent and, crying, after a week she finally could do that with her whole heart.

And she told me again how that poor young man came to work for us then, walked every day from his parents' yard at the south end of Number Four Friedensheim and helped her build

our sleeping and cooking houses, cut the bittergrass for the roof
and ploughed our land with that yoke of oxen, trained so well,
and learned to plant kaffir and Paraguayan beans and sweet potatoes and cotton too because Menno Colony already had built a
cotton mill. He helped us do our share of village work on fences
and road and school, for three years, always bringing his own
food for the day though he always ate it with us. It was he and
our little family—I was five and getting bigger and I shovelled
too—our family with my sister the oldest child left, barely sixteen, we tore away our first corral and built a larger one farther
back on our lot for the Beast, our Paraguay cow, and planted our
garden and years later, when we learned how, planted our Chaco
orchard, apricot trees and berry bushes and, even later, lemon
and orange trees here where our tent and our corral had first
stood, where it happened.

My mother told me nothing more. For her what happened
was gone. Heinrich Unruh was alive and only a little over eighty
years old, he would certainly have remembered something to tell
me, but why ask him? my mother said. On earth, if God is good,
you can sometimes forgive a few things long enough so you don't
have to drag them after you all the way into heaven before the
Throne of Grace. And anyway, she said, God already knows, He
understands it all, why should we turn over and over in our
hearts the little we know and the more that we don't? Let it rest
in the sand, there's enough sand for all of us here.

Adam asks me, "Have you forgiven that man?" And then he
says, very quickly, "I'm sorry. Please, forgive me."

After a while he says quietly, "That's really the second story
in the Bible. The two sons of Adam and Eve."

"I know," I tell him, and his eyes are so calm now and grey,

I know somewhere he knows about pain, or will soon. "I've read it so often, I still can't understand why Cain killed Abel."

"In the Bible it's because of God, and something about fruit and sheep."

"We don't have sheep, and I like oranges better than cow meat!"

We laugh a little again. Nothing to be said.

"How about God?" he asks.

"I don't think people need to kill each other about God. He can take care of Himself."

We are under the orange trees again. Adam has the longish, square face of the Wiebes I have seen in pictures, but black and white doesn't show those blue-grey eyes that turn a kind of steel when he looks at you long enough. I tell him we are standing where our first corral stood, our feet are on the spot.

He looks down at his polished shoes, dusty from Gran Chaco sand that grows every seed you plant into a miracle if only you can find enough water for it. A garden of Eden, if it had four rivers flowing through it. He says, finally:

"How could you live here, after that?"

"If you had come thirteen years ago, you could have asked my mother."

He laughs, lifts his fine doctor hands helplessly; I see that when he wants to, he can be even more evasive than I. So I tell him:

"I'm very glad. You are the first relative to come so far, to the Chaco, and that's good. Come."

We walk away from that spot, between the orange and lemon trees and through the wire gate into the schoolyard. Under a giant algarrobo six blond children—I count them, four boys in shorts and two girls in skirts—are swinging their strong bare legs and arms among the giant pods, hanging from the branches like long, pale monkeys, laughing and shouting to each other in their Spanish tangle of Lowgerman. Four are my grandchildren.

Adam says, "My mother is old. It would make her very happy, if you came to visit her. And me too."

"I think I have more relatives in Canada than you in Paraguay."

He laughs. "You could visit them all, at least as many as you like."

"We heard from Germany that the Communists are letting a few people out of Russia again. Maybe even some relatives."

"Have you heard any names?"

"One letter said a Peter Wiebe family is in Germany, from Kazakhstan, but long ago from Orenburg."

"Peter Wiebe from Orenburg!"

"It won't be our uncle."

We walk past the adobe school, which is also our church, and into the white blindness of December summer sun. East over the village pastures the vultures float high as they always do, riding the air on their giant wings. That's good, if they weren't up there we would know one of our cattle was dead. Beside us, in the field beyond the smooth fence wire drawn through holes in quebracho posts, five horses rest in the morning heat; a dapple grey mare suckles her foal. At the corner of the fence, between pasture and school, is the gravestone of my brother Vanya.

NINETEEN

BIRCH AND LILAC

Coaldale,
Lethbridge, Southern Alberta
1995

SUDDENLY NOW THE REMEMBERED river hills. The highway tilts beyond the hood of Adam's car, cuts down through green coulee slopes, bends again and there is the Oldman River: with a new concrete bridge—gone are the three black iron arches interlaced with bolts—poised flat and grey and speed limit over the brown water.

For him as a boy this river, cut sharp into clay banks and dry hills, always opened like the Bible storybook to John the Baptist standing in desert water to his waist, raising his arms, crying, "Behold the Lamb of God!" And a blazing dove sailing circles above the head of Jesus where he comes down through a dip of coulee, the water thick as earth to walk on. "It is I," says the numinous voice, "have no fear." And Adam snagged on the barbed wire of such impossible longings, *Do it, walk!* knowing himself no possible Peter, he could never find that first step of daring not to sink.

But the spring river remains, still swirls heavy as paint with soil carried from mountains, foothills, prairie. Swooping towards it now in his powerful car, Adam can see its eddies circle against the banks taut as ever, like innumerable Oldmen spinning dances in the deceptive evening light.

In an instant the road bends back behind him as he pulls the rush of the car left into the last lean of it, the sound under him changes hollow as concrete on sudden air. Stop, he has to.

Already he has crossed the river. In the silence of low, level light the prairie above cuts down into angled shadows. The valley folds open from the southwest like the wind lifting over him with a May whiff and whisper of sage, of wolf willow. He knows the stems of the water eddies reach down into the mud of the riverbed, but somewhere here too the Blackfoot forded, the Kutenai, the Gros Ventre and the Sarcees, many peoples and buffalo and finally horses, later a few manoeuvrings of paddle steamers carrying coal, and ranchers with tame cows and calves, a tricky ridge of stones always hidden by dense water or staggered ice. And above him—there—sheared clear as memory is the face of the cliff where the dinosaur bones emerged, first one vertebra bump revealed its small butt of stone with the next one fitted immediately against it, and then the next, he could feel the third, hey! I found something! He was burrowing bare-handed until the cliff shrugged and buried him to his shoulder in dry clay and Dorothy, leaning over him, screamed a little and vanished past him slick as mud slipping, she was clutching his foot. Saved.

And I shall see Him face to face,
And tell the story, Saved by grace!

334

A twist he never dared try on the male quartet, singing that, "Hey, where's Grace? I need saving!"

But *Albertasaurus rex* was no teen joke: "Our congratulations, the first sequential dinosaur bones unearthed along the Oldman River," the University of Alberta wrote them on letterhead. But Old Riediger, supposedly their high school science teacher, refused to think beyond his Scofield Reference Bible and the date carved at the head of Genesis, Chapter 1, B.C. 4004, or the engraved statement above it: "The events recorded in Genesis cover a period of 2,315 years (Archbishop Ussher)." So Dorothy bumped the petrified bones they had laid out in order on Old Riediger's desk, with the Bible she dutifully carried to every class.

"These are there," she insisted. "We found them in the earth. Bones of a once-living animal turned to stone, Adam dug them out, there's more of them in the cliff, look, Scofield writes this—'The first creation act "In the beginning God created" refers to the dateless past, and gives scope for all the geologic ages'—so why can't we say that?"

His distant cousin Dorothy Loewen so adamant, arguing absolutely like no girl ever did in the Coaldale Mennonite High School. "There's a gap of geologic age in Genesis between verse one and verse two, and these bones are *there*, deep in the ground above the river, we can hold them in our hands. We have to, because they're *there*."

His antediluvian teen past. This motionless blue evening— light, heaven, water, earth, the completed Third Day—is enough: quiet wind and clouds and land lie folded like flesh, and perhaps tiny cactus are already opening yellow on the lips of coulees around this silent, slipping river he can never forget wherever he searches, even to the Little Uran River which he saw in the dinted steppes north of Orenburg, Russia, between the round Hills of Number Eight Romanovka where the Wiebe and Loewen families herded their village cattle and perhaps lay in the first May grass. Did the boys watch the spring animals mounting each other, wait for the girls to appear along the skyline in the noon heat with water and bread—even there he recognized this Oldman swirling his tricky fingers into the secret, moist cracks of the earth.

To try and not remember is silly. Why else has he come? The funeral, his only, oldest, sister; a funeral is never anything but a looking back.

The long curve of highway up the coulee from the river becomes the grid road leading straight south as it always has: these patterns of giant cottonwood windbreaks, rising like tankers out of the sea, imprinted his boyhood recollection. And the farmstead houses remain at every half mile, the Great War Veterans' Colony farms weathering into grey behind the "modern" stucco bungalows that replaced them in the 1960s, or their steep, tiny barns—"Ready-Made" as they were advertised—all vertical boards and lean-tos as delicately gaunt as the Anglican church in gold-rush Barkerville. Canadian Pacific Railway land dedicated to what their designer circa 1919 may have considered bovine holiness—he never tried to milk a cow in a cloud of mosquitoes—the island farmsteads balloon in his head into picking long yellow beans in the heat, cutting green peas as the giant summer sun rose out of a rainbow of dew, irrigation mud and gumbo; breaking corn until his arms ran sticky with green milk; and beets, spring and summer and fall and forever bent over beets, thinning and hoeing and pulling and topping…there is simply too much detailed *place* for him here. He should just whistle on south until he hits Montana, Wyoming, curved Mexico, maybe Guatemala would be far enough, with its smoking volcanoes or the ball courts of Tikal, its narrow passages leading deeper into mountainous stone pyramids.

Where have you run to lately? Susannah will ask him at the funeral home, there will be a viewing, the usual mild curiosity in her voice after almost a month of not talking. And there's Coaldale, so quickly, one elevator cupola emerging above the red earth as his car lifts over an irrigation ditch embankment—stuck there by this arrow of prairie road once mud, then gravel, now Alberta-slick pavement and tar.

Nowhere, Adam will tell her. I told you, not this year.

You're finally motionless?

I'm not dead, I'm trying to think different.

They used to say thinking different was conversion.

I don't know, maybe they still do.

Coaldale spreads out more visible at its edges than he remembered, wider in trees and roofs along the hollow horizon of glacial Lake Lethbridge. One spring between university terms he walked field angles for weeks all around the town, counting each three-step swing of his measuring rod to triangulate the contract area of sugarbeet acres for the Canadian Sugar Factories Limited. The reason so many Mennonite people came here from Russia in the 1920s was the irrigated farmland with its labour-intensive beets—one winter evening they gathered to discuss, "Is the Mennonite Destined for Sugarbeet Cultivation?" and came to no further conclusion than that their Russian village past of wheat fields and cows and sheep gave them little, if any, guidance. But Adam's father, as usual, arrived there too late from their rocky homestead in the northern bush: by 1946 all the former CPR lands were already owned as certainly as if the Russian law of primogeniture were absolute in Canada as well and there was nothing he could afford to buy, he could only be a labourer for whoever hired him.

Na oba mien Jung. His mother's voice so earnest in Lowgerman, where the words for "boy" and "son" and "young" were all one, and her anxiety about his eternal soul's salvation unrelenting: But now my boy, the youngest, you go to school, become a good doctor, you go to the Mennonite High School where they teach the Bible too, not like the godless school in town and you miss your Eternal Life. Dearest loving mother, how had he so widely, even spectacularly, missed it? Years of unstoppable Charles E. Fuller *Back to the Bible Hour* preaching on the radio, with George Beverly Shea singing "I'd rather have Jesus than anything this world affords today"—no, that was thundering upstart Billy Graham—but certainly the Long Beach Municipal Auditorium with Rudy Atwood at the piano; his sweet mother watching from heaven would know exactly all he had missed in his half century since.

And on his right, past a windbreak, the field where the Coaldale Mennonite High School once stood flips open like a book, a ploughed field waiting to grow something as blank as his thought that for years he's missed being a doctor too—though he hasn't at all *missed* being one. Not one bit of the old conglomerate, dragged-together school buildings left; which included the first 1926 Readymade District Mennonite Church as long and straight as three two-by-four granaries nailed together end to end in one day of communal work; nothing left of the ball diamond or the open hockey rink gritted with dust from the west wind as everlasting as prayer, or the sound of singing, "Hallelujah! For the Lord God omnipotent ..." not even magnificent Handel could lift his immovable monotone into music. Every trace of school gone, seeded-to-salt gone. My dear sister Helen is gone, gone home—but there it still is: the immense roof of the old Mennonite Brethren Church, "no Sistern included," as he used to tease Dorothy. Shedding its cracked shingles above a few disoriented trees, sold when the church removed itself into town for a cinder-brick factory and an occasional kennel to harbour dogs; where he had heard a thousand sermons and could not remember one—but the songs, the *Heimatleeda* begun without introduction by the *Väasenja* and within a phrase multiplied into harmony by hundreds of throats, those songs scrolled through him still, more than ever. There his mother and father were "laid to rest," as it was said in English, but in Lowgerman they "had gone home," in the cemetery behind the church; his parents whom he had, with his "high and learned" behaviour, confused more and more in their old age

They had always thought, like most Mennonite parents— not thought so much as lived in blind, inexperienced hope—that no matter how many schools their child might attend, it would learn to know more in good Canada, but nonetheless continue to think in exactly the same way about its "soul's salvation" as it had when it heard only numberless repetitions of "born again" in this vast building, or the English Reverend, Charles E., or Charles Templeton briefly, or Bob Simpson or Billy Graham or Ernest C. Manning droning weekly from the Prophetic Bible Institute in downtown Calgary, Alberta, Canada—parents hopeful but also confused and concerned. And then more and more silently, sometimes desperately, worried. But loving you, praying to love you enough to lift you by God's inexplicable mercy to the heaven of life everlasting they knew awaited them, raise you to glory whether you knew enough to want to go there or not.

They were buried in that cemetery invisible behind the mass of the church. Not in family plots but, in the equality of their dying, laid under hundreds of tombstones no more than ten inches high: all equal in the eyes of God and safely gone home. Or to hell; there would be some of those too, burning fearfully and forever.

Helen certainly heaven-bound, already there and "waiting on the golden stair," Trish's song—where would Helen be buried? She and Joe had moved to Lethbridge and an English Baptist church decades ago.

The stucco face of the neglected, sadly desecrated building, its tiny Gothic-window eyes and the high, arched mouth of its separate men's and women's entrances curving down and out-ward in a bend of crumbling steps: broken concrete like every staircase he'd seen in Russia. Those men's steps, where once after the double Sunday sermon an older church "brother" he barely knew had drawn him aside and said very quietly, You're smart, if you want to go to university and need money, come see me.

You're lucky to be a Mennonite, Susannah said to him when he received the letter with five hundred dollars that helped him finish his last year of medicine. Mennonites help each other, they're good people.

Well, Adam said, John Martens certainly is good.

So...why do you always complain about them?

In the shadows of the setting sun, Adam sees the empty mass of the church gradually stare past him.

Dorothy lifts the coffee cup to her narrow lips and Adam can only think, Has she ever had a lover? Ever been unable to avoid the faint thought of desiring one? A question impossible for him to speak aloud to her—her hair has been coiled and tied into that severe control since...since the day after they both left high school, the few times he has seen her since then.

"Where's your handsome son now?" she asks.

He knew she'd start with family, but since when has "handsome" mattered to her?

"Joel."

"Vancouver," he says, laughing a bit, "at least that's where he said he was, I haven't got the bill yet."

"That's good, he calls at least, collect."

Her voice fades with her eyes rising to his, as sharp as he remembers them even after forty-five years and he thinks, Now she'll shift to Susannah, no, since Trish she writes to Susannah herself, maybe even phones, or visits her, she's too hopelessly thoughtful to probe about Susannah and me, she'll go straight to our mutual cousin David Loewen in Paraguay. Or to Russia, the most general comment, like "You were in Russia last summer, how was that?" She'll never say the only time we see each other is at funerals...but her glance crumples Adam's silly thoughts. In Coaldale Mennonite High School they understood each other like the books and maps they both swallowed whole.

"I always accept collect calls," he says, "no matter where from. One Christmas morning the phone rang so early..." Her singular attention holds him still, and he has a sudden desire to explain things, some small part of what has happened to him, moving as close as he dares to the acceptable edge of his unacceptably broken life, knowing that with her careful, considered

understanding—that's what she always was, direct and profoundly considerate—she will answer him, Yes, it's all right, yes.
No matter how many years it's been since he's seen her—and
recognizing that, he can only laugh and toss up his hands, he
must finish what he began: "—a call from Tierra del Fuego,
she—Trish—called once, Christmas morning at 5:30 and I was
of course sleeping and—"

He gets himself stopped before he explains who he was
sleeping with…dearest god, into this brunch he himself has
dragged Trish.

But she accepts him on the least threatening detail.

"Was it from Argentina, Ushuaia, on the Beagle Channel?"

They are no longer at a restaurant table in a hotel in
Lethbridge; they are bent over an atlas and the *Encyclopaedia
Britannica* in the narrow library of Coaldale Mennonite High
School and she's already reached the tip of South America while
he's still reading Uruguay and so he can ask her:

"Why do they call it Tierra del Fuego?"

"'Land of Fire.'" And she smiles. "The earth burning at
the last place on earth, maybe the Spaniards thought it was
hell!"

"No, no, Magellan was sailing around the world, why?"

"The Yaghan people who lived there wore almost nothing,
but they kept big fires burning on the beaches, and had wood
fires in their canoes when they fished, the women dived in the icy
water for shellfish. It really scared Europeans, the English too
after the Spaniards, narrow straits and mountains covered with
snow falling straight into the sea, and such naked people, their
bodies shining with seal grease and fire."

He can now only look at Dorothy, the plain Loewen fourth

or fifth cousin he once, for a year at least, tried crazily to imagine he wanted to marry and live with forever. That was what "marry" meant, then.

"You've gone there, haven't you," he says. Her hair is pulled back, gathered in a knot. Like my mother, he thinks. Trish never cut her hair like that.

Dorothy speaks into his thoughts. "I couldn't resist, when I was in Paraguay with Mennonite Missions. I took off two weeks and flew to Ushuaia, it's a green city on the blue Beagle Channel surrounded by white mountains. It's beautiful."

"'Beagle' as in Charles Darwin?"

"Yes, the great Charles whom Old Riediger tried all through high school to avoid. In 1834 he said the difference between the Yaghans and Europeans was greater than that between wild and domestic animals."

"Hey," Adam says, and they both bend forward, smiling at each other. "Do you still read the all-English and white-superior *Britannica*?"

"Not much." She laughs a little. "The University of Lethbridge Library is better. The Yaghans are like the Newfoundland Beothuks, all dead. Disease and hunting."

"Hunting?"

"Business and good sport. The English said they raided their sheep farms, so they paid a bounty of one pound sterling for each pair of Yaghan ears, matched."

"Shit," is all he can say.

"'Only the wind blows forever' is one of their few sayings that's still known," Dorothy says, and drinks a long swallow of cool coffee. "The wind's worse there than here in Lethbridge. An English missionary, Bridges, worked his whole lifetime on a Yaghan dictionary, 34,000 words, the last people on earth."

"Can anyone speak it?"

"No. I was reading a map, like we used to. Guess what I noticed, about Ushuaia, Argentina."

It's the old line of their old game; he grins at her, but for some reason he suddenly feels too sad for this, and much too ancient.

"I've lost all my guesses."

Her eyes catch his longing. "Latitude," she says. "It's halfway between 55 and 54 degrees south."

"Oh. The opposite of Waskahikan, 'home' in Cree, Miss Hingston wrote that my first day in school, that's 54.4 degrees north."

Dorothy smiles. "Too bad I wasn't there that day. I would have hid under your desk with you."

They both laugh at the memory of his English beginning with the terrifying planes. She lifts the last bit of eggs Benedict to her mouth as the waitress appears with a coffee pot and dips refills into their cups. Outside the May wind ripples long, dead stems over the coulees down to the Oldman River and the cliffs beyond, over the green grass sprouting where streets of whore-houses once waited for miners and cowboys and all the city men with their hats bent down to their noses.

Their silence together now is as empty, as easy as friends smiling; but then Dorothy disrupts it.

"David Loewen sent me two letters from Paraguay."

"I keep writing I'll send him a ticket," Adam says, "telling him to come to Alberta, come visit once more, but he says he's too old and I say, what's old, one day flying? He says now the only way he wants to fly is go to heaven."

She lays an envelope beside his plate. "He's heard more about the David Loewen brothers, and Sakhalin Island, from some relatives in Russia."

"He? Elizabeth Katerina told me she was trying to find out more from the KGB now, but she's said nothing in her letters, not about them."

"I think maybe they heard some lies."

"Lies? She would never lie."

"No no, not her—you read these. I made you a copy."

His fingers touch hers as he reaches across, their fingers curl together. Her grey eyes contemplate him with such, he recognizes it, profound concern. These letters will tell him another bit of that story and he will fly there, walk through the prisons Chekhov saw a century ago, and consider the outline of Sakhalin's burning hills his name-uncle could see from his cell window when his half-uncle Heinrich—he would have been Joel's age then, twenty-six—Heinrich the Communist, travelled four thousand miles to find him.

Dorothy's fingertips hook tight in his; she says, "She's still gone?"

He feels blindsided, and slashed. Only a Mennonite relative would dare say such a thing without a word of courtesy. Dorothy's face holds steady in the gentle tenderness it has in his best memories, but she also strikes him as so simple-minded that he cannot imagine what ridiculous teen longing could long to will itself to love exactly that in her: her directness blunt as a club down your throat.

He manages to growl, "She's not just 'still gone.'"

"Have you ever found anything?"

"Not a trace."

"So how can you know?"

"She bought a ticket on a ship that went from Patrai to Corfu to Dubrovnik and Venice, but she never got off anywhere."

"You followed up everything."

"Search files two feet high." He is far too loud for this stupid veneer restaurant, its ridiculous palm trees protected from the chinooks by glass and skylights. "One thousand seven hundred and three days, you want the hours too?"

"Adam."

"Even stupid me running around the Mediterranean and all over the world has to catch on: 'Give it up, Dad, I'm dead.'"

Dorothy does not flinch. She lifts her right hand open towards him and speaks as if affirming an oath:

"I don't believe it."

"You just can't think suicide."

"Is suicide easier than 'Look, Dad, I don't want to be found'?"

"Why would she be that cruel?"

"I don't know," Dorothy says softly. "But if it was suicide, why not leave her body where you could find it?"

"Sometimes I can only pray it was an accident."

"Accidents are usually trackable."

Adam's mind has turned to stone. "Don't you think I know that too," he says, getting to his feet.

Three flat paper boxes. Adam lifts the lid of the longest, and he feels its edge worn to the grain by his mother's work-flattened hands. Whenever briefly he came home in the years after his father's death, at some point these boxes would appear on her kitchen table, rest there between meals of borscht or deep-fried hamburger *Kotletten*, the snapshots inside them heaped in no order except her last shuffle. Her Canada Wiebe family in her hands, mostly posed in their Sunday clothes though on rare occasions working, their life caught in positions she could at last contemplate in a way impossible while living it. But Adam now sits with the pictures at his sister Helen's elderly chrome table. Helen "gone home" has left these random bits of family for whoever bothers to take them, as he is left with her husband Joe Tanguay in their seniors' apartment. Joe seated across the table with his grizzled head bowed between his hands. Tough, short blacksmith Tanguay, who with his steady pacemaker may well live into the next millennium.

The family midden. On top is his stocky mother, feet planted wide and arms crossed over her apron, leaning against a shoulder-high stack of Waskahikan firewood that stretches from one edge of the picture to the other; he himself sits on the woodpile, and on the ground below his feet Helen and Abram and Margaret rest on their heels; John must be taking the picture. Where is Helen's son Raymond, her little daughters Julia and Grace? It is spring, Adam knows he is nine, it is the day Abram brought him home on the wondrous train from two weeks in the Edmonton General Hospital and an operation for the ruptured appendix that almost killed him, Dr. Coglan said, they were very nearly too long getting him to the hospital. But there Adam sits high on split poplar, his face overexposed into a white blur under a grey cap, the thick scar of clamps and sewn buttons, which will grow wider with his belly, slowly healing, hidden under a buttoned jacket. And to the right of his boots Margaret's hair floats from her intense, open face, her arms rolled bare to her shoulders. He thinks again, as he always does: how could Mam let her be outside like that? Maybe it was just

Margaret being so swiftly, aggressively healthy in the sun bright against the white wood, I don't want to be sick all the time! But in less than a year the family surrounded by everyone in the church will stand around Margaret in her coffin, sentenced by rheumatic fever, incurable then. "Last night Margaret's heart tore off," he told Miss Klassen when she asked why he came to school so late, and she let him put his head down on his arms on his desk and the schoolroom was as quiet as if everyone had gone home. Until Olga, the other girl in grade eight, suddenly sobbed out loud. Fifty years this April in the Waskahikan Mennonite Cemetery, the church long ago pulled apart for logs and the floor collapsed into its cellar hole.

> Wonderful grace of Jesus,
> Greater than all my si-in;
> How shall my tongue describe it,
> Where shall its praise begin?

Margaret, sixteen then, in the church choir, singing. Old enough to be buried in the row for women, between the men's row along the outside fence and the children's graves backed against the poplar bush.

"Lots of times Helen would sit there, looking there," Joe says between his hands. "She sure really liked the old pictures."

"I do too," says Adam; and means it. The black Brownie box with the silver edges, a rectangle face of centred mouth lens that clicked on a spring and a smaller lens at each corner for eyes, you aimed that face, stared down into the viewer with the box steady against your stomach, found the shadows and between heartbeats flipped the trigger. When the mail came three weeks later there they were, eight instants that might fade thinner in the debris of your life, but not wear away completely.

Unless you placed them in fire. Like martyrs, translated into air. That could happen too.

Below the first layer Adam finds the posed image no Brownie ever captured, the one he brought back from Russia last year and gave Helen, a picture she could not remember ever having seen. Herself as a tiny girl in a long black dress and white, scalloped collar, barely old enough to stand on a chair, balanced by clutching the cummerbund of a young woman. "Yes, that's your mother, with Liena, your sister," ancient Elizabeth Katerina Loewen told him in Orenburg Susanovo, who had by God's ambiguous mercy outlived the war and ten years of Gulag in Magadan and permanent exile in the mining towns of Kazakhstan—"Is it mercy if God won't let you die living a life like mine?"—having subsumed the war, and subsumed Communism, and now outliving its "complete mess," as she called it, as well.

"My father, Alexander Wiebe, took that," she told Adam. "He was a wonderful photographer, oh, if I only had them all. When your father was in Anadol in the *Forstei* during the First War and he'd never seen Liena yet, they sent your father that one. But he never got it, it was lost or stolen or thrown away somewhere but this copy was kept here, in the family." She was adamant, "*Yo, yo, daut es Liena*," and Young Peter affirmed it too. Adam knew that it could well be Helen, an unrecognizable tiny child, but at first he could not believe the young woman beside her: in black, her dress to the floor, tight on the wrists and high around the neck with an immovable sadness on her face, that could be his mother, certainly—but the large eyes, the long nose and wide, full lips, such a sharp, almost awesome Central Asian beauty? He thinks, again: For forty-eight years I knew every touch and wrinkle of her skin, why did I never see that? Left buried in the pain of Communist Russia?

Was it there in Helen too, cute little Liena, fifteen years old when she arrived in Canada, his mother's first and the only daughter who survived her? Had anyone—Joe?—ever seen it— perhaps focused in passion? Adam has tried to imagine his parents making love. What did he hear and not comprehend in that log house? It must have been possible, in the dark.

Layers in the box. He shuffles Waskahikan bush and the shingled church with Abram and Leora in wedding clothes, grim as winter on the steps, clusters of family in Coaldale and Lethbridge parks, and cows in a field with the roof of the house where he lay under the rafters at night visible among distant poplars, and Firebag Lake with his brother John leading his new bride out of the water and another of himself at six, laughing as he pretends to ride black Carlo—patient, tongue lolling—by sitting on his tail, behind them the flat sod roof of the barn that always dripped a day after the rain was over. Adam has seen all this, forever, it's a bit stupid to sit here today, looking—if he digs much deeper he knows he'll find Susannah and himself smiling on their wedding day. But Joe is immovably unspeaking, presence is all he can endure and Adam doesn't yet want to read the letters Dorothy gave him, sixty years can wait one more day, and then among the greyish snapshots there appears a single sheet of a hymn he has not seen before. Page number 94, torn out, "Dearer Than All," and he knows it, of course, completely from the high school choir, everyone sang, even the monotones like himself who knew they never could:

Ye who the love of a mother have known,
There is a love sweeter far you may own....

Very strange. He has always remembered that line ending
"...sweeter far than your own," but it seems Alfred H. Ackley in
1915 actually versified an extra-sweet love far beyond mothers
and available purely as private property, one might say "redemp-
tive capitalism":

Dearer than all, yes, dearer than all,
He is my King, before Him I fall.

Okay peasant, flat on your face for king and love. Adam lifts the
page to Joe. "Did Helen like this song? It's in here."

Joe studies the sheet. He will need to shave before the
funeral, but he was seated in his chair beside the table when
Adam came in and he has not moved. Well, Raymond will be
here soon.

"No," Joe says slowly, and tears well in his voice as he turns
the sheet over, "it was this one she really liked." Number 93,
"Sweeter Than All:"

Christ will me His aid afford,
Never to fall, never to fall....

No falling flat for Christ in a song by J. Howard Entwisle. It was
the favourite of all male quartets at the Coaldale Mennonite High
School. If you could sing deep bass or high tenor in it you would
be elected student president and were sometimes permitted to sit
on the church podium with the row of grim preachers during a

school program. But Helen never went to school a day in Canada. When they arrived she went to work on farms where she said the farmers and the hired men were grabbing you all the time anyway, so why not get married, eighteen was old enough, of course, Mam said, and she learned to read English when little Raymond brought home his readers in grade one, her life endlessly repeating itself in labour and children.

"She sure really liked that one," Joe says, and hums the last line: "'Sweeter than all, sweeter than all.'"

He is weeping. And Adam finds under his fingers one of the amazing photographs Elizabeth Katerina gave him, taken by her father long ago in Orenburg, Susanovo. It shows little Liena about two years old, standing on a bench under trees in an orchard and leaning forward, her tiny fists bunched on a table covered by a white cloth. To her right stands tall Mariechen. That's your half-aunt, Young Peter tells Adam, she was worked to death in the Trutarmee, the labour army, in the Ufa coal mines during the Second War, she was the oldest child your grandfather David Loewen had with his third wife.

And the boy on the left, hair cut tight over his head and mouth pursed, who's that?

That's Mariechen's brother, your half-uncle Heinrich.

Heinrich?

The one in the Red Army, Heinrich Loewen the Communist.

Whose picture in spiked Red Army hat and Red Star uniform Adam has seen all his life, the cruel "artelistic" greetings signed with such a graceful flourish across the back. Adam asks his relations in Germany, in Russia, wherever he finds them, Why did Heinrich become a Communist?

They all tell him he was the sixth and last of those Loewens. David Loewen never had any children with his fourth wife Lienchen Peters. That was my mother's best friend, Adam says, she was the same age as my mother but Grandpa made her call her friend "Mama"; she could not forget that, even after fifty years in Canada. Yes, they say, that happened then, a young woman marrying an old man because he had a good house and land and grown children, if he was old enough you could outlive him, as Lienchen did; David Loewen was only fifty-four but those two had no children anyway. Adam asks, They were married the same year as my parents, 1914, and Mam called her first child Liena, why would she do that when she disliked calling her friend "Mama" so much? And some tell him, You should have asked her, and others, Maybe her father made her do that too, and others, Your father was the eighth son of Old Jakob Wiebe, not the sixth, and he fled with his family to Moscow with all those other thousands of Mennonites in 1929 and most of them were sent back to Orenburg by the GPU worse off than when they went, because they'd spent all their money and now the Communists knew they wanted to get out. But your family did get out, they even found Canada and not Paraguay. I know that, Adam says, I was born there—but Heinrich, did he ever marry, why did he become a Communist?

Huh! Who knows, even when he was little he was always *jaejenaun*, against everything. He was twelve and in school when Lenin sneaked back into Russia shovelling coal on a train into St. Petersburg, and then revolution and civil war and starvation and endless police and politics, they were building a new world so they had to burn the old one to ashes and kill everyone in it, it was the right time for the young to be *jaejenaun*, just against, against.

But Adam insists, Why would the Communists do that, when the Mennonites always lived in Russia in more or less communal villages, working together and caring for their poor, surely Marxist teaching fit that?

Why, why, you always ask why, there is no *why* with Russian Communists. Everything is the way they say it is and that's the whole situation. Marx said there is no God and he wrote about factories and workers, almost nothing about farming and villages, so all the Bolsheviks could do was destroy everything and make it up different, most of them had never been on a farm, they invented new taxes and turned churches into dance clubs and pig barns, the more it scared people the better. Each Mennonite family once owned its house and certain fields outside the village for crops, and common fields for village pasture, but in only two years of Stalin's first Five Year Plan they took that all away with impossible taxes, they had meetings and meetings until no one had time to work even when it was planting or harvest, they set up committees where the laziest and most useless who never knew what to do except follow orders were the highest bosses. And they obeyed Moscow to the letter though sometimes they couldn't even read a word of the orders—regular taxes and special taxes and then the worst tax—the "volunteer tax" as they called it, a joke, where you voted how much *extra* you wanted to pay because you were such a wonderful citizen you *wanted* to do extra, but if you said ten per cent, Moscow wanted twenty-five and they would just keep declaring the meetings invalid and finally have the room surrounded by GPU, watching until everyone voted twenty-five.

Weren't your Big Bosses elected Big Bosses?

Elected! There was never more than one nominated for any

position, the ones who'd never held a shovel in their hands, just vodka bottles and not even glasses either. They'd sit at the big tables with forms and stamps, and a Mennonite would have to read word for word what the orders said because if you couldn't read you'd certainly be elected the biggest boss in the local kolkhoz, and then you could go around every village with at least two GPU with guns looking at whatever you wanted and taking that as extra tax too, for yourself. No one, not the hardest-working farmer, ever had enough to pay taxes two years in a row.

But Heinrich became a Communist, Adam persisted.

Oh yes, Heinrich was David Loewen's youngest, he would never inherit any land and maybe that saved him from arrest, but maybe also being *jaejenaun*—that was always useful to Bolsheviks, and at twenty-one he could certainly read and after Stalin chased Trotsky to death and had his first and second Five Year Plans, Heinrich was already an officer in the army. But to survive even in the army you did what Stalin's political police, the GPU, "suggested." Nobody in Russia asked for reasons then, when they suggested anything you just did it; but to get permission to travel as far as Sakhalin, well, even for a soldier in uniform with papers in order, travel was very dangerous, and so far in winter! Yes, it was winter, Adam's relations said, so who knew what iron you could carry sewed into your felt boots.

But why, why would Heinrich kill his brother?

Because, they say, that's what Communists do.

Ancient Elizabeth Katerina, standing bent but fiercely strong among the lilacs of the Susanovo cemetery, told Adam one more thing: "You come here once from Canada when I'm ninety-one, God already knows we won't see each other again so we can say this aloud, no one will hear us here. I have written

letters to the army, and the KGB. In Siberia I met an exiled officer who knew Heinrich Loewen in the army. He called himself
Genrich Lvov, Russian for 'lion' like German 'Loewen,' and
somehow he slipped through Stalin's army purges in the thirties
and in 1945 he was a colonel who helped overrun Danzig, but
then in April a German sniper shot him on a street in Berlin-
Buch. I am writing letters, maybe I can find out more."

"Berlin-Buch," Adam said slowly. "That's where Hitler's
last bunker was."

Elizabeth Katerina broke off a sprig of purple lilac and held
it to her nostrils. "I only got as far as Danzig in '45," she said,
breathing deeply. "Only one side of the Marienkirche tower was
left, and the big beak of the Krahntor, walls standing like broken
chimneys, or posts. Oh, I could tell you stories—" She stops,
looks across the cemetery and the village to the distant hills.
"You come to Russia and we all tell you stories that are true—
stories true for us."

Adam holds the story of his tiny sister and Mariechen and
Heinrich in his hand, the picture of them in the spring orchard.
Nineteen seventeen, Orenburg Romanovka; austere children
with not one discernible wisp of joy or anticipation on their
faces. Letters that must be read. A past seemingly silent and
motionless as a frozen river, but the current is always there under
the ice. Though hidden, it flows relentlessly with time, distance,
enduring ancestors.

Not now. Now is the time to remember his loving sister.

> Sweeter than all the world to me...
> Sweeter than all, sweeter than all.

He holds the old picture in both hands. His sister Helen's round infant face with its button nose emerges from a white collar, so lovely and already so profoundly sad. Mariechen is long, slender, she looks calmly to the right across the heads of the two children beside her. Does she already see coal holes in the tundra? Heinrich, standing, is slightly taller than Helen on the bench. He's seven, a face of fixed stone. As if predestined.

And the old woman bent against the cemetery lilacs, her hands gnarled into hooks by freight trains on the Trans-Siberian Railway and Kolyma and gold-fields beyond frozen volcanoes, placed this picture in his hands. He finds he is crying.

It is Susannah who walks beside him down the sloping aisle of Seventh Avenue Baptist Church. Together they follow in procession behind Helen's coffin, Joe and Raymond leading, the other six children and their spouses with the grand- and great-grandchildren, brother John and his new wife Emily, into the moan of an electric organ whining the Fanny J. Crosby joys of heaven. Despite that, Adam feels happiness well up in him: his sister freed at last from her human concern and body ache, and Susannah momentarily so close that her sleeve brushes his suit: this is their third processional in three years—it's becoming our one, certain, annual ritual, eh? she said—beginning with his oldest brother Abram, then John's first wife Erica, and now that they are three months past eight years into their separation, he thinks again they might soon negotiate some version of day parole visits. Parole, from the French *parole d'honneur*, "word of honour" she asked him on the phone a summer ago without so much as a ripple of humour.

Why should we try to live together again?

We're married...we're lonely....

Speak for yourself.

I am.

Well, tough. Don't whine to me, I have great friends, excellent students, lots of work I enjoy.

Be honest, don't you still love me?

Don't you use "love" on me.

Don't you?

Does "love" for you mean "live together"?

It's a decision too.

How long might your decision last this time?

Ahead of them in the church, past all the mourners, at the bottom of the aisle the coffin turns right under the pulpit platform, and stops.

The pews are thick with people standing all around them, heads bowed, hands folded, and he feels Susannah nudge his hand. Three cool fingers, guiding him. Before him John turns, and Emily, into the pew reserved for them, and he follows.

In the pulpit above them is one of those all-purpose-mellifluous "Pastor Bills"; he reads the standard Bible verses with odd interpolations, and leads every hymn by braying into the microphone (was that his name, Bill Brayer?), his loud-speaker voice overpowering the organ; a man cheerful as cabbage and with less ceremony than if he were cooking borscht (which would certainly be beyond this necktied goof)—god, such ridiculous thoughts.

His sweet, venerable sister's body lies in that burnished coffin beyond the pews. At each family funeral Adam remembers down to his fingertips the texture of Margaret's flat, square box. It was covered with black cloth, every edge hand-stitched by

Mrs. Aaron Heinrichs; Mr. Abram Fehr bevelled together the spruce boards cut at Mr. John Lobe's sawmill, all corners mitred; the girls at Waskahikan School made the pink crepe-paper roses that covered Margaret's bare arms and spilled over into the open grave when the men, with Abram and John at their head, lifted her unevenly onto the grave planks and then closed the lid, nailed it carefully down. The women of the sewing circle had puffed the satin ruffles up around her shoulders and face so devastated by her long dying. Her black hair lies curled against her shoulders: Adam feels the brush in his hand snag, she sits up for a few moments on the cot in the corner of the room where they live and eat, his scribbler lying in her lap, and he has just tried to show her how he does long division, the number he must divide is 227 and Margaret makes him explain it, step by step, exactly, and what happens to the number that is left over, and then like every evening he tries to brush out her long hair that gets tangled from lying all day, sweating and tossing on the pillow, he tries to do it without hurting her. Addie, Addie, careful. There's a knot.

"When the roll is called up yonder I'll be there!" Pastor Bill bellows cheerfully over the quiet drone of the mourners; heaven is a one-room log school where you answer the roll every morning, Here.

Susannah brushes against his left hand; he realizes it is clamped in the grey cloth covering her right knee, her bones so exact in the wistful longing of his fingers he did not notice.

For God's sake, Adam! Her anger crackled on the phone. Look at yourself. Why should I believe you?

The minister is winding down a eulogy of little stories saccharine with Golden-Age hominess; Adam glances at the "In

Loving Memory" program for the first time, and realizes the funeral is more or less over. This minimal enthusiasm produced by a presiding cliché is it: no one who actually knew Helen will say one loving word over her coffin. Exactly the same thing happened at Abram and Erica's funerals: the few personal stories were told later, around small tables in the church basement after what remained of their bodies was far away and buried. And suddenly he feels this is grotesque. Every eye he can see is dry, glazed, sinking into this tasteless porridge poured over a good and gentle life. A final song, P.A. Bill and the relentless organ are dragging the congregation through the last line of "What a day, glorious day, that will be," and Adam touches Susannah's thigh for an instant—he does not dare look at her—and then he hoists himself to his feet. Emily and John glance up, startled, but shift their knees and he has edged by them, is standing in the aisle. And he walks down, past the end of the coffin and up the podium steps.

Pastor Bill is glaring at him, for once shut up. He bends a little, not surrendering anything, and Adam gestures, "Excuse me," and leans past him with a black shoulder angling in.

"Excuse me, I...I don't want to disturb" (it is an excellent speaker system, he can talk quietly) "disturb anyone, but I am Helen's youngest brother, Adam, and I feel...something should be said by family, about her...here, our good sister and wife and mother and grandmother, whom we loved. Like you can only love someone for a whole, long lifetime."

He almost makes the mistake of glancing at Joe's white face looking up at him, he knows it is, and Raymond beside him, but he concentrates on the coffin between them, directly below, the sprays of flowers on the glistening wood, the silver handles.

"Helen was born seventy-nine, almost eighty years ago on the steppes, near Orenburg, Russia, actually a village and colony built by Mennonites, Number Eight Romanovka they called their village. At fifteen she came to Canada, in 1930, in that 'miracle escape' over Moscow which our parents told us so often never to forget, even me who was born here in Canada, to always remember and thank God, all our lives. She was their first child, named after her grandmother Liena Loewen who had already died, and for me, born last, Helen was always an adult. And often when Raymond and I played together as little boys—we are the same age—it seemed his mother Helen wasn't just my big sister but my mother too, only much younger and so much fun, because she would sit on the floor and play string games with us, and blocks and cars.

"But what I...I want to tell you one memory of my big sister Helen; for me it's sharper than any family picture. It is the middle of a winter night, early March 1945, but all the kerosene lamps are lit in our house then, in Waskahikan, our homestead north of Edmonton. We are all crowded around our sister Margaret, in her cot in the centre room of the house, where she has lain all winter. My mother and dad, my brother Abram and I are there, and John sits behind Margaret, holding her upright in his arms so she can breathe easier. She flings her head from side to side, her long hair whips his face as she heaves herself around, she is burning inside and water runs down her face and out of her mouth, she screams in pain, weakly now, she has been burning up inside for hours, I think.

"And Helen kneels in front of her, she holds Margaret's hand tight between hers, we are all crying but she speaks so calmly, she is so strong, she repeats over and over Margaret's favourite words from Jesus: 'Do not let your heart be troubled; trust in God, trust also in me. In my Father's house are many mansions, if it were not so I would tell you. I go there to prepare a place for you, and then I will come again, and take you with me, so that where I am there you will be also.'"

Adam wipes his eyes, and finally he can look up. Faces blur into focus, the semicircular church is filled even to the narrow balcony, he has not imagined so many knew his quiet sister in her aging, there may be over four hundred people—and what does he know about her now anyway, decades of life gone by, she and Joe and their seven children with names like Tanguay, Wong, Lopez, Porteous and a solitary Loewen between them, those Russian stories ancient as piled stones, and several of her middle-aged children divorced and all their married-again spouses and twenty-two grandchildren and eleven great-grandchildren, if you could trust the "In Loving Memory" card. All their eyes looking at him: why is this crazy uncle interrupting the funeral, so rich he never has to be a doctor though he was one once and doing nothing and always running around somewhere in the world and who knows who goes with him.... It's for Helen, you witless nits, a few words over her body, the human being she was, you who knew her best, say it!

"I didn't mean to disturb anyone," he says quietly, and feels the words whisper in every crevice of Seventh Avenue Baptist Church. Directly below him in the pews is one tearful face smiling, certainly smiling at the silly apology in his tone; it is Susannah, so he can add more firmly, "I wanted to say something personal, for Helen. Please excuse me."

Adam gets down into the aisle without a stumble, but an arm catches him up. His wordless nephew Raymond at the corner of the coffin, exactly as tall and as old as he is; putting his arms around him, holding him tight.

Dorothy says, "My father's grave."

Nicholai Aaron Loewen
1906–1991
Orenburg Russia   Coaldale Canada

Adam looks up from the grey stone: his mother's father's first cousin, which makes Dorothy his fifth cousin at best, or sixth. The cemetery flat as a shorn grain field to the far May shrubbery of Coaldale bungalows: he thinks, Ohm Jakob Wiebe should have lived here, then lilacs mauve and deep purple would be blooming wildly along paths and between stones, and tall Siberian birch burn spring green in this evening light, like those crowded in dazzling wildness over Jakob's grave in Orenburg, Susanovo, no name markers anywhere to be found by pushing branches aside, the original boards rotted away to nothing; not even Young Peter could remember, only Elizabeth Katerina's memory to show him the hollow place where he could have read the date easily and perhaps deciphered the Cyrillic letters: *1879–1962. Jakob Jakob Wiebe.* In Mennonite Canada these power-efficient rows of stones designed for lawn mowers, and the great hulk of the neglected church across a parking lot, not forced to close by Communists but simply sold to the highest bidder. In Canada free enterprise can convert a church—even a Mennonite church built memorably and completely by community labour in two summer months in 1939—into a dog kennel faster than official atheists in Russia.

Susannah between them says, "Nineteen ninety-one."

Her black pumps, black stockings over the slender arch of her feet; that year in her voice the memory of their sad daughter, gone with not even a flat stone possible.

Anne Patricia Wiebe

1965

Edmonton, Canada

No date or place to add; nothing here or anywhere, if ever.

Dorothy's hand finds Susannah's, he sees them grip so hard their knuckles whiten. Dorothy says, "I told you, I don't believe it. The world is too big."

Anger surges in Adam, but abruptly Susannah turns and takes Dorothy in her arms. It is no funeral reaction, Susannah is kissing her, one cheek, then the other.

"Hmmm," she murmurs against Dorothy's hair pulled back over her ear, almost, Adam thinks, amazed, like the faint hum of her remembered lovering. "Where did your Mennonite parents find such a sweet name, 'Dorothy'?"

And Dorothy smiles, kissing her back along the turn of her chin. "It was my mother Hannah, they came to Canada in 1925 and when she finally got to go to school two years later she was so tall she insisted she belonged in grade five, and to prove it she taught herself English by learning to read *The Wizard of Oz* out loud!"

They hug each other, laughing at this lovely story, while Adam stands with his mind splayed empty. He has never heard this from the woman whose obvious childhood he always thought he knew. And then he hears his name called, his home name.

"Hey, Addie!"

John leaning on his cane on the gravel path, his new and cheerful wife hooked into his other arm.

"I forget," John calls too loudly in his deafness. "Where's Mam's grave? And Dad's, I want to show Emily, she'd like to see them, they're around here, eh—where?"

Adam has already joined them, gesturing, "This way," and they limp across rows of gravestones together. Only moments before they all stood around the opened ground while Helen's coffin was lowered, John's head above all the bowed mourners, his eyes closed facing up to the sunny sky. Adam thought then, he's thinking of his good Erica, her coffin sinking out of sight barely a year ago, and he says to his brother now, touching his cane arm, speaking directly into his hearing aid:

"This is a tough day, for all of us...so, how are you doing?"

And John laughs, an enormous gust of happiness bursting over the graves. "Oh, I can't thank God enough! He gave me two such wonderful women to love me, first Erica and now Emily! I'm so thankful, Addie, you know, how thankful I am? I can't even say it, Emily, she's better than anything I deserve, God is so good!"

His brother John, whom Adam in his childhood memory finds only grim, quiet and forever labouring at some drudgery: what has he missed, avoiding John in the past fifty years? They can simply laugh together, John and he, and Emily as well, quite obviously flattered, whom Adam has met only an hour before, very quickly, as the family gathered in the church vestibule to follow the coffin down the aisle, laughing all together in the cemetery of their mutual dead for seeming happiness in the mild May air, their sister's grave still open somewhere behind them and cars starting up in the parking lot, rolling over gravel, away. He glances across John to Emily and says to her, "That's wonderful, you're so good to my big brother."

He sees her motherly face lined with more than he wants to know. "Oh, it's not hard, he's very good to me."

John nudges him, voice suddenly alert. "Hey, your wife, Susannah, she came too…that's real good, are you together again, is it okay now, between you?"

A question only a brother whom you see once in two years at funerals, never weddings, would dare ask, deafly oblivious and loud so that anyone following, like Susannah herself with Dorothy, cannot help but hear. Adam says, as loudly, "Susannah's just behind us, she lives in Calgary, teaching at the university, and I live in Edmonton. Ask her."

Even short spring grass is difficult on a cane; John breathes heavily, it seems to Adam he can hear his mechanical knee creaking, surely he won't probe any further—but then, not looking at him, his brother persists:

"So, where does your boy stay?"

Adam controls himself. "His name is Joel, he's twenty-six years old and works as a computer programmer in Vancouver. Here. Here's Dad's place, Mam's is three rows up, over there."

John looks down at the small grey stone, breathing hard; and then he speaks in a rush, as if he had stored up these words for Adam until this moment together, to pour them over the two decades of their father's grave:

"I guess God is just good to me, I barely got three years of school in Canada and I stayed stuck with raising cattle and pulling calves every spring, Erica was real good at that too, and our kids are all married now and serving the Lord with nice

families living all around us and God gave me two such wonderful, loving women to care for me and Emily's kids are all married
too, and happy with good jobs—"

"John," Emily says, loudly.

Adam, stunned as he is, can only think that John never dared
say anything so thoughtless while Erica was alive—she'd have
told him to stop bragging a lot quicker than Emily—though he
certainly must have been thinking it all his life about me, who he
thinks has made such a mess of my rich and easy life—maybe God
is better to this self-satisfied bugger my brother than he knows,
and he's been so hard-working and believing the Bible word for
word all his life that now he thinks he deserves his wonderful
life—but if he mentions Trish so help me God—

"I'm sorry," John says quickly, touching Adam's shoulder
with his cane hand, "that sounded bad and I didn't mean that, we
all have pain, I've had pain, our whole family too, I'm sorry, I
know the pain you're feeling and I want to—"

"John," Adam spits in his plastic ear, "you know *nothing*
about how I feel. Just praise God he's so good to you and go feed
your big, fucking bulls."

"Hey, Addie, you don't have to swear, I didn't..." But Adam
gets past them both, over their father's grave, and finds by
instinct the black slab, the only one he really wanted to see.

Katerina Wiebe

1898–1982

AUF EWIG BEI DEM HERRN

That where I am, there you will be also; forever with the Lord.
Susannah and Dorothy are behind him. Susannah touches

367

his hand, says nothing, but Dorothy cannot help trying to be helpful: "Look, John didn't mean it badly."

"It doesn't matter...he's always thought that anyway."

Adam hears the whine in his own voice and he's ashamed, it's all too stupid for words. Anger between aged brothers standing over the green graves of their parents. He looks for the floating prairie horizon and sees the Orenburg steppes leading away into blue sky, the straw roofs of villages almost hidden in the valleys of small streams fed by springs, and his ancient uncle Ohm Jakob, white beard and long Wiebe nose bent over a shovel and planting row after row of birch trees and lilacs. "O Believer, Work and Hope," as the motto of *The Bloody Theatre, or Martyrs Mirror* taught, if only someone over the centuries anywhere in the bloody world would listen: the green and peeling white branches of the giant Susanovo trees, the glorious purple bushes rushing in windy sunlight over all those sinking graves, hidden and safely nameless.

"Work and hope," Adam says out loud. "On the steppes or the prairie, where we belong."

Susannah touched him. She and Dorothy are beside him over his mother's tombstone, and Emily and John also. He needs to explain himself, to say something good here, and he raises his voice so his brother will understand as well.

"Our father's oldest brother, Ohm Jakob they call him, worked in Orenburg Susanovo with a shovel till he was seventy-eight, planting birch trees. But in 1937 he was still in Number Eight Romanovka when Stalin decreed the New Constitution and then the purges began again, no more show trials, they just arrested people by the thousands, and one night the NKVD police came for Ohm Jakob. Their black cars always waited at the edge of the village and when it was dark they drove slowly without lights down the street, the way they had already come and taken our Onkel Peter. They hauled Ohm Jakob south over the hills to the city of Orenburg, three Black Marias in a convoy filled with men and women from the Mennonite villages, it didn't matter if little children were left behind without parents, they just had to fill quotas every night. Elizabeth Katerina told me black curtains covered the car windows but they knew when they drove inside the Grey Building that still stands on Kirov Street in Orenburg. She took me there last summer with our cousin Young Peter Wiebe, he and his family were with ours in Moscow, but he couldn't take me near it alone—she had to come with us—because he was inside there so many times, later. Everyone in a Black Maria knew exactly where they were when the iron gates slammed shut. They lined them up in the hall, and led them away one by one to register, and that night there were so many Ohm Jakob finally sat down on a chair in the hall, praying and waiting, and nobody called him. He was on the ground floor, with offices and cells on the two floors above, and he could hear 'interrogations' as they called them going on in the basement under him, sometimes he heard such long screams he could only cover his ears. But no one came for him, the grey police kept rushing past him with papers while he prayed, and finally he started to move his chair inch by inch, closer to the outside door. After three hours he was still there, but beside the door. It was locked of course, and he almost fell over, so exhausted, and a man came from the basement and asked him what he was doing. He said he didn't know and the man yelled, 'You can't sit here and fall asleep, out!' and he opened the door.

"We stood right across the street from that door, and

Elizabeth Katerina told me Ohm Jakob didn't know the man. Young Peter said to the end of his life Ohm Jakob believed that had been the holy angel of God.

"He walked away from the door in the free air, and the sun was coming up and people going to work looked away, no one said a word to him walking away from the Grey Building of the NKVD, the window shutters are never open even now, and the steel gates wider for trucks. In four days and nights he walked sixty miles back to Number Eight Romanovka, no one saw him on the steppe, he made sure of that, and next day he and his wife were gone. West over the Number Eight Hills to Orenburg Susanovo, where he grew a beard but kept his name, there were always four or five Jakob Wiebes in any Mennonite village. Every collective farm was ordered to plant trees, along roads and train tracks and between the huge fields, so the Susanovo Commune elected Ohm Jakob their head tree planter. Everywhere you go now, in the village and the fields and pastures and along the river there are birch trees, planted three or four rows wide along the wind side of roads and across the hills. Elizabeth Katerina and Young Peter and I walked there and sat under them when it rained. Some are two feet thick and as tall as cottonwoods."

Adam gestures to the cottonwood skyline of Coaldale half a mile away, and stops. He sees a large cluster of people gathered with him around his mother's grave; they seem to have been listening to this family story from the other side of the world. And he feels the perpetual wind that moves in southern Alberta: it is blowing a little harder, the air almost cool in the low, evening sun.

"Uncle Adam?" a girl's voice says, and he recognizes one of the pall-bearers. Helen's grandchild, Nicole Wong, her face like an oriental painting. "You were in Russia, talking to your aunt Elizabeth Katerina?"

Adam laughs. "Yeah, thank God for Lowgerman! She isn't really an aunt, a very distant cousin, but she was caught in the Second World War and afterwards the Soviet Army dragged her back from Danzig into Russia and she was sentenced to hard labour, and like Young Peter—he actually is my first cousin—she got her sentence cancelled after Stalin was dead and she..." He stops.

There is too much to tell; it cannot be spoken here in the open wind, too many people multiplied by all their living stories and he smiles at Nicole, her black, intense eyes. The faces around her are considering him with sad but also curious concentration. A family tells stories.

"Let's go back," he says, "to Lethbridge, and coffee, and I'll tell you more about your relations in Russia."

"Did you make a video?" A very young man, with a younger girl hooked on his shoulder.

"No, I took a camera, prints...come, I need coffee!"

And gradually, after they have all considered their great-grandmother's stone, including its translation:

Eternally/Forever with the Lord

the tangled Canadian family of Katerina and Abraham Wiebe, who alone of all their close Russian kin escaped Stalin in 1929, drifts in small, shifting clusters through the cemetery to the parking lot. We should be caribou, Adam recognizes, seeing them move and talk; our wandering life on the skyline an eternal search for whatever food will sustain us, too bad we don't have shovel hooves or natural enzymes to digest grass and moss, we can't smell Arctic lichen under snow; then nothing but good wolves would be pursuing us.

John limps close to him, and lifts the arm he doesn't need for the cane up around his shoulder. Adam puts his hand up on his brother's, feels it clasping him wide and strong, veined by heavy work, knuckles scarred by wrenches slipping, and for a short while they walk that way. The single mass of their shadow with its two heads reaches over the graves ahead of them.

Dorothy says beside him, "That Elizabeth Katerina Wiebe is about ninety, yes? And born in Gnadenthal, Ukraine?"

Adam tries to remember. "She said she was ninety-one, maybe she said Gnadenthal...there was probably one in every colony."

"I started a genealogical tree," Dorothy says. "I think her grandmother was a Loewen in the Judenplan Colony, married to a Benjamin Abram Wiebe."

"One more Abram Wiebe!"

Susannah says, "One more exalted father of a multitude."

And they laugh. "Just the two families," Dorothy says. "Wiebe and Loewen, just births and places and marriages and deaths," as if that would make the simplest story on earth. "I think I can find her ancestor connection with us, probably in Old Colony Chortiza."

Dorothy gets into Susannah's silver BMW; Susannah walks to the driver's side, and Adam follows her.

"Will you stay for coffee?"

"It's two hours to Calgary, I don't drive in the dark."

But he senses her hesitation, and before he can catch

himself he adds, "Best chance you'll ever have, meet even more of my numberless delightful relatives."

She glances at him. Her green eyes—they once would deepen into blue when they made love—tell him, You can be wonderful for a few minutes, but then you'll crack a joke and run. Or lie. And he knows like a knife in his heart that they will never stop loving each other.

So he adds, dead serious now, "If it gets late, there's two big beds in my hotel room. I use only one."

She opens the door, sits down behind the steering wheel, and swings her black legs in. The motor starts as the door closes clipped as a sentence.

TWENTY

THE HILLS OF NUMBER EIGHT ROMANOVKA

Lethbridge

1995

ANOTHER HOTEL ROOM AT NIGHT, but very different. The wind here drives up from the Oldman River coulees so furiously, determined to cave in the windows.

Adam says, "Young Peter finally did take me to Russia, it's perfectly safe now. He was practically Helen's twin, born the same day. His family had a big stone house in Number Eight, across from the school—'Stone Wiebes' they called them, though more for my uncle's character I think than the house— Helen was born in my parents' worker house at the end of the village. The stone house is still—"

"Listen to me," Susannah says into the darkness of the room.

She had disappeared under the blanket of the opposite bed, curled for sleep as she always did, and Adam had finally fallen asleep reading. But then he was awake because she was in bed with him. Behind him, her fingertips at his shoulder as if to keep him at a distance. He turns towards her, there are pyjamas and a sheet and half a metre between them.

She says, "Your Taunte Elizabeth, she lives in that place called Susanovo?"

"What are you doing?"

"Asking you a question."

"*Parole d'honneur?*"

"Half-day funeral pass, close relative."

"Correctional Services Canada never issues bed passes."

"Relatively close relative."

Adam thinks, Slowly, slowly; and speaks softly to her ear, "Her name is Elizabeth Katerina, a very distant cousin. She survived the German army retreat and the Soviet army overrunning them in Danzig."

"That village, Susanovo?"

And he is even happier, he recognizes her inflection. "Yeah, really, a Mennonite village has a woman's name. In 1911 an Orenburg Peters bought an estate on the steppe for his five sons and three married daughters, they were building the first farmhouse when his wife Susannah died. So, he named it."

"Amazing," she says.

"It's strange, after fifty years it's so easy to get there— one day. Fly to Orenburg from Frankfurt, hire a taxi over the hills for fifty dollars U.S. She has a little house made of railroad ties, it smells a bit like tar but that's all they had to build with, she's ninety-one and survived...you can't believe what she's survived."

"Does she believe?"

"Prayer and God, she says, that's why she's alive. Nine years of labour camp because she nursed old people in Germany. She says she can now let her past be what it is."

375

They lie motionless, their bodies parallel, quiet.

"There is mercy too, she says, though usually you can't see it when you most need it."

"'The appalling strangeness of the mercy of God.'"

"Who said that?"

"A priest, in Graham Greene."

"Ahhh." Adam remembers. "*Brighton Rock*, the girl at the end."

"Rose," Susannah says. "Just before she walks into the worst horror of all."

"'Curse God and die.' Elizabeth Katerina said she cursed, many times, but she never could die."

"Why not?"

"Come with me to Susanovo, you can ask her."

"I can't speak Lowgerman."

"I'll translate, and you can watch her answer. She's so strong, bent like curved steel, a gaunt, engraved...I'd say 'holy' face."

"You can talk to your lost cousins in your own language."

There is a surge, like a wash of sorrow between them, but he swallows hard, still so happy. "Mothertongue," he says, "best of gifts. I even taped her and Young Peter telling stories, and translated some into English."

"You have them here?"

"I brought one of his, for Dorothy."

"Read me something," Susannah says.

He says with a flip, "Reading could remind you of what we used to do in bed, out loud."

Her response crackles like ice. "You want me to leave?"

"I'm sorry, no no..." He touches her bare shoulder,

"Please..." and reaches across her carefully for the folder. "It's just so sad."

"That fits, we've just celebrated a good funeral."

Susannah's irresistible ability to make connections: he has forgotten so much about them together, even while he has remembered a few things too incessantly. Companionship, a beautiful word, he feels her warmth even though she is lying so straight, so far away from him. But she came to lie beside him. He turns on the bed light and fumbles with pages, to tell her the story of slight Young Peter, standing again on that Orenburg street. "The corner of Kirov and Ninth of January, there it is." Eighty years old and unable to look at the Grey Building. "I was in there," he told Elizabeth Katerina and Adam, "on the third floor in 1930, and in '41 and '48. And in the cellar eight times too. Many small rooms, waiting your turn, you could hear what they were doing to people. And smell it."

Adam finds the next place, and reads: "'...there was no such thing as "God" in Russia, and the NKVD—they kept changing their initials, first it was GPU, later KGB, but they always acted the same—the NKVD made sure we knew they watched us all the time, you can't imagine how fear controls you, but our village closed the windows and met Wednesday evenings for Bible reading anyway. I had the Bible and the room was always tight full and I read in German, my father Peter's Bible was the only one in Romanovka. In '48, the night they came, I was reading aloud John 15: "I am the vine, you are the branches. They that abide in me..."

"'And there was a pounding on our house door. As they always do. And of course it takes a while to get our door open, we always had the biggest men and women around the door so they can't get in too fast and when the pounding came I put the Bible back behind a stone in the wall and left the room, fast like I'd done two times before, but this time they are smarter: the two biggest ones are waiting outside the kitchen door when I open it. "We just want to ask you a few questions, nothing more, don't worry, Citizen Justina, he'll be back for night." Of course, but which night? Five years later, when Stalin was dead, Khrushchev made the "Cult of Personality" speech, saying things we would not dare think in our bluest dream, and then he reviewed all the ten or eleven, maybe it was thirteen, million political prisoners' records, and after almost seven years I was released just as quick, I could go not even into "free exile" as they call living anywhere except within five hundred kilometres of your home village, I could go, go home.

"'I was still alive because I am small and because I can keep books. Even sitting on a stool in a heated room all day you got barely enough food to keep a body as small as mine breathing year after year, but if you had to labour in the mines or forests in the terrible cold, especially if your body is big like yours, you don't last a month. Smaller people last longer, sometimes almost half a year, but me they would have stuffed with black bread gladly forever, sometimes even a fishhead in the soup, because every camp administrator has to have a bookkeeper to keep him ahead of the Boss who's all of a sudden there to check the endless records that have to be kept in the camps to avoid arrest, every turnip peel weighed and written down, and to have a prisoner who can add and is honest, well, every Overseer I ever had kissed me and cried when they took me away. By God's mercy, seven years into a twenty-five-year sentence and I am still alive, the food ration is the same to meet a quota for trees cut in waist-

deep snow or to add numbers all day, numbers like forests growing green in your head until your eye slides down numbers so
exactly not even the inspector with his electric machines can do
it faster, account books piled to the ceiling and thank the dearest
God who gives you this year after year mind of numbers and
denial, nothing more, "No, I did not... No, I never said... No, I
know of no one..."

"'The questions come at you at any time of any night,
always after the middle of the night, and only the numbers are
constant, solid as rock and the frozen spruce piled up like the
dead waiting for spring to be buried.'"

Adam stops reading. He could follow the sound of Young
Peter's voice in his memory, but momentarily cannot see his
words.

"That's more than enough."

Susannah says, "You've translated it beautifully."

"That's a problem, I think. Such a story, the better you tell
it, the less horrible it seems."

"Don't philosophize," is all she says. Then, "He did get
back?"

"Very suddenly... I can finish that bit," Adam says, shuffles
paper and reads:

"... 'the biggest men always die first, the women sometimes
last a little longer, but I'm small, I work inside, I last seven years;
until Stalin is dead. I get off the train at Platovka, different commune trucks give me rides and then I walk over the green Number
Eight Hills till I see our Romanovka roofs low along the sky. I
walk in the evening light, walk breathing the spring air and I reach
the cemetery where lilac bushes are blooming with a perfume
from beyond heaven. My mother is buried there under the lilacs,

no markers, only memory knows our graves. And then I walk to the centre crossroads of our village and open the door of our stone house, the same door where they took my father in 1937 and me three times. It's a Wednesday again and Liese Peters, who is reading, stops. She gives me back my father's Bible and I open it and read as if I had never left, aloud in that room crowded with the same silent faces, though I see that some are gone, read the words of Jesus, "They that abide in me and I in them, the same bring forth much fruit, for without me you can do nothing.""'"

Tears prickle in Adam's nose, behind his eyes. Words so comforting, and, at the same time, so appalling. And it seems to him that the brief and quiet sorrow he has felt today for his sister, this dream of Susannah so near him at last, is growing like a tree in their midnight room battered by wind; that every branch, every root, every twig and family tendril is nudging under the beds and around the light bulbs and along the edges of the ceiling, sprouting leaves like pain and the room is stuffed tight, he and Susannah are being wrapped, closer, in the green, unstoppable growth of their ancestors' suffering.

"'You can do nothing,'" Susannah murmurs against his neck.

She is so close he could taste her; but he does not dare. He can only say, "Young Peter…there's just the end, here…'That was my third return, but my father never came back once. They took him in 1937, and Stalin still lived sixteen years.'"

Susannah sighs. "That's good. If they want to tell their stories, that's very good."

"Some can, when they're old enough."

She turns off the light. "Yes, when the pain's leached out, a little."

Anger turns in him, quick as tension breaking in relief. "Goddamn Dorothy, I could have strangled her in the cemetery."

"Why? She's a kind person, and thoughtful."

"We're in a graveyard already, why drag Trish into it!"

"She knows who we're thinking about, she's telling us, 'I still have hope.'"

"Hope!"

Susannah says quietly, "She doesn't pretend Trish never existed."

"Good god, you think I do?"

"No. I think you're honest, about her. But most people do pretend, it's easier. Say nothing."

"Well, we can't think 'nothing' about her."

"We both know that." She shifts closer to him. "Tell me, about Young Peter's father, your uncle Peter who was sent back from Moscow in '29. He died in the Gulag?"

Her gentle breath; slowly Adam's mind relaxes. "No," he says. "They said he did, in 1960 the KGB sent the family a letter saying he died of a heart attack in a labour camp in 1944—imagine, sixteen years after!—but that was a lie."

"Do they know what really happened?"

"In 1990 the KGB records were opened and a granddaughter wrote for information. They got a letter that said the 1944 heart attack of her grandfather Peter Wiebe 'did not coincide with the truth.'"

"Did they say what did 'coincide'?"

"Oh yes. He was arrested on February 13, 1937—which they knew, of course—and put on trial August 13, which they didn't, convicted of working with a 'counterrevolutionary fascist organization,' sentenced to death and shot August 15, 1937. He had never left Orenburg prison. And they even sent them a picture of him, taken at the trial."

"God."

"The KGB kept exhaustive records, always 'cover your ass.'"

"Did they say where he's buried?"

"No, but it's obvious. Just across the Ural River from Orenburg, down in the wide valley there's a city park now, a suspension bridge across the water, and tall trees. Young Peter and I walked over there with Elizabeth Katerina. In '37 during the purge they took thousands of them into the valley at night to dig long, deep trenches, and then they shot them, into the trench."

Susannah says, tears in her voice, "In the city park?"

"It was military land in '37, then they made it a park. When the people found out ten years ago they'd been walking over bodies, they planted rows of birch trees, thick along the mass graves, and put plaques on each. Young Peter showed me his father's name tree."

"A birch tree. Growing."

"A green forest of them. Elizabeth Katerina said, 'It's good he died here so soon. Heaven is the best place for him to wait for us.'"

Their awareness of themselves, together, in this anonymous hotel room washes over them. And they understand they are enclosed in a sadness too enormous to be endured, of bodies sewn together by suffering, by torture, by faith, by hunger, by Stalin, by God, by hope, by their daughter, their only daughter, and they can do nothing, they can only, they must, move closer together. The edge of her mouth feels like skimmed honey. She enters him as he enters her. "Slow...slow..." Her tongue silences his tongue, and he does that, a motionlessness beyond memory or dream, they are discovering each other again as for the first time; but weeping.

The wind pummels the window. Susannah murmurs, "Adam."

"Susannah."

They lie on their backs; they are empty, profoundly comforted. In Lowgerman they could "walk from here and beyond the moon."

Susannah offers, quietly, "I was in Saskatoon, at a Canadian lit conference. A woman there told me something about my father's family."

"Is it dreadful too?"

"No, nothing like yours."

"What is it?"

"My dad's ancestors were from Russia too. His name was actually Loewen."

Adam lies still in amazement. If he had ever so much as dreamed Mennonite about Bud Lyons, he would have bumped into that Lions/German Loewen possibility—only last summer he heard that his Soviet uncle had turned Heinrich Loewen into Russian Genrich Lvov—all he can say to Susannah, foolishly, is:

"You and I may be related."

"Maybe, ten or forty generations ago. This elderly Justine Toews told me her grandfather and my dad's grandfather were friends in Russia, her grandfather was the David Toews who helped thousands of Mennonites immigrate here in the twenties."

"David Toews, head of the Canadian Mennonite Colonization Board?"

"Yes—I thought you'd know of him."

"He's the main reason my parents got to Canada, he talked Prime Minister Mackenzie King and the CPR into it."

"I keep telling you, Mennonites are good people."

"Sometimes—at least to each other. How did she know David Toews knew your dad's grandfather?"

"Letters. They wrote to each other in North America, all their lives. They were friends as boys, when their parents trekked into an Asian desert in 1880 to be ready to meet the Second Coming of Christ."

Adam stares at the grey stucco of the hotel ceiling. Not in his bluest dream, as Young Peter would say, could he have imagined what she has said.

"Your Loewens followed that mad millennialist Claus Epp?"

"Mad? Who was Claus Epp?"

"Mennonite history has lots of strange stuff growing in the cracks. Have you gone to Idaho to follow this up?"

"No."

"Well, the *Mennonite Encyclopedia* in the University of Calgary Library will tell you enough about crazy Asia Epp."

"You think they were crazy, that Dad was hiding that?"

"No, no, please, most of the families left Epp, long before he gathered them on the hills for the minute he predicted Jesus would come, but never did of course."

Susannah is silent, and Adam adds, "Want me to try and track your Lyons-Loewen family?"

"Leave it alone!" She twists in his arms, suddenly fierce. "Maybe I don't want to know. My father had all his life to tell me what he wanted me to know. If he wanted his past to die with him, maybe, if I love him, I should leave it alone."

"Okay okay. On the other hand, my mother would say, The

blessed dead are in heaven and there they know everything any-way—but it might help us, to know a little something on earth."

"Did she ever say that?"

"No, but she believed in 'the cloud of witnesses' always in heaven, watching us on earth."

"So that's what you're trying to do, snooping around so much, get the jump on heaven?"

Adam snorts. "I might not make it there, so I better know here."

"I can't stand your smart alec jokes."

"I'm sorry." And he touches her. She gives him back her elegant hand; it feels thinner now, but oh so marvellously warm in his. "My aged sister barely buried. But there's so much, once you start—that's just a bit about the Wiebes, and now your dad—I haven't even dared read the letters about my Loewen uncles."

Susannah says into the darkness, "Maybe you should start thinking about your mother. If she's been watching from heaven, what has she seen you do?" And she stirs suddenly, sits up. She is clasping her knees through the bedsheet. "So many dead—I want to know how Elizabeth Katerina stayed alive!"

Adam can say nothing. She has given him such tenderness, so unexpectedly, but in the grey room her tone makes his long searches self-centred; a hounding of the ghoulish: is there something worse I can uncover? More lies? While avoiding my own.

"And that Peters," she says, "and his village Susanovo."

"You...want something named after you?"

"What are you naming?"

"Maybe the old homestead, at Waskahikan."

"Oh. You always said you'd never go near 'that backwoods mudhole.'"

"I changed my mind."

"Really." She is parallel and distant again in bed; she sounds almost sardonic. "So?"

"They've cleared it all off, the big hill is one bare field."

"A bare hill. You could plant birch trees."

For all the dead. Something else he had not recognized by himself.

"Yes," he says. "'Work, and hope.' At last."

Their arms and thighs touch. Her long, round body along his makes him shiver again. His erection brushes her thigh, but she does not move.

"Could I use your name?"

"For what?"

"The homestead. 'Susanovo.'"

"Where you were born." Then she adds, "I refuse to be dead."

"Hey, that's not what I..."

But it seems the lightness of her body along his helps his body understand what she is saying; before his mind can grasp it. Live as far apart as they may, for as long as they will, they can never fully fathom either their mutual, indivisible love or their grief unless they live through them together. If they dare.

She answers his thought. "Dorothy does not believe it."

"She said that to me too."

They have not made love for over eight years; he cannot reach for her again if she does not turn to him. Neither of them has ever been in this bed, in this impersonal, numbered room which is always, and only briefly, inhabited by strangers. Not even the sleeping clothes they moved aside are familiar: they are only as they know themselves and each other at this moment, their bare bodies and the years of their life together so long ago, inside a cotton sheet and memory. So separate.

If he asked her, Why did you get into bed with me, she'd answer, Don't make me regret this.

Susannah says, "The story of your sisters, it was lovely."

"That silly minister…but I apologized later, he—"

"Shhhhh," she says. So separate. But after a moment, "The Book of Common Prayer has 'Forms of Prayers to Be Used at Sea.' You three were always all over the world, so every day I said the one for travellers. But then I thought, we all travel on roads now, or air, so I made up my own."

Her fingers touch Adam's face, and he waits while they move along his eyelids, his nose. Her fingers reach his lips, and he feels her prayer as he hears it:

"O God our Creator, you are present in every place anyone can be. When you speak, the crooked is made straight and the waves of the sea fall still; you make the clouds your chariots, and you walk on the wings of the wind. O loving Creator, protect I pray these my dear ones who are far away, and travel. And bring each of us, wherever we may be, safe to our journey's rest."

If Susannah and Adam are together, they are sleeping.

TWENTY-ONE

BONES OF THE ATACAMA

Chile

1995

I WAS BORN ON SUNDAY, JULY 25, 1965, in the maternity section
of the University of Alberta Hospital, Edmonton. That gave me
my most useful adult possession, a Canadian passport.

On my twenty-fifth birthday, which I didn't celebrate, in
the Turkish desert of Goreme, I finally made the decision I had
pondered for years: I changed my name. Going from Anne
Patricia Wiebe to Ann Patricia Wilson shifted me into a world
of colourless English where unavoidable questions are never
asked at border crossings, especially airports, and certainly none
in snoopy conversations about ethnic Mennonite possibilities.
Or, worse yet, questions about the blood spoor of relations fled
and scattered in unexpected places anywhere on earth. Only
Smith or Brown could have served me better, and I decided they
both sound too easily assumed for simple, honest disappearance.
"Wilson" moved me even closer to the end of the alphabet than
"Wiebe": in a list or demand roll-call I would have time to

388

consider various answers to inevitable questions as the final Ws approached.

July 25 is my saint's day, Anne. In the Eastern Church tradition they say Saint Anne was the wife of Joachim and mother of Mary of Nazareth. All I needed to do was drop the Green Gables *e*.

And Spanish is the most necessary second language in the southern hemisphere, which is big enough for any lifetime of disappearance.

"But why learn Spanish in Australia, of all places?" Jorge asked me, and I brushed it away with a laugh and a question myself: "Well, why are you teaching it here?" And he growled, "That's easy—exile by our glorious Generalissimo Perro-chet!" He had already taught me enough to understand his mispronunciation of Chilean dictator Augusto Pinochet's name in that twisted pun, "General Dog-shit," and our burst of laughter was loud, even for a harbour bar during the Sydney January Festival.

But today is December, the unavoidable festival is Christmas, and I am in Santiago where Jorge refuses to return as long as the General is alive. At a street kiosk among the streaming shoppers on the Paseo Ahumeda, "the capital city's main pedestrian throughfare" as the *Lonely Planet* guidebook informs me, I choose a map of Chile for its title, *Travel Vision Map, Rutero Chileno*. A thin booklet for an extremely long, dagger-thin country, its tip buried in the ice heart of Antarctica at Polo Sur. I need vision, perhaps there is one here, why have I never walked in Chile before? Why only Peru and Ecuador, even the close tip of Argentina (Mennonite Paraguay is more than easy to avoid). And as I count out 2,900 pesos—ten Australian dollars, or Canadian too, if it still mattered—I feel fingertips touch my arm: a woman in the vicious sun of the street's canyon. Her slender hand offers me a paper. Before I look up at her, I sense like breathing that her face will be worn grey from staring at it:

"My dearest Josepha." And then the single English sentence explains that "All my Love! John," is now at home and he will not be able to return to her from the United States. Dearest indeed. The woman's black eyes, so beautiful with tears about to slip over her ivory skin. "*Schade*," I apologize quickly, and hand the paper back. "*Ich spreche nur alemán.*"

The wide, flowing Santiago street shrieks with voices, diesels roar and fume at crosswalks, vendors offer everlasting Coca-Cola and empanadas *fritas*. Under plastic shelters down the middle of the crowds street painters swiftly smear canvases with snow-lined peaks, bucolic forests. A barrier wall is sprayed: "*Pinochet asesino*" and below it, trailing into the broken sidewalk, "*Clinton asesino igual que Pinochet*," an elementary political debate neither the daily *El Mercurio* nor *El Epocha* will ever make public. Over the heads jostling past I can barely recognize the square surround of the classic Spanish Plaza de Armas: one side of its park has been ripped out into a gigantic hole swarming with yellow-helmeted workers who are filling it in again, slowly, with the concrete and black steel prongs of a subway extension. But beyond that devastation, the plaza fountain still sprays and drips under superb, giant trees. Around the fountain Santa Clauses sit with sweating children on their laps in cardboard sleighs attached to wooden reindeer, and from high in the gnarled pepper trees, dangling pods like giant ebony earrings, "Rudolph the Red-nosed Reindeer" resounds with a Tex-Mex rhythm—inescapable—I slip by, shove, manoeuvre myself away.

Beside the steps of the cathedral the thick crowd eddies

around a small space: two Mapuche grandmothers tap a hand drum, quietly, relentless as a clock beating. "Return Our Land" says their sign wrapped in weathered plastic. In 1541 their ancestors very nearly obliterated Pedro de Valdivia and the town he first laid out on this very spot in Spanish squares, but as Jorge always said, with Europeans in the Western hemisphere nearly was never enough, not nearly. And even completely is inevitably reversed sometime.

Nothing is forever, he told me, not even time.

And I find a high, amazing silence. Arched, cavernous Catedral Metropolitana built on the sometimes shaking earth of faith in Santiago del Nuevo Extremo, as they still called this place in 1745. So mercilessly far from the beneficent Santiago de Compostela of pilgrimage Spain that you had to pass through the ocean hells of Tierra del Fuego to settle among its earthquakes; the terror of God's shuddering, arbitrary and fathomless wrath.

Nevertheless, on this afternoon of Christmas Eve, 1995, the tile floor does not suddenly crumple, the immense pillars lean and split. I hear only an infant laughing, delicate as a scatter of beads in the near darkness of this world extremity I have searched out; I am beginning to fear, uselessly. I may have gone too far at last. Along the transept of the aisle ahead shines Mary's perfect china face crowned with a golden cross, the Jesus on her arm her tiny mirror image, exact to crown, eyeshadow, pertly bowed lips, long curly hair and brocade dress down to his toes. A long banner over them:

Maria, Hija Predilecta Del Padre Dios, Ruega Por Nostros

Yes, Mary, Mary, sweetly favourite daughter of God the Father— your mother's name mine, does that make us daughters, and sisters?—plead, please plead and never cease, you and your perfect baby, who in this late light appears to be an exquisite daughter Jesus, her tiny right forefinger pointing forever upward to heaven, oh, plead for me, pray for what until now I have never yet known or acknowledged I need.

There are coloured bulbs ahead, blinking. They outline the roof of a huge crèche to the right of the golden altar burning with seven golden candles. Donkeys, camels, shapes of people and adoring sheep larger than life, lights blinking electrically like an Edmonton December house memory, here where the only snow can be cotton, the manger with its waiting hay empty. Tonight during the mass the necessary plaster, or perhaps plastic, baby will be borne in and deposited there.

Suddenly, loudspeakers crackle along the cavernous nave and aisles, they mutter into a Wurlitzer "Jesu, Joy of Man's Desiring." Man's desire indeed. Ineradicable Bach shoves me past altars and stations of the cross, past a "Relique San Macrim Martyris" exposed in glass below a side altar, its naked legs brown like polished wood and half-naked torso contorted as if hanged, past an altar dedicated to "Santa Teresa de los Andes, 1900–1920," her anorexic image blessed—so declares the letter screwed onto the wall—by Pope John Paul II on 24 March, 1993, the unrelenting tin racket declaring in Johann Sebastian undulations forever and forever that the bleeding wounds of Jesu Christi have set him, him at least if no one else, free, free forever!

Down Avenida O'Higgins, in one glance thundering past the superb iron filigree of Gustave Eiffel's Central Railroad Station, in twenty-five minutes I'm back where I arrived this morning: the essential airport. I point to the largest name on the first page of my map. "Iquique, *si!*" the woman sings; my knapsack is on my back, no need for a passport. The plane rises into a red Pacific sunset, crimson light fleeing to Australia but we are all belted in place and pointed north, fleeting north. I consider my map and see Iquique is only twenty degrees south of north, getting too close, and I concentrate on the stark, shadowed mountains below me, black blocks and pyramids with twisted rivers blazing gold long enough to satisfy any obsessive Spaniard. Abruptly the light cuts into the ragged lines of brilliant surf, seemingly motionless, but I know waves are smashing at the continent, breaking it. The sea has endless edges but never an end. To fall from the sky here, to smash, fuse indistinguishably into cinders of volcanic sand, as Jorge's blessed Pablo Neruda wrote in "Yo Volvere":

> afterwards, when I am not alive,
> look here, look for me here
> between the stones and the ocean.

To be so lucky.

"*Wohl mir! Jesu Christi Wunden*"—Good for me, the wounds of Jesus Christ—red cinder Chile momentarily stopped that song in my head; but not the memory. Mother, mother, I know very well that there are two quite different poems for that Bach harmonization because you told me, always an incarnation of a comp lit prof. You explained so clearly that the older poem was "*Jesu, meiner Seelen Wonne*," a continuous contemplation of the soul's glorious rapture brought on instantly and forever by Jesus. But the other text, used with exactly the same melody and harmonization, was all chain bondage and gaping wounds. You said, "In English they sing mostly the rapturous joy of the soul soaring to uncreated light, but in German it's always the sin and bloody guilt one, see. The only difference between them is the key. The bright G for 'Jesus, joy,' and this sombre F."

And you bent over me at the piano, translated the last line to the very rhyme as you played so darkly:

> Sin's huge debt and my soul's dread,
> Made of me the li-i-i-ving dead.

Mother, why did you make me understand this? The music was enough.

At the plane window below my left elbow, west is grey space and black ocean. Nothing remains possible but east; perhaps in that direction, over the thin blade of this continent and then more ocean, finally Africa? How can it be final, continual east can finally only carry me west again? The plane trundles down to land on the Tropic of Capricorn, the Aeropuerto Cerro Moreno outside Antofagasta. In the shadow of the airport's largest building I leave the file of passengers disembarking and turn left into darkness; wait. Finally the plane roars away, north towards Iquique where my ticket, if it should be traced, will say I landed. No one will trace it.

Silence. A white simmer of night insects I will never, thank god, recognize. I can search for stars. The sky is unrecognizable, I cannot even find the Southern Cross where I sense it should be. It seems momentarily as if I have never before looked up into the night sky. Christmas Eve. Perhaps I am lucky.

The *Lonely Planet Travel Survival Kit* still holds true next morning:

Outside the larger Chilean cities, women travelling alone are objects of curiosity. You should interpret questions as to whether you are running away from parents or husband as expressions of concern. Scandinavian women (or women who look Scandinavian) may find that some Chilean men associate them with liberal attitudes towards sex and pornography.

I know I look Scandinavian, but overnight in Antofagasta I have not yet had to try and put a Chilean man (they can be "very *machista* but rarely violent in public behaviour towards women") to shame by "responding aggressively" in my memorized Spanish. Perhaps they are all resting from their Christmas midnight mass. Or drunk. And no one, not even the massively mothering concierge at the residence off the Plaza Colón, asks me about running away. She has her teenage daughter to shout with.

The empty Christmas morning bus crawls northeast up the two-hundred-kilometre incline into the sun of the Atacama Desert. We follow the narrow railroad; the highway over the bus driver's shoulder is a black tar ribbon in a stunning abstraction of grey and tan and reddish ridges that lift to cliffs, long plateaus, hills, mountains. It cuts through the thick adobe and rock warrens of nitrate towns left roofless on the sand and whistling, moaning wind in the staggering light. The eventual city of Calama is wiped upwards against the slope of hills below the mountains of the largest hole ever dug into the earth; even on Christmas Day the copper dust drifts east from it high and splendid as the unreachable clouds of heaven. On the grey road beyond dusty Calama, the city irrigated into green by the Rio Loa flowing from the Andes, the driver tells me over his shoulder that a four-hundred-year drought ended here in 1973, only to begin again immediately.

In 1973. "They made you hear the screaming," Jorge told me. "From under the stadium seats, especially at night. You had to smell the terrified. The CIA Americans taught them very well: torture is first of all a place in the mind."

The perfect desert, Atacama, not a cloud to rain, not a single sprig of green plant visible anywhere. Though they say enough morning dew is possible to open grey sticks into sudden flowers, possibly once or twice a year on a spot somewhere. The perfect cone of Volcan Lincancabur rises blue into six-thousand-metre snow on the approaching spine of the Andes. In the first and last oasis, trees sheltering the village of San Pedro de Atacama, the bus stops behind the adobe museum, where skeletal bodies hunched inside clay urns hug their bone and leather knees against their bony leather chests. What relative is looking for them? Whom do they remember? The giant algarrobo and pepper trees of the Plaza de Armas separate Conquistador Pedro de Valdivia's mud house from the narrow whitewashed Iglesia de San Pedro, its dark waves of algarrobo rafters overlaid with pale slices of cactus logs.

As the stupendous heat of Christmas cools a little, people stroll along the paths of the plaza arm in arm. Bars begin to blare Tex-Mex, dogs smell each other intimately at street corners and fuck fast in circles of staring attention. Dogs and men and children only, never hurrying women. I join a small bus tour onto the Salar. Thirty-nine degrees, forty-two in cloudless sun, flat baked salt and pale water two centimetres deep. The impossible jointed legs of flamingoes walk in the water as if on transparent skin, their luminous, doubled bodies meet, bowing to themselves at their

black beaks when they feed. I kneel in the salt baked round and
jagged as coral boils. It gleams against my brown knees, blinding
me, smashingly white, far whiter than snow...Lord wash me and
I will be whiter...they say salt water is closer to human blood
than—who told me that?—I begin to walk slowly back towards
the empty bus, concentrating on the stark distance of the farthest
volcano, but I am the bare, tanned skin of my arms, my long legs,
the crunch and dark spread of saltwater-blood oozing at the crust
where I place my feet. I can only walk faster.

"Everything happens," Jorge said. His chest and armpits
and inner thighs were circled by thick knobs, as if screws with
gnarled, ragged heads held him bolted together in burn patterns.
"And it all stays inside you," he said, "like a splinter, like rusty
steel. It gets worse, it never just heals out."

"So, what is to be done?"

"You ask me?"

"Can't a person decide, something?"

He faced me sitting in my lap, our legs and arms joined
around each other.

"You and your perfect Canadian 'decide,'" he said. "You
have to get inside yourself, and cut it out. Or encrust it."

"What?"

"You carry it, but it is sealed off. Encrusted."

"The English medical term is 'encapsulate.'"

"Mine is short, and rougher."

Jorge said. But I know only walking, always walking, away.
Through devastating dust, past shade trees and irrigation canals
like pencil marks drawn in the sand and paths made by goats
climbing between rocks, like Greece but blacker, and piled into
walls. I stop high above the twisted valley of Rio San Pedro—

every name here is conquering Peter, every solid rock on which to nail another Jesus—I am on a hill veined with the stone walls of the *pukara* where the Inca/Atacamas made their last stand against Pedro de Valdivia in 1540. The Atacamas did not have nearly enough either, of anything. Below are adobe walls, village roofs traced among the oasis trees, the distant flat of desert rises gradually to an endless, undulating skyline anchored in immense volcanoes. Superb in the moonlight, like altars. No, deeper... like rising prayers. If only.

I said to my mother. "Right," I said. "Just right: a song for wounded living-dead Mennonites."

"Trish, Trish," she said then, quickly, "it wasn't a Mennonite who wrote the words, it was—"

"Like a fuckinawful Hollywood movie," I interrupted her because I already knew I knew everything it was necessary to know. "Sing 'The Menno-night of the Li-i-i-iving Dead.'"

Under the clear moon this futile fortress of defence is spread over the mountain around me like a thick, dark Inca weaving. You are here now; so are they; they will certainly overwhelm you. What is to be done?

And my mother, Susannah Lyons Wiebe, is holding a book. I am leaning against her knee and watching the book, and slowly, like the book opening between her hands:

> With the fire of life impassioned,
> In the love of jo-o-oys unknown

very slowly in the blue moonlight my mind opens.

Morning brightens behind the desolate mountains. I can walk only northeast, up the sharp river valley towards the spine of Andes between Chile and Bolivia. Black-faced sheep with lambs surge out of high speargrass for their Boxing Day drink from the stream, the shepherds wait for them, a woman in dark trousers, a quick black-and-tan dog, a man, until they cross where the water clatters over rocks. An hour later there is an open stone sheepfold, gnarled branches bent over a corner shelter, and on the plateau above that a small tower. A church, set in wide and completely empty space, made of baked earth, the top of its red walls level with my head, a domed door fastened from inside. The white tower at its corner opens in the four directions for a hanging bell. I stoop into the tower, pull the rope, and the single toll rings along the valley and comes back faint with its thin edge of iron. Not the round, full "bo-o-o-om" of a Buddhist prayer log swinging back. Comes again.

Trish Wiebe.

I have heard my name. I wait. I turn carefully in every direction in the fierce sun around the small, red church. My name is Ann, do you hear, Ann Wilson.

Nothing moves. I slip into my pack and walk to the faint track switching back and forth up to the next plateau. I climb too fast, the church becomes a red and white flicker, impossible to see unless I blink and search for it, and I breathe my body down into a distance-climbing rhythm until at last the tiny building is gone; only desert cliffs and erosions and tiered plateaus of gravel surround me, empty as crushed paper.

Sky. Tremendous, eroded cliffs burning into high noon above me: there are the ruined fortress walls of Catarpe, built by the Incas so they could watch the valley in either direction. Their conquest and repression of the Atacamas only a shade less ruthless than Spain's oppression of both, the eternal human litany of fear at the core eddying around small ease and much, much pain. A narrowing barranca opens down, I clamber into it, feet and hands. The volcanic walls glisten with veins of minerals, feathered slabs of feldspar, and a gash split by rock-shift and water opens beside me. Deep, deep inside, where the black layers tilt together, from some narrow split sunlight gleams on odd, unrockishly knobbed, splintered, curved tan and white protrusions.

Bones. It must be. I drop my pack, I face the gash and lay myself face down along it, stretch myself thin and wriggle in. I feel my shirt hook, rip along my back; one bra-strap snags on rock but loosens and scrapes past when I squeeze lower, squirming forward, reaching until the rock lowers to clamp itself onto my head. My fingertips can almost touch them, long ends knotted, leg bones perhaps, they are set immovably in a runnel of sand washed hard as concrete. Through split rock the sun's finger of light is pointing, *look here, look for me here—*

I pull in a long breath, twist to lay my head flatter, sideways, and hunch ahead, squeeze the last centimetres until I can feel them, feel and see my fingers just at the corner of my eye, the knobbly grain of their age and surface impressed like the cellular filigree of a leaf. My left shoulder and breast are crushed, a volcanic tip is hooked down into my left ear, but my reaching left hand can still move and if I stare straight ahead to where the rock closes on darkness, at the peripheral edge of vision I can see the shadow, even as I feel the edge, the slender fluted comma of a human rib.

> This at last is bone of my bone,
> and she shall be called wo-man,
> because she was taken out-of-man.

Genesis, my father Adam says. Even the Hebrew pun replicates itself in English. His square face, the heavy Wiebe jaw lightens into his surprising smile. So suddenly gentle it might seduce anyone, if only for the moment it may last. Truly a DNA story, you lovely bone of my bone.

I am your daughter.

You are. And so, scientifically speaking, more bone of my bone than your mother can be. As you are hers more than I.

I am, I will always be, a double daughter.

It seems the Chilean earth has shrugged softly, tighter, and I am held without breath, held firm and immovably at last. Or at least long enough, by the earth encrusted. No more deciding.

TWENTY-TWO

HOMESTEAD

Waskahikan, Northern Alberta
Calgary
1996

TO GET INTO THE COPSE they have to push between brush over their shoulders, scrub willow, saskatoon, sharp, scratching rose-bushes and wild cranberry, their berries freeze-dried by winter; but after a few crunching steps the bush opens suddenly, upwards, and there are the tall aspen. Their white, branchless trunks crowd around the two grey buildings, bend over them in the giant curves of the perpetual northwest wind, so tall the sky is spring green, a tropical canopy drawn above them.

Adam thinks again, How can they be here, these immense trees? The yard was clean as a swept steppe, the chickens grazed the grass to the ground and the only tree nearer than the shelter strip north of the garden was the huge spruce beside the out-house where the magpies squabbled while you sat—there is no spruce. Beyond where it grew is the thickest tree of all, a black poplar—*schundt* his father declared them, trash, the roots suck up every drop of water, the first tree to clear away and never bring into the house, no heat in that wood, just pulp leaking soot from the stovepipe—but there it grew, on the edge of the space where the sod-roofed barn once was; almost a metre at the base. Fifty years.

There is a bluster of wind, too high to feel but he can hear the rush of it as the aspen flicker far above him and bend east, swing, circle back in their rooted give and return and, staring up, it seems he is standing on a tall ship, its great masts heel as he leans to remain erect on the tilting deck, the green-blue sails bulge before the wind and he staggers, his hand finds a balance on the nearest mast of a tree and instantly he feels the earth's motion, even as he hears and sees it; as he leans again with the white mast and is carried, driven hard through the heaving sea.

"Sir?"

Ground returns, solid beneath his feet. He has never travelled on a sailing ship.

"Mr. Wiebe? Are you all right?"

Alison beside him; she is a tall, heavy woman, but her hand is lighter than a leaf on his shoulder. He turns to her small smile: he had not met her before she and Joel arrived in Edmonton last night, and he thinks again that maybe Joel is lucky, really lucky—no, not luck, Adam's mother said when she first saw him through the maternity window, so broad and black-haired and heavy and roaring loud enough they heard him through the thick glass, your boy is blessed.

"Thanks, thanks, I'm fine—" Adam hesitates before Alison's steady gaze. "You don't have to call me 'sir,'" he tells her again.

"I know...."

She shrugs, and he smiles with her. He says, "I was feeling… Flickering aspen, when the wind comes and you touch them, you can…seem to…feel their sound."

She lifts her hand to touch the tree, her palm and fingers listening. "A tintinnabulum?" she asks. "Susurration?"

He hisses an echo in her ear, "Susurration."

They draw it out into rhythm with the poplars high over them, their cloud of leaf voices singing.

Adam gestures up. "The voices of those who have died before us."

Alison stares at him, and he tells her mildly, "I'm not crazy. Just a comforting way to think of leaves and wind. For me."

Her smile returns, but uncertainly, as Joel comes crunching through brush around the corner of the frame house. He ducks under the branch spikes of a tree crashed into the caved roof. "Dad, this is wild," he says. He runs his hands down the grey siding. "And beautiful clear cedar, so soft, it's grainy as cloth."

"Never painted," Adam says, "just gentle Alberta weather."

Joel laughs, patting the wall. "This house cost a lot, two floors, cement foundation—and you always bragged your homestead was so poor! Romantic crap."

"No crap, that wasn't our house. Orest Homeniuk built it, when we moved away and he bought the land for back taxes, one hundred eighty-seven dollars."

Alison gestures to the black log mound beside them. "You didn't live in here?"

"That's where we lived."

"Huh?" Joel takes four steps and he is beside her, the eave of the rotting roof comes barely to his forehead. "God, I thought this was maybe your chicken barn, or the pigs."

"No no, that was our sweet little home in the north. Good thing Orest never tore it down, see how neatly the corners are fitted?"

"Sawn off so trim," Alison says, fingering axe marks. "But the logs aren't sawn...what is this?"

"Trimmed flat, by broadaxe. John could trim two sides of a log straight as a string. That wall's stood sixty-five years and look at it: still straight."

"Uncle John chopped all these logs flat?"

"Sixteen years old." Adam taps Joel's shoulder. "They don't make them that way any more."

"They don't have to." Joel bends down to the windowsill just above his feet. "The window's low enough to walk through."

"And the trees are so huge," Alison says. "What happened?"

"That big frame house was never lived in, it was never finished. We left in May '46, and Orest started cutting spruce and sawing lumber and building—everything but the cedar is wood off this land—as soon as he got title, but he died just after Joe, his son, got back from the war. Heart attack."

Beside them that tall, narrow, almost ghostly shell surrounded by the white trunks of trees swaying slightly, back and forth as if to bar the black openings where windows and doors have never been. Adam sees apprehension in Alison's eyes; almost, perhaps, fear.

He tells her, "Joe Homeniuk fought for land, foot by bloody foot in Normandy and the Battle of Holland. He said he and his buddies were killed and killed for it, and when he came back land couldn't be what it was for his father, or us Mennonites. Land was our living, our life and food, but for

Soldier Joe land was what you either had or didn't have, it was business. What land grows you sell, grain or trees or cattle, it's all for sale, and you buy and sell land like shares on the stock market, buy low with borrowed money and mortgage and buy more and sell high and always make a profit. He wouldn't live out here in the sticks, thirteen miles from the railroad. He built that castle on the bluff in Boyle and the Toshiba Products plant we passed in Rowand, he sold his lumber mill to them six years ago. Tens of millions, and he still owns half the country."

Alison asks, "And you bought this back from him?"

"Yeah. One small piece, our homestead quarter, after two years' negotiation. He cleared every square inch to grow crop— he did that to all the land he owned—he bulldozed the barn and the sheds and the trees, even the muskeg, all up in smoke, but he didn't torch this little copse, these—houses."

"So, how'd you persuade him?"

"We made a deal: I'll never touch them either."

"I don't get it," Joel says. "Why?"

"This is the last thing his father built. And I'm the only person born on this place."

"A real good guy."

"As the Cree say, 'Blood runs thick and long and forever.'"

Joel guffaws. "Not on the Internet!"

Adam's feet sink in half a century of leaves, the roof so low he can rub the end of the highest gable-log with the palm of his hand. The wood sifts dust on his fingers. Abruptly he leads Alison and Joel around to the gaping hole of the door in the centre section of the long log mound, and ducks in. The old house space is no larger than a granary, and crowded with long drapes of paper like tattered hides hanging from the ceiling. There is no place for feet: the floor has vanished, collapsed in debris into the cellar hole.

"It's just rotten paper," Adam says to the two hesitating in the doorway. "Wrapping paper, paper bags, newspapers, we pasted them all together with flour and over the walls and ceiling the last winter, to try and keep the wind out."

Alison murmurs, "It's an installation. A tight space of art hangings."

"And you can read it!" Adam laughs, and feels a surge of happiness that she is here. "Look at this one, the *Zionsbote*, 'Mittwoch, den 22 März, 1938'—Mom always saved the *Zionsbote*, she must have been desperate, pasting them all over."

"This is amazing."

"It wasn't then, we were just cold. This one centre room was the house they built first, fall 1930, five people living in it. Helen was always away working, and then she got married. Kitchen and living and sleeping room all one, then two years later they cut out doors in opposite walls and added the bedrooms at either end. That one is where we kids slept, Margaret in there on a cot behind a sheet hung exactly to the middle of the window so we all got some evening sun, and John and me on this side in a double bed, me against the corner wall and no reading in bed at night, no light anyway. When Abe or Helen came home they'd sleep on Margaret's cot and she either on a mattress on the floor, here, or in Mam and Dad's room over there."

Alison and Joel are halfway in, leaning around the tattered, hanging papers, peering into the dark space of the bedroom. Their arms are tight around each other and they are so close to Adam, their presence so vivid in this tiny place, his first home, that he is filled with sudden, wonderful longing. And he hears the voice of his mother remind him in this waiting air—she is frying potatoes, she is scrubbing clothes, she is ironing, he is turning the milk separator where the milk and cream arch out of opposite spouts and the wood she thrusts into the firebox of the stove sprays sparks against her hand. "Little children," she repeats the Watchword, "play and trample in your lap, big children walk on your heart"—some, Mamma, yes, but not every one. These grown children are now so near to him, he recognizes what he is feeling is contentment; almost as if he can, finally, stop thinking he must make up his mind.

Joel has turned and is bent past him, peering between the tatters. "Where did Margaret lie? When she was sick?"

"In this room. Her cot was against that wall, the kitchen table over in the middle."

"God, it's all so tiny...."

"Actually, it's very good for a long-term patient. Never alone, in here she was always with the family, right in the middle of what's going on."

"I mean the whole...five, six people living in here, fifteen years?"

"It was close and warm in winter, in summer you mostly lived outside, cooked..." His son staring at him. "Like Mam said, we always had enough to eat, and at night no Bolshevik ever hammered on the door, not even a Mountie!"

After a silence Alison says, almost at his ear, "You were born in this room?"

"No," Adam says, and sees the black space in the middle of the right wall, past where the stove and the woodbox he had to keep filled under the washbasin stood in the corner. He gestures, "In there." The ground has heaved up inside the darkness that all afternoon moved deeper into the small room with its eastern window. Four times he has returned here and he has never yet gone into that room, nor asked himself why; his mind, when he looks there, is simply blank, and he thinks perhaps it is because this is the first time he has come here with someone alive. There is no smell inside these ruined walls with their gaping doors and windows, the long spaces of mud fallen from between the logs: during fifty years of trees and night and day and every weather the kitchen sank, the bedroom rose as if the earth must turn, adjust itself into some comfort after their momentary existence here, his fleeting birth. His mother and father there in bed, once upon a time, holding each other.

Once this was their home. Each time he has now returned more of his child's family memory is packed into this space, and it is Margaret's room. Dead at sixteen, but she is sitting there on her cot, he is trying to brush out the tangles of her long, black hair.

He says aloud, "We better go around outside. It's easier to look in the bedroom, from the window."

Joel says, walking beside him, "When Grandma got that picture from her brother, in Russia, with him in the pointed army cap, they were living here?"

"Yeah, they had cleared a few acres in the bush, and used the trees for this little starting house. That was good, Orenburg has no trees to build anything, and this cost nothing, just work...."

"Wasn't his name Heinrich?"

Adam says, before he thinks, "My name was once Heinrich."

"What?"

He regrets his words, but now he must continue. "For about eight years. My dad registered my name that way, though I didn't know it."

Joel asks, even more puzzled, "Were you named after that uncle?"

"I don't know. Maybe after eight weeks of my yelling Dad figured out I'd always be *jaejenaun* too."

"What's that?"

"Always against, against whatever's going on, you never want to do what you're told."

"Oh yeah," Joel says. "I can see that."

"Never mind," Adam says, "that's another story, don't scare Alison too much on her first visit—anyway, they never told me anything about me and that name. But my Loewen relatives in Russia have now got more information about him. It seems by 1945 he was a Red Army officer, and he was killed by a sniper while they were taking Berlin. Your great-uncle Heinrich was Colonel Genrich Lvov, a Soviet war hero."

Joel has stopped, and so has Alison; they hear the distant rush of a vehicle approaching on the gravel road that passes the copse.

"Crazy," Joel says at last. "Did they hear for sure what happened with that other brother, on Sakhalin Island?"

"Peter David Loewen," Adam says heavily, and leans against the ancient wall whose very grain he remembers; if there were no trees, it would be deeply warm from the spring sun. He has avoided telling Joel about Elizabeth Katerina's letters, and he especially does not want to talk about them here...but something must be said. He says, carefully, "Teacher Loewen they called him. They say he was solid, with wide shoulders and thick black hair like yours, a hard handgrip, but the—Genrich Lvov going there, to see him in prison…carrying a knife…Maybe that never happened."

"Onkel David in Paraguay said Grandma had heard it," Joel insists. "She told him for sure…but it's a lie? Brother killing brother? Mennonite killing Mennonite?"

His mother had doubtless said those Lowgerman words, *Massa*, knife, and *spetje*, stab. But words about facts happening half a world away—especially Lowgerman words—could change, grow, slant, lean into a more cruel and relentless form of torture. In words carried across continents you meet them all somehow, both the living and the dead. Sometimes even yourself.

Adam says, slowly, "I wouldn't say it was a lie. Family stories…names…the facts can get a little changed, shifted, but they're based on something that happened. Usually true enough."

"But killing is killing."

"Maybe Heinrich never carried a knife—but by working for Stalin's system, he did kill his brother."

The gravel roar of the car has passed away on the road north. The road was always two tracks leading to Boyle, he would stand here half-hidden by this corner of the house and watch the slow wagons draw past, steady farm *schrugge* nodding in the sun, the grind and thud of wheels on stone. His hand touches a clump of chinking still caught between the house logs. He mixed it, tramping the mud down in the pit with his small naked feet, Margaret too, and John, and Pa brought forkfuls of straw…now this bit rubs to dust under his fingers, dribbling away.

He says aloud, "My father told me I yelled a lot, when I was a baby. Screamed, I guess, often at night. Maybe he named me

Heinrich because for me something seemed to be always wrong too, like my uncle, I was *jaejenaun*."

"Jaejenaun," Joel repeats, as if tasting it.

"People who somehow aren't satisfied, who always look for 'different.'"

Alison sings, "'Mary, Mary, quite contrary, how does your garden grow?'"

"That's it, contrary."

Alison says, "My mother always says she should have called me Mary."

"Hey!" Joel says in mock alarm. "You never told me that!"

They are around the low bedroom window, laughing a little, and they hear a car door thud. Somewhere outside the brush of the copse that hides them. They straighten up, listen. Above them green sunlight cuts streaks between the tall, pale trees.

"Adam? Are you there, Adam?"

Adam had not wanted to talk about his uncles at the homestead. He had wanted to look through the window space with Joel and Alison, into the little, dark log room where his mother had given him birth; he wanted to walk out across the open field with his children and up the hill, to show them the beaver dams on the height of land.

From the field below, that long hill he wanted to walk up on the Waskahikan homestead looked like the Orenburg steppes, where he and Young Peter walked with Elizabeth Katerina, talking, the day before they drove to the city of Orenburg and went to the Grey House. Then she had led them down the great staircase into the valley, and over the walking bridge across the Ural River from Europe into Asia, led them under the giant cottonwoods of the park until they came to the murder trenches.

There they stood, silent. Adam looked down row upon row of memorial birch, walked between them in a daze, trying not to think of earth ripped open for bodies, bodies not neatly laid out side by side like a hand gesturing over a bed but bodies exploded, thousands of bodies crumpled on top of each other as they crashed backwards, blown apart by a single exploding bullet, marvellous human bodies like those he had once cared for so tenderly, sprawled in deep ditches here; brutally disconnected. And then he saw the beaver stump, at his very feet.

Where the edge of the undercut bank dropped into the Ural River turning past, the gnawed stump of a tree. Not birch. Adam touched the tooth marks, felt the scalloped striations, the tuft and splinter of the centre break. Just where the river turned towards Orenburg City high on the distant cliffs. Not birch, an alder stump, where on the river's edge in the eighties the human bones were first washed out. He had taken a picture of the river and the bend and the stump. Beaver would not cut down birch but they might learn to gnaw bones, his cousin Young Peter told them as they stood together beside the Ural, who could say what even the animals had to do to stay alive in the Soviet Union.

But when Adam returned to Edmonton, in his developed picture he found only the edge of the muddy clay bank and the water and the summer wall of green trees across the river. Neither of his cousins was there, nor the beaver stump he remembered more certainly than anything else. Maybe there had just been too much, first the story of the building and then the murder park and then the river and the bones exposed and the birch trees, and finally his own discovery of the beaver—that stump was in his camera viewfinder; of that he was absolutely certain. And Young Peter too, and at least the edge of Elizabeth Katerina's dress, they were there in several other pictures, he took rolls, but somehow after all those stories, each one worse, his camera had avoided them both beside the beaver stump, that was too much. But the stump was still right there; if he could shift the picture half an inch left you would have to see it, and both of them standing beside it. All he could do now was remember that, and believe it.

Alison had never in her life, she said, seen more than a picture of a beaver. So come, he intended to tell her and Joel now, walk across the field and up the hill at the back of the homestead, where they've dammed up ponds along the height of land. Lots of trees fallen the wrong way and left to rot, and more than enough black poplar and blackening aspen stumps among all the beaver paths and deep dug canals that you can look and put your hands on. When they dammed up the water to protect their houses, the beavers revealed that it is a true height of land.

Which he never knew as a child. Then the swamp beyond the hill only drained away north, every spring, but now the beaver dams had caught and contained the water that became Firebag Creek where it fell away north to Firebag Lake and the Athabasca River, Great Slave Lake, finally the Beaufort Sea, and in the opposite direction a series of backed-up sloughs and islands and much longer southern dams made the water muddle south through muskeg and swamp and finally into White Earth Creek to the North Saskatchewan River and Hudson Bay.

When he was a boy he could not know this. There was no map he could read to tell him that their homestead land and the long eastern hill were folded over the continental divide, but now that the beavers had revealed it, he would build a new log house on the hill, he had told Joel and Alison driving up from Edmonton. A beautiful house, long and safe, with room enough for everyone to look in all directions, and a veranda along the front facing east so that every day they could look out over water that flowed in two directions, north and south; any raindrop or flake of snow could split and slip into seas a continent apart.

And he would plant lanes of birch trees on the whole quarter-section of poplar and spruce and clumps of willow Joe Homeniuk had bulldozed clear into one huge field; plant rows, avenues like those leading back from the Ural River where the Orenburg people strolled on sunny holidays. Young Peter said the orders had come from Moscow to open the river valley as a park for the faithful citizens who had helped destroy the Fascists in the war, though the German armies never got near Orenburg, but then the river washed out the bones and they discovered they were walking on layered, murdered people and they built a high iron-picket fence around them and planted birch trees inside. After Adam took what he thought was the beaver stump picture he turned his back to the river and took another one, which did show exactly what he believed he remembered: the path worn through a gap in the black iron fence and the long lanes of bright birch opening far away to Elizabeth Katerina and Young Peter, very tiny against the triangle of sunlight and the heaped memorial of round, grey stones gathered out of the river and mortared together:

To You Nameless Martyrs Who Were Innocent
and Shot in the Criminal Repressive Years of Stalin
and Who Are Buried Here
1937–38
You Will Be Eternally Remembered

Each white birch tree nailed to a name burned black Cyrillic into a brown board. They walked all afternoon deeper and deeper into the trees, and Young Peter transliterated Tumanov, Reimer, Brodsky, and finally his father:

Wiebe Peytor Jakovlevich 20.6.1880–15.8.1937

Thousands and thousands of trees shot through the back of the skull. Hauled here from Orenburg Prison, which was visible from the bridge over the river they had walked crossing from Europe into Asia. With one hand braced on the scrolled iron railing of the bridge, far from the Grey House where he was tortured, Young Peter could only point at the prison—the long roof and numberless tiny windows rising out of the trees—and the other Orenburg buildings that he had been inside three times, the first right after the GPU forced their family to return from Moscow to Orenburg and "Your parents got out," he said to Adam. He was still a boy with a body smaller than a boy but he was the oldest son of a kulak who had tried to run. A giant prisoner adopted him, a vicious man sentenced to life for murder took him for himself, curled his huge, gnarled body warm around him so he could sleep, kept him safe from other prisoners; he did nothing to hurt him. Without him, Young Peter said, he would have been dead, certainly the man was a killer but also perhaps an angel, who knows how strangely God lets them come to us, he said, though he saw the prisoner smash a man's head once and once with one kick crush another's genitals into his belly. There was nothing but fear between criminals and political prisoners thrown together in a small cell where only twelve men at a time could lie in bunks and on the floor to sleep and fifteen had to stand packed between them waiting their turn, sleeping on their feet and sometimes collapsing on the others as if shot. The names of the innocent and weeping dead, killed for no other reason than being alive and unable to stand any longer, Young Peter said, are nailed and written here on the birches by those who remember them and believe so completely that by faith they see what they know is written on the white bark of the tree of life.

Under the tall aspen that shroud the mouldering homestead cabin, Joel exclaims, "That's Mom!" He shouts, "Mom!" and charges away towards the sound.

And as Adam moves quickly to follow him he can only think, Susannah has never come looking for me...not in nine years, only that one marvellous night in Lethbridge...he shoves himself through the brush, out of the copse, holding the branches back for Alison crowding behind him, and he sees the two figures beyond his car. Susannah, beside her "one and only extravagance" the silver BMW, and Joel already there suddenly leans over the hood, his broad body folding down between his braced arms as if he had been slugged.

"Susannah!" Adam shouts, running. "What? What?"

Her mouth opens and she begins to run as well. To meet him, he hears her word, he sees her face shine as if she were speaking out of a blazing fire.

Trish. Trish. It is all he can think, her name, Trish.

"It was her, Adam, I know her voice!"

She is on the 10:45 evening flight from Dallas to Calgary.

"Four hundred twenty-five kilometres from here to—no, we charter a plane, Edmonton Municipal, thirty-three minutes' flying and we—"

"It's still another five hours, we'll just have to sit there and wait—"

Joel lifts his head. "And all our cars in Edmonton, why not drive like hell, who gives a shit about tickets and—"

Adam is running for Susannah's cellphone, yelling, "I want to wait in the Calgary Airport! Sit there! Right there!"

Adam is with Susannah pointed south on Highway 63, his Toyota with Joel and Alison in the rear-view mirror, a Learjet ready in Edmonton. The huge farmsteads hiding behind their square rows of shelterbelt whistle past.

How can you look at someone returned from the dead?

Will you see her walk through an airport double door?

A rotting house sinks slowly to its knees in an open field, the running steel lines of railroad dip down into the setting sun. Adam sees himself with a shovel planting birch trees over the open hill and down to the creek below the cliff and along the northern swamp willows and around up over the hill again and down to the beaver ponds on the height of land—beavers let paper birch live— planting thousands of birch—not in straight rows like his Onkel Jakob in a regimented commune but in circles. He will burn all the names of every ancestor he knows into boards, buy a truckload of cedar and use every alphabet invented for any language so wher- ever on earth they lived or died their names will be read and understood, burn names deep in Egyptian hieroglyphics and Hittite and Mayan and Inca and Etruscan and every other shape of writing known to the dead until the names on the trees come around and round again as endless as a ring rolling.

She is on an American Airlines jet. Hurtling towards Calgary, Susannah said.

He says out loud, "How can I believe it."

Susannah says, "Have you told Joel about your Sakhalin uncles?"

Adam stutters, "I told…him about them…and my names, yes."

She insists, "About Heinrich and Peter? Exactly what Elizabeth Katerina found out?"

"Not very much, only that some of the story may not be true."

Susannah explodes with a cry of rage; if she were not driving, she might be beating him over the head. "You promised me! You promised me last summer, and every call since then, that you'd tell him the records show Peter Loewen died on Sakhalin after the war, three years after Heinrich was buried in Berlin! What is the matter with you? You promised."

"Take it easy, take it—"

"Don't you ever learn anything? How important something can be to someone else, beside yourself?"

"It's just so contradictory, the facts don't make sense, what they say happened doesn't—"

"Just you tell Joel all the facts you know. If it's important to him, let *him* make whatever sense he wants."

"Okay, okay," Adam says. "Okay."

Susannah glances swiftly at him, then back to the coming, vanishing streaks of the highway. She drives as if she were threading a needle.

Before the double double-doors opening and closing in the glass and concrete international arrivals area echoing with persons repeatedly paged but apparently never lifting a receiver to be heard by an ear waiting for a voice, to the right of the arrivals barrier in the Calgary International Airport, there is a circle of five people.

If they were facing outward, they would resemble muskoxen of the High Arctic backed around young to confront their lifelong enemies. But these face in upon themselves: they are bending gradually closer together, intent upon the slowly tightening sphere they make, closer feet, rounded bodies, bowed heads. It could well be a family: a mother, a son, a father, a daughter- or son-in-law, one daughter or two. Between the slabs of echoing airport glass a globe of quiet gathers about them, it seems they are trying to look into each other's eyes, to search out all of themselves at the same lasting instant while their hands and arms grope around and beyond the person pressed against them for the next. Trying to feel every bone in every individual body, and feeling at last their hearts beat the conviction of their enduring love.

TWENTY-THREE

A LADDER OF ANGELS

The Einlage
Danzig
1652

FROM THE MOMENT OF OUR BIRTH, dying carries us towards the moment of our death. I am close now, kneeling in this soft, black ground pulling out turnips one by one. An old man has time. Time to feel earth between his fingers down to its very dust. After all, my name is Adam.

Ground sweet enough to place in your mouth, to taste and see it is good.

For thirty-five years I was chief engineer of the fortress city of Danzig, but like all Mennonites, our family had no permit to live in its tight stone buildings. Fortunately. In our row village of Neugarten, between the shadows of the Bishop's and the Hagel's Hill, we all had deep black soil for gardens, and though every army that besieged Danzig burned Neugarten to the ground while we fled inside the walls with a few possessions, my wife Anna and I agreed: a garden was worth it. A burned house can be rebuilt, but flowers cannot grow between cobblestones. Even when the city invited me, for my services, to build three houses inside the Wagon Gate for my family, we never lived in them. Then in 1637 our sons Abraham and Jakob received royal permission to dam and drain the floodplain of the Nogat River opposite the city of Elbing, and for the past fifteen years, while we continued working in both Danzig and Elbing as engineers, Wiebes have diked and ditched and drained the Einlage, as it is called. With other Mennonite families we have built both row villages and scattered farmsteads on raised mounds, as we built them long ago in Friesland. Once mostly wild water rushes grew here, but now the Einlage orchards and dike trees hide the spires of St. Nicholas and St. Mary in Elbing far across the river.

Actually, I do not live only in the Einlage. The city of Danzig also permitted me to buy land and build a house at Pasewark, a village overlooking the dunes of the Bay of Danzig. But my Anna is gone home and I have come to live here with Jakob's family for a little while. I like to pull up their fat garden turnips, which the grandchildren tell me are really only fit to be eaten by cows.

I refuse to smile, I tell them cow milk is excellent, of course, but raw, crisp turnips help give you strong teeth. And I show them mine: squarely solid, at least in front, see, I've eaten garden turnips all my life. But Trientje, Jacob's last daughter, does not believe mere words. Her quick fingers have to feel as far as they can inside my mouth.

"Grousspau!" she exclaims. "Your hind teeth are all gone, where are they?"

I fondle her ear and whisper they're like hair, old men don't need so many to look beautiful like little girls, and for a moment

I can see belief widen her unblinking eyes. Touch and hearing, she is almost ten and I pray the dearest God she lives long; what a woman she will be.

I am hunched on my heels in the rich delta garden, and I feel Trientje's fingers brush the edge of my beard. "Why do you always plant turnips?" she asks. "Nobody likes them, just you."

My Anna, God give her peace, would have laughed with me to hear her; Anna didn't much like cooking turnips either. She always insisted life was a feast we could enjoy with pleasure and great gratitude, that we personally had enjoyed so much that surely to describe life as a kind of "continual dying" was considering it from the wrong side of the table. And I said true, God in His mercy has given us much, but which is the wrong side? Burned villages are easily rebuilt, but children killed cannot be reborn.

How do you know?

Nor the memory of their agony and dying erased.

Yes, Anna said then. That may be harder than being born once again.

Trientje is nudging me gently. "Grousspau, why?"

"Why...what?"

"The turnips." She is still too young to be impatient with me in my aging. "I asked you twice."

She turns her warm face to me as I draw her close; she gives a small grunt of happiness as we kiss. It is required that Mennonite grandfathers, especially those known in public, appear wisely dignified and distant; they cannot possibly kiss even their grandchildren—except when hidden by the trees in their gardens.

I place the last clean turnip on my small pyramid. "Come,

we'll leave them here, these old things, your great-great-grandmother already ate turnips in Friesland." And I use her sturdy shoulder to get to my feet. "We'll find something different, something sweet for you."

"Yes yes!" she cries, skipping her hand into mine to the lilt of her voice. "Potatoes! Ohhh, the potatoes!"

Oh, the dribble of stranded facts running in an old man's memory, like the unruly dance of his grandchild on the ploughed earth around him as he walks. A new word, *eadschock* is what we call potatoes in Prussian Lowgerman, a neutral compromise for the many Dutch dialects we carried here over the last century, the very sound of which reminded too many of us of our endless Dutch disagreements. The word means "earth" and also "sixty," I think, which is how these marvellous tubers seem to multiply into every possible shape in good soil. I've been growing them larger and larger from the tiny balls Jan Adriaenz Leeghwater first brought me from Holland in 1628.

"These come from the New World," he said, "from mountains too high to believe, but they will grow anywhere hidden in the earth, they'll feed you even if the Swedish cannon smash every Danzig wheat ship and granary."

For years I had invited him to come and help me redesign our outdated bastions; we needed a second harbour channel and should enlarge our walls to include the Long Garden, so we would have more food to withstand the next siege. We were so endlessly beset by whatever army had a fleeting advantage in the Wars of the Polish Succession, complicated by the Thirty Years War of Religion and Holy Roman Empire, that we never had sufficient time to rebuild the bastions, leave alone extend our fortifications. But then, suddenly, Jan Adriaenz did arrive, as usual by an obvious miracle: he and his small potatoes were aboard the first Dutch ship to venture into the river after the immense spring floods of 1628 forced King Gustavus II Adolphus and his dreadful Swedish army to abandon their siege of Danzig. That very August, while Jan Adriaenz helped me design the new walls around the Lower Town and the Long Garden, we heard by sailors' rumour that the largest warship ever built, the *Vasa*, had been launched for Gustavus Adolphus in Stockholm. It carried double-tiered bronze cannon that could fire twenty-four-pound balls over a mile, that is, it could destroy Danzig from the Bay without sailing up the river. But then, while thousands of Swedes cheered from the bank and every flag flew, the *Vasa* had barely moved past the royal palace when a cross-wind caught its huge sails and, top-heavy with armaments, it keeled over, water poured in at all its massive gun ports, and it sank before their eyes in the deepest trench of Stockholm harbour. Praise be to God.

Jan Adriaenz said, "If Gustavus Adolphus had sailed those *Vasa* cannon to the mouth of the Vistula, how long would Danzig have held out?"

"But he didn't! Water swallowed them at the first puff of wind."

"In four months," he said, "God has saved Danzig twice."

By water and by air; for the time being. As Danzig's master builder, I had to ponder war: our independent city, a strategic and rich prize for any conqueror, was fixed in its place, set immovably on the earth inside the triangle formed on two sides by three rivers and on the third by the westerly line of hills anchored by the Bishop's Hill. Beyond any walls we could build, our best defence was the water of the rivers; when we opened our control dikes and sluices, water flooded the approaches to the city on two sides to confound any attacking army. The strongest offence against us was, of course, ever more fire from ever-larger cannon, and for this our western hills, which before gunpowder were a fine defence as well, were becoming our greatest problem. For if a general attacked from the west and forced his way up to their tops, he was not only above the flood but also above the walls; the city lay below him, open to whatever destruction his cannonballs could wreak.

The world was not only the water and air that saved us momentarily from the Swedes, it was also earth and fire. And all four must be controlled, together and in combination, for protection and peaceful shelter from our rulers' unending war.

An added lesson: not controlling three of the four elements destroyed Gustavus II Adolphus himself, the most devout Protestant and brilliant warlord of his age. In November 1632, at the battle of Lützen against the Roman Catholic Army led by Wallenstein, towards evening the gory field became obscured by drifting fog, and the impulsive King of Sweden may have lost his bearings; in any event, he galloped between the opposing battle lines of Wallenstein's cavalry and the Swedish foot soldiers and he was fatally shot by his own expert musketeers.

Water and air and fire in yet another unexpected, and deadly, combination. Only earth could save Danzig, Jan Adriaenz and I decided. Our thick bastion walls were built of earth dug out deep to create the moats, and faced with thin stone barged from the mountains. Under heavy cannon fire the stone would break, but the wide, exactly sloped dam of earth behind it would absorb the force of the cannonball without serious damage. Our fortifications facing the delta and the three rivers began at the north point of the hills, at the Corpus Christi Bastion, and curved around in an immense half-circle of fifteen bastions, in a line of fourteen curtain walls almost two miles long, to the hills at the Gertrud Bastion—a true stronghold.

The problem was the straight line of wall from the Gertrud back to the Corpus Christi Bastion. That wall fronted the western hills that overlooked the city; it was almost a mile long and dangerously low because we had always counted on the hills to protect us. How could that wall be strengthened? There was so little usable earth along the Raduane Canal with its swampy, bottomless marshes. The Bishop's Hill had more than enough earth, even boulders and rock, to build up the wall. The question was how to get that earth from the hill and across the marsh and canal to the wall.

We have always moved earth, the City Councillors told me.

Yes, by building roads and bridges and ramps, by hauling with sled, cart and wheelbarrow, by shoulder yoke and buckets. So?

So. I had to decide. Carry the earth in endless tiny shovelfuls, drag every grain and clump of it over miles of ground the way the Children of Israel slaved for the Egyptians? Had we learned nothing about the *placedness* of earth, its possible motion, since the desert pyramids of Genesis?

After he returned home, Jan Adriaenz sent me letters by ship. He told of the continuing voyages of sailors from Hoorn; of Adrian Block who had once wintered in Man-a-hat-a; of Willem Schounen who was the first man to finally sail around the cold and storm-ripped tip of South America and named it after his home port, Cape Hoorn; of Peter Minuit who had settled twenty-four Dutch families, including four Mennonites, at

Man-a-hat-a after he traded rights to the island from the Indians for goods worth twelve Dutch guilders, and renamed it New Amsterdam.

"With such a name," Jan Adriaenz wrote, "and land so deceitfully purchased, I think it impossible they will ever build a heavenly city."

I wrote back, "It is as well then that I sailed east."

He replied, "Or, perhaps, if you had gone west you could have prevented it. I hear now they are digging a harbour canal and building walls to protect themselves, I think, from the Indians who certainly know they have been betrayed."

I could only answer, "I struggle enough with our 'Old Europe Christian' walls and ditches, what would I do with walls for New World Indians?"

His letter in return seemed sad: "Walls are always what they are, no more, no less. And so it should be also with Christian actions, wherever we are on God's earth: caring and fair to others as we wish to be cared for."

Words of Jesus, seemingly as impossible in Dutch trade as they would be futile in facing Swedish cannon. If one dared utter them.

"You are a brilliant engineer," Jan Adriaenz concluded. "But still, I think, too little illogical. You once called me 'the man who walks under water,' well, I gradually discerned the diving bell when I stopped thinking only about water and pondered its relation to air. To solve the earth problem of your western wall, you need to think different; perhaps more about fire."

I tried, but in my case these two elements did not seem to link as co-operatively as the two in his. My problem was a relationship of motion, not stasis, and useful fire must be, I think, largely static; when it moves it usually explodes and is to that extent dangerously uncontrollable. Water, on the other hand, is always in motion and relatively controllable. The problem was earth. The base of the Bishop's Hill must remain as it was, a solid anchor of our protection; therefore the earth for our wall must move down from its top—which, if it were lowered, would also lessen the advantage of enemy cannon placed there. A water sluice down from the top of the Bishop's Hill, sloped on supports across the valley, marsh, canal and moat, would carry the needed soil down in the continuing wash of a stream. But how would you, for one, get the carrying water to the top of that great dry hill, and two, even harder, get it back up again after the soil had settled out? And three, the settling would take too long. Three problems for one.

Water, water. The beauty of it moving, the drinking sounds of it under clear ice. Water is so heavy it always seeks low; over the high Bishop's Hill there is nothing but air. We are not birds pointed like feathers to walk or drift on it; birds are too light to harness and men are too heavy, when we try to fly we merely fall and smash. The best we can do is build ladders to climb step by heavy step up, be there in the air momentarily, and retreat slowly down to earth again, stand ladders against the steep sides of the hill, one stream of people climbing up with yokes and empty buckets, a second stream with buckets filled coming down, in an endless circular motion on ladders, like the ladder Jacob saw as he slept with his head on a stone, and sleeping saw a ladder with its top reaching to heaven and angels going up and down on it and God there standing over him. A ladder set on the earth and leading up to the very gate of heaven, and down again. Angels moving up and down continuously.

It was before dawn when I stood on the Gertrud Bastion, the southern anchor of Danzig's curved wall where it turns straight north. I was staring across the valley at the Bishop's Hill. Jacob in Genesis said when he awoke from sleeping on his stone, "Truly God is in this place and I never knew it." It seemed to me then that even after twenty-six years I did not know this place either, nor what was in it, though I had built so much of it. I was asleep, but asleep somehow wrongly—perhaps I should ask our ancient stonecutter Jan Adam Wens for a stone on which to lay my head.

November 13, 1642. The blazing rim of the early winter sun rose on the edge of the earth behind me. It was already so far south of east that, as I faced the Bishop's Hill from the Gertrud Bastion, it laid the shadow of Danzig's western wall all across the middle of the hill. The wall was too low, and much too thin.

A bird perched beside me on the parapet of the bastion. A tiny bird, in the dawn light it shone on the grey stone like a star. Then it opened its wings, which were amazingly large for so tiny a body, and launched itself into the air of the valley, a spot of light lifting and lifting up in waves until it crested the tip of the Bishop's Hill. Its flight like a string of light reaching across the valley.

The next day we received the message that on November 13 our son Jakob's wife, Ruth, had given birth to a daughter in the new village they were building in the Einlage. They had named her Katerina, in Lowgerman Trientje. Purity.

When I first held her—her tiny face was closed, she was sleeping—they told me she was born at dawn, and I remembered the line between light and shadow that I had seen laid across the Bishop's Hill. Level on the earth as only light can be at the instant of sunrise, and I realized it had revealed to me the precise difference in height between hill and wall, that I could measure it as exactly as I could the width of this tiny perfect nose.

And I saw. The machine was already there, a machine like a line of light in air. I had been merely blind.

Connect hill and wall with a string. Like the flight of the bird, like wool that sags and unwinds between the round ball of it and the continuous pull of knitting needles making mittens, here use a strong rope, unbreakably strong like the ship ropes Holland now twists out of the incredible sisal fibres it brings from the New World, connect a continuous circle of this rope from hill to wall and back up again, attach to that rope the necessary yokes of buckets, fill them with earth on the hill and the weight of the filled buckets will carry them down and across the valley marsh and up to the top of the fortification wall, because it always remains lower than the hill and at the same time the circle will be returning the empty buckets back to the crest of the hill. Human energy will be needed only to fill the buckets on the hill, and to tip them empty on the wall. The earth can be moved without pause, in buckets hung on a continuous rope.

It took me a year to develop the right size of rope and work out all the problems of exact balance and bucket attachment, the rope and pillar supports. But once started, the aerial rope-train worked perfectly. All over Europe people heard of it and came to see Adam Wiebe's "Jacob's ladder" as they called it, came to stare and praise me, write stories in papers and books, even songs.

And one morning, when the workmen arrived to begin their work, I stepped into the first empty bucket myself and, like the shovelled earth, swaying a little, I was carried slowly along the crest of the Bishop's Hill and then, suddenly, dropped out into space; and then even more suddenly dropped from light into the twilight before dawn lying level across the valley. Moving steadily, riding the waves over the supporting pillars, I knew I was neither bird nor angel. I was a human being suspended in air and shadow approaching an earthen city. When I was lifted up again into the brilliant sunrise over the Wiebe Bastion that anchored the long Wiebe Wall (as the Council had now named them) and the workmen tilted me out, I found myself weeping for happiness.

Trientje is gathering the purple potatoes as I lift them out of the soil with the shovel, rubbing them clean, piling them in small heaps. She has been talking, as she does endlessly, language such a charm and lisp between her small teeth, telling me, "…this one is even bigger, oh look! Do you think, Grousspau, did Jesus dig up potatoes sometimes too?"

"They didn't…" But I stop, say to her bowed head, hair so neatly braided. "Where he lived, maybe they didn't have potatoes."

"They would have," she says confidently. "Jesus could dig up anything he wanted to, and when he…"

Her voice sings on, the sky above the garden and orchard trees shines in a whitish mist, like a shroud of diaphanous wool woven to hide us; safe. War is coming, the twenty-six-year truce between Poland and Sweden—I think their kings are cousins, or perhaps half-brothers—is almost over. Across the river my son Jakob, Trientje's father, is strengthening the walls of Elbing for the Swedes who under the truce have controlled it for a quarter of a century; in Danzig my daughter Anna and her husband, Abraham Jantzen, live in one of our houses inside the Wiebe Wall at the Wagon Gate and are growing very rich operating a brandy distillery. My oldest son Abraham works steadily for the

Polish defence on Danzig's second line of city fortifications, the high bastions and curtain walls connecting the Bishop's and Hagel's hills west above the city, which together with the Scottish Highland mercenaries—if they can hire enough of them again, with their bony knees and terrifying swords—will keep Danzig acting as if it were independent until the Swedes once and for all blow our walls to pieces. If they possibly can. In fact, most of Danzig's surrounding villages are already blown up. To provide enough rubble to build the new walls on the ravines and slopes of the two hills, Abraham has torn down eight villages, including Mennonite Neugarten and Stolzenberg. He is now using the Jacob's ladder, powered by horses walking around a wheel, to lift the village stones and timbers up to the tops of walls they are building even wider than I made the Wiebe Wall, because Swedish cannon are now even more powerful than we estimated. And their deadly pikemen are no longer needed in attacks; a knife called a bayonet can now be attached to every musket to make a pikeman out of every musketeer and every musket into a double killing machine: at long range by bullet, or body to body by stabbing.

I dig. Trientje, on her knees, gathers. Her busy little fingers and mouth. When the winter storms and ice are past in late March, I will return to live in my small house at Pasewark, and walk on the dunes. The spring of the year, the Bible says, is the time when kings go forth to war. I will sit on the high sand there and look north across the Bay of Danzig to the sea, to watch for tall ships approaching. The redesigned Swedish warships, coming again. Perhaps God will be merciful to Danzig, perhaps the Polish army and the Dutch navy can drive them off. So many will be killed. Perhaps God will be merciful to me, and I will not be there to see them come over the water before the wind. Terrible with banners.

At my feet Trientje exclaims, "Oh oh, you cut one."

And so I have. Cut it in half, the white meat of the *eadschock* like two precious coins shining in the black earth.

But I have dug too long, and now straightened up too fast. Nausea uncoils in my head and stomach, spreads like the ancient warmth of desire I can still feel, sometimes, so easily remember when I see the shape of a bright body bend. The sky spins with it, a taste edging into my mouth; anchored on my shovel I lower myself deeper into it until I rest on my knees, tilt my face down to Trientje's hands burrowing at the split potato, the earth and potato smell of it.

She is Trientje now. When she is old enough to marry she will become Trien, and years later, God keep her safe and it please Him, somewhere in the world she will be Grossma Triena.

"Here," I say, and our hands grub in the earth together. We each nudge out one piece and hold it, touch them together like a toast. Our spring and autumn jubilee. I give her my pocket knife and she laughs; with her left hand she cuts a thin slice from hers and one from mine. Then we place them on each other's tongue. Potato fresh from the earth, sweet and sharp as coming winter snow, moist together in our laughing mouths.

ACKNOWLEDGMENTS

Parts of this novel, in very different form, have appeared in *Canadian Fiction Magazine*, *Kunapipi*, *Malahat Review*, *More Than Words Can Say*, and *The New Quarterly*. I thank their editors for first publishing this fiction. Also, I sincerely thank the Canadian Broadcasting Corporation for originally commissioning a version of *Sailing to Danzig* as a radio play, and Carol Dyck of Edmonton for composing the music for the broadcast in August 1986.

Beyond the standard Mennonite history texts, the following books were particularly helpful.

Auss-Bundt, Das ist: Etliche schöne Christliche Lieder, wie die in der Gefängnus zu Passau in dem Schloss von denen Schweitzer-Brüderen und von anderen rechtglaubigen Christen hin and her gedichtet worden.... Basel, Switzerland: n.d. [1550, 1838 (?)]

Braght, Thieleman J. van, trans. Joseph Sohm. *The Bloody Theatre or Martyrs Mirror of the Defenseless Christians Who Baptized Only upon Confession of Faith, and Who Suffered and Died for the Testimony of Jesus, Their Saviour, From the Time of Christ to the Year A.D. 1660.* Mennonite Publishing House, Elkhart, Ind.: 1886; Scottdale, Pa., and Kitchener, Ont.: Herald Press, 1987.

Cuny, Georg. "Die Maler Deneter und Seemann," *Mitteilungen des Westpreussischen Geschichtsvereins,* 1913, pp. 48–54.

Curicken, Georg Reinhold. *Der Stadt Dantzigk historiche Beschreibung...1645.* Amsterdam and Danzig: Johan & Gillis Janssons, 1686.

Epp, Jacob, trans. and ed. Harvey Dyck. *A Mennonite in Russia.* Toronto: University of Toronto Press, 1991.

Friccius, Carl. *Geschichte der Befestigungen und Belagerungen Danzigs.* Berlin: Veit & Comp, 1854.

Janzen, Anna. *Eine Beschreibung der Ausreise von Deutschland nach Russland.* Baunatal, Germany: Manfred Sinning, 1995.

Klassen, Peter. *A Homeland for Strangers.* Fresno, Calif.: Center for Mennonite Brethren Studies, 1989.

Penner, Horst. *Die ost—und westpreussischen Mennoniten.* Weierhof, Germany: Mennonitischer Geschichtsverein, 2 v., 1978, 1987.

Penner, Horst. "Die Wiebes." *Mennonitisches Jahrbuch.* Newton, Kans.: 1951, pp. 14–20.

Rempel, John, and Paul Tiessen, eds. *Forever Summer, Forever Sunday: Peter Gerhard Rempel's Photographs of Mennonites in Russia, 1890–1917.* St. Jacobs, Ont.: Sand Hills Books, 1981.

Thiessen, Jack. *Mennonite Low German Dictionary.* Steinbach, Man.: Hanover Steinbach Historical Society, n.d. [2000].

Visser, Piet, and Mary Sprunger. *Menno Simons.* Altona, Man.: Friesens, 1996.